RIP CONVERSE

CALLIE
AWAKENS
BOOK 1

Copyright

The characters and events in this book are fictitious. Any similarity to real persons, living or dead, is coincidental and unintended by the author.

1st eBook edition: June 23, 2021
1st Paperback edition: June 23, 2021

Dedication

This book is dedicated to my younger brother Courtland who passed away this past year. I will always remember him for his rich and playful sense of humor and his brilliance as a jazz and pop pianist and composer. He lived his entire adult life as a player in the LA music scene which distanced us geographically from one another. I hope he's okay wherever he is now and laying down some serious tuneage.

Thanks

Many thanks to my wife Louise for putting up with my odd writing hours, help with cover design, social media, and emotional support in this fourth published work of mine, to Donna Rich for her exquisite proofreading, and to Freddie Douglass and Gene Rogers for their beta reading, comments, and suggestions, and to Meredith Norton and Dawson Biondi for their teenage perspective, thoughts, and suggestions on Callie. All of you helped make this a better work.

And a special thanks to Wayne Stinnett who was kind enough to loan me one of his iconic characters (Billy Rainwater) in this 1st book in my Callie series. Wayne is the author of the twenty-one-book Jesse McDermitt series and the five-book Charity Styles series. I have long enjoyed Wayne's work and heartily recommend all of it. Wayne is a great guy and tremendously supportive of other authors. It was fascinating and a little bit spooky to discover that both of us (independent of one another) were working against the same villains, in the same city, at the same time, and for a brief twenty-four-hour period our stories and characters overlapped. We decided to collaborate and to include various synced dialogues between *Callie Awakens* and his new release, *Rising Tide*. Thank you, Wayne, for your collaboration and support. If you enjoy *Callie Awakens*, you'll absolutely love *Rising Tide*.

Table of Contents

CALLIE
AWAKENS

Prologue

Esteban Cordilla wasn't in any particular hurry and absently tapped his fingers on the steering wheel in time with the beat of the Los Hermanos Flores song, blaring out of the radio. The air conditioning in his white, eight-year-old, Ford Econoline van had never worked properly, and the open window next to him provided no relief from the blistering waves of heat that rose off the black pavement. It only insured a uniform temperature of discomfort between the inside and outside air.

Hijo de puta, hace calor (Motherfucker, it's hot)! he thought to himself.

He was in the industrial area of North Fort Myers and slowed as he arrived at his destination. He drove around to the backside of the rundown building, backed up to the rollup door, and honked twice. Several seconds later the overhead-door jerkily started to rise. Once it had risen high enough, he backed the van in puffing perfect, little, white smoke rings out of the tailpipe. One of the cylinders in the van had a bad valve and with each turn of the camshaft, the bad cylinder would add its oil laden contribution into the exhaust mix every time that cylinder fired.

Until 2012, the building had been a respectable auto body shop filled with honest workers doing an honest day's work. The building had then sat vacant for seven years and fell into disrepair from vandalism and neglect. In 2019 it had been repurposed by Esteban's organization into an exclusive clubhouse for the lost, violent, morally bankrupt, uneducated, unskilled, drug addled, thieving, whore mongering, members of MS-13.

Esteban was the number two man in the Fort Myers chapter and the most senior member of the gang in age (thirty-one). His senior citizen status was due entirely to his out of scale prison build, his amoral character, and a preference for resolving the simplest of disagreements with extreme violence. He was well qualified for the management position he held within the organization.

Once inside, he stuck his left arm out of the window, made a circular motion with his index finger, and the door was lowered again. He turned the key off and listened as the engine dieseled several times before finally stopping. "Pedazo de mierde (Piece of shit.)" He muttered out loud, then shouldered the dented door open, stepped down, and was greeted by his boss.

"Esteban, bueno! You must have found a new one for me." Observed Diego Alturaz as he walked over.

"Sí, Jefe."

"Good, that's good. Let's have a look."

Esteban was casual and relaxed about the contents of the van, walked to the rear, opened the door, and tipped his hand inwards like a game show hostess showcasing a new television set on *The Price is Right*. Inside on the grease-spotted metal floor was a what looked like a pile of dirty laundry covered by a blanket. Esteban reached in, pulled back the blanket, and revealed a struggling, clearly terrified, sixteen-year-old female. She was bound, gagged, and blindfolded, and hyperventilating from struggling against her bonds. Her dirty face was streaked from tears that had washed through the dirt on her cheeks; the smells of fear and urine, acrid and powerful as they wafted out of the sweltering van.

Diego waved his open hand past his nose several times. "Jesucristo cabrón, que olor (Jesus Christ, what a smell)!"

Esteban's only response was an uncaring shrug. A group of eight gang members shuffled over and clustered around the open door at the rear of the van and assessed the young girl inside with cold, flat, dead eyes. All of them were absolutely deaf and blind to her terror, and they discussed her looks and her body features with no more feeling than they would some new lowrider with glass-pack mufflers and an interesting set of rims.

The scared girl was filthy and a bit old for Diego's taste, but injecting new girls with crystal methedrine and then running a train (gang raping) on them was the quickest way he'd found to turn otherwise hostile kidnap victims into compliant, dependent, income-producing prostitutes. He also understood "team building" without ever having attended Outward Bound

2

or a single management seminar and the power that providing fresh meat to his troops on a regular basis conferred.

"Bones, put together a syringe full of crystal and barbiturates for this one and get her started on her new life. Then go into my office and get an eight-ball of nose candy for the boys to help them get in the mood. It's in the top right drawer of the desk."

Diego turned back to Esteban. "Bring the girl inside to the rec room, undress her, hose her down, and then turn the boys loose on her until she's appropriately respectful. And make sure they don't get too excited and damage her like the last one."

RIP CONVERSE

Chapter 1

My name is Catherine Addison Babich and I'm fifteen years old. Most people call me Callie. I don't wear glasses, play the violin, compete in international chess tournaments, and wasn't adopted from Asia or India. I'm not a member of any math club and I've never been in a spelling bee. Despite my obvious lack of supporting qualifications, I have an IQ of 162 and an almost photographic memory. When I say "almost" I don't mean that I retain photographic still-shots of pages in books like some people, it's more that I'm able to process and retain complex step by step processes better than most. If I watch someone do something or I read how to do something, I simply never forget it once I've seen it.

Both of these gifts were "free," but I pay a price for them every day in the form of social isolation. I like to think that I don't need other people, but all of us do. We all need people for validation and a feeling of self-worth. These things are so important that they're right at the top of Maslow's hierarchy of needs, above food, water, and shelter. As a result, all of us are in a near constant quest for the recognition, validation, and reverence of others. Sometimes our search is conscious, sometimes not. What a strange dichotomy it is that we first need to be accepted into an unremarkable homogenous group to be recognized for those unique things in each of us that set us apart.

So, what does somebody who is bright, curious, ambitious, self-directed, focused, and deliberate do if they're completely uninterested in virtually all of the things that completely absorb their peers like social media, television, team sports, gossip, and clothes? What if all of your family members and the people around you have very average IQs and no one you come in contact with on a daily basis reads books or has any interest in the outside world or sees anything wrong with treating women as a somewhat inferior challenged subset of the male species? What if no one recognizes or applauds you for working hard and for outstanding achievement? What if you are shunned by your classmates simply for always doing the work and answering the teacher's questions correctly?

You end up isolated, alone, un-validated and always feel like you're on the outside looking in. Once you sense this isolation, you either modify your behavior to be more like those around you, or you accept who you are and try to move forward without them.

When I first started noticing that I wasn't a part of any group, I didn't understand why inclusion was important, and for longer than I now care to admit I instinctively did things that would make me more like those around me. I'd dumb myself down and say nothing or pretend I didn't know the answers to the teacher's questions when in fact I did. And I'd participate in and do things with my peers that violated my own sense of right and wrong just so I could be part of the gang. I did these things instinctively in my quest for acceptance and validation; until one morning something happened that made me realize that compromising my behavior just to feel less lonely, was no longer going to work for me.

I was twelve years old and showering. My hair was full of soap and my eyes were screwed shut. I'd locked the bathroom door out of habit to prevent family members from inadvertently walking in, but the old-fashioned lockset securing the door was never intended as a serious security measure and proved nothing more than a low speedbump that slowed, but did not stop, the deviants outside from getting in.

****

Both of the lock picker's hands were filthy, his nails chipped and broken. The key in the old lockset trembled ever so slightly as he manipulated it from his side of the door with a screwdriver. He felt the initial contact and paused to smile before slowly resuming and gently pushing the key backwards out of the lock. Once clear, it fell end over end to the floor and landed silently on several pages of newsprint that he'd slid under the door in advance. Besides deadening the sound of the key as it landed, the newspaper also allowed him to pull it back under the door to his side.

Once he had it in hand, he proudly held it up in front of his three co-conspirators and smiled cruelly. All of them were dressed in filthy jeans, camouflage shirts, and mud laden work boots. They looked like extras from *Deliverance*. They shuffled their feet impatiently leaving clods of dirt on the floor.

"Come on, let's do this!" one of them whispered. He looked back nervously over his shoulder down the hallway.

"Yeah, don't jerk us around. We've been waiting for this for a long time," said another.

"Patience boys, good things come to those who wait."

He quietly inserted the key into his side of the door and started turning it.

****

Do you remember how shy and self-conscious you were at twelve? I could barely stand to look at myself in the mirror. I was spindly, my breasts were just a dream, and I hadn't gotten my period yet. In short, I felt and looked nothing like the women I saw idolized daily in magazines and on TV and was seriously struggling with my self-image. Still a tomboy, I had not yet begun to look on boys and men as anything other than somewhat crude unwashed creatures and certainly didn't yet think of them in sexual ways. I still naively believed that men and women were of the same species and must therefore share similar values. I was also still in my early phase where I was willing to compromise my instincts and behavior to better fit in with those around me.

The first clue I had that something terrible was about to happen was when the warm moist air around me shifted ever so slightly as it will when air starts pouring out of a ceiling vent when the air handler clicks on or off. But we had neither central heat nor A/C in the house I grew up in. My subconscious registered the shift, but it wasn't until I heard the metal curtain hangers slide along the shower rod that my conscious mind kicked in and said to me, *You better check out what's going on.* It never even occurred to me that some other person or persons might be in the bathroom with me.

I quickly rinsed the soap off of my face, turned off the water, swept my hair out of my face, and wiped the water off my eyelids. I still remember how silent it was in that bathroom once I shut off the water. I finally open my eyes to see what on earth was going on with the shower curtain. Standing there, less than two feet away, were my brothers and their two open mouthed friends, all of them staring at me and my wet, naked, teenage body.

How would you have felt? At the time I would have preferred Norman Bates from that Hitchcock movie *Psycho* and his big ol' kitchen knife stabbing into my body that morning.

Less than a second passed before I reacted and covered myself, but in that instant, I knew that the horse had already left the barn, that the bank had been robbed, and that something priceless had been stolen from me that I could never recover. Images of me were now permanently etched into their memories. I felt horror and crushing embarrassment, then sadness at the treachery of my brothers, then rage, and finally deep sadness again; all within that instant of time.

The scream that came out of my soul and the abject look of horror on my face as I collapsed to the floor of the tub and tried to hide all my private parts at once, instantly conveyed to those four retards that what they'd just done, crossed a line. It wasn't just another one of their pranks that they'd high-five each other over later. No, what they'd just done was indefensible on any level and a real crime against another human being that all of them would carry around and remember with shame for the rest of their lives.

All four of them pointedly averted their stares, looked down at the floor, and then shuffled silently out of the bathroom and down the hall to my brothers' room. They'd taken something very personal from me that I could never regain, and they knew it before my scream reached the other end of the house and alerted Mam that something bad had just happened.

CALLIE AWAKENS

Mam hadn't punished my brothers since they'd become teenagers. They were simply too big, and she left corporal punishment to Daddy. But that day, she made an exception.

After rushing down the hall and into the bathroom in response to my scream and taking in what had obviously happened, she kind of lost it. It's the one time I remember her taking a principled stand against something and did she ever.

She assessed the scene of the crime in less than a second. The bathroom door and the shower curtain were both still open. I was on the floor of the tub, naked and sobbing, with my arms wrapped around my front, desperately trying to disappear. She didn't say one word, she simply wheeled around, marched into my brothers' room, pushed their two friends roughly out of her way, tore the curtains down off the window, extracted the curtain rod, and then commenced to beat my two brothers bloody. I mean she whaled on them.

Before you get all horrified and start calling child services, consider the crime and their ages. My brothers were not innocent little boys. They were fifteen and sixteen at the time. Secondly, the curtain rod was not one of those solid, quality ones from Restoration Hardware that would have broken bones and caused concussions. It was just one of those cheap, two-piece, telescoping, lightweight ones that costs about two dollars at Target. The way she went right for the curtains and stripped out the rod, you'd think she did it every day.

Once armed, she whaled, and she whaled on my brothers until the rod was twisted into two mangled pieces. My brothers cowered afterwards on the floor hurt not so much by the rod but rather from the vehemence that they had witnessed in our mother. Normally, she was like a mouse around the house and careful not to cause controversy of any kind. On this occasion though, she let it out. That mouse roared and my brothers heard it. Someday I'll have to ask her why or how she had the presence of mind to even think of using a curtain rod as a disciplinary tool.

After, she threw the mangled pieces to the floor in disgust and simply said, "You boys think that was something, you just wait until your father gets home."

I had put on a robe while my mother was beating them. After she finished, she came back into the bathroom and gathered me into her arms. "Callie, I don't know what's wrong with those boys. Are you okay?"

"I don't know, Mam." I'd sobbed. "I can't believe anyone would do something like that to me."

"Hard to believe, isn't it?"

Hearing that story come out of my mind I realize I still have a couple of resentments that I need to work through. I could say, "it was nothing" but that wouldn't be true. It *was* something and it made me realize several things that I'd been clueless about until that morning. I realized I was very different from men in general and my brothers in particular. I would never, ever, even think of singling out and objectifying another human being the way they had me. It simply isn't in my DNA and it's against my nature. Most importantly, that was the instant in time where I made the connection that validation and acceptance are only likely and valuable if they are confirmed on you by people who share similar values and standards. They're worthless otherwise and I decided at that moment that I would no longer compromise my values or my behavior for anyone.

I still want and need attention, recognition, and validation, but from that day forward I made a conscious decision to no longer dumb myself down or compromise any aspect of my behavior to get that attention. I simply couldn't and wouldn't be a part of any group that could do something so despicable and unfeeling to another human being. It just wasn't worth it, and I stopped following my brothers and their friends around looking for their acceptance.

I've matured some over the last three years and no longer feel like Gumby, but one thing has not changed, I still want to be seen and acknowledged for who I am and what I've done; for my principles, my values, and my accomplishments, not for how I look. The "shower day" incident reduced me to a thing and made me all the thirstier to be recognized for what I'm capable of doing and who I am, as opposed to just being a pretty face. I will be nobody's object.

To his credit, when Daddy got home later that day and heard what had happened and saw the look in Mam's eyes when she told him, even he understood that it was important that he punish my brothers for what they'd done to me. Some things just cannot be allowed to stand if there is to be any harmony in a family. Despite his love and pride in his two boys, or perhaps because of it, he took my brothers out behind the woodshed (literally) and took his belt to them till his arm was tired. They couldn't sit for two days after.

That incident changed several things. I think it's when my brothers first realized that there were consequences for their actions, and they took their first baby steps into adulthood. It was when I came to understand and believe that men are different from women and that if I were ever going to ascend to where I wanted to go in a male dominated world that I would need to be even tougher, more focused and self-directed, and less of a sycophant around them.

They were never going to let me into their club and rather than humiliating myself further by trying to get into a club that didn't want me, I decided to start my own. This club would have exactly one member and it would be anchored by my high standards and guided by the unwavering arrow of my moral compass. I was done compromising my values so that I could feel less alone.

RIP CONVERSE

Chapter 2

My parent's given names are Frances and Harley; my brothers are Damon and Harley. We live just outside the city of Fort Myers, Florida on the Caloosahatchee River; about a thirty-minute skiff ride upriver from the Gulf of Mexico.

Our home is off a no-name, single lane, paved road that goes exactly nowhere. It inexplicably stops a half mile past our house with nothing at the end of it; no warning, no turnaround, nothing. It's like the road man suddenly got dementia and simply forgot where he'd been paving the day before. I've been told a developer paid for the road back in the 70's with plans of putting up a vacation resort at the end of it, but he must have had dementia too as there's nothing at the end of that road but fields full of cow flop, swamp, and the river.

We live in what's called a "shotgun" which was the most popular type of house in the U.S. between the Civil War and the 1920's but is seldom built today. The name came about because a person could fire a shotgun through the front door and the pellets could travel the length of the entire house and go right out the rear door without hitting anything. It's about the cheapest house you can buy or build. The rectangular shape sits atop cinder blocks spaced every eight feet or so. This is fine until you have a wet summer or get the storm surge from a hurricane. When the ground gets overly wet the cinder blocks tend to sink into the ground. As a result, every few years Daddy and my brothers have to jack up one side of the house or the other and shim it to equalize things. The best way of telling if the house is getting off-kilter is to drop a lemon on the floor in the kitchen and then watch where it rolls and comes to rest. That's the side of the house that needs lifting.

Because of my IQ, I entered first grade almost a year early and then several years later skipped sixth grade which made me almost two years younger than my classmates. This age difference in combination with my academic record and driven personality distanced and alienated me from them. My parents have never had to ask me if my homework is done or tell me to read a book or stop watching TV and go outside and play. I do those things naturally. As a result, I've grown up less supervised than most kids my age.

I'm extremely self-disciplined. I started to run just four years ago, but already I've done four marathons and had three, top five finishes. While I'm really proud of my running achievements, the unintended consequence is that it further alienated me from most of my peers who all seem to be trying to do the absolute minimum to get by.

Sexism is probably the biggest obstacle I've faced growing up. I grew up surrounded by men who don't think of women as equals. As a result I've had to fight for every scrap of power, relevance, and recognition I can get. I don't know why this is so important to me, but it is. I don't want to be invisible. Our household and most of the community around us is highly patriarchal. I don't know whether this is due to lack of education, income, geography, or something else, but it's real and it's there.

Neither Daddy nor my mother finished high school. She got pregnant with my oldest brother Harley their junior year and they both dropped out. Their life options were limited as a result, and they've had to work like dogs every sunlit moment since. For reasons I do not understand Mam seems quietly accepting of Daddy's sexism.

He's a shrimper and has been his whole working life. He keeps his boat, *Damon & Harley* tied up on San Carlos Island when he's not out in the Gulf trawling. It's also where he offloads his shrimp and fuels her. My relationship with him has always been difficult. He's a hard man who's been shaped by a hard life. I wouldn't call him a violent man, but on more than one occasion I've seen him use his fists to underscore a point or mete out justice as he sees it.

He's always called me "Girl," as though my gender were my most distinguishing feature. I think he loves me on some level, but I don't remember him ever saying so. I've always craved his attention and approval but could never figure out how to get it. Daddy is simply brimming over with conflicting messages that he got from his daddy about women and their place in the world and when someone's only exposed to one way of thinking growing up, it tends to make them myopic.

I get all that; that's not what bothers me most about him. What really bugs me is that he's always treated me differently than my brothers simply because I'm a woman and must therefore be imbued with all sorts of deficiencies and weaknesses as a result. I don't know where the stereotypes he has in his mind came from. Mam is not some weak-willed, overly emotional woman. She's always been someone who gets things done, never complains, and doesn't gossip. She isn't overly emotional or nonsensical, nor is she a "nagger." She's all business all the time and holds up her end of the partnership without making demands. She's one of those people who does things simply because they need to be done.

I was just six years old when I first noticed Daddy's sexism. Back then I would silently watch his eyes during dinner as he would listen to my brothers endlessly prattle on about their juvenile exploits and adventures. His attention was always rapt, the pride and approval in his eyes plain as day. He'd stare at those two like every breath they took was some sort of precious miracle.

When I'd try to get his attention, he'd briefly look over at me, but then immediately shift his gaze and attention to reconfiguring the peas on his plate or picking some imaginary bit of debris out of his water glass. It was as if he suddenly remembered that I wasn't important and that the chance of me saying something that was remotely interesting to him was impossible just because I was a woman.

I hated how that made me feel then, and I still hate it today. Sometimes, in frustration, I'd make non-sensical motions with my arms or silently mime words at him testing whether or not he even saw me. His complete lack of interest in me or my life was palpable. I could have quoted scripture, in tongues, from memory while juggling five balls and I doubt he would have looked directly at me. Granted, my physical world was very small and not terribly interesting at the age of six, but wasn't I just as much of a construct of him and my mother as my brothers were? He hadn't ignored them. Couldn't he have feigned some tiny interest in me or my life? I would have done anything he asked of me, but he never gave me a clue as to how I could gain his love and approval.

Mam's a little better and usually calls me Callie like I'm a real person, but she's always sought and embraced the invisibility that I resist. She's a good woman, but I can't remember ever being inspired by anything she's ever done or her possessing anything special that I wanted. Her willingness to accept second class status as a "woman," without complaint, baffles me. I discount her for this and many of my memories of her are cloudy or not there altogether as a result. I know she was always physically present for me as I was growing up, but I've either forgotten or blocked many specific memories.

When I look at her, I want to feel as though we're players on the same team and that we have a soul connection. I want to feel gushing gratitude, gentle love, and deep awe for her principled ways. I don't feel any of those things though, just a sense of sadness that she accepted the status quo of the sexism surrounding her. If she has any dreams, I'm unaware of them.

My two brothers, Damon and Harley Jr. are complete Neanderthals and totally objectify women. They called me "Gator Girl" when I lost my baby teeth, and "Tits" when I started wearing a training bra, and "Rag Girl" when I menstruated for the first time. They've never seemed to consider the feelings of others when they speak and treat me and women in general as though we exist to simply serve in a supportive role filling their stomachs, picking up after them, incubating their babies, and minding male offspring until they can drink, hunt and fish. To put it in the plainest terms, my brothers and most of the boys I grew up with are myopic morons and retards. They all think they're damned geniuses and know everything about everything, but they don't. And don't start on me about my use of language. I'm not from New York or Boston where everyone goes all a-faint when you call a spade a spade. Where I grew up, we spoke plainly. I know using the word "retard" is offensive to some. I assure you I would never use it when addressing someone who was born developmentally disabled, I'm not that sort of person. No, the way I use it against my brothers and most of the other boys I grew up with, I mean it to be offensive, like a wet slap in the face. I want a word that hurts and has some sting to it.

CALLIE AWAKENS

A defining moment for me when I was quite young was when I decided that I wanted to become a ship captain. I was just six years old at the time and knew I wanted to be a Master & Commander and go where I pleased, when I pleased. I wanted to be able to find my way through the most challenging swamp, to feel the wind in my hair and scream through meandering switchbacks at full throttle while giving understated waves to other boaters with a casual/cool look about me. I wanted to be able to come down off a plane, spin the wheel, and coast to a perfect landing at the dock. And even though I didn't know it at the time, more than anything, I wanted that look of pride, admiration, and respect that my father so easily conferred on my brothers and withheld from me.

The day I decided I would become a captain; I was out behind our house catching lizards in the log pile. That probably sounds odd to some of you but that's the sort of thing kids my age did in the rural setting I grew up in. After a while I grew bored and walked out onto our short dock, climbed down into Daddy's skiff, and took the helm. I'd been in my father's boat plenty of times, but I hadn't yet been allowed to try driving it on my own. I sat down at the steering console and started playing out my fantasies. I knew what everything did and turned the wheel one way and then the other and periodically adjusted the throttle, making engine sounds. After about fifteen minutes of doing this, I got sleepy and lay down in the bottom of the boat. The summer sun was hot and after a few minutes I fell soundly asleep listening to the undulating waves of sound produced by thousands of male cicadas in the forest around our house.

Mam was inside beading at the time. She makes intricate bracelets and necklaces out of incredibly tiny bits of semi-precious stones using lapis lazuli, leopard skin, unakite, red agate, rose quartz, yellow tiger eye, and others. Because the stones are so small it takes considerable dexterity and concentration to string them.

She'd looked out the window regularly while I was catching lizards to check on me but got wrapped up in one of her bracelets and time disappeared on her. When she finally left the kitchen table to have a look out the window I was nowhere in sight and she decided she'd better have a look and went to the back door and called out for me a number of times, she later told me.

I didn't hear her with my head on the cabin sole of the boat below the gunwales. They acted like a sound barrier along with the Spanish moss hanging off the oaks around our house and muffled her calls.

"Cat…. Cat…. Callie!" *Where's that girl gotten to?* Mam wondered and came down the back steps and into the backyard. When she got to the log pile, she called out again.

"Callieee!"

When there was still no answer, she started getting nervous and ran around to the front side of the house calling my name out over and over again. Then she ran back into the backyard and started anxiously looking out over the swampy river water. Had I somehow fallen in the river and drowned? She ran out onto the dock at that point, right past the skiff without thinking to look inside. She started to sob and cried my name out once again as loud as she could from the end of the dock.

"CALLIEEE!"

I heard her at that point and sat up in the boat.

"What, Momma? What is it?"

She turned back towards the skiff, jumped down, gathered me up in her arms and hugged me to her breast.

"What were you doing? I thought you'd drowned."

"I'm okay, I was just taking a nap in Daddy's boat."

"You should have come into the house if you wanted to nap. You've got no business in this boat."

"Don't say that, Momma. I'm going to be a captain when I grow up."

"Cat, that's just foolish talk. Where on earth did you come up with a silly idea like that? You come into the house with me now and help me with the bracelet I'm making. I need your clever little fingers to pick out twenty-five pieces of leopard skin."

Chapter 3

What do I look like? The very first thing people notice about me is that I'm physically tiny, just five feet short. I wish looks and stature weren't such powerful determinants of how we're all treated in this world. I don't think of myself as a beauty. I don't even like the term. When I hear my brothers or other boys talk about some girl as being "really pretty" it always seems to me that whoever they're talking about becomes just that, and nothing more. It's as if her physical appearance becomes her entire identity. I can see as easily as anyone else whether or not a man or a woman is attractive, but my next thought is always, *I wonder what he or she does and what they're thinking.*

Anyway, I have shoulder length, dirty blond hair that's average at best. It's unruly and doesn't take direction well. It does what it wants when it wants.

My face is nothing special, it's just a face. I don't have fancy cheek bones or a patrician nose that sets me apart. It's covered with freckles that extend out to both sides and under my eyes. Truth be told my nose is a little smushed and when I laugh, I sometimes snort if I really get going.

My lips are full, but not the pouty kind men fantasize about. My teeth are anything but perfect. They're white, but orthodontics is not in a shrimping family's household budget and my top two middle teeth have a little gap between them and they twist ever so slightly away from one another which makes them look as though they aren't speaking. I'm also missing a tooth on the left side, right behind my canine. Harley found a golf club in someone's trash when we were little kids and wanted to show me how far he could hit a pinecone with it. I was standing too close behind him and his backswing got me, dislodged a tooth, and left me with a small scar that comes off the side of my mouth.

My arms are striated and sinewy from hard work and running, my stomach is flat, thanks to my workout regimen, and my legs are also strong and defined from running.

I saved the one feature I like about me for last. It's my eyes. They're gem-quality jade in color and clarity. Tiny, yellow, starbursts resembling sunflower petals surround black pupils and then explode outward in thousands of micro-rivulets of a unique grey/green color. People stare at my eyes for a second too long when I'm introduced, and sometimes, I even catch people I've known for years studying them, trying to figure them out. They must break some sort of eye rule.

In summary, I'm a ninety-pound, short, flat, average girl with a wild head of hair and a face and mouth full of distracting imperfections. I have the musculature of a Kenyan long-distance runner and I've got really cool eyes.

Chapter 4

The meat of my story begins at the end of my junior school year in 2020 at the age of fifteen. Something happened to me that spring that changed the entire trajectory of my life.

I'd been dating a boy named Christopher that I'd started seeing right after the pandemic started in February. He was two years older than me and my first "boyfriend." In early May he tried to take something from me that I was not yet willing to give up.

Some of my classmates had started dating and having sex as early as twelve, but that wasn't the norm in our small, conservative, Southern town and certainly not for me, the ostracized outsider. My universe of potential suitors was minuscule and further reduced in size by my own strict standards. Christopher was the first boy that had shown any serious interest in me that was reciprocated. He would walk me home after school on the few days that we actually had school in February of 2020. That was the year of the great Covid-19 pandemic from China and school was an on and off affair that entire year. Chris and I would study together, do school projects together, run together and on occasion discuss books that we were reading although he wasn't as big a reader as I. Going to the movies, parties, field trips and other activities that involved groups of people were simply not options with the Covid-19 virus running rampant around the country, and many of those activities were banned. Because of all this and by virtue of the fact that we lived quite close to one another, we ended up spending more time in close proximity to one another than would have been the norm. He seemed to care about what I was thinking, who I was as a person, and what I wanted to be. I was flattered by this attention and to some degree it helps explain my blindness to his true nature.

One afternoon we got kissing in Chris's family barn. We'd done it before, but I'd always stopped things short of having sex with him. For the first half-hour he was attentive, complimentary, gentle, and adoring, but on that particular day some filter in him got shut off and when he finally realized that I was serious about hanging onto my virginity, he turned mean and scared the hell out of me.

The whole time he'd been saying all these sweet things to me hoping to wear me down. But when I finally pushed him away after having pulled his hand out of my jeans for probably the tenth time, and firmly telling him "'no," his true nature came to light.

That day, instead of apologizing and backing off as he'd done in the past, he rolled me onto my back, straddled my upper body, held both my arms at my sides and said, "Cat, enough of the cock teasing. If you won't give it to me, I'm going to take it."

I looked up at him, incredulously. I'd never once heard language like that come out of his mouth and what he said infuriated me on a number of levels.

I was instantly white-hot angry. "Say what!" I shouted up at him.

I'd never had the slightest inkling that Christopher had a crude, aggressive, dominating, side to him. He'd professed on numerous occasions that he cared about me, and been thoughtful, considerate, and accommodating to a fault. I remember looking up into his eyes after that statement and didn't even recognize the person staring back at me. It was like his mask had fallen off and, in that moment, I realized that everything we'd shared up to that point had been a deceitful act on his part. He was a living lie and worst of all, I'd completely fallen for his act. I was as furious at myself, as I was with him.

"Like hell you are!"

My words seemed to encourage rather than discourage him and he smiled smugly. "I'm going to fuck you, little Callie-girl. I know you've wanted me from the moment we met. You can fight me, but it's a waste of time."

I started struggling at that point and tried to get him to release my arms. "Christopher, stop! Please! I'm not your little girl and you're scaring the hell out me. Get off!"

CALLIE AWAKENS

My pleas were pointless, however, and he kept leering at me with this stupid expression on his face. I think all the blood in his head had traveled to his nether regions and my pleas fell on deaf ears. He pulled my tee shirt up and roughly pawed at my breasts. I shook my head from side to side and tried to squirm out from underneath him.

"Christopher, don't do this!" I pleaded and struggled some more. He was about six feet tall and had almost 100 pounds on me. My struggling was completely ineffective, but I kept up my resistance and realizing he wasn't going to stop, I yelled out for help hoping that one of his parents might hear me.

He put his left arm across my upper chest pinning me to the floor, then put his right hand over my mouth to stifle my cries. I was seriously starting to freak out at that point and with almost no thought at all, I reacted to his hand over my mouth, by biting it.

He pulled it back, swore, and then hit me in the mouth with his right fist to shut me up. I immediately tasted blood, and then watched with increasing horror as he reached back, grabbed a bandana out of his back pocket, and stuffed it into my mouth. Then he reached down with the same hand, to undo his pants.

I was completely stunned. I couldn't believe he'd just hit me and then stuffed a rag into my mouth. Those were the practiced actions of someone who had raped before. How on earth could any human being instantly transition so completely from adoring boyfriend and confidant to a dangerous, predator/batterer like that? And how could I have failed so spectacularly to see this side of him and to read his true nature?

He had to lean forward and bend over to keep pressure on my chest with his forearm and at the same time reach back to undo his pants. I realized this was going to end badly very shortly if I didn't think of something in the next few seconds. My mind was racing as I continued to buck and squirm beneath him, and I tried to think of something, anything, I could do to get out of the predicament I was in. I remember feeling nauseous too and wondered if throwing up on him might cool him off. Then suddenly, out of nowhere, I remembered a fight scene I'd seen in a movie I'd watched with my brothers. Two prison toughs had been battling it out with their fists and had ended up grappling on the floor. One of the two prisoners had straddled the other in much the same way that Chris was holding me down. He was punching the other inmate from the same superior position that Chris held over me. I remembered how quickly the fight had ended, however, when the one on the bottom in the defensive position had suddenly snapped his head forward and head-butted his opponent right in the face. I wondered if I could do the same thing to Chris.

I was absolutely determined that he was not going to take my virginity from me by force, no matter what, and I started planning as to how I would do it. Christopher was totally focused on getting his pants undone and perhaps not paying enough attention to me. Despite the pressure of his arm on my upper chest pushing me down, I sensed I had enough range of motion in my neck to lift my head far enough to make contact with his face, if I could just get him to turn back towards me and look down at me. I bided my time and waited as he seesawed his pants down over his hips. Once they were down around his knees, he turned back to face me and gloat for a second before going to work on my pants. I wanted him to keep facing me and stopped struggling just long enough to let him think I was becoming compliant. I remember him smiling down at me probably thinking that his charm was working. I smiled back and silently mouthed the word "yes."

"So you do want it," he observed delusionally.

I nodded. "Oh yes, Chris, I want…!" I screamed.

As the last word came out of my mouth, I snapped my head forward, as hard as I could, right into the middle of his face. I put every ounce of strength I had into the strike. It was a really clean, hard hit and I distinctly remember both feeling and hearing his nose break. I bet my head went from 0-50mph in the short distance it traveled.

Immediately he released the pressure on my chest and sat straight up. I sensed a new opening and an increase in my freedom of movement, and I snapped my forehead into his face a second time, even harder than my first strike, right into the orbital bone under his left eye, cracking that also.

I finished the statement I'd started before my head butts. "What I want, you freak, is to bash your damned head in!" I screamed.

He rolled backwards off me howling in agony and brought a hand to his shattered nose.

"You bitch! I can't believe you just did that to me!"

He was on his side on the floor next to me at that point with his jeans and underwear around his knees with blood and snot pouring out of his flattened nose. I scrambled to my feet, pumped and still absolutely furious at him for trying to rape me. He was crying from the pain and his entire face was starting to swell. But I felt absolutely no remorse for what I'd just done and instead of kneeling down to see if I could help him, I instead picked up my foot and stomped down as hard as I could on his crotch. He cried out again and folded himself into a fetal position.

"You asshole! I can't believe I fell for you!"

God I was angry. I'd thwarted his rape, but I felt absolutely humiliated. As I straightened my clothes and collected myself, I ran the entire incident through my mind again and got so mad I kicked him again; this time in the thigh for good measure and spit some of the blood out of my mouth and onto his prostrate form. The last thought I remember having in the barn was that *spitting wasn't ladylike*, but I didn't care and ran all the way home. I wasn't fearful of him following me. I knew I'd really hurt him and that he wouldn't be walking let alone running after anyone for a while. I simply wanted to get as far away from him and the entire incident as quickly as possible. My failure to see through him is what shook me the most.

By the time I reached home, I'd settled down enough to realize that I didn't want any of my family members to see my split lip and I came in quietly through the back door and successfully got to my room without running into anyone. Once in there with the door closed, I started shaking and allowed myself some tears as I thought about what had almost happened. I swore at that moment that I would never allow myself to be physically overpowered and intimidated by a man ever again. I think Chris's arrogant assumption that he could physically dominate me bothered me as much as his attempted rape.

It didn't end there, however. My split lip and bruised mouth were going to be impossible to hide from my family. I was ready to let the whole thing go. To my way of thinking I'd learned an important lesson and I knew that Chris would never bother me again. The rape had not happened and the damage I'd done to his face seemed adequate punishment. But I was fearful about what might happen at the dinner table that night. I cleaned up my face and lip as best I could in the bathroom and then stayed in my room until Mam called us all to dinner an hour later.

I was the last to sit at the table and subconsciously kept my head down. I didn't want to lie to my family, but I also didn't want to give them the details as to what had happened. There was no telling how my father or brothers would respond.

I'd been having scraps with Daddy on a pretty regular basis by this time. We most frequently fought over me wanting to do things he didn't approve of or saw no point in. That spring, for instance, I'd been adamant about wanting to spend the summer on *Damon & Harley*, shrimping with him and my brothers. I still wanted to be a boat captain and I needed the sea time and experience I would get on the boat to qualify for a license. He thought me becoming a boat captain was a stupid idea and a waste of time and didn't believe that a girl could meet the physical challenges of shrimping and he'd consistently told me, "no."

"What happened to your face, Callie?" my mother asked after putting a plate in front of me and gently reaching towards the hurt area.

I petulantly pulled back from her hand. "I'd rather not discuss it, Mam."

Conversation stopped around the table, and everyone looked over at me.

"Answer your mother, girl," my father ordered.

"What part of 'I'd rather not discuss it' was I unclear about? I told you all I don't want to talk about it."

"Don't get fresh, young lady.," my father warned threateningly.

"C'mon, Callie, tell us what happened?" my brother Harley prodded.

"I told you, I don't want to talk about it."

I could tell from their persistent interest that it was absolutely out of the question for me to tell all of them that a boy from school had tried to rape me. I was terrified of how they'd react. The attempted rape of a girl in our family would be a huge insult to all of them. I knew each of them cared about me and my well-being to some degree, but family pride was a big deal in our family and an attack on one of us, was an attack on all of us. If I told them the whole story, I knew the entire thing was going to spiral out of control.

"It's none of any of your business. Just leave it!" I shouted, and then pushed off from the table and fled to my room and listened for the next few minutes to the four of them discussing it. They speculated quite a bit back and forth and then my father directed my mother to go get it out of me.

She knocked a few moments later.

"What?"

Mam came into my room and sat down on the edge of the bed. "Callie, you need to tell us what happened. It's clear that somebody hit you."

"Why? Why do I need to tell you? It doesn't have anything to do with any of you. It happened to me, and I took care of it. There's no need to let the whole thing get bigger than it is."

"Your father really wants to know."

"Why, because his macho pride is at risk?"

"Well, I imagine it's because he cares about you and wants to make sure it doesn't happen again."

"Bull. Just tell him I got into a fight at school with another girl. He won't care so much about it."

She got an angry look in her eye. "Are you telling me it wasn't a girl that did this to you?"

"I didn't say any such thing. Just tell him what I said. If you think it will make him feel better, tell him she got the worst of it."

I didn't know it at the time, but my father was standing right outside my bedroom door and had heard every word. He burst in.

"Goddamnit, girl! Did a man do this to you?" He grabbed me by the shoulders and shook me.

I looked up at him, angry. "I don't want you and my brothers getting involved! It was nothing I couldn't handle and the reason I'm keeping this whole thing to myself is because I knew that you and my two retarded brothers would totally wig out, just like you are now!"

"You're going to tell me, Callie! he stated definitively.

"No, sir, not gonna happen." I shook my head.

He kicked the newel post at the bottom of my bed. "You are grounded until you tell me who did this!"

"What? You're going to ground me for defending myself? That is so messed up!"

My father raised his open hand as if to strike me but didn't. Maybe even he appreciated how ironic it would be for a man to strike a woman for not telling him what man had struck her. He stormed out of the room.

There were very few secrets at our school though, and by the end of the next day my brothers had found out what happened to me and they in turn told my father. Just as I'd feared and speculated, the three of them piled into my father's truck and drove over to Chris's family's home that evening. They hadn't been drinking moonshine and didn't drive over there with loaded shotguns, a noose, and my dog Crab Claw baying in the back, but they were every bit as determined and crazy as an old-time lynch mob when they left our house.

****

Christopher's father heard them as they screeched to a halt in his driveway and went out on the front porch.

"Bring your son out here, right now, Angus!" my father shouted.

"You're joking right, Harley?"

"You'll find out how much I'm joking! I'm serious as a heart attack. There's nothing amusing about this situation, Angus. Bring him out here right now. Me and my sons would like a word with him."

"Well I'd be hard-pressed doing that considering he's in the hospital with what your daughter already did to him!"

My father and brothers looked at each other, totally befuddled.

"What she did to him! What on earth are you talking about? All we've heard is what he tried to do to her."

Christopher's father shook his head before responding.

"That girl of yours broke up his whole face is what she did. His nose was destroyed and the bones under his left eye were cracked. I expect he'll be in the hospital for several days and then need expensive plastic surgery to put his face back in order. I won't even say what she did to his privates. He might never be able to father children! I don't approve in any way of what Christopher might have tried doing with your daughter, but she's lucky she's not in jail for what she did to him."

My father was completely flummoxed and uncertain as to what to say or do next. He shuffled his feet and thought for a moment before bringing his head up and looking Christopher's father in the eye again.

"Angus, you tell your boy when he gets out that he's not welcome in our home or anywhere near our daughter. If I ever hear of something like this again or he threatens her in any way, he best be prepared for a proper beating from me and my boys."

"Oh, you needn't worry about him messing around with Callie in the future. I think he's terrified of her. Serves him right. He's still got me to deal with once he's healed up. I'm sorry this whole thing happened, Harley. I apologize sincerely from our family to yours."

My father stood there without saying anything more for several seconds. He'd gotten everything he needed to satisfy his Southern male pride. Apparently, our family honor had already been successfully defended by me, and Christopher's father had just delivered a heartfelt apology.

"Well, all right then; I guess. I'm glad you have the situation in hand. Too bad there had to be this unpleasantness."

"I'm sorry too. And, Harley?

"What?"

"Good luck with that girl of yours. What is she, five feet tall?"

"Sounds right."

"She's got a strong head on her, in more ways than one."

****

When Daddy got back to the house, he called me out of my room.

"Catherine, what on earth did you do to that boy?"

I thought for a moment before answering unsure of whether he was pleased or angry with me.

"I told him, 'no' and when he tried taking what was mine anyway, I smashed his face in with my head and then stomped him in the crotch."

As my words sank in, Daddy actually smiled and looked me right in the eye for several seconds before responding further and, in that instant, for one tiny second, I glimpsed that same coveted approval he so easily conferred on my two brothers.

He caught himself though and averted his gaze. "You did well, Catherine. I probably shouldn't say that, but certain people need a beating on occasion, and from what I've heard, you did a credible job."

He started to walk off, and then turned back. "You're no longer grounded."

I was speechless for a moment because my father had never let me off punishment before. I decided the moment was ripe to push for more.

"Does that also mean I can go shrimping with you and my brothers this summer?"

"No, girl, that does not! I'm proud of the way you handled yourself with that boy, but the ocean is no place for a little bit of a girl like you. You can do better than life on a shrimp boat with your brains and that hard head of yours. Get interested in something else."

I didn't get my way on shrimping with him and my brothers that summer, but I did, and I will never forget it, get his respect and admiration for one quick moment for smashing in Christopher's face. That was also the only time I ever remember him calling me Catherine. What a family.

I was already an outsider at school for the all the reasons I talked about earlier. Perversely, the incident with Christopher took me even farther away from my peers and left me feeling part of exactly nothing. Instead of coming out the villain, Christopher had somehow ended up as the handsome favorite that had been unjustly wronged by the freak, brain-girl that no one identified with. Adding in the fact that I wouldn't be shrimping with my brothers and father for the coming summer and didn't have an alternative job of any sort lined up left me feeling like a complete loser as school was closing. That brings me to my Aunt Nancy Liddell from Boca Grande and the profound influence she had on me and the trajectory of my entire life that summer.

Chapter 5

Aunt Nancy is my mother's older sister. Mam and she are opposites. If you met them on the street, you'd never guess that they'd shared the same home, parents, and upbringing as children.

Mam has always been introverted, quiet, unopinionated, deferential, modest, and plain. She discontinued her education when she became pregnant with Harley in her Junior year.

Nancy, on the other hand, was noisy, highly opinionated, brash, and deferred to no one going through high school. She went on to become highly educated, stylish, powerful, and rich as can be. Where my mother has always drawn her entire sense of self from her husband and family, Nancy cast her husband aside when she grew bored with him, and they never produced children. Unlike Mam, Nancy went to college, lived in New York and Chicago, became famous in her own right as a publisher, and then sold her company for a fortune at the age of thirty-eight. Why they're such complete opposites is anyone's guess. Maybe one of them got dropped on their head as a child. Certainly, I'm as different from my brothers as night is from day and we all had the same parents.

Aunt Nancy lives on an island named Boca Grande which is one of the most expensive zip codes in the country. It's just an hour away by car and about the same by fast skiff. Despite her living quite close to us, we seldom visited her as a family more than once a year, and never for more than a day or two as no one in our family but me felt comfortable on Boca Grande. The chasm between our respective lifestyles is vast and Nancy and my parents share not one single common interest. I think she and my mother both regret this, but they've never been able to get around it. Neither is openly critical of the other, but between my aunt's outside interests and the demands my father and brothers put on Mam, the two sisters never grew close and spent little time together. Our family visits had tapered off to nothing by my fifteenth year.

Life on Boca Grande is like an alternate universe to life on the edge of the Caloosahatchee River. Even as a six-year-old girl I'd sensed this. While the two places are geographically close to one another, in reality they're light years apart. Thinking back on those early visits; before we'd even get in the truck, my parents and brothers would get tense and voices would get raised around the house. I was too young then to get the nuances of feeling inferior because of the clothing you wear or the car you drive, but I could sense how awkward going to visit Nancy made all of them feel. I liked going to visit her because her house was so beautiful, her pool sparkled, and her beds were so comfortable. I couldn't imagine anything more glorious. I liked Nancy because she was attentive to me and considered every one of my words when I spoke. She would look me in the eye and respond to my questions thoughtfully. That made me feel special and important.

During this period when I was feeling like a loser with absolutely no plan for my summer, the house phone rang, and I answered it. Mam was out shopping. I was home alone.

"Hello."

"Catherine, is that you?"

I recognized her voice right away and smiled before speaking.

"No, I think you're mistaken. Callie isn't here right now. You're speaking to a loser."

"What? A loser? Hardly, dear girl. What's going on. How are you really, Catherine?"

I loved that she called me Catherine and "dear girl."

"I'm fine." I started.

"Well you don't sound fine!"

"No, ma'am, I guess I'm really not," I admitted.

"Well spit it out and tell me what's going on. And it's Aunt Nancy or just Nancy. I'm still hot and 'ma'am' makes me sound like some frumpy old thing in a moo moo. I'm just barely forty for Christ's sake!"

I laughed outright, forgetting how refreshing it was to talk with her.

"I'm sorry, Nancy. I've just been really wrapped up in some stuff that happened here and can't seem to get out of my own way today. I really had my heart set on shrimping with my father and my brothers this summer and they just aren't having it. I'm feeling rudderless."

"Well this whole damned spring has been a mess with this pandemic and these lockdowns. What's the 'stuff' you're wrapped up in?"

I was embarrassed about what had taken place between Christopher and me, but knew I couldn't hold anything back from her. I had to think for a few seconds how to phrase it. "A boy got fresh with me a couple of weeks ago and I put him in the hospital."

"What! Are you alright?"

"I'm fine, but the whole thing made me even more of a pariah with my 'friends.' Mainly I'm just trying to figure out what to do with myself for the summer. I really wanted to go shrimping with my father, but he says girls don't belong on shrimp boats which is a total crock."

"You still have your heart set on becoming a ship captain?"

"Yup, but I'm not making much progress on that front."

She paused for a second and then blew me away with her next question. "Well, why don't you come spend the summer with me?"

I was flabbergasted at her suggestion. The idea of getting away from my family, my dorky non-friends, and the possibility of avoiding Christopher had tremendous appeal. And to do it while living on Boca Grande with the coolest woman I knew was some sort of fantasy dream.

"Oh, Nancy, I'd love to do that, but I've got a feeling I could never talk my parents into it."

"And why do you think they'd have a problem?"

I hesitated for a moment not wanting to offend her. "They're funny about Boca Grande."

"Boca Grande is just an island like any other."

"I know, but it's loaded with rich people."

"And that makes it bad?"

"Well, Daddy's weird. He can't relate to rich people and he'd probably think their influence would be corrupting or some other foolishness."

"I know what you're saying. Not about the rich people being corrupting but about your father. Let me talk with Frances. Is she there?"

"No, she's out shopping. She'll be back in an hour or so."

"Leave it to me, Catherine. I'll talk to her later and see if I can't make it happen."

"Thanks, Aunt Nancy. I really appreciate your offer, but I won't get my hopes up."

"Hang in there, Nancy's on the case."

"Okay, nice talking with you. I'm glad you called."

Nancy called back later that afternoon and spoke with my mother. I'm still not sure what the conversation was between them and how it all went down, but I'm guessing my mother probably understood on some level how awkward the whole thing with Christopher was for me in the community. The bottom line was I was ultimately allowed to go to Boca Grande that summer and absolutely everything in my life changed.

Chapter 6

Mam drove me to Aunt Nancy's two weeks later. Daddy was unavailable (and I'm sure pleased) as he was off on a trip with Damon and Harley on the *Damon & Harley*. Notice how the boat's name isn't *Damon & Harley & Catherine*? That fact wasn't lost on me, and I arrived still thinking about and resenting the fact that I wasn't shrimping with them and getting required sea-time for my captain's license. Despite those resentments, I was excited at the prospect of spending the summer on Boca Grande and spending time with Aunt Nancy. After we paid the outrageous $6.50 toll the residents charge to go over the tiny bridge that leads onto the island, my mood improved.

After you cross the bridge, you travel across a causeway that leads onto the island proper. The view from this vantage point is stunning. To your left and paralleling the road, are the old stone trestles that once supported the track of the railroad line that used to connect Boca Grande with Fort Myers, Naples, Tampa, and the rest of the world. These supports are granite block and rise just twelve feet above the water. In-between them, sport-fishermen in their boats cast into the water around them hoping to catch some of the fish that shelter below. On the other side of the trestles is the Cape Haze Aquatic Preserve and the shore of the mainland in the distance.

To your right sits the pristine inlet and shores of Little Gasparilla Island and the pass that boats travel through to get to the West side of the Island and the open Gulf of Mexico. Everything on Boca Grande is landscaped and lovely and even the water surrounding the island seems to change to a more beautiful color as you cross the bridge. I lowered my window as we crossed the causeway and breathed in the sea air. I'd never spent time away from my family and I suddenly felt very independent and grown-up as if a new chapter in my life were beginning.

Nancy's house is on the West side of the island, right on the Gulf of Mexico. It's a monstrous, rambling, Spanish Colonial Revival home built in the early 1900's and has eight bedrooms and five bathrooms. It's stucco with traditional red barrel-tile roofs. The porch that wraps around the main house is twelve feet deep and there are covered breezeways that connect the various parts of the house. The shade provided by these overhangs cools the ocean breeze before it blows through the windows. Nancy seldom uses air conditioning and prefers instead to feel and smell the outside air as it blows through the house. The structure sits on a four-acre parcel of land surrounded on three sides by a ten-foot-tall stucco wall. The side of the house facing the Gulf, is open. Between the house and the beach there's a pool surrounded by a marble piazza.

When you arrive at Nancy's "beachside cottage" (as she calls it), you drive through imposing iron gates and then onto a pristine, raked, white-pebble driveway that makes popping sounds as car tires run over it. Both sides of the winding driveway are filled with beds of hibiscus, rhododendron, dogwoods, myrtles, jacarandas, ornamental grasses, palms of all sizes, and dozens of flowering perennials. Her grounds are meticulously maintained by three full-time gardeners. At the end of the driveway near the house she has a five-car garage and an attached greenhouse that houses a multitude of plants and seedlings including twelve different mature camelia trees that produce blossoms about five months of the year.

I know nothing about art and interior design. Nancy calls her taste and furnishings "minimalist." I can tell you that what there is in each room is unusual and beautiful and her paintings, sculptures and furniture pieces are all unique and clearly one-of-a-kind. And despite each one demanding attention, none of them are pretentious or garish and all of them work effortlessly well together.

There are exposed, rough, wooden, beams overhead throughout the house and perfectly finished wood floors at your feet. When you walk inside you are almost overwhelmed by the delicious smells of fresh flowers, furniture polish, and the Gulf wafting in through the dozens of open, divided light windows.

CALLIE AWAKENS

After Nancy greeted us, her housekeeper Rosario served the three of us a delicious lunch consisting of New England lobster rolls, the best salad I'd ever eaten, little pastries, and iced tea that had all been sourced from *Newlin's* about four blocks away. My mother was as uncomfortable as I was at the opulent surroundings and after various attempts at finding some common ground to discuss with her sister, and failing as usual, she simply stood up at the end of lunch, thanked her sister, admonished me to be on my best behavior, and then simply left.

Nancy came back into the house after seeing her off. "Well, that was awkward. Let's go talk in the living room, shall we, Catherine?"

I followed her out to her large living room that faced the Gulf. Nancy sat down on one of the two pristine white couches that faced each other. I remained standing, terrified of sitting on anything so white. The closest thing we had to white in my house was dark gray, and I was scared I'd stain something if I sat down. I was dressed in a "Bait Shack" t-shirt, worn cutoff shorts, and running shoes. I wasn't dirty, but I felt that way.

"Sit, sit."

I looked around for a blanket to put down.

"I don't want to get anything dirty."

She cocked her head at me, stood up, and hugged me. "Catherine, don't be silly. I know this is a bit of a culture shock for you, but it's just furniture."

"But it's white furniture!"

Nancy laughed. "It's going to be a long summer if you can't feel comfortable in my house."

"I hope my coming wasn't a mistake, Aunt Nancy. I'm very excited about being here and really grateful that you offered, but it's going to take me a little time to get comfortable with all this." I swept my hand around the room. "It's nothing like I'm used to."

She thought for a moment. "Okay, try this. Just do what I do." Nancy turned around, sat back down on the couch, and then smiling, drew her legs up, swung her body around, and lay back on the couch with her sandal-clad-feet on the cushion. Then she leaned back in an exaggerated Cleopatra pose. "Like this."

I took a breath, smiled back at her, sat down and after double checking that there wasn't something on my sneakers, put them up on the couch and reclined, mimicking her. She smiled at me again, then threw a cushion at me and giggled. That was our beginning.

"Now that all of that nonsense is out of the way, catch me up on your life, Catherine."

"What part? I don't really have one."

"Nonsense, of course you do. Start out by telling me what in the heck happened between you and this boy and what he did that compelled you to hospitalize him."

I said nothing for a few seconds. She was so direct and what she was asking was embarrassing for me. I wasn't used to being spoken to so honestly and directly.

"Okay, I was starting to really like this boy at school named Christopher."

"What did you like about him?"

"Well, he was the first boy who would listen to me. I felt like he was interested in who I was as a person. We'd do school projects together, run, and, you know, hang out. He's tall, and muscular and he's got these really nice eyes and his hair is long and kind of falls into his eyes...."

"He's a dreamboat, got it. How old?"

"Seventeen."

"And you're what, fifteen?"

I nodded.

"And he hit on you a little hard?"

"Well, actually no. He hit me, hit me."

"Like, with a fist?" She mimicked a punch with an incredulous expression on her face.

I nodded. "He cut my lip and bruised my mouth."

"Bastard! There's never, ever a justification for that. But just for context, what were the circumstances?"

"We were, you know, kissing."

"Just kissing or were you doing more?

I blushed. "I was just kissing, but he had quite a bit more in mind; like everything."

"And you said, 'no'?"

I nodded.

"And he said?"

I hung my head, embarrassed. "He said, 'I'm going to screw you little girl.' Then I said, 'Like hell you are!' Then I struggled to get out from underneath him and called out for help. When he put his hand over my mouth to shut me up, I bit him."

"Good for you!"

"That was when he hit me and stuffed a rag in my mouth."

"Cocksucker! Oops, Aunt Nancy isn't supposed to use language like that."

I burst out laughing.

"And then you gave him some sort of 'adjustment,' I assume? You must have done something besides bite him to put him in the hospital?"

I'd never heard that expression before but nodded. "Yes, I 'adjusted' him with two headbutts; one to the nose and the second to one of his cheekbones. Oh, and I stomped him in the balls for good measure."

Nancy had a very intense look on her face at this point; like she was seeing something in me she hadn't expected. I expected her to sympathize with me next. She didn't.

"What did you learn from this experience?"

I had to think for a second. "I guess the biggest thing I learned was that I wasn't the judge of character that I thought I was and that maybe I'd trusted someone too much without enough information." I shrugged.

"Men can be total assholes." Nancy observed.

I maintained eye contact with her after her observation and then, with a serious expression on my face and an admonishing tone said, "Language Aunt Nancy, language." I was completely deadpan in my delivery.

She looked at me disbelieving at first and then burst out laughing.

"You're a piece of work, Callie."

Her comment felt like a compliment despite being phrased as a negative.

"Thank you, Nancy. You know, I'm laughing about it now, but at the time, I was terrified. I realized I wasn't nearly as smart as I thought, and I also realized how physically vulnerable I was to a bully like him. I didn't like it. I got in a few lucky shots, but I never want to find myself in a position like that again where I'm physically intimidated by anyone. I felt really defenseless. There aren't a lot of options when you're my size."

Nancy got a faraway look in her eyes. "I know. So, tell me some of your hopes and your dreams. We haven't had much contact over the last couple of years".

"I still want to be a ship captain, a real licensed captain and drive big ships."

"Any particular reason?"

"I want to be looked up to and respected. I want to be in charge and in control."

"Do you mean a shrimp boat captain like your father?"

"No…, something more than that. I'm angry at my father right now. He says a shrimp boat is no place for a woman. He's such a chauvinist and I can't stand being told I can't do something because I'm a woman. It just makes me want to do it more."

"There are lots of ways you can get looked up to and respected. Are you sure this captain thing is something you really want?"

"I'm sure." I nodded with assurance.

"Well, I know some interesting and powerful women. Let me give all this some thought and I'll see what I can think up to help you. In the meantime, how do you want to spend your time while you're here on the island? Do you want to lie around the beach all day, work, learn something new, what?"

"I'd like to work, ideally something where I could advance my sea-time hours. I also love learning new things."

"How do you advance sea time hours?"

"In order to sit for your captain's license, you need to document 360 days at sea. You can include all time spent on boats eighteen feet or longer and anything more than four hours away from the dock counts as a day. So, I'm going to look for some sort of job that gives me that."

"What about fun? A girl's gotta have fun."

"I'm not sure I'm very good at fun. I'm always studying, running, or swimming. Running's my big thing. I've already done four marathons, but seeing as you have a pool, I'm going to work out in that a lot this summer too."

Nancy seemed surprised at what I'd told her. "I wish I'd had your energy and drive when I was fifteen. I seem to remember that sleep was my favorite thing when I was that age. All that aside, I have a feeling that you and I are going to have a ball this summer and I'd like to start out by making a suggestion."

"What's that?"

"As I'm sure you've noticed from your past trips here, Boca Grande is a little more stylish than Fort Myers.

I rolled my eyes. "I've noticed."

Nancy smiled. "How would you feel about letting your incredibly rich, old aunt take you out this afternoon for a little clothes shopping? The last thing I want is for you to feel awkward or uncomfortable while you're here and there will be times when you'll want something more fashionable than tee shirts, cutoffs and sneakers."

"That's a very nice offer, Nancy, but I can buy my own stuff once I get a job."

"I know you can, and I respect you for wanting to, but I'm frightfully rich and easily bored, and with no kids of my own, I'd really enjoy doing that for you. Besides," she added. "I've got this massive, heavy purse that my financial adviser insists on constantly filling with cash. You'd really be doing me huge a favor if you'd help me empty it and allow me to purchase you a few modest rags."

I wasn't comfortable with the idea of her spending money on me. I wasn't used to being given anything and had to think about it for a few seconds. I sensed that her desire was sincere and not some way of gaining any sort of power over me. I also didn't want to start out our summer together by saying "no" to her. "Aunt Nancy, the last thing I want to do is disappoint you and if letting you spoil me is the only way we can avoid that, then so be it. Let the shopping begin."

"Excellent, let me go grab my purse and then we'll take one of the golf carts into the village."

"Can I help you carry it?"

She looked at me with a perplexed expression on her face.

"Your purse; I wouldn't want you to hurt yourself."

Nancy recovered quickly. "Aren't you adorable."

"I've got my learner's permit you know." I told her as we walked through the house. "May I drive?"

"Of course."

We walked out into the garage through the kitchen door. She pressed a button on the wall, all the lights came on, and one of the five overhead doors rolled up. In the stall directly in front of us there were three golf carts. In the adjoining stall there was an immaculate, black convertible with the top down with a radiator emblem that said, *"Bentley."* It immediately caught my eye. I'd never seen one before but had seen pictures of them in automobile magazines. "What a cool car, Aunt Nancy," I said, instantly falling in love. "Are you sure you wouldn't be more comfortable in that?"

"Oh, don't be silly, Catherine; most assuredly not. That would be pretentious for just running into the village. And besides, you're far too young to drive the Bentley. That is a motorcar that one drives only after having driven all others. And if we do have occasion to go off island this summer, you will drive my utility vehicle."

I looked around the rest of the garage to see what she was talking about. "You have a truck?"

"A truck? Certainly not," she said with umbrage and waved her hand towards another gleaming black car. "I have a little Range Rover I use for mundane chores like shopping."

Chapter 7

That afternoon we bought bags of really nice and mostly casual clothing at *Boca Grande Outfitters* and *Fugate's* including two simple summer dresses from *Lilly Pulitzer's*. I had never in my life had so many new things and I'm embarrassed to say, I loved it.

Nancy introduced me to a number of her friends and neighbors as we shopped and walked around the quaint, little, village of Boca Grande. Everyone was very nice, but when several of them asked me about my plans for the future and I told them I wanted to be a captain, I noted that a disconnect of sort seemed to take place. Several of them also asked me what universities I'd applied to for the following year as if it were a given that I would be attending college. In my circles, college wasn't a "given" and I started to feel embarrassed when I admitted that I hadn't really given it a lot of thought. Neither of my parents had been to college and my brothers would be lucky if they finished high school. Their questions did, however, plant a seed in me.

Nancy and I talked as we drove back to her cottage in the golf cart. On Boca Grande everyone drives either a bike or a golf cart when going from one place to another.

"Thank you for all the incredible clothes, Nancy. I don't think I've ever owned anything as nice as the ones you bought me."

"You're entirely welcome, Catherine. You have no idea the pleasure it gave me to be able to do that."

We rode in silence for a block before she spoke again.

"You're a good student, right?

I nodded. "Yes." I admitted honestly. "Straight A's."

"Have you really not thought at all about going to college?"

"I've thought about it, but not seriously because I'd need to work for a couple of years before being able to afford the kind of school I'd want to go to. I just don't see the point of going to some below average community college just to be able to say I went to college. All those people asking me about it today made me realize that maybe I should be thinking about it more though."

"Good; ship captain is an admirable goal, but if you also had a college degree it would open a lot of other doors. Once you're the best captain in the Gulf of Mexico you might decide to do something completely different, and trust me, the world already has plenty of vapid, uneducated females. You've got a rare spark and I'd hate to see it extinguished."

Her words felt like a nice compliment, and I made a note to self to think more about college again.

Right away I settled into a workout routine and ran or swam every morning early before it got hot, and I learned my way around the island as I ran. After a few days of this I started recognizing people who were also out at that time of day. Many of them were fishing charter guides, landscapers, contractors, and other working stiffs. I identified with them more than most of Nancy's friends and after waving a few times as I ran by, I started stopping here and there, introducing myself, asking questions, and basically trying to identify possible opportunities. I became kind of a "thing" on my early morning runs and after a while people started smiling at me as I ran by and yelling things like, "run, Callie, run!" like Forrest Gump's girlfriend exhorted him when he was fleeing the mean boys on bicycles. After running or swimming I would usually take a shower and then have breakfast with Nancy.

After, I would help her maid/cook Rosario around the house or lend a hand to her husband Jesús in the gardens and around her small estate. Nancy didn't expect me to do any of this and had pointed out that was the reason she employed laborers. When she'd find me doing dishes, vacuuming, raking the driveway, or pruning alongside Jesús she seemed taken aback. Eventually, however, she acquiesced and seemed to accept that was just who I was.

Jesús had two others helping him with grounds maintenance; his twenty-one-year-old son John who was just like his father and another man in his mid-twenties named Matèo. He had more tattoos than I'd ever seen on a human being, and I wondered if he had gang affiliations. He kept to himself but creeped me out for reasons besides his tattoos. When I'd ask Matèo something, he would never look me in the eye when he answered, but I'd frequently catch him staring at me from a distance. I asked Jesús about him one day.

"Jesús, what's the deal with Matèo? He hardly says a word."

"I think that's just the way he is. He's not the best worker I've ever had, but my son John and he were good friends when they were younger, and he told me that Matèo was trying to break away from the gang life. I told John that I'd try him for a while. He hasn't bothered you, has he?"

"No, he just seems to look at me funny sometimes. I just noticed all the tattoos and wondered about the gang thing."

"Yes, I think he was part of MS13 years ago, but he says, 'no more.' In El Salvador where we all came from originally, almost everyone is part of the gangs at a certain age. He told me he is no longer involved, and he shows up on time every day, so I try not to judge."

I smiled at him. "You're a good man, Jesús."

"Thank you, Callie."

During my second week on the island, over breakfast one morning, Nancy told me that she'd invited a friend of a friend over for a casual early supper that night.

"She owns the ferry that runs between the Gasparilla Marina and Marco Island. She's agreed to talk with you and see if she can find you some sort of a job on her boat."

"How big a boat is it?" I asked excitedly.

"I gather it isn't a big ferry; I think she told me it's sixty-five feet, but if you can get the job, it would at least enable you to get started on your sea time."

I jumped up from the breakfast table and hugged her from behind. "You are so cool! Thank you, thank you, thank you!"

"Catherine, control yourself. Young ladies should never gush."

"Oh, horse pucky!"

"Horse pucky? I've always wondered, what is that?"

"It means horse shit."

45

"I am rather clever, aren't I?"

"Yes, you certainly are."

"Well, it's not like I gave you a Lamborghini with the trunk full of cash and a tank full of gas. It's a manual labor job and it's far from certain. She's a nice woman though, who'd love to help another aspiring sea-woman if she can. She does have several reservations, however. Your age is one problem and there are also some minimum standards you'll have to meet. You need to be CPR and advanced first aid certified to get the job. You also have to be willing to load and unload the ferry at each stop. She said it's pretty hard work and she's not sure it would be something you'd be physically capable of."

"You don't understand; that's exactly the type of job I want! It would be perfect for me!"

"She told me that some days they carry construction materials. Do you really think you can lift sixty-pound bags of concrete and gravel and handle loads of pressure treated lumber?"

"Nancy, I can do anything, if I'm given a shot."

"Well, her name's Melissa Trent. She'll be here at 5:30 this evening."

I gave Nancy a big, wet, kiss right on her forehead. "You're the best! Now I feel guilty for actually believing all those horrible things your neighbors and staff said about you when I first got here." I was messing with her.

"Ingrates, each and every one of them," she agreed playing along with me.

"Don't we know it Aunt Nancy." I nodded my head in mock agreement.

"We certainly do. Now, run along and go lift some weights or run 5 miles while I get this slobber off my forehead."

I kissed her again in the exact same spot and then literally skipped out of the house like a nine-year-old. I wanted to share my excitement with someone else and went in search of Jesús to see what he was up to. I also had a question I wanted to ask him. He was out at the front gate, painting the mailbox.

"Hola, Jesús, the most talented and attractive man in the world."

He stopped painting and smiled at me. "Buenos Dias, Miss Callie. And what pray tell has you smiling and telling lies so early in the day?"

46

"I have an interview tonight with a woman about a job on her ferry and I'm very excited about it."

"And why does a beautiful young girl like you wish to work on a ferry?"

"Because I want to be a captain of big ships and the only way I can get a license is to first get sea-time and experience. I've wanted to be a captain since I was six and Aunt Nancy invited a woman who is a captain to come for dinner tonight to meet me and interview me for a job."

Normally I would have brindled at Jesús's question about women wanting to work on a ferry as being sexist, but I knew him well enough at that point to know that he both liked me and also respected me for the hard work I put in at his side without complaint on an almost daily basis.

"Miss Callie, if that is your dream, then I have no doubt you will become a very good one."

"Jesús, I have a question. We have extra bags of the driveway stones, right?"

"Sí, of course. Why do you ask?"

"Part of my job will be to load and unload this ferry every day and the woman who might hire me is worried I won't be physically up to the job. Where are they? I want to practice lifting them."

"They are in the shed next to the garage."

"Cool, thanks."

I ran back down the driveway to the shed he'd spoken of. There were thirty or more bags in there underneath a tarp. The bags were only fifty pounds and not the sixty-pound variety, but I wanted to see if I could lift them. I squatted in front of the stack and pulled one into my lap. They were heavy, but careful to keep my back straight, I picked one up from a squat, hugged it to my chest and walked out of the shed and into the driveway. Both Jesús and his son John were leaning on their rakes looking at me as I came out. They looked at each other and nodded approval.

"What do you think?" I asked.

"Very good." Jesús offered. "May I make a suggestion?"

"Absolutely."

"See if you can get it up on your shoulder. I think you'll find it easier to carry that way."

I thought about it for a second, got my left hand under one end of the bag and pitched it up onto my shoulder. He was right. It was easier to carry. A thought came to me.

"Jesús, is there any chance that about 5:30 this evening you might just happen to be raking this end of the driveway and need some help?" I winked at him awkwardly several times.

He got it right away. "Well, normally we quit at 4:30, but seeing as I have personal errands to run this afternoon, I'll be staying late to catch up with my work. Help is always welcomed."

John laughed and smiled. "You two are a pair. I guess I'll be working late this evening also. Glad to help you, Callie."

At 5:00, I went looking for Nancy and found her in the living room. "Anything special you think I should wear this evening?"

"I don't think so. You're basically applying for a laborers job. I don't think wearing a dress is going to help you get this one."

"Good, I was hoping you'd say that."

At 5:20 I went out to the front of the house. Jesús and John were chatting and raking the driveway near the front door where cars pulled up. I gave a thumbs up to my co-conspirators and when we heard the sound of car wheels turning onto the gravel driveway from the main road I quickly ran into the shed, hoisted one of the fifty-pound bags onto my shoulder, and walked out to the area Jesús and John were raking. I casually looked at the car for a moment as it pulled up, then flipped the bag of gravel off my shoulder and onto the ground. The woman in the car got out and stood watching for a moment as Jesús reached down with his pruning knife, slit the bag open, and then dumped it out.

"Need any more of these, Jesús?" I asked.

"No, Miss Callie, thanks, that should be plenty."

I dusted my hands off on each other then walked over to the car, stuck out my hand and introduced myself.

"Hi. You must be our guest this evening. Melissa Trent, right? I'm Callie, Aunt Nancy's niece."

The woman standing before me was about 5'10" and powerfully built. I only came up to her breasts and stood as tall as I could trying to maximize my size. When she grasped my hand, I made sure to give her a firm handshake.

"Hi, Callie. Yes, I'm Melissa. What are you three up to?"

"I was just helping Jesús with some gravel while I waited to greet you. I help with chores outside when I'm not doing other things. I'm grateful that you're willing to speak with me about a possible job."

"Nancy's a big fan of yours, but I can't promise anything yet. You're two years younger than the people we generally hire for this job. I can see you're fit, but the job involves a lot of hard physical labor. And honestly, you're not the beefy sort of person we generally hire."

"I understand, ma'am. I'm grateful even for your consideration."

Nancy came out of the house. "I see you two have met."

"We have, and I have to tell you, I'm already impressed with your niece. It's refreshing to meet a young person who looks you in the eye and speaks directly. I'm lucky if I can get grunts out of my nephews and nieces."

"Come in, come in. Rosario made a delicious supper for the three of us. Why don't we eat it outside, on the ocean side?"

"Sounds lovely, Nancy."

I made a good enough impression on Ms. Trent that evening that she offered me a conditional job. I would first have to take Coast Guard required classes in CPR and advanced first aid. If I got the certificates, she agreed to take me on three days a week to start with a two-week trial period. I agreed to come down to the landing at Gasparilla Marina the next morning to look over the boat, hear a more thorough job description, and ride with her on their route to Marco Island. I was ecstatic.

Gasparilla Marina is just off-island on the mainland and Aunt Nancy suggested I take one of the guest bikes to ride there. It was about a five-mile bike ride.

I packed a lunch the next morning and biked to the ferry landing. I got there fifteen minutes early and stood at the dock looking over the sixty-five-foot aluminum crew boat. Even though she was a working boat, I could tell Melissa took pride in how her boat looked. Lack of cleanliness was something I'd never understood about my father's shrimp boat and all the other shrimp boats in his fleet. All of them looked like garbage scows and I'd never understood why. Every shrimp boat I'd ever seen looked like she was just ten minutes away from going to the bottom.

Melissa's ferry *Gulf Runner* was clean and completely squared away. The paint on her hull was unblemished and all her lines were coiled neatly. I fell in love right away. It was only 7:45 a.m. and I didn't yet see anyone around, but I heard the sound of metal on metal from inside the boat and noted that one of the two engine hatches on the rear deck was open.

"Ahoy, *Gulf Runner*." I called out in a loud voice. No answer. I called out again and still received no answer. I looked around the dock-front and grabbed a scrap piece of 2"x4" out of an old fifty-gallon oil drum that was being used as a trash bin and gently knocked on the side of the hull with it mindful not to scuff the paint.

The noises inside stopped, and a head appeared through one of the engine hatches at deck level.

"Oh, hi, Callie. You're a bit early. You want to help me below here in the engine room?"

"Good morning, Ms. Trent."

Melissa screwed her face up into an uncomfortable look. "That's not going to work. Just call me Melissa."

"Good morning, Melissa. I'd love to; help you, that is."

"Leave your knapsack up on deck and then climb below. Mind where you step coming down. There isn't a ladder. Just step on the engine and climb down as best you can. Once you get down here there's plenty of room."

I followed her instructions and climbed down into the engine room. "Wow!" was all I could manage once I was below. The engine space was huge, and I found I could stand upright in it without any problem. Melissa had to stay bent to avoid hitting her head. There were two monstrous green engines facing fore and aft and a third slightly smaller engine mounted sideways behind them, against the rear bulkhead.

"Ever been in the engine room of boat this size before."

"My father's shrimp boat is the same length, but he's only got a single motor and it's much smaller than these." I gestured at the main engines. "These are huge!"

"These old aluminum Breau Boats were built for speed and moving men and equipment in the oil fields."

"What are the engines?"

"The mains are turbocharged twelve-cylinder GM 1271's. They can push her along at thirty knots."

"Wow, my dad's boat just has one eight-cylinder motor. I don't think his boat can do over ten knots."

"I'm not surprised. The two boats were built to do really different things; this one was built light with an open cargo deck so it can go fast. His was built to pull a trawling net with tons of drag across the bottom at lower speeds.

Okay, the first thing I'm going to have you do every day when you're working is to come down here and check all the fluids in all three engines. That includes engine oil, transmission fluid and radiator coolant. All three, every day. You're also responsible for checking the water level in all six of those marine batteries. You'll also be checking all the hose clamps on the cooling hoses, visually inspecting for oil leaks of any kind anywhere, checking the bilge for water level and also for any signs of leaking oil."

She went over to a small tool bench alongside the generator, picked up a bound notebook and held it up.

"See this?"

I nodded.

"This is a maintenance log for everything that goes on in the engine room. You make a note of everything you do down here. If you add oil, transmission fluid or water to anything, you note it. If you change the oil or a filter on an engine, you note it. You note the day, which engine, and the engine hours at the time each bit of maintenance is done. You note if something is leaking or if it looks worn. Everything gets noted, even if you just replace a fuse or a bulb. This enables me or anyone else to come down here, take one look at the log and almost instantly tell the mechanical health of the vessel. Is one of the engines burning more oil than another, is the stuffing box on one side leaking more than the one on the other side, are we burning out bilge pumps for some reason?"

Melissa got down on her knees and took a flashlight out of her pocket. She turned it on and pointed it to where the shaft of one of the engines disappeared through the hull. See how there's a drip coming every three or four seconds where the shaft enters that box?"

I nodded.

"That's the stuffing box. The shaft goes through there on the way to the propeller. It allows the shaft to spin freely without water from the outside leaking into the ship. Some stuffing boxes use a flax type of material to get a good seal. This one uses grease. If it starts dripping faster than that, and it will after a few days, you need to turn this fitting here two turns. When you do that, it squeezes some grease into the stuffing box which slows down the leak. You want some leakage, but not too much. Understand?"

I nodded again.

She moved up to the front of the engine and placed two fingers in the middle of one of the fan belts running off the flywheel. She applied some pressure with her fingers. "See how much flex is in this fan belt? That's about the right amount of tension. As the belts wear and get exposed to all the heat down here, they tend to stretch. If they have too much play in them, they'll start slipping and either wear out prematurely, or break. If that happens you won't have any alternator or maybe the air conditioning will go out."

"What's an alternator?"

"Good question and I'm glad you asked instead of pretending you know. The alternators are here and here." She pointed to them. "They produce electricity which charges the ship's batteries which in turn provide the entire ship with electricity for running lights, refrigeration, radar, navigation instruments, etcetera. Follow me around and watch as I do each of the things, I just mentioned. Next time I'll have you do it while I watch. You'll be an expert in no time.

"Once a month or every 100 engine hours we'll change the engine oil and the fuel filters. The last thing I like to check when I'm down here is the throttle and gear shift cables for the main engines. Make sure nothing's loose or about to fall off. When you're coming into the dock the last thing you want is to lose control of one or both of your engines. Other than those things I just mentioned you also want to wipe down the engines and make sure it stays tidy down here and that everything is in its place. If the engines are clean all the time, an oil leak will stand out like a sore thumb.

One last thing; knowing exactly where everything is on a boat, all the time, is essential. For some reason when things go wrong on a boat, they go wrong at the worst possible time, and you don't want to be wasting time looking around for a tool or discover that the batteries in your flashlight are dead when you need it most. I expect you to be diligent about putting tools away and maintaining things like flashlights and fire extinguishers. Am I being clear?"

"Yes, Melissa, crystal."

She smiled and gave me a little punch on the arm.

"Good. Oh, and I signed you up for your CPR and emergency first aid course at the Fire Department this week. It's a four-hour certification course and it's at 1:00 pm on Wednesday. I'll take care of the course fees for you."

"Thank you, ma'am... I mean Melissa. I'll be there. By the way, we never discussed what you'll pay me."

"It's minimum wage, $8.46 per hour to start. If you're still with me at the end of July, I'll give you a review and a raise if you're doing a good job. I like you, Callie. You pay attention and I think you'll be good with customers. You cannot be late though. Understand? There are no free passes on this. On days you're scheduled to work, if you don't show up, I'm screwed. I'm not allowed to leave the dock with passengers unless I have at least one deckhand. I might be able to find a replacement on short notice, but probably not. So be here without fail if you're on the schedule."

"Yes, Melissa, absolutely. You can count on me."

"And, Callie, if you can't handle the freight part of the job, no hard feelings. You're a small woman. Size isn't something any of us can control."

"I'll handle it."

RIP CONVERSE

Chapter 8

Diego Alturaz was holding court and sharpening an already very sharp machete with a small honing stone back in Fort Myers. He ran the stone up one side of the blade, and then slowly down the other. The smell of toxic, old, auto-body paint remained strong in the clubhouse despite the fact that fifteen years had passed since the building had been used as an autobody shop. The gang still used the large central section to work on their cars, but all the other ancillary rooms were now used as either sleeping or common area party rooms for members of the gang who didn't live in regular houses.

He turned his attention to the other three gang members sitting in his office. The one called "Bones" had a black eye and several scabs on his face. "Bones, que pasa? You're not looking so good. Did your pendejo hermana (stupid sister) beat on you or was it one of your putas (whores)?"

"No, it was the Lake Boyz, jefe. We messed them up worse though."

"I should hope so, but it's time they learned some respect. I was talking with Santiago when I was in Miami earlier this week and he is not pleased with our performance. He expected faster growth, more drug sales and more prostitution and protection revenue. You think we're living some sort of *West Side Story* here, bro, where we and the Lake Boyz have little fights, and everybody keeps their honor?"

"What's *West Side Story*, jefe?" Bones asked.

Diego shook his head. "Really? What I'm saying here is that this beating them up shit isn't working and if we want to grow and increase profits, the fastest way of doing that is to take market share from them. That means we are going to have to take a more, shall we say, serious approach with the Lake Boyz."

"What is it you have in mind, Jefe?" Esteban asked.

"They need to learn respect for us, and for the blade. Starting today, whenever you run into Lake Boyz, I want you to chop the motherfuckers up. Comprende! I want these stovepipes to tremble in their sneakers and piss in their pants whenever they see MS-13. Bones, you can start today. Take two or three of the younger ones who still need to initiate, find the mofos who beat on you, and then slice and dice them until their own mothers couldn't identify the pieces. Clear?"

"Diego...I mean, jefe, this isn't like El Salvador. If we start chopping up locals, it's going to bring some serious heat down on us."

"I don't give a fuck about heat! Are you MS-13 or are you some pussy assed faggot? Would you rather have heat from the police or heat from Santiago? I'm supposed to be producing.

Bones acquiesced. "It shall be done."

"Jefe?" Razor interjected.

"Sí."

"I have an idea. Another way of really hurting them would be to take away their puta revenue."

"And how would you do that?"

"Take away their putas."

"What, you think maybe I should send them all away on vacation or tell them all about finding Jesus? How would I take them away?"

"Kill them, Jefe, simply kill them."

Diego started to object and then caught himself. The simplicity of the idea intrigued him. "Let me think about this, Razor. It's not that bad an idea. In the meantime though we need young, white, innocents under seventeen. That's what the demand is for and those are the ones that bring top dollar. Esteban, that will be your next project. Find me putas like that."

"It's not the same as snatching illegals and homeless tramps. If we start doing that, we're going to bring heat."

"Are you all fucking deaf! I know that. You're still not getting it. If we don't produce Santiago will kill us as an example and then get someone else to do it. If we need fresh trim, we take it. That's our way. You need to man-up and grow a pair!"

Diego let his words sink in before speaking again. "And, Razor?"

"Sí."

"I also want you to hustle on more school-distribution of spice and fentanyl. We are missing that boat big time especially with the younger kids. Put some of our grade school age members on that."

Razor nodded his accent.

"Okay then, the meeting is over. Get busy."

Razor and Bones left the room. Esteban stayed behind.

"Que?" Diego asked.

"Jefe, I expect you know that if we start snatching little white girls out of suburbia that's going to be a whole lot different than chopping up Lake Boyz or killing their hookers. The police will come at us hard."

"I don't give a fuck."

RIP CONVERSE

Chapter 9

So began my first boat job. The physical part sometimes took everything I had, but I did it. Every day was different. Some days there were lumber and other construction materials like concrete, but most of our cargo was fresh seafood and other specialty foods destined for Marco via the Fort Myers airport. Once the freight was all loaded, all of it then had to be lashed securely to prevent it from shifting on deck.

In addition to maintaining the engine room and loading freight, I also had to learn about fire extinguishers and our firefighting system. In the case of an engine room fire the procedure was to first shut off the fuel lines and then to starve the engine room of oxygen by shutting all the exterior ventilation ports feeding the engine room. They were on deck along with the central fuel shutoff. If the fire continued to burn after I'd shut off both the fuel and ventilation vents, Melissa could activate a fire suppression system from the bridge. The chemical deployed by the fire suppression system removed any remaining oxygen in the engine room.

For deck or cabin fires I was supposed to use one of the six dry-chemical extinguishers or one of the two fire hoses. The pump for the fire hoses ran off the main engines so if we didn't have engine power, we didn't have pumps. I was also responsible for taking tickets when the passengers boarded and for doing the USCG mandated safety briefing at the beginning of every trip. I was a busy girl, but I loved it. As my knowledge grew so did my confidence.

The thing I enjoyed most was the time I spent in the wheelhouse with Melissa. After two weeks and proving my commitment and abilities to her, she started giving me wheel time and sharing her considerable experience freely as we traveled back and forth to Marco Island each day. Once we got off the dock, I would stow all the dock lines and fenders and then after walking around the entire deck making sure everything and everyone was secure and, in their place, I'd join Melissa in the wheelhouse. I was like a sponge as I absorbed navigation techniques, radar and GPS operation, rules of the road, chart reading, passing agreements between other vessels, day signals, and emergency procedures. Once every two weeks, Melissa would stage both fire and man overboard drills. She believed that total familiarity with systems and procedures was necessary to effectively prepare for real emergencies.

During the first month I made only one mistake. We'd just left the dock and I was coiling the dock lines when I got into a discussion with a passenger and simply forgot to bring in the inflated rubber fenders that hung over the side whenever we were at the dock. I had no idea what an incredible "no-no" it was to leave them hanging outside the rail while underway. Shrimp boats almost always have all manner of buoys, floats and fenders hanging on their sides. But trim, well run, commercial fast-ferries never, ever, have fenders hanging over the side when underway. The first inkling of trouble came when another commercial vessel we knew came over the radio to vocalize their passing intentions.

"*Gulf Runner* this is *Myers Run* on 13. We are a half mile astern of you and overtaking. One whistle, Captain?"

Melissa looked astern of us, saw the high-speed catamaran ferry coming up behind us and picked up the mic to answer them. "*Myers Run, Gulf Runner*. One whistle it is Gary, my starboard side. How are you today?"

"I'm well, Melissa. Did you want me to stop so we can raft up?" We both heard him chuckle before he released his mic button.

"What do you think he means by that?" I asked with a quizzical expression on my face. I knew it would be highly irregular for us to stop out in the Gulf and raft up with another boat in anything but an emergency. Melissa thought for a second before responding and then walked outside onto the starboard wing of the bridge and looked down. She came back into the wheelhouse with a pissed-off expression on her face and picked up the mic.

"*Myers Run, Gulf Runner*. Thanks for offer but no need for you to stop unless you're short a worthless deckhand and want to take this one off my hands."

I paled before speaking again. Melissa had just called me worthless and sounded really mad.

"Oh crap," I said out loud.

"Oh crap' is right, Callie; you left the fenders out! I can't believe you did that!"

I jumped out of the captain's barber chair, giving her the wheel, but didn't really understand her level of anger.

"Not a problem, Melissa, no worries, I'll get them in right away," I said somewhat submissively.

"No worries? Next, you'll probably tell me to chill. You're not going to do that, are you, Callie?"

"No, ma'am, absolutely not. I'll go get them right away."

"Yes, you will." Melissa muttered something else under her breath as I sprung for the wheelhouse door. "Callie."

"What?" I stopped.

"Do you know how many drinks I'll have to buy him to make up for your oversight?"

I shook my head.

"At least three, and he drinks top shelf. I'm docking you a half day's pay for your failure to observe proper marine etiquette and thereby making me look like an asshat. If my vessel doesn't look squared away, I don't look squared away. Do I not look squared away to you, Callie?" She sounded like an angry drill instructor at this point.

"Of course you are," I stumbled out. "You're the best...."

"Then why are our fenders dragging alongside our boat like some drunk, half-assed, weekend, fisherman?!" she shouted. "Whose fault do you suppose it is?"

"It's my fault, Melissa. I was the one who forgot to bring them in when we left the dock."

"No, Callie, wrong."

I looked up at her, totally confused.

"If a passenger fell over the side and we were unable to retrieve that person because you left the man overboard ring line in a rat's nest rendering it unthrowable, whose fault would that be?"

"Mine?"

"Wrong again. Does my boat remind you of the Federal Government? Running a ship isn't like government where some politician gets to skate free by sacrificing some lower-level flunky. The captain of a ship is responsible for anything and everything that takes place aboard his or her ship. At the Coast Guard inquiry, I would take the fall. They're not going to give me a free ride because my unlicensed, fifteen-year-old, deckhand failed to coil it properly. They're going to blame me because I didn't notice my equipment was in disarray or I failed to have proper procedures and training in place insuring it didn't happen. In the maritime world all fingers are always pointed at the captain, all the time. I'm responsible for every single thing that happens on this boat including your oversights. That's why I've got the license. I'm supposed to notice every single goddamned thing on this vessel. Right now, I look like an ass. I don't like looking like an ass. If you can grasp that, it's easily worth a half day's pay and you'll thank me one day." She nodded her head at the door. "Go. Get the fenders in, and when you're done, I want you to come back up here and write in the back of the ship's log, 'I will never make Melissa look like an asshat again.' And do it fifty times!" she added.

"You're kidding, right?"

She glared at me. "Do I sound like I'm kidding?" she bellowed.

I nodded. "Got it, you're serious."

Chapter 10

My relationship with Aunt Nancy continued to grow in new and interesting ways. I came to realize that she wasn't in fact retired. She had sold her publishing business, but she still served on four different boards of directors. Two were major corporations and two were non-profits. She was also actively looking at possible acquisition opportunities.

"I'm too young to retire, Callie. The truth is, I love to work."

"I get that, I like my job too."

She smiled at me and ruffled my already messy hair. "Melissa tells me she's thrilled she hired you and thinks you may have what it takes to be a good captain."

"She actually said those things?" I was thrilled that Melissa was saying good things about me. Just a week had gone by since I'd had to write "I will not make Melissa look like an asshat." in the ship's log fifty times.

"She did. She also said you were punctual, respectful and a hard worker. I'm extremely proud of you."

That was the first time in my life anyone had ever told me they were proud of me.

"Callie, one of the boards I serve on is a battered women's shelter in Bradenton. The other night I got into a discussion with another board member after the meeting about ways some of our women can recover their shattered confidence and defend themselves in the future from batterers. She told me about a Krav Maga instructor they have coming in to give classes and it made me think back to the conversation you and I had the first day you were here about how someone your size can defend herself against bigger opponents. Are you still interested in that?"

I nodded. "Very much so, but what's Krav Maga?"

"I gather it's an Israeli martial arts discipline. Remember how you told me you never wanted to be defenseless again like when that boy hit you and tried to take advantage of you?"

I did remember and still thought about the attack almost daily. "I remember."

"The woman who's going to be teaching a class at the shelter is going to be there three nights from now giving a demonstration. Any interest in going and seeing what it's all about?"

"I'd love to."

"Great. I'll pick you up when you get off work and we'll drive up together and check it out. We can stop in Sarasota on the way back and have dinner. Bring some clean pants and a blouse with you to work so you have something to change into after."

Three evenings later, Nancy pulled up to the ferry dock. I was putting the hose away after rinsing the salt off *Gulf Runner*. I held up a finger for her to wait, dashed into the restroom and pulled on clean pants and a blouse.

Normally, on our off-island trips we would take the Range Rover and she would let me drive. That night she was driving her Bentley convertible which she had not yet let me drive. I threw my knapsack into the backseat and buckled up in the front. The top was down, and the air conditioning was on. Despite all the ventilation, the smell of rich leather permeated the air as I sat back in the luxurious seat.

"This car is so bad," I observed.

"Bad! What on earth are you talking about? I paid almost $240,000 for this car. I think it's one of the finest motorcars money can buy!"

"I didn't mean bad as in *bad*; I meant bad as in *good*! This car is awesome! I would kill for this car."

Nancy smiled; she'd known what I'd meant. "It is rather nice, isn't it? I've always felt that any moment in life can be dramatically enhanced when experienced in a Bentley."

I loved this outrageous side of my aunt. I couldn't feign "airs" like she sometimes did and didn't try. I was a tomboy/grease monkey/deckhand, and I knew it. She wasn't. She was an elegant, self-made, millionaire who had every right to put on airs. In public she never acted that way, but in private with certain people she would do it as a way of making fun of herself. Despite her wealth she never took herself too seriously and was always finding new and interesting ways to give back. The battered women's shelter that we were headed to was a perfect example of this.

"I don't care what they say about you, Aunt Nancy, I think you're okay."

She responded with her fake outrage. "Who? What are they saying? Tell me now, Catherine! I've been exceptionally good lately."

I knew perfectly well she didn't give two craps what other people thought, but I could always get a rise out of her when I played that game with her.

An hour into our trip we were stopped in a radar trap on route 75. A very serious State Trooper approached the car and asked why we were traveling 85mph in a 70mph zone. Instead of answering his question, Nancy said, "Officer, first of all I'd like to compliment you for doing an outstanding job protecting public safety. I know that I for one, will drive onwards with much greater confidence knowing that a man of your obvious integrity and dedication is on the job and reining in thoughtless lawbreakers."

Nancy could do that; talk in the third person as though she was someone else and get away with it even when she was caught.

"Lady, really?"

Nancy smiled up at him, transparent as could be, and then doubled down.

"I apologize for putting you in the position of having to stop me. My outrageous, badly-behaved niece was responsible. She can be very distracting, and hopefully your traffic stop will serve as a reminder for her that there are consequences when you break the law. She should have known better."

I looked back and forth between her and the Trooper aghast as she threw me under the bus, wondering if he was believing one word coming out of her mouth. I jumped in to defend myself.

"What! How! That is so unfair! I'm responsible—"

She cut me off mid-sentence.

"Callie, you need to stop right there. Don't make this poor man's job any more difficult than it already is. Apologize right now and assure him that you will never do it again."

"Do what again!"

"Callie...really."

The Trooper burst out laughing, no doubt grateful for a comedic break on an otherwise tedious day.

"Lady, you are a piece of work. Never in all my years of doing traffic stops have I heard such a flagrant line of BS." He shook his head and then pondered the situation for a few seconds.

"I'll tell you what, I'm going to give you an A for effort on your BS, but on the speeding, you need to slow it down. Consider this a verbal warning on the speeding. I'm serious."

He shook his head then continued. "And tell the 'bad influence' seated next to you that she needs to be less distracting in her behavior." Then he muttered under his breath, "I can't believe I just said that."

Nancy smiled up at him, batted her eyelids a few times and smiled.

"Thank you, officer, I assure you, I'll have a serious talk with her the moment we're back on the road."

I shook my head as we pulled back onto the highway, then leaned forward, and put a hand behind my back and started rubbing it."

"What's wrong with your back, Callie?" Nancy asked with a big smile on her face.

"Do you have any idea how much buses weigh? I can't believe you just did what you did."

"Oh, don't be such a stick-in-the-mud! He knew I was kidding around. Have some fun once in a while."

I shook my head.

The class we attended that evening was conducted by a woman almost as small as I. She was maybe 5'2" and 110 pounds. She was dressed in form-fitting leggings and a tee shirt.

"Good evening, everyone. My name is Eva Dahan. I'm Israeli by birth and I've been in the U.S. for six years. I'm a second level black belt in the fighting style called Krav Maga." She paced for a few seconds and then continued.

"Krav Maga is a personal defense/fighting system used by the Israeli military and taught to all incoming recruits. In English it means close combat and was developed by a man named Imi Lichtenfeld in the 1930's in Czechoslovakia as a self-defense system for Jews who were increasingly being targeted by anti-Semites in pre-WWII Europe. It's a combination of boxing, wrestling and judo moves and it's highly effective against attackers when practiced correctly. It enables me to defend myself against much larger or multiple attackers.

Many of you here have been punched, bullied, or otherwise brutalized by men who are usually bigger and more aggressive. If you are tired of being someone's punching bag and are willing to put in some work, I can teach you an alternative."

She paused for a moment, then continued. "With Krav Maga, like many other types of fighting techniques, the first rule is to always try to avoid confrontation. If simply walking or running away is an option, then you should take it, every time. Even better is to never get into the situation in the first place. Many of you were abused by your abuser multiple times before ending up here at the shelter. Avoiding an abuser after the first incidence is a good example of what I'm talking about. I know your situations are frequently complicated by marriage and children but be very certain, abusers don't suddenly stop. Usually they escalate which is something I know you'll be working on with your counselors here.

"Avoidance of trouble is where the similarity to other martial arts disciplines ends. With Krav Maga, once avoidance and fleeing have been ruled out, the next thing you do is to apply immediate overwhelming force to your opponent's weakest points and press your attack until they are completely neutralized." She let that sink in for a moment and then repeated herself. "Overwhelming force, applied to your opponent's weakest points, until they are completely neutralized. I am *not* here to teach you how to strike an opponent in such a way as to cause them to withdraw. This is not a polite fighting style like fisticuffs. Once you decide fighting is your only option, you will be using devastating force that results in serious physical damage to your antagonist, things like broken joints and bones, smashed teeth, shattered knees, gouged eyes and worse. Once you make the determination to defend yourself you will learn to apply this force in an explosive, continuous, unrelenting way until your opponent is no longer viable. Krav Maga is an attitude of destruction. I teach people how to become street fighters because it takes a ruthless, anything goes, attitude such as this to overcome an adversary who has physical advantages over you whether it be a gun, a knife, their size, or their numbers. This attitude of destruction will become your advantage.

"Let me give you an example of what makes Krav Maga very different from most other fighting styles. In boxing you try to strike your opponent in the stomach, kidneys, or face. Those are typical focus points you would target. Instinctually you avoid the crotch, the neck, the fingers, and toes. When practicing Krav Maga you learn all those areas are in fact target-rich areas for you. If you hit someone in the neck and damage their trachea, they're out of the fight. If you break just one finger in a boxer's hand you have effectively neutralized that hand. If you break a person's toe or toes, their movement is severely restricted. If you take out someone's eyes, they are blinded. If you crush someone's testicles with repeated knee strikes, they are neutralized. If you break someone's wrist or shatter one of their knees, the fight is over."

She moved her eyes over each of us. "I notice all of you cringed at different points as I was describing these target areas. Make no mistake, Krav Maga is very, very violent when done correctly. That's another reason it must never be used with the casual attitude of a fisticuff competition. You should always attempt to avoid, de-escalate, or flee a potentially violent situation before using your training.

Krav Maga is for those times when none of that works and you are certain someone is going to either kill or seriously injure you or someone else. There is some calculus you will do coincident with your weakness assessment of an opponent. If someone attacks you with a knife or points a gun at you, that requires a different response than someone who pushes you in a violent manner. For the 'pusher' I may be able to stop my defensive strikes after a single knee to their testicles or breaking their nose. If someone attacks me with a knife, then we are playing in a different ballgame. If that person is themselves cut or stabbed while I am disarming them, I will not lose sleep over it. After all, they initiated it and I am defending myself. Same thing with a gun. If someone points a gun at me, I will do whatever is necessary to take it from them. If I break their hand or their fingers in the process, so be it. If there are multiple attackers, I may be forced to shoot one or more of them once I disarm the gunman. It's about surviving and doing whatever is necessary to neutralize the threat."

She paused and paced for a moment collecting her thoughts then continued.

"In addition to teaching you violence avoidance techniques, physical strikes, and continuous motion attack, we will also look at weakness assessment and making use of ad-hoc weapons available to you in your normal everyday environment. I'd like to begin this evening by demonstrating several techniques with Carl here. He's one of my students. I will start by taking a basic Krav Maga fighting stance."

Eva stepped back from Carl with her right foot back, raised her hands to head level with both palms open and forward and nodded once to Carl to proceed. Carl very aggressively attacked Eva in a variety of ways including, strikes at her head and body, choking from behind, with a rubber knife and finally with a plastic gun. Eva would occasionally slow down her response to a threat and demonstrate her response in slow motion.

She made her destruction of Carl look effortless. I knew it was a demonstration with a somewhat compliant opponent, but Eva's determined focus on Carl's weakest points like his eyes, throat, fingers, testicles, and knees with repeated blows using the edge of her hand, her elbows, her feet, her knees, and her forehead quickly revealed the core principals of Krav Maga and how devastating her strikes would be to a real attacker. At every juncture where she paused for emphasis, she subjected Carl's joints, bones, and soft points to cringeworthy abuse. At no point did she pause to access her damage or to catch her breath. She would instead press each one of her attacks mercilessly until Carl was on the ground and it was clear that he would have had a crushed trachea, a broken arm, broken wrist, crushed testicles, gouged out eyes or a shattered knee. I was very impressed and could see how a fighting style like hers would be the perfect thing for a small person such as me.

At the end of the class I waited until everyone had thanked her for the demonstration and then walked over to her feeling somewhat self-conscious.

"Hi, Eva. I'm Callie." I held out my hand.

She shook it and gave me her full attention. "It's a pleasure to meet you, Callie."

"I really enjoyed your presentation and wondered if you have a studio or gym near where I live? I'd like to take some classes with you."

"Where do you live, Callie? I gather you're not a resident here at the shelter."

I shook my head confirming her assumption. "Right now, I'm living with my aunt for the summer on Boca Grande. In the winter I live near Fort Myers."

"Actually, Fort Myers is my home base where my studio is." She smiled and then bent down, reached into her duffle, and then handed me a business card.

"Call me this fall when you get back. I'd love to have you as a student."

"Thank you, I will."

Chapter 11

During my summer with Aunt Nancy I swam three days a week and ran four, alternating days. The next day was a swim day and I got up at 6:00, dressed in a one-piece swimsuit, grabbed a towel and after stopping in the kitchen for a glass of juice and a bottle of spring water, headed out to Nancy's pool on the beach side of the house. I spent ten minutes stretching and then did fifty pushups and one hundred sit-ups. The sky was just starting to lighten with the tropical softness of the Gulf, and I dove into the pool, full of optimism for the day ahead and did the first of one hundred and twenty-eight laps.

The water temperature in the pool was eighty-five degrees and I barely felt it when I dove in. I would generally swim twenty laps using a crawl stroke then do two to four laps doing a backstroke, and then repeat until I reached one hundred and twenty-eight. I wasn't trying to beat any particular time when I swam, but I always kept moving at a solid pace, with no breaks. After I finished, I dried off, then did another fifty pushups and one hundred sit-ups and stretched out a second time.

When I re-entered the house, I could hear Rosario in the kitchen and poked my head in before continuing to the shower. "Good morning, Rosario." I offered with a big smile.

"Good morning, Miss Callie. Did you have a nice swim?"

"Very nice."

"Can I make you some breakfast this morning?"

I looked at my watch. "Some fruit and coffee would be nice, thank you, but today's a workday and I have to be down to the boat by 8:00."

"We have quite a bit of chicken left over from last night. Can I make you a chicken salad tortilla?"

"Yum, you're spoiling me. I feel guilty that I'm not making it though."

"Nonsense. It's my job. Besides, I love making you things. You get your shower and when you're out, it will be ready to go."

My bathroom at Nancy's is the size of my entire bedroom at my parents' house. That's where the similarities end. My bathroom at Nancy's has white marble floors, ten-foot ceilings and dozens of those tiny low-amperage lights like the ones they use in jewelry stores. The shower area is enclosed in spotless thick glass and there are three shower heads that pummel you with gallons of hot water simultaneously. I took a relatively quick ten-minute shower and after drying off stood in front of the full-length mirror mounted on the back of the door as I started to brush some of the tangles out of my hair. I liked who I saw looking back.

I was still shorter and less endowed than I would have preferred, but I no longer felt like the awkward, underdeveloped geek I'd felt like when my brothers and their friends had pulled back the shower curtain on me three years before. I felt powerful. My face looked healthy from all the sunshine and outdoor work I was doing on the ferry, my shoulders were ripped, my breasts, although small, were definitely there. My stomach was flat and also ripped, and my hips flared in a complementary way. I turned around and stood on my toes. The muscles in my butt and my calves were defined and strong. I felt good about myself. I'd never be a magazine beauty, but my physical strength in combination with all the practical knowledge I was accruing on my job made me feel whole, together, and confident.

I realized the time was flying by and quickly dried my hair, threw on a sports bra, underwear, a black polo shirt with *Gulf Runner* written on the front, and a pair of khaki shorts. Then I took one last look in the mirror and smiled. I felt older and more mature than when I'd arrived four weeks earlier. I had responsibilities now and people trusted me. I put on a pair of running shoes, packed my boat shoes and foul weather gear jacket in my knapsack, and headed out to the kitchen to pick up my lunch and to say goodbye to Rosario and my aunt.

That day on *Gulf Runner* started out as most others for me. I was the first one there and after snubbing all the lines and bringing *Gulf Runner* tight to the dock, I climbed aboard and went through my engine room check list making sure everything was ready to go. I was closing up the engine room hatches when Melissa arrived.

"Morning, Callie. Everything shipshape below?"

"Yes, Melissa."

"Good; it's a light freight day, but we've got a group of twenty seniors from one of the local assisted living communities booked in addition to the regular walk-on traffic, so make sure the restrooms are tidy and there's plenty of spring water on ice."

Restrooms were part of my job. In addition to keeping the toilets and sinks clean, floors swept and paper products on-hand, it was also my responsibility to deal with the marine toilets when they clogged. Usually, I could solve most issues with a good plunging, but not always. Sometimes the marine heads had to be taken apart and parts replaced. I hated this part of my job, but Melissa told me early on that's where every single deckhand starts, and that good captains are familiar with every single system on their ship.

The people from the assisted living community arrived fifteen minutes early before general boarding started at 9:30. Because so many of them were dependent on walkers and canes, Melissa had me start boarding them early so they would have some place comfortable to sit out of the heat. She also started the engines early in order to provide A/C to the cabin area. The weather forecast for that day was for SW breezes at ten to twelve knots, mostly clear skies, and temperatures in the low nineties. The last two people to board were two men in their thirties who almost missed the boat. I had already closed the boarding gate and watched as they came across the parking lot. Both were drinking cans of beer and didn't seem very stable on their feet. One was tall and skinny, and the other was average height but really overweight.

"Hold the boat there, little lady!" the overweight one shouted. Already I didn't like him. Besides being a slob, I hated it when people called me 'little lady.' Melissa looked down at me from the wing of the bridge and we exchanged a look. I wondered if she wanted me to board these last two obviously marginal passengers. I could tell she was debating it but when they held up their tickets, she nodded yes, and I re-opened the gangway gate and let them aboard.

Responsibility for the passengers fell on me, the lowly deckhand. The captain is always in the wheelhouse making sure the boat is running correctly and that we don't run aground or collide with other vessels. On a small ferry like *Gulf Runner* taking tickets and handling the lines were just two of many responsibilities I had. The deckhand is also responsible for passenger comfort and safety, all mechanical issues that can't be sorted out from the bridge, firefighting, medical emergencies, and a dozen other things the average person never thinks about.

When you work on a boat and must deal with the general public every day, you can't help but mark people in your mind as they board. This one will need some extra help, that one's a jerk and probably won't leave a tip, this one might leave a tip if I give him/her some extra attention, this one doesn't listen, this one is physically impaired, this one is drunk. I marked the two guys who boarded last as Slim and Bubba and expected both would be difficult. They didn't disappoint.

Once everyone was aboard and the gangway pulled onto the dock, I slipped our lines, jumped aboard, shut the stanchion post gate, coiled the lines, and pulled the fenders aboard while Melissa idled across the waterway and out into Gasparilla Sound. I went into the passenger cabin and did the safety briefing.

"Hi, everyone. Could I get your attention please?" I started and then waited for all the conversation to stop before continuing. Everyone but Slim and Bubba politely stopped talking. I tried talking over them at first.

"My name is Callie and I'm your deckhand today. The trip over to Marco Island usually takes two to two and a quarter hours depending on the sea-state. The weather today looks pleasant so it shouldn't be too rough a ride. Please let me know *before* you hurl if you're feeling seasick." I paused for a few seconds as people nervously laughed. "I'm required by the Coast Guard to go over a number of safety items with you, so please pay attention."

The Bub brothers continued to talk, laugh, and rib each other after I continued. "Excuse me, gentlemen?" I paused, waiting for them to stop, but they kept on.

"I remember when I had my first beer too." I said in a loud voice to the rest of the passengers. They laughed and Slim and Bubba stopped after realizing they were the butt of my joke.

I then proceeded to tell everyone the locations of the life preservers and other safety equipment and what to do in the event of the boat sinking. Then I described where they could and couldn't go on the boat, proper use of the marine toilets, and lastly suggested that they should feel free to leave me a tip in the tip jar if they were pleased with my performance as a deckhand,

"Fat chance of that," Bubba muttered loud enough for everyone to hear.

I didn't take the bait and respond and after concluding my safety briefing, made my way up to the wheelhouse to join Melissa as she slowly brought *Gulf Runner* up on a plane and then to our cruising speed of twenty-five knots.

"How does it look below?" she asked.

"With the exception of the 'bub brothers' who boarded last, there shouldn't be any problems. A few of the people from the retirement home aren't very steady on their feet, but as long as they stay seated, they'll be fine."

"You want to take her?"

Melissa slid out of the barber's chair as she offered me the helm.

"Thanks."

Melissa stood next to me for about a minute and watched me as I acclimated myself. "Remember, Callie, head on a swivel. Keep scanning your instruments in addition to looking around us 360 degrees. A lot of people get fixated on their course and lose sight of the bigger picture like traffic around them. Don't get tunnel vision. Keep an eye on your oil pressure and temp gauges. On the nav side you want to be alert if any one of your instruments starts disagreeing with another. If you're looking at the chart plotter and you notice the fathometer is suddenly not agreeing with what you're seeing displayed on the plotter or the image displayed is no longer agreeing with the reflected returns on the radar, then you've got something going on which you need to resolve."

"So, which one should I believe if two different instruments start disagreeing?"

"It depends. Most people tend to put the most faith in the chart plotter, probably because it looks high tech and has a pretty picture. In my experience the more complex an instrument, the more things there are that can go wrong with it. For the plotter to work correctly it needs to be triangulating off a minimum of three satellites in outer space. Usually there are seven or eight visible to the antenna which increases the accuracy of your position. But if there's anything wrong with the processor, the antenna, or with the satellites the plotter might be giving you a garbage position. Simplest is always best so I suggest visually verifying landmarks and buoys wherever possible." Melissa reached over and turned the GPS to standby. The screen went dark. "What are you going to do now Callie?"

I panicked for just a second as *Gulf Runner* and our course line disappeared from the screen. Of all our instruments I relied on the nav-plotter most. I smiled, feeling very clever and pointed at the radar. "I can see Cayo Costa point clear as day on the radar. I can also see the Jug Creek Shoal Light and the outer channel markers for the Charlotte Channel out in the Gulf."

Melissa smiled back at me and then turned the radar to standby. The screen on that also went dark. "Okay, smarty-pants, you just had an electrical malfunction somewhere between the engine room and here and _all_ of your electronic navigation systems have gone out. You've got forty-five passengers below that you're responsible for. What're you going to do now?"

I looked at her blankly trying to think. I was at a loss. I'd really believed I had things down cold between the GPS and the radar and in an instant, she'd removed all my primary aids to navigation and blinded me.

"Okay, now just for the purposes of this demonstration and because I don't want to stop the boat, turn on the autopilot."

I did as she had told me and engaged it.

"Look around us now and see if you can't identify a minimum two points you can positively identify visually."

I did as she'd instructed. "Cayo Costa off the starboard bow and Jug Creek Shoal Light off the port bow."

"Good. Now, take magnetic bearings to both of those points and then plot both lines on the paper chart. Where they intersect is where you are. Once you know where you are, you can then plot a course on the chart to where you want to go."

I turned red with embarrassment. "I don't know how to take a bearing and I don't know how to plot it on the chart."

"I didn't expect so." She turned both the radar and the GPS back on.

"That's what I want you to work on next, chart plotting. I'll show you right now how to take a bearing and during our layover on Marco, I'll show you how to do basic plots. Then I want you to take a chart and some parallel rules home tonight, and practice."

"Thank you, Melissa." I responded with humility.

"You're welcome." She moved closer to me and extended her arm and her hand right past my face down my sight line. Then, looking like she was going to chop something, pointed her hand at Jug Shoal Light and then dropped her hand on the compass.

"Look down my arm towards where my hand is pointing. See how the bottom of my hand is going through the middle of the compass?"

I nodded.

"What's the compass reading under my pinkie?"

I sighted down her hand noting she was pointing to Jug Shoal. "It's about 135 degrees."

"Excellent, write that down."

She moved to my other side and did the same thing with her hand pointing this time to the end of Cayo Costa. "What's that reading?"

"218 degrees?"

"Let's call it 220 degrees. Again, good."

We were both suddenly distracted from finishing our exercise as Slim and Bubba stumbled up the deck and towards the bow. They were both laughing, and Bubba pointedly ignored the "No Entrance" sign hanging on a chain in the very bow. He stepped over it and went into the V of the bow. Then he assumed the pose of Leonardo DiCaprio on the bow of the Titanic and started shouting, "I'm the king of the fucking world!" while Slim took pictures of him with his cell phone.

"Callie, do me a favor and go down there and get those two morons out of my bow. They're making me very nervous."

"Will do, Melissa." I slid out of the helm chair and quickly exited the pilot house towards the bow. There were two metal pipe railings running around the circumference of *Gulf Runner*: one at knee height and the other at stomach height. Passengers were prohibited from going all the way into the bow so that what was happening now, never happened. By the time I came down off the bridge and walked to the bow, Bubba had climbed up on the knee-height rail with his lower thighs braced against the upper rail.

It was an incredibly stupid and dangerous thing for someone to do. If his feet slipped or a wave threw him off balance, he'd go right over the bow and likely get run over by the ship. Noting the situation Melissa was already reducing power and starting to slow *Gulf Runner's* speed as I got to the bow.

"Hey, mister! You need to get down off there right now!" I shouted. Slim kept taking pictures.

I slowed my approach so as not to startle him. I was hoping I'd be able to grab him by his belt and pull him down into the boat. Melissa continued to slow *Gulf Runner*. I could tell she was trying to do it gradually enough so as not to precipitate him pitching over the bow. I stopped right before I got to him and tried to reason with him.

"Mister, that really isn't safe. Please come down off there." We'd slowed to about ten knots by that point.

"Who's that, Herb?" he shouted. "Is it the tiny little deckhand?" He turned his head and looked at me. "You gonna arrest me for having a little fun, shrimp-girl?" He put both hands up into the air and started pretending he'd lost his balance and was swaying from side to side and back to front in an exaggerated fashion. "Oh no, this is sooo scary!" he said in a mocking way. Of course, the next thing that happened was he lost his balance for real and pitched headfirst right over the bow.

Melissa chopped both throttles and put both engines in neutral to stop our propellers in case he went directly under the boat instead of alongside it. I rushed to the rail on the side he'd fallen. I could tell from the way he bumped his way down the side of the boat that he was unconscious. His face was in the water, and he wasn't struggling.

Normally in a man overboard situation I was trained to first put on a life preserver myself in case I needed to go into the water to aid the person who was in the water. Then I was supposed to throw the man overboard ring to them once Melissa had maneuvered the boat close to the person who'd gone overboard. After they grabbed on to it, I was supposed to pull them alongside and then deploy a ladder that went from our deck down into the water. There wasn't time for any of that though.

With hardly a thought, I dove over the side and started swimming back to him as soon as I hit the water. He was still face down and not moving.

CALLIE AWAKENS

Despite having put both engines in neutral the moment Melissa saw him go over, *Gulf Runner* still had forty-nine tons of momentum and traveled several hundred feet beyond the point where she'd shifted into neutral, before finally drifting to a stop. Melissa came out of the rear door of the wheelhouse to the second set of controls. The rear-facing oil-field controls gave her an unobstructed view of the stern and enabled her to drive accurately and safely, in reverse. Several passengers had by this time migrated out of the passenger cabin to the open rear deck and were anxiously looking back and forth between Melissa and the two of us in the water.

The second I hit the water I swam as fast as I could to Bubba and once I reached him, I got an arm around his neck and pulled his face backward out of the water and assessed him. He wasn't breathing. His forehead was bleeding from hitting his head on the side of the boat when he'd landed in the water, but I could tell it wasn't a major injury and I thought back to my CPR class and the ABCs that had been drilled into us; Airway, Breathing, Cardiac. I knew it would be several minutes before we would be able to get him back aboard to start proper CPR and tried to think of how I could breathe for this fat slob in the water. The last thing I wanted to do was put my mouth over his. I shouted at him several times first. "Hey, mister, breathe! Come on, breathe!" I had his neck in the crook of my arm and was flutter kicking below the surface burning quite a bit of energy in my effort to keep both our heads above the surface. I put my ear up to his mouth, still nothing.

I realized I was going to have to do the unthinkable if I was going to save him. I was already starting to tire some as I treaded water and struggled to keep both of our heads above water. He was truly a whale of a man and must have weighed at least 300 pounds. I took several deep breaths and pulled his face towards mine, put my mouth over his and gave him a strong rescue breath. All the air immediately exited through his nose before it could go into his chest. I'd forgotten to pinch his nostrils and hyperextend his neck.

I set up again, this time canting his head backwards and hyperextending his neck. Then I reached around with my left hand and pinched his nostrils, put my mouth over his, and blew again. With that breath, his chest expanded, but it did not result in him breathing on his own. I continued to give him rescue breaths.

On the fifth breath he spontaneously sputtered and started flailing his arms. After several gasping breaths he began to heave and then vomited, covering me with a foul-smelling combination of beer and seawater. I dunked my face in water to wash it off. His friend was leaning over the rail yelling something at me as Melissa backed ever closer to us and I listened to him for a second.

"He doesn't swim!" his friend yelled.

Great, I thought to myself. *Here I am with no flotation device for either of us and I've got to try and keep this candidate for* World's Biggest Loser *afloat.*

Bubba's eyes suddenly opened and realizing where he was, he completely freaked out and started pawing at me and pushing me under the water in apoplectic panic. It was like he expected he could climb on top of me to get out of the water.

I managed a quick breath before he pushed me under. I briefly struggled against him to swim back to the surface, but quickly realized that I was no match for a panicked, 300-pound man and instead of fighting him, I did the opposite and simply relaxed and let him push me further down until his own head started to go beneath the surface. He let go of me instinctively and went back to a frantic dog paddle. I calmly surfaced several feet away and tried to think what I could do next to keep him from drowning. I tried reasoning first.

"Mister!" I shouted. "Listen to me. If you stop struggling and simply do what I'm doing, you'll float. Look at me, I'm hardly moving, and my head is out of the water. I won't let you drown."

He made eye contact with me for a second and thinking I'd gotten through to him; I swam closer to him again. He'd fooled me though, and as soon as I came within reach, he lunged out and grabbed one of my shoulders. Once he had the first one, he grabbed the other one with his other hand, and again tried to climb on top of me. I found myself completely submerged again with my head under water.

He was really starting to piss me off. He'd latched onto my polo shirt with both hands in a death grip and unless I figured out a way to break his hold, he was going to drown me. I calmed myself and tried to think what

CALLIE AWAKENS

Eva the Krav Maga instructor would do in a situation like the one I was in. I couldn't kick him effectively because of the dynamics of being in water and I couldn't strike him with either of my hands either because he had my shoulders in a death grip. I reached up with both my hands on either side and put my hands over the top of his. They felt like iron claws. I sensed I had just enough room to grab onto his left index finger and started trying to bend it back once I got my thumb under it. If I could break it, he'd likely lose the ability to hold on to me with that hand.

I couldn't budge it though; his finger was stronger than mine. Normally I could stay underwater for more than two minutes without breathing but trying to keep both of us afloat and then struggling with him had winded me and I was starting to become concerned. I could probably hold my breath for no more than fifteen seconds longer. Without giving it much thought I brought my knee up into his crotch with as much force as I could muster and got his attention. Reflexively he curled inward pulling his knees up toward his head and I was able to bring my right hand up to my left and got a good grip on his left-hand index finger with both of my hands. Once I had a good grip on his finger, I didn't hesitate and bent his finger back, until it snapped. He screamed out in pain and let go of my shoulder with that hand. I twisted my whole body away from him and swam down below him again, using the last of the oxygen remaining in my lungs. He let go with his other hand at that point.

I swam out and away from him and looked toward the boat when I surfaced. It was only ten feet away. Melissa had come down to deck level from the bridge and was now leaning over the rail with the man overboard ring in one hand and a life preserver in the other.

"You all right, Callie?"

I was too exhausted to verbally respond but nodded yes while I caught my breath. "Throw me both." I finally managed.

Melissa threw the heavier life ring first and then followed it with the life preserver. I put one arm through each so as not to lose them and then swam the life ring over to Bubba. He was keeping his head out of the water but just barely. I didn't want to get too close and pushed the life ring the last three feet, maintaining my distance.

He seized onto it and immediately stopped flailing and struggling. I took a moment to get into the life preserver. After snapping the strap in front, cinched it tight and I turned to him.

"What's your name, sir?"

"Roger."

"Are you okay?"

"I guess, but I don't know how to swim, and I'd feel a whole lot better if I could get back on the boat."

"I'll help you do that, but first I want you to try and relax a little and take a moment to catch your breath."

He nodded and took several deep breaths.

Melissa opened the gate in the railing and lowered our emergency boarding ladder over the side and hooked it over gunnel. Then she slowly took up tension on the line attached to the life ring and explained to Roger what she wanted him to do.

"Sir, I'm going to pull you to the ladder and once I get you here, I want you to grab onto it and climb up to me. Understand?"

Roger nodded his head and reached out for the ladder as she pulled him alongside. He got one hand on it and both feet on the bottom rung. Then he reached up with his other hand to grab a step higher and howled out in pain.

"That little bitch broke my finger on this hand; I'm not sure I'll be able to pull myself up with that hand."

"That little bitch just saved your life you ungrateful slob and you'll be lucky if I don't break all your other fingers once you get up here. Stop whining like a baby and pull yourself up!"

I smiled at Melissa's admonishment. The only time I'd ever seen her near as mad was when I'd failed to bring in the fenders and we got called out by another boat.

"Roger."

He looked down and back at me. "What?"

"I'd do what she says, you don't want to get her mad."

Roger slowly made his way up the ladder and once he reached the deck rolled over onto it like a beached whale. He stayed that way, breathing hard, and holding his injured hand looking like he expected sympathy from the rest of the passengers. One of the elderly male passengers who was using a walker shamed him instead.

"You better thank that young girl. She just did one of the bravest things I've ever seen anyone do and what did you do? You tried to drown her near as I could tell. Seeing what you did in the water made me embarrassed to be a man."

I stepped off the ladder onto the deck as he said the last part and Roger looked up at me. I expected he was going to apologize. He didn't, and instead said, "I should sue you."

I just shook my head as I shrugged out of the life preserver. Melissa looked at me and said, "Callie, get all this mess shipshape and stowed and then come up to the wheelhouse. We need to get back underway."

I nodded at her that I understood then shut the gate and put the ladder away. Several of the passengers complimented me on my courage and disparaged Roger.

"You did well, young lady. That was very brave. I can't believe what that man tried to do to you."

Instead of agreeing with them I found myself trying to make excuses for his behavior.

"He must just have been terrified of drowning."

"Still, you don't climb on top of someone who just brought you back to life, even if you're scared. It's just not right."

The more I thought about it, I had to agree. I thanked everyone for their kind words but felt very self-conscious about all the attention I was receiving. After I finished coiling the line for the man overboard ring and putting it back into its bracket, I asked if anyone needed anything, and then made my way back up to bridge in my wet clothes.

Melissa went from an idle back up to our cruising speed as I closed the wheelhouse door behind me.

"What were you thinking when you jumped over the side after him, Callie?"

Her tone was admonishing. I knew that there was no way she could have seen what I'd seen from the rail, so I started to explain. "I could see as soon as I looked down that he'd hit his head and was unconscious. He was face down, so I knew I had to move fast. They told us in my CPR class that the sooner you get to an unconscious person and start trying to resuscitate them, the better your chances of reviving them." I paused for a second then continued. "I didn't think much past that. I saw what needed to be done and did it."

Melissa took a moment to frame what she was going to say next. "Callie you're a strong swimmer and courageous. I respect you for that. But I want you to think about the bigger picture for a second. What should you have done differently? He damned near killed you in the water. What's the procedure we've practiced?"

I thought about it before responding. "I'm not sure," I admitted. "We never talked about recovering an unconscious victim in our practice sessions. I knew it would take you several minutes to maneuver the boat alongside him. I also knew I'd have to go in the water eventually even if it were just to rig a life sling around him so we could get him out of the water with the cargo boom."

"You're right about all of that, but what's our procedure?"

"To put on a life preserver first?"

"Yup. And how long do you think it would've taken you to reach into the deck box in the bow and strap on a life preserver?"

I saw where she was going with her critique. "Five or ten seconds?"

"Exactly. Think about it a little more and game it forward. He very nearly drowned you. If he'd succeeded what would my options have been? I've now got two people face down and likely drowned in the water. Would *I* then leave the boat to try and somehow get both of you aboard? Would I ask one of the elderly passengers to go in? Can you see the impossible situation you left me in? My primary responsibility is to all those elderly passengers down below. Can you see how your impetuous act threatened everyone?"

I colored and then nodded, embarrassed at my shortsightedness. Hearing her explain her options and putting myself in her shoes I could see her point immediately. "You're right, Melissa. I should have thought about it more before I jumped in."

"Callie, when you become a captain it's not just about driving the boat and looking good. Just about anybody can do that. A good captain spends very little time driving the boat. A good captain doesn't even have to think about piloting the boat. He or she should be thinking about everything else happening around them and gaming things forward in their head, constantly. What would I do if this happened? What would I do if that happened? Do you understand where I'm going with all this?"

I did get where she was going. It made total sense the same way learning and understanding every single system on the boat made sense. I nodded feeling embarrassed. "I totally get it. I only saved five or ten seconds by jumping in without a life preserver and in the process lost sight of the bigger picture and my primary responsibility to you and everyone else aboard."

Melissa nodded. "Exactly. Someday I expect you're going to be a great captain, but a big part of that is cerebral." She tapped the side of her head. What she said next totally surprised me.

"What're you doing Sunday?"

I cocked my head at her confused by the sudden subject shift. "Why, what are you thinking?"

"I think you're ready to take the next step up and I'd like to spend a few hours working with you Sunday on close maneuvering, docking, and what I call my 'captain overboard' drill."

I felt like I was going to explode with happiness as I biked home at the end of the day. I hadn't given my close brush with drowning a second thought. Of far more importance was the fact that Melissa was going to teach me how to dock *Gulf Runner*! I'm not sure you can appreciate what a big deal that was for me and my evolution as a captain. Being trusted to handle a sixty-five-foot, forty-nine-ton, twin engine boat at the age of fifteen felt really big.

Aunt Nancy and I shared a light dinner together on the rear patio facing the pool and the Gulf that evening. We liked it back there for the unobstructed view of the sunsets. I told her all about the incident with the two drunk passengers as we ate, how one had fallen over, how I'd jumped in after him, given him rescue breaths, and then gotten him breathing again."

"And once he was breathing, he was able to swim to the boat on his own?" she asked.

"No, it turned out he didn't know how to swim either."

"What a nightmare! So how did you get him back on the boat?"

"It got a little dicey at that point, but ultimately Melissa was able to throw the life ring to him and pull him to the boat."

"What do you mean 'a little dicey'?"

"He struggled some, but it wasn't a big deal."

Nancy had this ability to cut to the chase which I admired, but I was wary of doing or saying anything that might jeopardize my job and I wanted to keep her respect for me and my judgment, intact.

"What does 'struggled some' mean? You mean he struggled with you, right?"

"Yea, no biggy, I handled it." The second I said that I realized I sounded over-confident. It had actually been a very dangerous situation that I'd gotten myself into.

Nancy's stare bored into me. She tapped her wineglass with a fingernail. "Handled it how? Come on, Callie, tell me. I can always tell when you're minimizing."

"It got a little difficult in the water with the guy. He basically decided climbing on top of me like I was some sort of an island would keep him from drowning. It got pretty scary for a while," I admitted.

"So, what did you do? He was 300 pounds, right?"

I nodded and wondered what words to use. I remembered back to our discussion about my physical altercation with Christopher in the barn and the word Nancy had used. I shrugged and used the same word she had. "I gave him an 'adjustment.'"

She'd just taken a sip of her wine and sputtered some of it onto the table, then laughed.

"What sort of an adjustment? I can't wait to hear what my ninety-pound niece did to the poor 300-pound gorilla."

"I broke his index finger to make him let go of me."

"You did what! God, Callie, you're tough. You mean you just took his finger and broke it? I don't think I'd ever have had the presence of mind to try something like that. And he just let you go?"

"Not quite, I also had to knee him in the groin."

"Of course you did, dear girl. How did you even think of doing something like that?"

"It was something the Krav Maga instructor Eva said at the beginning of her demonstration. The second time he got his hands on me I realized he really was going to drown me to save himself, and if I didn't do something to disable him, then he was going to succeed."

"I'm just glad you're all right. It sounds like you had a very close call."

We ate in silence for a few moments and then Nancy had a thought.

"Hey, don't you have a birthday coming up soon?"

"Next Tuesday, I'll be sixteen."

"Anything special you want?"

I thought for a second. "Thanks for asking, but I don't need a thing. This whole summer has been an incredible gift. You've already been amazingly generous."

RIP CONVERSE

Chapter 12

G*ulf Runner* only ran between the Gasparilla Marina and Marco Island six days a week. Sundays were our down-days and as I biked to the marina, I was both excited and anxious. Melissa was going to meet me at 9:00 a.m. I got there at 8:00 and after I completed my regular engine room checks I went up to wheelhouse and sat down in the helmsman's chair and looked over all the instruments and then at the combination throttle/shift levers and the wheel. All of it suddenly looked different as I contemplated actually controlling the multi-ton ferry within in the close quarters of the marina and not smashing into anything. I was seeing everything through new eyes.

Normally when we left the dock or idled up to it, I was always down on deck either preparing the fenders and lines for docking or putting them away. When we were underway Melissa would occasionally have me adjust our course and speed, but I'd never actually been in the wheelhouse with her when she was leaving the dock or returning to it. I'd never actually seen her manipulate the controls as she maneuvered the boat in close quarters. I really had no idea how she was able to maneuver *Gulf Runner* in tight spaces and dock her as gently as a lamb.

We were tied at our normal berth on the outer face of the marina dock and as I contemplated all of this, my heart rate increased, and I started to sweat. I literally had no idea as to how I would get us off the dock without scraping the side of the boat or hitting the boat in front of us or the one behind. My panic attack was interrupted by the sound of the gangway opening and then closing down on deck and several seconds later by the sound of Melissa's footsteps as she walked through the passenger cabin and up the steps into the wheelhouse.

"Morning, Callie." She looked at me sitting in the barber chair. "The view out the window's a little different than the one you see as a deckhand, isn't it?"

I looked over at her, feeling completely out of my depth at the prospect of maneuvering Gulf Runner and it must have shown.

"Don't worry; we all had a first day. You'll do fine."

"Right now, just getting off this dock face seems like a big deal. I guess I never really thought about it from your perspective."

"First thing is, relax. I'm not going to have you do anything today that I don't demonstrate first. I know you've got zero experience driving a twin-screw boat. First, let's warm up the engines and listen to the weather. We won't be going far today, but I expect we'll be a few hours practicing and you always want to have an idea of what the weather's going to be for the day. You can go ahead and start both engines and let them warm up."

I made sure both were in neutral, turned the key and then pressed the starter button on the starboard main. After it was running and the RPM had settled at 800 rpm, I repeated the process on the port main and then I started the generator.

"Now check all of your oil pressure gauges."

I did; all three engines were in the green zone.

"Good. Now turn on your GPS, Radar and VHF and switch to the weather frequency."

I did as she suggested and then the two of us listened to the computer-generated voice that gave us the weather for our area. I let it play through two cycles to make sure I didn't miss anything. We were forecast to have Northeasterly winds at five to ten knots in the morning increasing to ten to fifteen in the afternoon, partly cloudy skies, with high tide at 11:30 a.m.

"As a rule, you might want to write that info down."

I leaned over to port and wrote down the pertinent bits on the scratch pad lying next to the paper chart.

"Okay, follow me."

I followed her down the stairs and through the main cabin out onto the rear deck. "What are we doing here?"

"One thing I always like to do is visually check for good healthy streams of cooling water coming out of all three exhausts."

She peered over the stern first and then the port side. "See how all three exhausts have a good healthy flow of water mixed in with the exhaust?

I nodded.

"If you've got no flow or just an intermittent flow on an engine, what would you suspect?"

I considered it for a moment. "Maybe the sea strainer is full of weed?" Checking and cleaning out the sea strainers for seaweed was one of my morning maintenance chores. The sea strainers catch anything that might interfere with the flow of cooling water getting to each engine.

"Good guess, but what if your sea strainers are clean and you still have poor flow?"

I racked my brain. "I don't know."

"There are two other things it could be. You or I might have shut off the raw water intake to do something and then forgot to turn it back on. The only other thing it could be is the impeller. We haven't replaced one of those yet, but all three engines have them. It doesn't matter whether it's a closed freshwater cooling system or an outside seawater system. Both of them need something to circulate the water through the cooling jacket of the engine. Next time we change out the oil or the fuel filters I'll show you how to replace one.

The next thing you want to do is simply stand here on deck for a few seconds and get a feel for all the things going on around you that will affect the boat. Feel the wind on your face and note the direction and speed of it. Look down into the water at a crab pot, a mooring or one of the pilings and look for telltale eddies or other signs of current. Current and wind will both effect the boat the moment we undo the lines. We've got quite a bit of sail area."

I cocked my head to the side. "What do you mean? We don't have any sails."

"Think of anything above the waterline as a sail. If the wind is blowing it will exert force on the entire boat in the direction the wind is blowing. If the lines were off the boat right now and the wind was blowing from the starboard side, what effect would you guess that would have?"

"It would push us away from the dock, right?"

Melissa nodded. "And where's the wind now?"

I felt the wind on my face and looked out into the anchorage and then at the flag flying from the marina flagpole. "It's coming from the northeast and will tend to blow us against the dock."

"Good. See any current?"

I looked out over the side at an empty mooring ball about 100 feet away from us in the channel. There were no telltale eddies of water visible. "Don't see any."

"Okay, follow me."

We climbed the short ladder up to the stern-facing set of controls and Melissa pointed to various obstacles around us.

"We've got a boat tied up fifteen feet in front of us, another tied up twenty feet behind us, and the wind is blowing us against the dock. We can't just put the boat in forward or reverse and drive away from the dock because the wind will tend to hold us against the dock. If you just try to drive it straight out of here, it won't work. We'll just end up dragging the side of *Gulf Runner* down the side of the dock and then hit either the boat in front of us or the one behind.

The way we're going to do it is I want you to first hang one of those big ball fenders over the starboard bow, tie it on to the second stanchion-post back from the bow and then lower it to pier height. Then go ask Jason in the fuel shack to help us with our lines. I'll have him untie all the lines except for the spring line leading forward to the bow. I want you up here in the wheelhouse with me. Once he's done that, we're going to drive forward against the spring line until the bow starts pivoting off that fender. Our stern will simultaneously come off the dock towards the channel. Then I'll create some slack in the line so that Jason can get it off the cleat and we'll have him throw it over our rail."

I followed her back through the cabin and up the stairs. "Will we be steering from the wheelhouse or the stern station getting off the dock?"

"Both. If I get you to take away anything today, I want it to be a calm, measured, thought-out approach, to everything you do. We're not in a rush to do anything. It's far more important that you have a firm plan in your mind and equally as important, that you've clearly shared that plan with whoever is helping you. If you ever find yourself yelling at your crew or other people on the dock, it's because your plan was flawed, or you failed to adequately convey it properly to the people helping you. Prizes for speed and how cool you look are never awarded, especially on a commercial vessel. Your primary responsibility is to get off the dock and return to the dock with the same number of people you started with without hitting anything or hurting anyone in the process. Anything else is bullshit. And there are no stupid questions, so if you're unsure of something or I'm unclear, let me know. Got it?"

"Got it."

I hung the fender ball as she'd requested, then asked Jason in the fuel shed to help us with our lines. He agreed and I went back up to the wheelhouse. Melissa opened the side door in the wheelhouse to facilitate communicating with Jason.

"Jason; take off the bow, the stern and the stern spring. I'm going to pivot her on the forward spring. Once my stern's out, off the dock and in the channel, I'll give you a nod and you can take off the bow spring and throw it aboard. Clear?"

"Yes, ma'am."

She waited for him to get the lines off.

"Lines off, Melissa," he shouted.

"Watch what I do, Callie."

She bumped both throttles into forward for just a second and then shifted both back into neutral. It was just enough thrust to idle us forward and take the slack out of the remaining spring line. Once the slack was out of it, she advanced the port throttle into forward again at idle speed, turned the wheel to Starboard, and *Gulf Runner* started pivoting on her bow against the fender. The stern immediately started to move away from the dock and out into the channel. Once *Gulf Runner* was at the angle she wanted, she shifted into neutral and leaned out of the door.

"Jason, I'm going to do some touch and go's with Callie. We'll be back in a couple of minutes. When we come alongside just put that same spring back on if you would and then stand by to release it again after our stern pivots out."

"Will do, Melissa. You want it off the cleat now?"

She nodded and he threw the line over our rail. "Okay, follow me, Callie."

I followed her through the rear door in the wheelhouse to the stern controls. She advanced the starboard engine into reverse and the Port engine to forward, got us the rest of the way clear of the dock and then straightened the boat in the channel. "Okay, Callie, your turn. Your stern is now your bow. Keep your wheel straight and using just your engines continue backing in a straight line up the channel."

"Aren't we going to go back into the wheelhouse and steer from there?"

"Nope. You have far more control of a twin screw using your engines to pull you. I want you to get a feel for exactly where your pivot point is using the twin screws, and this is the best way of doing it. Pick a boat or some point across the anchorage and try and back in a straight line towards it using just your engines."

So began my first day of driving. We practiced docking and maneuvering for three hours. Jason looked like he wanted to kill me after I did seven landings and departures in a row. I didn't do everything perfectly, but I got the basics down and a solid understanding of how to maneuver a twin-screw powerboat. One exercise she had me do was turning the boat in several 360-degree circles without going forward or backwards. She found two empty moorings about ninety feet apart and Melissa had me stay between them and spin *Gulf Runner* in a tight circle without hitting either one. By the end of the day I knew I could back the boat and safely pick-up Melissa without chopping her up in the props if she were ever to fall overboard.

Melissa was a captain's captain and I think I will carry her lessons and especially the way that she gave those lessons, forward for many years. She was always calm, discussed each principle until I understood it perfectly, and then gently coached me through the execution of each maneuver. I felt privileged to learn from her. She was patient, thorough and meticulous. I hope that someday I can in-turn teach others in the same manner.

I explained everything we'd worked at to Nancy over dinner that evening.

"Nancy, did you know that twin-screw vessels like *Gulf Runner* have counter rotating propellors?"

"I had no idea. But I'm certain you'll tell me."

"Are you making fun of me?"

"No, I'm sure it's absolutely fascinating. I can't wait to hear about counter-rotating propellors. Don't keep me in suspense for a single moment longer."

I ignored her sarcasm. "Well, it's important because if you don't yet have any way on and therefore no water going past your rudders then...."

I looked up. She was staring at me with a huge smile on her face.

"You _are_ making fun of me!"

"I most assuredly am not. Any knowledge that could so animate someone as smart as you must be of great importance. I am absolutely stuck to my seat with anticipation."

"You are not!"

"Well, I am having some difficulty in figuring out how I could personally put this knowledge to good use in my own life. That aside, clearly the concept of counter-rotating propellers and the resultant effects on the port and starboard snickle snackles added to the thrust and the folderol generated by gaseous wind will, as I'm sure you know, impact and impinge on various critical maritime laws."

"Exactly, and if you take the sum total of your maritime knowledge and integrate it with the brain of a barnacle you would end up with a brain-dead barnacle plus the additional parasitical drag it tends to cause when growing on a hull beneath the waterline. Ipso facto, porto and starboardo."

"Porto? Starboardo? Really, Callie, even I know those aren't real words. You're just showing off your command of that odd language you sailors speak to one another. And, if I'm not mistaken, I believe you also just implied that your dear, dear Aunt Nancy is brain-dead. I'm shocked and deeply injured that you would speak to me in that manner."

I got up out of my seat, wrapped my arms around her, leaned down and whispered in her ear. "You poor baby, it must be heartbreaking being you and having to put up with such a snotty little niece. Just remember, I think you are one of the coolest, most special, aunts a girl could ever have even if all the things your neighbors say behind your back are true."

She reached back and put her hand on the side of my face. "I'm so glad you came into my life this summer, Callie. Seeing life through your eyes has given me a whole new outlook on my life. I've got a lot of things to do, going forward."

I could tell she was serious, and I put our funny banter to the side. "What sorts of things?"

"I used to have your energy and optimism. I also had your determination. You've made me realize that I've just been coasting along since I sold my company. I've just been sitting here in in my posh, little, beachfront cottage in Boca Grande going to cocktail parties and driving my swank little Bentley around. Nothing I'm doing right now is important, or productive, and my inestimable talents are being wasted."

"That's not true. You have your projects like the women's shelter which are very important. At least to the women there." I added.

"You're nice to say that but believe me, I can do much more. And I'm far too young, talented, and wealthy to not be doing it. With the money I've been able to make, I can do anything I set my little heart on. Every day I watch you go to your mostly menial job schlepping concrete and lumber and putting up with the unwashed masses on that ferryboat so you can pursue this captain's dream of yours. You don't have a nickel to your name, you never complain or gossip and somehow you have a smile on your face every day! You just keep the pedal to the metal and your drive blows me away. It's made me realize that if everyone pursued life like you, the sky would be the limit for our world. I need to get up off my ass, get back in shape and get my cerebral cortex back in the game. I'm not exactly sure of what that will end up looking like, but it will entail giving more back and making it possible for more people like you to live up to their potential."

"That sounds like big stuff you're thinking about."

"It will be. And a lot of it will be thanks to you."

"That's BS, Aunt Nancy—" I started, but immediately felt awkward at my language and presuming to know better than her.

She pulled back. "Catherine, language! A young lady never uses course language like that, it's so fucking common."

I resisted the urge to linguistically compete with her and picked up on her thoughts. "Nancy, you've always had that in you. It's how you got where you are. You've just been on a little break, fortifying yourself for the next five miles of the marathon."

She was silent for a few moments, then looked me in the eye and spoke again. "You're so smart, Callie, and I'm not talking book-smarts. You are going to do some great things. And while we're on the subject of brains I want to discuss the potential atrophy of yours. I actually got you two birthday presents, one of which I'd like to discuss with you now. The other will remain a secret till Tuesday."

"Okay," I offered cautiously trying to think why she might be thinking my brain was atrophying.

"What's the deal with you and college? Have you really not given it any thought?"

I didn't respond right away. I had in fact been thinking about it quite a bit in the weeks since our initial discussion. But her comment felt like it was also criticism of my decision to pursue the captain's license, something I'd put considerable effort into over the course of the summer. I'd thought she approved of that. "Of course, I've thought about it, but what's wrong with learning a good skill like captaining?" I came back defensively.

"Nothing, Catherine, nothing at all. I wasn't criticizing you. I'm sure you'll be a great captain and also make a perfectly respectable living wage doing it. I couldn't be any prouder of you and how you've attacked your goal for the entire summer. But besides being that, and beautiful, and athletic as hell, you're also a brain. I'd hate to see that side of you wasted. I'm not suggesting that you give up your dream of being a Captain, I'm merely suggesting that you can also be quite a bit more if you set your sights higher."

Now I really felt self-conscious. "Yes, I'm smart I suppose. I know I've got a really high IQ, but school's never been a challenge and I guess I just assumed college would be more of the same. Honestly, I've always felt as though I could get farther on my own and that any time I spent at a community college would be wasted."

"Why do you put the limitation of community college on yourself?"

I looked at her, held up my right hand and rubbed my index finger and my thumb together. "Money," I reminded her.

"What if money wasn't a consideration? What if you could go to any college in the world that you wanted?"

"Honestly, I'd have to think about it. From what little I know about Ivy League schools and the other top colleges; they're places for snobs and theorists. I'm not either. I'm a doer. I'm a simple girl from a, let's be honest, poor Southern family and I wouldn't fit in. They'd make fun of me the same way the rich kids at Fort Myers High do."

"They make fun of you not because you're poor but because you're a threat. Competence intimidates."

"Maybe, but trust me, they also make fun of me because I'm poor and I don't have the right labels on my clothes."

"Do you know how stupid that sounds?"

"It's real."

"I'm not talking about the clothes; I'm talking about you. That you would care is stupid. It would be like me actually giving two shits about what my neighbors think of me."

"Nancy, how can I take you seriously when you use such language?"

"Callie, in the three weeks you have remaining here I want you to give this some serious thought. I would be honored to pay for any higher education you want, anything. It could be Harvard, MIT, Oxford. It could even be the Naval Academy for God's sake. I would look at it as a sound investment in a brilliant future. The only stipulation or repayment I would ask is that at some later date after you've succeeded beyond your wildest dreams, I want you to pay it forward to someone else who you think has the same potential that I see in you."

My eyes teared up. What she was offering me was huge and I was immensely grateful. "That's an incredible gift, Nancy, really. I'll give it a lot of thought. No one has ever had as much confidence and faith in me as you and your offer means a great deal. I do have one question though."

"What."

"Does this mean the Bentley is off the table as a birthday present?"

She reached out and ruffled my hair which I absolutely hated unless she was doing it.

I got serious again. "I meant to ask you; would you like to ride over to Marco Island on the ferry with me one day before I leave?"

"I'd love to, Callie! Let me look at my calendar." Nancy swiped at her phone several times and looked back up. "I've got two doctor's appointments and some tests on Monday, but what about Tuesday?"

"Tuesday would be great. I'll ask Melissa. What's up with the doctor appointments? Have you been feeling sick?"

Nancy shook her head. "Nope; nothing in particular. I go in once a year for bloodwork and a physical with one doctor and I see a dermatologist twice a year simply because I'm a Floridian and tend to get a lot of sun."

CALLIE AWAKENS

Tuesday was my birthday and I rushed through my engine-room duties and then loaded the freight as quickly as I could. Nancy pulled into the parking lot at 9:10 just as I opened the gate to board the fifteen passengers, we had going over with us that day. Melissa came down off the bridge to welcome her aboard.

"Welcome aboard, Nancy. I can't tell you what a pleasure it's been for me having your niece as my deckhand this summer. She hasn't been late once and has performed every aspect of her job in an admirable way with the exception of just one, regrettable day."

Nancy looked at her confused and surprised to hear anything negative about me. "Which regrettable day was that? Young Catherine here has failed to mention anything but positive accolades from you."

I couldn't believe Melissa was going to embarrass me in front of Nancy with her lame story about me failing to bring in the fenders. It was like I'd committed some unpardonable sin that could never be forgiven. "Melissa, you aren't going to tell the story of the fenders again, are you?"

"I certainly am." She turned to Nancy. "Believe it or not your niece did something so awful that I've been the joke of the entire waterfront since. It's a day that will live in local infamy."

I rolled my eyes and Nancy put on her concerned face. "That doesn't sound like the Callie I know."

"I know! Normally she's attentive to a fault, brilliant in the engine room, not afraid to get her hands dirty, shows great judgment and never forgets anything I tell her; in short, an almost perfect deckhand."

"So, what did she do? I'm dying to know. And before you tell me let me first extend my sincerest apologies for her on behalf of our whole family." She turned to me. "Catherine, I can't believe you would so something that would disappoint Melissa this much." She turned back to Melissa. "What did she do?"

"Well, believe it or not Callie failed to bring in the fenders one day and we drove halfway to Marco with them bouncing along our side in the water. We must have looked like drunken clowns auditioning for some sort of maritime circus and as a result I was the butt of every captain's joke for weeks afterward when word got out. I'm still buying free drinks for them as a result. Can you believe it?"

Nancy was silent for several seconds and looked down at me with a disappointed look on her face as she tried to gauge the shame I'd brought on the family. I couldn't believe Melissa had made such a big deal out of it.

Nancy finally spoke again. "Melissa, that's awful! I can't imagine how I would have felt if she'd done that to me. I probably would have fired her!"

"I know, right?" Melissa agreed with indignation.

"I'm curious though, there's one thing I don't understand."

"What's that?"

"What's a fender?"

There was silence for a second or two and then both Melissa and Nancy both broke up into uproarious laughter, with me as the joke. I'd been set up by the two of them and completely fallen for their little skit.

"Oh, you two are about as funny as a bad case of shingles. Jeesh, I can't believe I'm still being ridden for that one tiny oversight."

"Callie, you've been great this summer, really. I couldn't be more pleased. We were just having a little fun." Melissa looked at her watch. "We should shove off. We're three minutes behind schedule. Callie, bring Nancy up onto the bridge with you and then take *Gulf Runner* off the dock. I'll do the lines today."

At first, I thought I'd misheard her and looked back at her with a confused expression on my face. Was she pulling another prank on me?

"Really?" I asked incredulously.

"Of course, really."

I don't have to go into all the details of what happened next beyond telling you that seeing the look of pride on Nancy's face as I stood behind the controls and twin screwed a commercial ferry flawlessly out of her slip, at the age of fifteen, was one of the proudest moments of my life. Melissa let me drive the entire way to Marco Island, had me dock *Gulf Runner* there, and then also drive the return leg after our layover. I talked Nancy's ear off the entire trip explaining everything I knew about oil pressure, engine temps, bilge pumps, radar, GPS, fathometers and passing agreements between vessels. I even took a second swing at explaining counter rotating propeller shafts to her. I don't think she understood a word I said or cared about any of them one wit. She just cared that all those things were important to me and if I loved them, then she would love them also.

CALLIE AWAKENS

RIP CONVERSE

Chapter 13

I got home from work Tuesday night at 6:00. Nancy was in the living room watching the news.

"Hi, birthday girl. Do you feel any different?"

"Just that now, I can get my driver's license."

"Yes, that was a big milestone in my life too. Remember how I told you I'd have a surprise for you this evening?"

I nodded. "Of course. Don't tell me that you've finally decided to part with your Bentley. You really shouldn't."

"Oh, I'm sure that's what I must have been thinking. Not. Go get changed and then come down for dinner. Your surprise should be here by then."

I cocked my head dying to know what she had in store for me. "Cool, what or who is it?"

"It wouldn't be a surprise if I told you now, would it?"

I came down the stairs fifteen minutes later curious as to what my surprise birthday present might be. There was someone in the living room sitting across from Nancy with her back to me as I came down the stairs, but I couldn't tell right away who it was. She started to turn towards me.

Nancy looked up also, as I came down the stairs. "Callie, you remember Eva, right?"

Eva stood up and held her hand out to me.

"Of course. Hello, Eva." I smiled and shook her outstretched hand. "It's very nice to see you again. I still have your card and was planning on calling you in two weeks once I get home. Aunt Nancy seems to have gotten ahead of me."

"Your Aunt Nancy is quite a fan of yours. She was just telling me about your summer and your job on the ferry. Nancy said that you make handling a commercial ferry look very simple."

I blushed realizing that I was the topic of their conversation. I was really proud of what I'd accomplished over the summer, but at the same time I wasn't quite sure of how to respond with any sort of humility, or without over-sharing on the subject. Eva obviously wasn't here to talk about boats and my summer job, so I deflected and minimized. "My boss lets me drive occasionally, but I'm really just a deckhand. So, I'm curious, what are you two cooking up together?"

Nancy answered for both of them. "Knowing that this Krav Maga business is something that you want to pursue, Callie, I thought I would help you get started. I've arranged for Eva to give you private lessons over the next two weeks. Eva told me that if you work at it, she can teach you quite a bit in that time. She's got some vacation time she'd been planning on taking and Eva's going to be staying with us as our guest for the next two weeks."

Eva jumped in. "I don't get much free time off, Callie, but when your aunt offered me a room on this beautiful island while I'm teaching you, I couldn't say no. During the day when you're working, I plan on going to the beach, catching up on my reading, and doing some shopping. On your days off and mornings and evenings, you and I will work out together. Think you have the energy for it?"

I didn't have any reservations at all as to having the energy. "Absolutely Eva. That sounds awesome!" I walked over to Nancy with a big, beaming smile on my face and gave her a hug. "Thank you, Aunt Nancy, what a cool birthday present." I took her hands in mine and maintained eye contact for several seconds to underscore how pleased I was.

"I heard you on your very first day here when you told me about that dreadful boy who hit you and tried to take advantage of you. And even though I didn't say much at the time, I got a little freaked out about that man off the ferry who tried to drown you. You have the heart of a lion Callie, but unfortunately, it's in the body of a lemur. I don't want you to feel physically intimidated by anyone ever again. It will also be nice to have a trained security expert on staff, even if it is just temporarily. The only security on this island is the outrageous toll they charge to get on."

I scoffed at Nancy's suggestion that any security was needed on Boca Grande and turned to Eva. "I think that the last crime committed on this island was probably twenty years ago when someone on their way to a cocktail party double parked their Rolls Royce for two minutes to run into *Newlin's* for a wedge of Brie."

Nancy and Eva both chuckled and then Nancy turned to Eva. "Let's eat, shall we? Rosario made us a roast, risotto and also picked some fresh garden tomatoes. I also believe she made a crème de cacao for dessert. While we dine perhaps Eva will share some of her background and how she came to be an instructor in this deadly art she practices."

The wind was blowing that evening and we decided to eat inside instead of out. I went out into the kitchen to see if I could help Rosario serve as Eva and Nancy got settled at the table.

"What can I do, Rosario?"

"Nothing, Callie. You go sit and enjoy your guest. I can serve this, it's simple."

"Let me at least help serve the soup, I'm already out here."

"No, you're going to insult me if you don't sit. This is my job. Let me do it."

I gave her a smile and a hug. "I'm sorry, of course you can."

"And it's your birthday. Now go, out of my kitchen!"

I returned to the table. "Rosario definitely doesn't need my help."

Nancy turned to Eva. "Tell us where you're from, Eva, how you became a Krav Maga instructor and something particularly embarrassing about yourself."

"Nancy, Eva just got here and isn't used to you yet." I leaned towards Eva and feigned a whisper. "She's like this. I don't know where she gets it but be strong because she's relentless."

"Catherine, don't ruin my fun. I just like to cut through the normal BS and Eva is a guest in our home."

I looked at Eva, raised a hand to the side of my head and made circular motions with my index finger around my temple. "Aunt Nancy can be a little loopy. She thinks 'guest in my home' means license to torture. She does this kind of thing to me all the time."

"I don't mind. I actually find it refreshing. Israelis are direct like this also. I was a bit of a shiksa growing up, so I'm used to it."

"What's a shiksa?" I asked.

"It means I was a bit of a non-conformist or maybe a rebel in English."

"All interesting women are." Nancy interjected.

"Yes, well perhaps, but my family and especially my father didn't approve of a great deal of what I did. As result there was always tension between us and I decided early on that I wanted to be out of our home and on my own as soon as I was of age. My father had something else in mind. He expected I would meet a nice Jewish boy, get married, and have lots of Jewish babies right away; oh, and be deferential to both him and my husband. I, of course, wanted to do the exact opposite. After I completed High School, I immediately entered the IDF for my mandatory two years of service."

"What's the IDF?" I asked.

"Israeli Defense Force. It's mandatory military service and it's required of everyone unless you are Arab or ultra-orthodox. Much to my father's disappointment I failed to meet the old-fashioned Jewish boy he'd hoped for and instead fell in love with a goy just after I completed my two years of service."

I looked at her again confused by the word.

"Sorry, a goy is someone non-Jewish which is a no, no where I'm from. Even worse, Eric was a pro-Palestinian activist in Israel to protest Israeli policy towards Palestinians. He was only there for two months before the government revoked his visa and sent him back to the States, but our relationship was extremely passionate. My father was furious, refused to let him enter our home and also forbid me from returning until Eric was out of my life. That, of course, pissed me off and made me want Eric more."

"Eva, language," Aunt Nancy said quietly with a cautionary tone.

Eva paled, obviously embarrassed. "I'm terribly—"

I interrupted. "It's okay, Eva, Nancy swears like a sailor when it's just her and me. It's an inside joke between us. Don't worry, you'll get used to us."

Eva smiled nervously at both of us, confused by our banter. "Long story short, as you say, I got a green card from the U.S. Government and came to the U.S. in pursuit of Eric. You can probably guess how that story ended."

I looked down at her finger for a wedding ring. Nancy saw my glance and spoke.

"I'm going to guess you woke up one morning here in the States next to this Eric fellow and as much as you hated to admit it, realized that your father had been right, you'd been a fool, and that this Eric chap was a complete loser."

"I still wouldn't say my father was totally right in his actions, but I would agree with you that I was a fool, and I also did come to realize that Eric was a complete loser. How did you know?"

"I could tell from the moment I first heard you speak at the women's shelter that you were principled and cut from some strong cloth. I expect you likely came to the realization that for all its mistakes, Israel is your home and an idea that you were proud to be a part of. That it was something worth fighting for and that sleeping with Eric was like sleeping with the enemy."

"That's pretty much it."

"What about the Krav Maga? How did you get started and end up a teacher?" Nancy pressed on.

"All Israeli recruits are introduced to it in basic training."

"Yes, perhaps, but I also suspect that very few become instructors and get as competent at it as you are."

Eva paused overly long before responding again. "I just really liked it and found I was good at it."

She put her head down a little quickly and took a bite from her plate. "Rosario is a very good cook." Changing the topic.

I looked over at Nancy and she gave me a very subtle wag of her head. We both knew there was more to her story, but clearly Eva wasn't willing to share it with us yet.

Nancy had a full-size workout room in her home which I'd never seen her use. I showed it to Eva after dinner and she said it would be the perfect place to set up the equipment that she'd brought with her. She and I made several trips back and forth to her van and set up tumbling mats, a speed bag, a heavy bag, a grappling dummy, and two duffels full of gear that included, headgear, instep guards, boxing gloves, MMA gloves, focus mitts, fake knives, and fake guns. We set it all up in front of the large floor to ceiling mirrors that covered the front wall of the space.

"Let's not start till tomorrow night Callie, that was a big dinner."

I put a hand to my stomach silently signaling that I agreed.

"I like your aunt, she's quite a woman and not really what I expected at all."

"She's a trip all right. I'm glad you weren't put off by her. She can be super-direct which takes a while to get used to. She's got an incredibly kind heart though."

"I can see all of that. I can also tell that she thinks a great deal of you."

"Yes, I'm quite lucky." I replied somewhat wistfully. "Is there anything I can do for you or show you before I head off to bed, Eva?"

"No, I'm good. I think I'll have a short walk on the beach before I turn in. I've never had a beach right outside my door and this 'cottage' of your aunt's is really something."

"Yes, it's a beautiful place. In the morning I generally get up by 6:00 and either run five miles or swim before I head off to my job. I've usually got time for breakfast between 7:00-7:45 if you're up."

"I'll plan on it. See you in the morning."

I got up the next morning at 6:00, pulled on a swimsuit and went out to the pool. Before starting my laps, I stretched out for several minutes, and did my normal fifty push-ups and 100 sit-ups. Then I dove in. I'd been working on my underwater endurance the previous week and swam my first lap entirely underwater. After my turn, I swam more than halfway back before finally surfacing and settling into my first twenty laps of crawl stroke. I pushed myself hard, fueled by endorphins and the simple joy of feeling alive. I'm not sure what makes one workout different from another, but that morning I felt my strength increasing instead of decreasing with each lap.

When I finished, I briefly toyed with the idea of also going for a run, but I wanted to leave some time for coffee with Eva before going to work and settled for eighty sit-ups instead of my normal fifty and when I did my push-ups, I clapped my hands at the top of each one.

After doing some stretches at the end, I looked out over the beach towards the Gulf and spontaneously ran out of the pool area onto the beach and sprinted down it until I was winded, about a half mile. Then I stopped, with my hands on my hips, breathing hard and looked out over the Gulf. I felt incredibly powerful and lucky to be alive. I ran my feet through the wave wash as I walked back to the house thinking about Aunt Nancy's offer of college. I wasn't yet sure what I would do, but the seed she'd planted was definitely growing.

****

Nancy had given Eva the guest cottage for her time with us. Eva was also up early and hearing sounds of life from the front of the house, wandered into the living room just minutes after I started my workout. Not wanting to interrupt me she curled up at the end of one of the couches and watched.

Rosario peered into the living room from the kitchen and seeing her, walked in.

"Good morning, Miss Eva. May I get you some coffee or a juice?"

"Hello, Rosario, good morning. I'd love some coffee. I'm just enjoying watching Callie work out. Does she do this every morning?"

"Oh no. Miss Callie only swims three or four days a week. The other days she runs. That girl is like the wind. I don't know where she gets her energy, but I've never seen anything like her. She never stops. When she's not working at her job or running or swimming, she helps me around the house or my husband with the landscaping."

"Wow. I was just trying to think if I ever had as much energy as her. Is she ever like other teenagers? I mean doesn't she ever sleep late or watch TV or text with her friends?"

Rosario thought about the question for a few seconds then shook her head. "No, not Miss Callie. She says life's too short to waste time doing those things."

****

I wrapped a towel around myself once I got back to the pool area and walked into the living room. Hearing voices in the kitchen, I went in and joined Rosario and Eva.

"Buenos dios, Miss Callie. You're looking particularly happy this morning. Can I get you a coffee or juice?"

"Buenos dios, Rosario, and good morning, Eva. I'd like both if you don't mind."

"I watched you work out, Callie. It was inspiring and I think I'll use some of my time here on the island to step up my own aerobic fitness."

"I love days like today. Do you ever have workouts where the more you do the more you feel like doing, Eva?"

She smiled at me. "I think I know what you mean. I tend to focus more on drills and strength training, but watching you makes me want to work more on my endurance. Would you mind if I joined you for some of your workouts?"

"Not at all, that would be fun. Tomorrow's a running day, I can show you most of the island if you're up for it."

"Great! What time do you get home from your job?"

"Usually by 5:00."

"What would you think about us starting your Krav Maga training right at 5:00 and then eating supper after 7:00?"

"Works for me. Rosario, what's the dinner plan for tonight?"

"It's very flexible. I was going to leave the three of you a big, green, garden salad, cut-up fruit, lobster salad and crème brûlée. You can pull it out of the fridge whenever you like."

I gave her a hug. "Can we eat it now? I'm really going to miss you when I go home to my family?"

"You'll be fine, Miss Callie. I know you've been paying attention to how I make everything all summer. You'll just make it yourself."

"I know just enough to be dangerous in the kitchen."

"You better hurry; it's already 7:30. I'll have a lunch packed for you by the time you get out of the shower."

I gave Rosario a kiss on the cheek and turned to Eva. "I'll see you tonight at 5:00, Eva; I'm really looking forward to it."

"Have a good day, Callie."

My first training with Eva was not what I expected when I returned home at the end of the day. She had me put on a pair of MMA gloves and then asked me to watch her. She turned and faced the padded striking dummy, went up on the toes of her left foot, and then did two very quick snap kicks to the dummy's face with her right foot.

"Try that, Callie. Kick Dan in the head, hard if you can."

"Dan?"

"Yes, Dan the dummy. It helps to know your opponent."

I smiled, went up on my left foot the way she had and made two pathetic kick attempts as she'd instructed. Both were low, not terribly powerful, and slow. "I think I'm too short to kick that high, Eva."

"Actually, you're plenty tall; you're just not flexible enough. We'll work on that. Right now, I'm trying to get a feel for your body, your limitations, and your mindset." She turned until she was facing Dan again with her hands up and open in the normal Krav Maga ready stance and then after quickly rotating her body right, rotated back left and drove the heel of her right hand into the Dan's face several times. With each strike his head snapped back almost a foot.

"Now you, Callie. For now, just use your right hand. Strike through your target with the heel of your hand."

"Wouldn't a fist have more impact."

"For now I'd like you to use palm strikes. It's too easy to break a finger when you close your fist. Turn right first and then rotate your entire body left as you strike through your target. They real power doesn't come from your arms; it comes from turning your whole body as you strike."

I struck out at Dan's face like she'd told me and made good contact in the face area with each strike, but Dan didn't move and seemed impervious to my strikes.

"Get closer to him, Callie. Remember, you're trying to strike through him, not hold him off. Your body language is saying, 'don't mess with me.' It wants to be saying, 'I'm going to kill you.' Get into his space."

I tried several more strikes and got Dan's head to move an inch or two each time, but I knew the striking force I was applying was nowhere near what Eva had demonstrated.

"Okay, stop for now. Come, sit on the floor facing me."

I sat.

"Put your feet together with your knees out to the side. Pull your feet inwards till they are touching each other and pull your heels as close to your groin as you can. Then, using your elbows, push down and try and get your knees to touch the floor. This is called a butterfly stretch. The goal is to have your heels touch your groin and for your knees to simultaneously touch the floor. Every day I want you to focus on this exercise and then also on groin stretches." She stood up, spread her legs apart several feet, then bent one knee halfway and leaned on it with her elbow, leaving the other leg long and extended and sat down into the stretch of the elongated leg. "This is another inner thigh and groin stretch. Do these two exercises every day, both sides, several times a day. Eventually, you will have a much greater range of motion and arc when you do your kicks.

The main thing I'm going to be working on with you right now, is mindset. All women I've ever met, including myself, start out with a deficient mindset." She held up her hands in a defensive manner and started backing up. "When you display body language like this you are saying, 'please don't hurt me.' That is not what you want to say. You want to say this." She tucked in her head and pressed a forward-moving attack in a series of blinding palm strikes but also constantly moving forward, leaning into an imaginary attacker, striking over and over again. After ten or twelve palm strikes, she grabbed her imaginary attacker with both hands behind his head, pulled him down and then simultaneously brought her knee up into his face repeatedly. "That is the Krav Maga way."

"I see the difference and know my hits were weak, but how do I change my mindset?"

"Drills, practice, getting hit, and learning not to fear getting hit. Then more drills, more practice and sparring. Certain techniques like disarming armed opponents require considerable finesse and technique, but they too can be learned with repetition. For the remainder of tonight though, we are going to just work on your stance and palm strikes with both hands."

She turned to the equipment pile and put her hands through two focus mitts, turned to me, and pushed me roughly. I almost fell over. "Come on, Callie, hit me like you mean it!" She was bouncing on her toes and held the mitts to either side of her face. "Get in your stance. Now, right hand only, strike, strike, strike. Now your left hand, strike, strike, strike. Harder! Drive through my hand! Harder, harder!"

After every set of strikes she would get into my space and roughly push me or punch me in the chest or arms in order to annoy and motivate me and get me used to being hit and not flinching.

I started to hate the focus mitts. No matter how hard and how many times I hit them they were always right back in my face. I also didn't like getting pushed and hit, but after an hour straight of it and discovering I wasn't going to break every time she hit me or pushed me, I found myself fearing contact less and able to press an attack on her and the mitts. Whenever I would slow down or start to tire, instead of letting up and suggesting we take a break, she'd push me harder. "Come on, Callie! Do you think your opponent will wait for you to catch your breath? Strike through my hand! Put him down! Again!"

The next morning I met Eva in the kitchen for a glass of juice before we started our run together.

"How do you feel this morning?" she asked with a smile on her face.

"Good, I'm good; a little sore perhaps," I replied.

She nodded at me, we put our juice glasses in the sink and went out to the front yard to do some stretching before our run.

"Shall we start with some of those butterfly stretches I showed you last night?" She didn't wait for my response. She just put her heels together and sat down directly into the stretch. When she reached the ground, both heels were still together but in her crotch. Her knees were splayed outward and touching the ground, and most impressive of all, she never touched the ground with her hands. She turned her head backwards to see how I faired.

I smiled at her, put my feet together and started downwards. She'd made it look simple. Halfway there I realized that she'd been using muscles that

I'd not yet developed. My legs started to shake, I groaned out loud, and fell over onto my side.

She burst out laughing. "You okay, Callie? Maybe a little tender?"

I was embarrassed initially but then started laughing along with her. "I'm good! No problems at all unless you include being crippled from the waste downwards. My God, what did you do to me last night?"

Despite being much more flexible than me, Eva was not as aerobically fit, and I had to modulate my pace that morning. I didn't mind though as we immediately fell into an easy camaraderie. She was intelligent, fun, and sometimes even silly. Besides respecting her Krav Maga abilities I also found myself liking her as a person. She also kept moving me forward with the Krav Maga during our run. Even as we walked the final half mile for a cool down, she had me "shadow striking" as I moved. First one side, then the other, then kicking one side, then the other. And always she would verbally coach me.

"Drive into it, Callie! Kick through! Strike through! Decimate your opponent! Elbow to windpipe, elbow to windpipe! Now, knee to face, knee to face! This is not ballet, this is Armageddon, act like you mean it!"

During the second week of Eva's training the two of us were returning to the house after a long run at the water's edge. Eva was doing her normal drill instructor thing coaching me through my kicks and strikes as we walked. "Come on, Callie, you're hitting like a butterfly again. You're not dating your opponent; you're trying to drive his balls into the back of his throat! Excellent, now crush his windpipe! Again!"

It was a still morning with barely a breadth of wind and our voices were carrying more of a distance than normal. Unbeknownst to us, Nancy was enjoying a leisurely breakfast at the edge of the pool and had heard Eva as she coached me up the beach. We weren't aware of Nancy until we stepped up off the beach and onto the marble piazza surrounding the pool.

"Oh, isn't this just precious."

Eva and I looked up startled at the sound of my aunt's voice and stopped. She was dressed in an elegant silk robe, calmly sipping her coffee.

"You two are just the sweetest things. 'Crush his windpipe and drive his balls into the back of his throat'? Did I get that right?"

Eva blanched. "Ms. Liddell, I'm terribly sorry. You're absolutely right. That wasn't language I should have been using with Callie."

Nancy stood. "Certainly not. Catherine is a young, impressionable, delicate flower who cannot be exposed to such things. Even I, at my ever so slightly advanced age have difficulty hearing such things. I should terminate you for corrupting her."

Eva was now mortified. "I assure you, Ms. Liddell, it won't happen again."

I doubted Nancy was serious and I didn't want to abandon Eva. "Aunt Nancy, please tell Eva you're joking."

"Joking around! I don't believe my ears!"

I turned to Eva. "Nancy must be feeling cranky about something."

"Hush, Callie, I think she's serious."

Nancy certainly looked serious, and I suddenly felt guilty for the way I'd spoken to her and started to apologize when all at once she put her hand to her head, wobbled several times, and then fell backwards into the pool disappearing beneath the surface.

Eva freaked out and immediately jumped in after her and pulled her to the surface. "Callie, quick! Help me get her out."

I looked down at Aunt Nancy. Her head was in Eva's arms, motionless, her wet hair was plastered across her face. Eva was genuinely concerned.

I was suddenly very suspicious. Nancy was never faint of heart or of body and her falling backwards into the pool with her robe on while holding her head had seemed overly dramatic. If she'd really been mad at Eva or me, she wouldn't have fainted, she wasn't the type.

"No, I don't want to get my sneakers wet." A second later my suspicions were confirmed when I saw Nancy crack a tiny little smile. I now knew she was doing one of her things.

"Hurry, Callie!" Eva implored.

"No, she's not worth saving. She needs to sink or swim on her own."

"Callie! You get in here, right now; I'm not joking!"

I sighed once and then jumped in next to them. "Okay, I'll take her," I said to Eva. I replaced Eva's arm with one of my own under Nancy's neck and with the other started tickling Nancy's waist under the surface. She immediately burst to the surface laughing.

"You two are so easy!"

Eva was flabbergasted and looked back and forth between Nancy and me. "You mean that was all an act!"

"Of course, it was! You should have caught on when I said Callie was an impressionable, delicate, flower."

Eva pushed a handful of water at Nancy. "I thought you were serious!"

Nancy had quite a laugh at our expense and then turned somewhat serious.

"All this does bring up an interesting question. What is my sister going to think when I return her daughter home next week and she asks Callie what she did on her summer vacation? I can hear Callie now. 'Mam, it was such a cool summer, I trained with an Israeli assassin Aunt Nancy hired so I could learn the killing art of Krav Maga, and she also taught me how to swear like a depraved sailor. Want to see me crush someone's windpipe and smash his balls into the back of his throat?"

"That's an exaggeration, Nancy, and you know it. I also learned how to drive a big passenger ferry from Melissa, how to make a mean crème brûlée from Rosario, and how to prune bonsai from Jesús. Oh, and let's not forget all the outrageousness I learned from you."

"Yes, all highly coveted skills for women to be adept at in rural South Florida shrimping families."

I looked over at Nancy in her silk robe and Eva in her running clothes; all three of us wet and slightly disheveled from our unscheduled trip into the pool and a warm feeling of gratitude suddenly washed over me. It was a memorable life-moment for me standing there with those two incredibly strong women that I both respected and admired greatly. I hoped I would be able to keep both of them in my life for many years to come.

On the last night of Eva's stay with us we were cooling down and stretching out on the mats.

"You're going back to your family on Sunday right, Callie?"

I nodded. "I'm not looking forward to it though. This last year of high school is going to be torture."

"Why? Most kids love their last year of high school."

"There's just no challenge in it."

"Won't it be nice to see your family?"

"I guess, but you'd have to meet them to understand why I have such a difficult time with them. My mother's the exact opposite of Nancy. She's quiet and doesn't seem to have an opinion on anything. My father's quiet yet opinionated and thinks a woman's place is in the home. My two brothers are morons and if they can't shoot it or hook it, they aren't interested in it. I think the only book in our house is an old copy of the Joy of Cooking that my mother got from her mother."

"I know what you're saying. My mother and father are very similar. But you need to remember that despite all their faults, they produced you. And whether you like it or not, you are them. We are all the sum of our parents and other family members."

"That's a frightening thought! They didn't teach me to drive a boat or learn self-defense or to run a marathon or get straight A's."

"Ah, but they did."

I looked at her confused.

"Where do you suppose your intelligence or your drive or your attention to detail came from? Do you think you created those things yourself? Think about it some and try not to be too hard on them. They did the absolute best for you that they knew how. Think about this summer and the wonderful opportunities that you enjoyed with Aunt Nancy, Melissa, Rosario, Jesús and me. Who gave you permission to do that? Do you think this was an easy decision for them? Do you think it was easy for them to let you go? I'm sure Nancy and this entire lifestyle of hers must be very threatening to them on some level. They also had the faith and confidence in you to make good decisions this summer. Maybe you've been too hard and judgmental of them?"

I thought about what she was trying to tell me and realized the truth in what she was saying. "How'd you get so smart, Eva?"

"Simple, I made all of the same mistakes myself. You and I are like sisters. My father and I will always butt heads, but I do respect him and care about him even if I seldom get along with him. I doubt I'll ever understand my mother's almost blind devotion to him, but I can still respect her loyalty."

I thought about Mam and her relationship with Daddy. "Thanks, Eva, I'll think about all that." I paused for a moment. "I have another question for you. You know how much Aunt Nancy means to me, right?"

"I do."

"I want to do something really nice for her to thank her for everything that she's done for me this summer. I've saved a couple of thousand dollars from my job, but what the heck can you buy for someone who already has everything? I'm stuck."

Eva thought for a second before responding. "I'm not sure I should be saying anything on this subject because it was told to me in what felt like confidence, but I think it's important. Have you given any thought to your aunt's offer of college? She thinks of you like her own daughter, and I know she's worried that you might not have set your sights high enough and that you not going to college would be a big mistake."

I was deeply touched by Eva's words at what Nancy thought about me. "I've thought about it a lot actually. It's an incredible offer. I'm definitely interested, but I want to give her a gift, not get one."

"Strange as it sounds, accepting her offer would be a gift of inestimable value to her; much better than a new cashmere sweater or a clay ashtray."

On Sunday I put two garbage bags full of clothes into the trunk of Nancy's Bentley. She'd offered to buy me a suitcase to carry my clothes in, but I think she understood my reasons for not accepting her offer. I tearfully hugged Rosario, Jesús and John goodbye in the driveway. "Thank you, all of you, for everything. I had an incredible summer and each of you means a great deal to me."

Rosario hugged me again. "Don't be a stranger, Miss Callie. I hope we will see you soon."

"I hope so too."

Nancy put her hand on my shoulder as we turned towards the car and said, "Callie, I have a little headache, would you mind terribly driving?"

I was concerned. "Really? I mean, are you okay?"

"No, you fool, I'm fine."

Sometimes I'm a little dense. She was going to let me drive the Bentley! "Yeesss!" I ran around the front of the car, got in the driver's seat, and moved it forward. Jesús was smiling at me.

I ran around to the driver's side, got in, did up my belt and waited politely for Nancy to get settled in the passenger seat. "All set?" I asked.

She nodded. I put the car in drive, waved again to everyone, and slowly pulled away. Funny the things you remember about moments in time. Beyond the sight of Rosario, Jesús and John standing there, I vividly remember the sound of the Bentleys tires scrunching over the tiny, white driveway stones, and the smells of blooming frangipani and iced leather coming out of the A/C ducts as we drove up the driveway. It had been an incredible summer.

"They are good people."

"Yes, they are," Nancy agreed. Before we turned out of the driveway and onto the main road, Nancy opened the glove box and pulled out a small, wrapped box and held it out to me.

"I'm going to miss you a tremendous amount, Callie. I got you this little bauble so we can stay close."

I put the Bentley in park and looked at her quizzically for a second before accepting and then unwrapping the box. It was a new iPhone12 Pro Max.

I shook my head knowing it cost over $1,000. "Nancy, I can't accept this."

"Whatever do you mean? Did I get the wrong model, the wrong color?"

"No, of course not. It's incredible!"

"Did you want something else? You can have whatever you want; it's only money and Heaven knows I've got plenty of that."

"No, don't be silly."

"Silly? I guess you must not want it then." She reached for the box to take it back.

I clasped the phone to my chest. "Don't you dare touch my new iPhone!"

"Huh, I thought so." Nancy smiled obviously pleased with herself. "You do like my gift."

No one had ever given me such an extravagant gift before and I sat there just staring at it for a few seconds before unclipping my seat belt and leaning over to give her a big, wet, kiss on the cheek. "Thank you. It's a wonderful gift."

"I should think so."

I turned to her with a serious expression on my face. "Nancy?"

She looked over at me. "What?"

"You know how the neighbors are always saying incredibly mean, awful things about you?"

"I do. Tell me something I don't know? What kind of a world do we live in where a woman of my obvious caliber, charm and beauty is so thoughtlessly derided? Don't believe a word they say."

"Oh, I don't, you taught me better than that. What I wanted to say was that despite the awful way they talk about you, I adore you. You're the best aunt any girl could ever dream of having."

"Of course I am and how astute and very sweet of you to notice, Catherine."

"You know, the iPhone is very, very nice…"

"And?"

"It's certainly a surprise, but I was certain you were going to get me a Bentley."

"Aren't you funny, but the phone will have to suffice for now. Also, I would be derelict in my duty as your temporary guardian if I failed to point out that no one should start out their driving career in a Bentley. In order to properly appreciate a motorcar such as this you must first drive a series of shitboxes and of course also get a driver's license."

I had only been playing with her, of course, and pressed the "on" button on the phone. I watched as it lit up and booted. "I love it, Nancy. As soon as I get home I'll sign up for an account and get a number assigned. You'll be my first call."

"I don't think that will be necessary."

"Why not?"

"Do you really think I would give you a phone that didn't work?"

The phone finished booting and I pressed the phone icon. Her name and number were in the #1 Favorites position except instead of saying Nancy Liddell it said, "Incredible Aunt Nancy."

"Did you know my address to set up billing?"

"No need; what kind of a gift would it be if you had to pay a pesky bill every month? Don't be ridiculous; that triviality is taken care of."

"That's incredibly generous. I don't even know what to say."

"Nothing more is required. Just make sure you let me know what's going on in your life this winter."

"I will. I promise."

I looked both ways and then turned out of the driveway and onto the main road heading off island. I gave it a little gas and the twelve cylinders under the hood brought us up to the 35-mph speed limit in first gear. The smooth power of the turbocharged Bentley engine was awesome.

"Nancy, on a more serious note; while we're on the subject of gifts, I have something I'd like to give you."

"Aren't you sweet for thinking of me; but I really don't need a thing."

"Well, it's kind of an odd, backward gift and I'm not really sure if it really is a gift."

Nancy looked over at me, curious. "Okay, I'll bite. It sounds interesting which means I might like it. What is it?"

"I decided that you're right about college. I haven't picked a school yet, but I've decided to apply to some good schools and see if I can get into one." I was uncomfortable with accepting gifts like the one she'd offered me and after pausing I added, "And to let you pay for it, of course, if I get into one."

Nancy sat looking straight ahead and was silent for a few moments. Several tears rolled down her cheeks. She wiped them away as quickly as they fell. "Damned allergies."

I reached over and put my hand on top of hers. "I'm touched that you're touched."

"Don't be silly; I'm not 'touched' as you so casually refer to my emotions. I was simply calculating how much you going to college will cost me and was deeply saddened at the loss. I hope you know that money doesn't grow on trees."

"I know." I replied with appropriate respect. I let several seconds pass. "Thank God you've got plenty of it." I reached over and squeezed her hand.

"I know, right?"

An hour and fifteen minutes later we turned onto the no name road leading to my driveway. I pulled over to the side before we reached my parents' house.

"Probably best if you drove from here," I said to Nancy.

I didn't want to drive up to our house in Nancy's swank convertible and give any false impressions to my family. They were critical enough of Nancy's wealth and lifestyle and I didn't want to exacerbate that.

Nancy understood without me saying a word and we switched seats before turning onto our dirt driveway. My father's truck and the truck my brothers now shared were parked haphazardly in front of the house. Mam and Daddy were sitting in two old aluminum chairs in the shade of the front porch. They both got up as we pulled to a stop. Nancy shut off the engine.

It was uncomfortably silent for a second or two as we undid our seatbelts, and I opened my door. I remember feeling very aware of leaving one world (the luxurious, pristine, Bentley) and stepping back into another (the dirt driveway and cluttered front yard of my parents). I wasn't uncomfortable or embarrassed. It was my home, and all the very familiar sights and smells were in fact comforting and welcoming. Before I could carry the thought any further, however, our rooster, Cogburn, came squawking around the side of the house with my Plott Hound, Crab Claw, hot on his tail. The awkwardness of the moment instantly evaporated.

I didn't know how much I'd missed Crab Claw until that moment and jumped out of the car and intercepted him before he could jump on the side of Nancy's gleaming black car. He recognized my smell right away and started squirming uncontrollably in my arms and didn't seem to know whether to lick me or bite me with joy at my return. We fell into the dirt with me laughing and him licking and whining.

Mam and Daddy came off the porch and met Nancy at the bottom of the steps. Mam gave her sister a welcoming hug; Daddy nodded his greeting.

"Nancy, it's good to see you. We were wondering if we'd ever see Callie again. The place seemed kind of empty without her this summer. I hope she was well behaved," Mam commented.

"Frances, we had a wonderful summer together! What a joy it was to have someone with Callie's energy and drive around. She's really a credit to you both and the job you did bringing her up. I'll confess, I toyed with the idea of driving away with her. Everything about the last couple of months was a pleasure and I hope you'll do me the favor of letting me spend more time with her in the future."

CALLIE AWAKENS

Mam blushed. Daddy just stood there and after looking at me covered in dirt from dog wrassling, looked back at Nancy and said, "Well, good to hear, I guess. She can be a bit willful."

Nancy didn't bite and instead said, "Worked out just fine; we were like two peas in a pod."

Daddy looked into her eyes. "I can believe that."

"Would you like a glass of iced tea, Nancy?" my mother offered.

"Yes, I'd enjoy that."

"Callie, your brothers are out back working on the skiff. Why don't you go say hello?" my father suggested.

"Yes, sir." I brushed some of the dirt off the short sleeved, Polo shirt I was wearing. When I pushed myself off the ground, I could tell both my parents noticed the hard, defined muscles in my arms. "Come on, Crab Claw; let's go see what Harley and Damon are up to." We ran off around the side of the house and then out onto the dock.

"Well look who's here, Harley. If I'm not mistaken it's our long-lost shrimp of a sister."

"So it is, Damon."

They both smiled at me and in spite of their ribbing I was surprised at how good it felt to see them both. "Ah, yes my moronic brothers the retardo twins. What are the two of you busting up back here?"

Damon bent down to the outboard which was tilted up. He had a piece of wire in his right hand and was poking it into the cooling water exit port. "We're not busting anything, Callie. We're fixing it. It keeps overheating and we've got a really lame stream of cooling water coming out. Don't you worry your pretty little head. It's complicated."

"Sounds like the impeller. Is that the original one?"

Damon and Harley just looked at each other. I didn't have to say another word. "Come on up to the house and say hello to Aunt Nancy if you're of a mind. I can fix that for you later if you don't get it squared away."

I turned on my heel and ran back towards the house with Crab Claw on my heels barking up a storm. After we careened around the corner I went over to Nancy's car, popped the interior trunk release, and grabbed my two garbage bags of clothing. "I'll be right back," I said to Nancy and my parents as I brought my things into the house.

Nancy stayed about an hour talking with my parents. When she was ready to leave, I walked with her to her car and opened the door for her.

"Well, this is it, kiddo," she said.

We looked into each other's eyes, teared up and then hugged.

"There's a lot of pollen here alongside the river," I suggested. We laughed at each other.

"Yes, I expect there is. Callie, I don't need to tell you how much I enjoyed this summer and getting to know you. All I can think about right now is how empty my cottage will feel without you and next summer. Will you be back?"

"Of course. I've got to get through this winter first."

"You will, just play the game, bide your time, do the next right thing. I don't have to tell you any of this."

"I know. One good thing will be Eva. I'm going to work my butt off for her every spare minute I'm not in school."

"I really like her too. She's a powerful and smart woman, even if she is an assassin."

I chuckled at Nancy's exaggeration. "Not as powerful and smart as you."

"Well, of course, that goes without saying. Okay then."

"Okay then." I reached out and hugged her again.

"Don't leave the school applications too long and let me know what you're thinking. Oh, and Callie?"

"What?"

She leaned towards me and lowered her voice. "With everything you do, crush their windpipes and drive their balls into the back of their everloving throats."

I smiled. "Language, Aunt Nancy, language. How do you ever expect me to become a proper young lady with language like that?"

"I don't, ever. You just continue to be the woman you are."

Chapter 14

I started classes again September 1st, and once I got my school schedule pinned down, I got back in touch with Eva, and we put together an intense five classes a week schedule for me at her dojo. It wasn't one-on-one instruction like I'd had at Nancy's, but a side benefit was having students of varying capability that I could spar with.

Getting to and from her downtown Fort Myers dojo was problematic, however. My mother was only occasionally available to transport me so the second week of September, I sat for my driver's license test and then set out to find a car I could afford. I had about $3,500 I was willing to spend out of my summer earnings. Finding something reliable that I also wanted to drive, was challenging. I confess, I turned my nose up at a number of mechanically sound cars, but because they looked like complete pieces of crap, I just couldn't do it. I'd been spoiled by Aunt Nancy's small fleet of luxury autos and in the end, after a knockdown drag out fight with my parents, I decided to buy a motorcycle.

I didn't have any motorcycle experience at the time I made the decision, but Damon and Harley had an old, beat up, Yamaha 125cc dirt bike that they used to knock around in the woods surrounding our property and in exchange for me agreeing to do their respective chores for a couple of weeks they agreed to teach me the basics and to let me use it and practice with it on the road that ran past our house and in the woods surrounding our property. It just barely ran and was loud as hell.

At some point most of the muffler/tailpipe had rusted off and the two of them had cobbled-on a piece of vacuum cleaner pipe that they'd stolen from Mam, and hose-clamped it on as a substitute. It worked reasonably well at redirecting the exhaust, but it got red hot after a few minutes, and I had to be super careful not to burn myself on the pipe when riding around. On my third day riding the bike I learned two important lessons about motorcycles, the hard way.

I was driving on the ad-hoc dirt track my brothers had created in the woods and was practicing shifting and seeing how fast I could go around the track. I was leaned over in a left-hand turn when all at once the chain came off the rear sprocket and locked up the rear wheel. I fell off and the bike ended up on top of me. I didn't break any bones, but the bike and that red-hot vacuum cleaner pipe ended up coming to rest on my legs and I got a nasty burn across the back of one of my thighs. Once I'd gotten out from underneath it and shut it off, I hobbled into the house hoping for a little sympathy and medical attention from Mam. I got the medical attention, but not the sympathy.

"Callie, this is exactly the type of thing that can happen on motorcycles and why your father and I don't want you to get one. Now, lie down on your bed and let me have a look at it."

I did as she instructed and lay face-down on the bed. I'd been wearing shorts when I fell and pulled the hem up on the burned leg.

"I'll bet that smarts," Mam noted unnecessarily after looking at it.

"You have no idea." I moaned.

"I'm going to get an ice pack and then I'm going to have to clean it."

She returned a minute later with the ice pack and warned me. "This will hurt a little at first, but it should make it feel better after a few seconds." She lay the pack on the burn which was about six inches long and an inch and a half wide.

She returned again five minutes later with a pan of warm water, some antimicrobial soap, Bacitracin Ointment, a clean washcloth, and some tweezers. I looked over at it all on the bedside table. "What are the tweezers for?" I asked."

"To pull off all the dead skin."

"What dead skin?"

She pulled away the first piece and I almost leapt off the bed it hurt so bad.

"Oh, that dead skin!" I yelled.

"Sorry, Callie. Infection is the biggest problem with burns like these. It's got to be done."

Mam worked for about ten minutes pulling all the burnt skin away from the middle and the margins of the wound, washed the area with clean water and soap and then dabbed on some of the Bacitracin.

"That should do it." She said once she finished. "I'm going to wrap it with some none stick pads and gauze for now, but after a couple of days it would be better if you just rolled up your hem on that side and gave it as much air as possible as it heals. Keep it clean and put fresh ointment on it twice a day."

"Thanks Mam."

"You're welcome."

The lessons I learned that day were, don't ride a motorcycle without protective clothing, and maintain your machinery. If I'd checked the chain tension and tightened it as needed, it never would have jumped the sprocket. Riding in shorts and a tee shirt had been just foolish.

Despite the accident I was still determined to get a bike and used my brief time laid-up to scour Craigslist and Cycle Trader for used bikes. I finally located a low mileage 2014 Ducati Monster 796 at a really good price. The nineteen-year-old owner had lost control of it once and taken it down on its side. There hadn't been any collision or frame damage and he'd had the cosmetic damage repaired, but once he started riding it again, he realized he'd lost his "heart" for it in the accident. He just wanted out and was willing to accept $3,500 instead of the $4,800 or more it was likely worth. His loss was my gain, and I purchased the bike that same day. I took the required two-day motorcycle certification course the following weekend and was finally mobile!

For those of you unfamiliar with motorcycles, Ducati's are very light, exceptionally fast, Italian racing bikes. I liked it over many other motorcycles I looked at simply because I could sit on it and touch the ground with both feet. It wasn't an ideal mode of transportation, especially when it rained, but it was mine and it was my first vehicle.

The Ducati was incredibly powerful compared to the Yamaha and I had a number of close calls during my first few weeks operating the bigger bike in traffic. This taught me to never assume that cars saw me coming and to expect rather than hope that they wouldn't do things like pulling out in front of me. I also dropped the bike over on her side twice walking her back into parking spaces. I wasn't hurt either time, but all these things combined to sensitize me as to how easily I might be hurt if I were ever to dump her on the road going fifty-mph. I ended up investing in a set of leathers in addition to the full-face Bluetooth helmet I'd already purchased.

Initially I took the longer, slower, secondary roads to Eva's dojo. Only after I was completely comfortable driving the big Ducati did I finally dare to take her out on Route 75. It was scary at first, but once driving her became instinctive and I didn't have to spend all my time focused on the mechanics of shifting and braking, I came to love her. The sense of freedom I felt on the Ducati was like nothing I'd ever experienced and every time I pressed the starter button and heard her engine come to life, my heart would start to beat faster, not from fear, but rather from excitement. I loved driving her and decided she needed a name. I named her Velocitá (pronounced vee-lo-chita).

The pandemic was still raging around the world and sometimes we had in-person classes at school and other times they would close, and we were relegated to remote learning once again. Either way I found that as long as I did my reading for all my courses, I was able to maintain my straight A average with very little effort. My time with Eva and her Krav Maga classes were what gave my life meaning and purpose that Fall. I got incredibly good in a short amount of time simply because I spent every free moment either taking classes or sparring.

Nancy and I talked every week and once I started looking at colleges in earnest, we talked every few days. I was conflicted because on one hand I still really wanted to do the captain thing and thought that going to a college like Mass Maritime or the Merchant Marine Academy at Kings Point would be excellent places to advance my maritime future. If I did either of their four-year programs, I would not only graduate with a four-year college degree, but I would also graduate with an unlimited tonnage, all oceans, 3rd Mate's ticket and would have the requisite sea time and experience to sit for a 500-ton captain's license. It was interesting what I learned in the application process. The 3rd mate, unlimited tonnage license was in many ways a bigger license than a 100-ton or 500-ton captain's license. If I stuck to that career highway and did a year as a 3rd mate, then a year as a 2nd mate and a final year as a 1st mate, I would have the prerequisites to captain any ship regardless of size by the time I was twenty-four. Pretty heady stuff for someone my age to think about.

The time commitment scared me though. Was I really ready to dedicate seven or eight years of my life to this pursuit? And if I went to the Merchant Marine Academy, I would owe either a five-year stint in the armed forces, on graduation, or five years in the maritime industry and then eight years in the reserves.

Applying to more traditional liberal arts colleges didn't feel like the right option either. I was worried that they would be nothing more than advanced high schools like the one I was attending, unchallenging with little emphasis on practical skills. I dismissed technical and engineering schools like MIT, Stanford, and the like simply because I couldn't see myself in an office or a laboratory. I loved getting my hands dirty and doing things. I was frustrated and could feel the application clock ticking. I called Nancy and asked for her opinion yet again, in mid-October.

"Nancy, I'm lost on what schools to apply to and need your help. When I started this whole 'captain' thing, I was thinking about it in terms of having a license to captain a shrimp boat or a supply boat in the oil fields or maybe a big yacht or a ferry. I had no idea that it was even possible for someone in their twenties to get an unlimited tonnage captain's license. How cool would it be to be a supertanker captain at that age?"

"I would guess that it would be a very big deal. I think one thing you should be trying to do as you evaluate options is asking yourself what your strengths and weaknesses are. I know you're bright as hell but every single one of us has strengths and we also have weaknesses. I think you should also ask yourself what you want your life to look like in ten years, twenty years, and thirty years out. I know thinking like that at sixteen is difficult, but assume you'll be successful at achieving your goal and then ask yourself what your day-to-day life would be like and what other options you'd have. What if you wanted to get married or have kids? Can you do a job like that and have any sort of home or a home-based life? What if you wanted to own a business down the road?"

"I guess I'm not really thinking about any of that. I'm only sixteen as you noted. I just think it would be really cool to have that much responsibility."

"I can see the attraction, but it's a huge amount of time to invest in a reasonably narrow field of endeavor."

"What do you mean?"

"Take your job with Melissa as an example. Let's say you got your captain's license two years from now and she offered you a full-time job driving her ferry. Would that be something you could see yourself doing for the rest of your life?"

I thought back to my summer for a few moments. I'd certainly enjoyed the learning process with Melissa, but there were also many days where the job felt routine and boring once I'd learned how to do it. "No, I don't think so. I think I'd want to do more."

"You mean you'd want to drive a bigger boat; one with larger engines, more complicated systems, more crew, more cargo, more passengers?"

"Yes, exactly." Even as I said it, I began to see where she was going.

"What about once you know all the ins and outs of that bigger ship and the one after it and the one after it? Knowing you as I do and having watched how you approached things this past summer, I would think at some point you might start to feel like a bus driver and become bored no matter what the size of the ship was."

"I guess that's possible."

"Don't get me wrong. I've got no doubt that you could easily become a supertanker captain by the time you're in your mid-twenties and I'd be incredibly proud of you if you did, but you'll be putting in a tremendous amount of time to accrue a relatively narrow body of knowledge that won't necessarily qualify you to do much else besides that."

"I get that, but couldn't you say that about almost every profession or trade; that virtually every one of them requires a specialized, narrow, body of knowledge? I know I can learn or do anything. I really believe that, but I'm kind of lost as to what you're suggesting. I can't go through my whole life just learning new skills. What's the point in that? I'm a doer not a theorist."

"I know you're a doer, Callie. I saw that every day when you were with me this summer with your boat job, your workouts, the way you applied yourself to learn Krav Maga; even the way you so naturally worked alongside Jesús and Rosario tells me you're a doer. I guess what I'm suggesting is that maybe you're both?"

"Both what?"

"Both a doer and a theorist. Why do they have to be mutually exclusive? Why do you have to be one or the other? I think you're bright enough, disciplined enough and motivated enough to be both. Just the fact that you even understand this conversation and what I'm asking you to consider is incredibly perceptive."

"You've lost me. I was hoping you could help me decide where to go to school and what to study and now I'm completely lost. I feel farther away from knowing what I should do next than I did when I picked up the phone."

"I'm just trying to talk you through the process of making a decision."

"Well it's not helping. Can't you give me a clue?"

"No. It's important that you be the one who decides what the next right step is."

"Nancy, you're driving me crazy! Come on, just give me a clue."

She was silent for a few moments. "I gave you one."

"Well, I missed it."

"What was the last thing I said?"

"That it was important that I be the one who decides."

"Before that."

I struggled for a second recalling our conversation. "You said something about talking me through the process of a decision."

"Exactly."

"Exactly what? Talking, process, or decision?"

"I need to go now and water the forsythia."

"Nancy! You've never watered a plant in your life."

"Bye."

I sat there on the end of my parent's dock for ten minutes after Nancy hung up on me going over and over our discussion. I felt more lost than ever. Deadlines for college admission applications for the following year were quickly approaching and I hadn't a clue where to apply or what to study. I tried thinking through her "clue." What part of "talking me through the process of a decision" indicated whether I should go to Mass Maritime, MIT, Stanford, or Harvard? And who said I could get into any of them? Her questions about marriage and children felt completely irrelevant. I needed a husband like a trapeze artist needs a table saw and decided to let it all roll around in my brain some more. I looked at my watch and realized I had a class at Eva's Dojo in forty-five minutes and went into the house and changed into the black leather biker pants and riding jacket I'd bought the week before. On hot days, the pants and the jacket were a torture to wear, but the second skin both items afforded, in combination with the armored pads in the shoulders, elbows and back of the jacket would likely save me from disfiguring injury if I were ever to go down on my bike. I packed my workout sweats into the small knapsack I'd taken to carrying everywhere and headed out into the kitchen.

"I'm going to Eva's to work out, Mam. I should be back by 9:00."

My mother looked me up and down. "I don't know if I'll ever get used to seeing you in all that black gear, but I'm glad you wear it if you're going to ride a motorcycle. And watch out in that neighborhood, Cat. I hate you going there at night, especially with those two middle schoolers being abducted and all else that's been going on in that area of the city."

"I'll be careful, Mam. Good thing I'm almost a lethal weapon."

"Callie, you're a tiny bit of thing, not a Navy Seal. You be careful; I'm serious."

"I know, I will be." I went outside, started Velocitá, snapped my cell phone into the bracket next to my tach and after strapping on my full-face helmet, briefly checked that my phone had paired with it, de-selected the inner smoked lens, pivoted the modular chin/face shield into position and climbed on.

Every day I drove Velocitá, I appreciated her more. I liked the fact that she wasn't a "rice burner" and the throatier exhaust rumble belied her better torque at lower RPMs. She was a lady but just barely. When I'd first started driving her, I'd been very tentative in my acceleration and especially cornering. I felt as though the bike were going to slide right out from under me on corners. Then one day by chance I stumbled across a YouTube video of professional motorcycle racers competing in something called the Isle of Man TT and had watched in absolute awe as the racers went through the thirty-eight-mile island course with their bikes tilted nearly horizontal at average speeds of 137mph and top speeds over 200mph. I'd no idea that motorcycles could be pushed so hard and since watching those racers I'd pushed myself and Velocitá a little harder each day when road conditions and traffic permitted.

Once I was out of the driveway and on the main road, I opened the vents in my helmet to the max and put Velocitá through the gears, smiling the whole time. She provided a release for me like no other. Running, swimming, doing marathons, working on my Krav Maga, studying, and driving the ferry were all activities that required me to be responsible and disciplined. Driving Velocitá was my very private release from responsibility. Some people my age chose drugs, alcohol, sex, or video games as their escape; I had Velocitá.

Eva shared space with a Pilates instructor named Laurie. Neither had enough students to afford the commercial space they were in on her own, so they'd leased the space together and then subdivided it into two separate areas. They were located in the Dick's Sporting Goods plaza near the airport at Page Field on South Cleveland Avenue. There were two ways for me to get there from my parents'. I could take all secondary roads which was a shorter distance and more interesting, but it was also slower than taking Bayshore Drive and then Route 75 despite being five miles longer in distance. Both routes required me to cross the Caloosahatchee River and I decided to take the Bayshore/75 route that evening because I was starting to run tight on time.

I turned onto Bayshore from Donald Road and brought Velocitá up to 70mph. I found myself thinking about my mother's warning as I headed out the door. We didn't have any crime to speak of in our neighborhood, but the greater Fort Myers area had been struggling with an increasing crime rate for several years and had become downright dangerous in several areas. The causes were two-fold, increasing drug use and gang-related violence. We'd always had some gang activity in the poorer neighborhoods of the city, but lately MS-13 had taken root in our little city and been responsible for a number of horrific attacks. They'd recently attacked two teenagers from the Lake Boyz (a rival gang) with machetes and when police attempted to arrest one of the perpetrators, the gang members had fought back resulting in their deaths and the wounding of three police officers.

That type of in-your-face violence by gang members against police was something never seen before in Fort Myers and the cops were pretty wound up at the shear effrontery of it. There had also been a startling number of unsolved abductions of teenage girls in recent weeks. Several of the young girls that had gone missing were runaways and drug addicts and their absence or disappearance was easily explained away by the police, but the previous week, two well-known, responsible, thirteen-year-old middle-schoolers had disappeared walking the short distance from school to home. Neither were considered likely runaways and they'd simply disappeared without a trace or a clue as to who may have taken them. As a direct result, we'd all been warned the week before at a school assembly to be extremely careful about where we went, to travel in groups, and to avoid gang members at all cost. Both MS-13 and the Lake Boyz were being looked at as suspects, but none of the missing girls had been recovered and no one had been arrested yet.

I accelerated as I entered the long, straight, on-ramp to 75S off of Bayshore and briefly brought Velocitá up over ninety before backing down the throttle and merging with traffic at about eighty. At 80mph she purred like a kitten at around 4,500 rpm. Eva and Laurie's place was quite near Page Park where two of the recent abductions had taken place. I'd keep a sharp eye out. I wasn't so much concerned about myself as I was other girls my age from school and the young druggies I occasionally saw on the street.

Eva spent a great deal of time emphasizing the need for heightened situational awareness in all of us. "Heads on a swivel." She would say over and over. "How can you avoid or flee danger if you aren't even aware it exists? Your best chance of survival is always improved if you can plan and assess a situation before it reaches critical mass. That can only happen with awareness. Look around you, all the time and game things forward. If you're in a crowded movie theatre ask yourself if a fire broke out or a shooter entered, what would I do? And do this all the time before something happens. Just as important, ask yourself what everyone else around you will do.

Don't go into that trance that ninety-five percent of the people around you perpetually walk around in where they're either staring at their cell phones or daydreaming. Use your eyes, your ears, and your nose. Most importantly, listen to that quiet inner voice when it speaks, not just the loud voice of thought and opinion that talks endlessly to you. Listen and respect the quiet observational voice that observes the other voices in your head. That quiet inner voice is the important one. It is true awareness.

You cannot avoid something or flee it unless you are aware of it. If you do have to fight, your chances of survival go up dramatically if you have assessed the threat, determined your opponent's weaknesses, and availed yourself of a weapon. That weapon might be something you already have, or it might be a weapon of convenience. Either way, a weapon in hand at the time of an attack is far better than trying to find one or think of one after you've been hit, or someone is choking you."

The idea of someone snatching young girls off the street for likely use in the sex trade got me wound up on several levels. First because it involved men trying to use generally superior physical strength against weaker subjects for their own gratification, and second, because these guys seemed to be targeting increasingly young, innocent girls. That hit too close to home and I was determined that would never happen to me again. As I turned West onto Colonial Boulevard after exiting 75, I decreased my speed to about forty-five in deference to the heavier traffic.

Melissa always talked about gaming things ahead, just like Eva, and I knew the more trained and automatic my responses to a given situation, the more brain I would have available for observation and problem-solving. This was equally true whether captaining a boat or physically engaging an opponent in combat. It really applies to everything in life and as I entered the heavier traffic on Colonial, I automatically dialed up my awareness. I had learned my very first week driving Velocitá that everyone driving a car is determined to extinguish the life of every motorcyclist. Well, maybe not everyone, but if I drove "as if" every one of them was out to kill me, I'd have a far better chance of survival. Cars turning onto roadways in front of me was immensely popular, closely followed by people cutting me off. On two occasions elderly snowbirds had locked up their brakes nearly plowing into me from behind.

***

Esteban's standing orders from Diego were to continue procuring more young girls for the sex-trade side of their business. Over the past two months he'd brought a total of five to Diego. Three of them had been young druggies. The two most recent were two junior-high age girls who'd been at the wrong place at the wrong time. He'd snatched the two thirteen-year-olds as a pair, walking home from school together. All five of the girls had initially been brought to the autobody shop to be "broken in" by other gang members. The three druggies were groomed and kept in line by Bones who collected money from them and kept them high on crystal. Diego had developed a thing for the two junior high girls, and he'd dedicated two rooms at the shop for gratifying himself with them and when not, he rented them out. He planned on keeping them until they became too worn out or diseased.

That evening Esteban was out in their white "snatch van" with Javier and Darian, two younger members of the gang. They were his pickup crew. Esteban was powerfully built and thirty-two-years old, which brought him senior citizen status in the gang. Every square inch of his body was tattooed with spiderwebs around and across his face, barbed wire around his arms, MARA SALVATRUCHA across his front and MS 13 on his back. His shaved head was also tattooed as were his neck, arms, legs, and fingers. He was pumped with prison type muscle and almost six feet tall. His stature and physical power were directly responsible for his relatively old age.

Javier and Darian were both eighteen, skinny and in general less threatening in appearance than Esteban. All three of them wore earring hole expanders. Javier and Darian had tattoos, but in the newer fashion they tended to be mostly beneath their shirts and trousers. After they'd snatched the two junior-high girls it had immediately become more difficult for them to find potential prey, especially at night. Word got around fast when young girls with strong ties to the community disappeared.

On this particular evening they were cruising the Page Field area looking for young druggies again. They didn't bring as much money as fresh high schoolers, but they were easier to find and also out at night. The trick was in finding and taking them with no witnesses. Normally they would cruise near areas where drugs were sold, follow a girl if she were alone, and then snatch her where she crashed or used.

They were following a scruffy young thing in filthy jeans that they'd seen scoring drugs in a parking lot off of Cleveland near Page Field. She had short, dirty black hair with died purple streaks and a telltale stumble to her step.

"Darian, what do you think?" Esteban asked.

"She looks good, I'd do her."

"You'd screw a rock pile if you thought there was a snake in it," Javier jibed.

"I'm not fucking around, you two! Yes, or no? Do you guys think she'd clean up okay?"

Darian nodded. "Sí, I think so."

Javier also quickly agreed, anxious to avoid confrontation with Esteban.

They were a block behind her on Cleveland, but traffic was moving at a speed requiring them to drive by her repeatedly as she shuffled along the shoulder. They couldn't just roll up on her and pull her into the van because of the number of people likely to see them. Esteban drove past her for the third time. She was oblivious to what was going on around her and was looking down at her feet as they drove by.

"She does have a cute little ass. I'll pull into the next parking lot and we'll wait for her to walk by us. At some point I'm sure she'll head into the bushes so she can do her fix." Esteban noted. He pulled over into the parking lot of a Denny's near the edge of the road and the three of them watched as the girl walked through the underpass beneath Colonial and continued South on Cleveland.

***

I downshifted Velocitá as I exited off Colonial and then stopped at the light at the bottom. I planned to make a left on Cleveland when the light changed and watched as a girl my age made her way unsteadily down Cleveland on the other side of the intersection. She was dirty, carried a knapsack, and wasn't moving as though she had any specific destination in

137

mind. I couldn't help but compare myself to the drugged-out girl and think how lucky I was to have a place to live, transportation, and goals in my life. It was a long light and Velocitá didn't like idling at low rpms for long periods. I goosed her throttle several times to keep the engine running. The light finally changed, I kicked Velocitá into gear, eased out the clutch, and gently accelerated into my turn. The young girl looked over at me briefly as I passed. Her face was hollow, her eyes empty and dead. I nodded to her in acknowledgement, but I don't think she noticed.

Eva's dojo was just three blocks away and I stole a quick look down at my phone. I had nine minutes before class started and on impulse, I pulled into an Italian Ice place I frequented a block before Eva's.

***

Esteban continued to watch their target as she made her way down the side of Cleveland. Once she'd gotten a full block away, he pulled out into the intersection in the right-hand lane and waited for the light to change. He could still see the girl. When the light changed, he accelerated going as slow as he could with traffic. After driving a half block, he was pleased to see the girl leave the roadway and walk into a parking lot ahead of them.

***

After I got my Italian Ice, I walked back outside to eat it as fast as I could without giving myself a frozen headache. I liked the sugar rush I got from the ice and leaned up against the seat of Velocitá as I ate it. I was parked behind the Ice shop as there was no parking on the street side of the building and watched the young girl I'd seen walking, shuffle off the roadway and into the lot where I was parked. Then I watched her as she continued diagonally across it and then up the side of the parking area along the treeline. She seemed to be heading to the back of the lot where trucks made deliveries to the big box stores.

138

CALLIE AWAKENS

Twenty seconds later an older model, white, Econoline van pulled in and instead of parking, continued along the same treeline that bordered the side of the parking lot at a slow rate of speed in the direction the girl was going. I got a brief look at the driver. He had tattoos all over his face and alarm bells started going off in my head. Without a doubt, the people in the van appeared to be following and stalking the young girl.

I took three steps, dropped the balance of my ice in a trash can, put on my helmet, swung onto Velocitá, and engaged the starter. Then I pulled forward just enough to see past the corner of the building, down the treeline, and watched as the van turned sideways and then stopped right behind the girl, just ten or fifteen feet behind her. She was completely oblivious to the threat. I knew instinctively that they'd turned sideways to block the view of anyone who might drive up that side of the building and I guessed that they were either going to assault or take the girl against her will. There wasn't time to think. If I was going to intervene it had to be immediately. They would have her in the back of the van within the next few seconds.

Clueless to the threat I'd be facing, I gunned Velocitá and roared up the side of the building, went around the rear of the van, and then drove thirty feet past wanting to leave myself an out. I threw out the kickstand and leapt off the bike leaving Velocitá running.

Two young men were on either side of the girl holding her by the arms and walking her towards the side door of the van. She seemed completely oblivious to what was happening to her. I was relieved to see that both of the abductors were relatively small in size and neither appeared to have a weapon.

"Hey!" I shouted. "Let her go, now!" It was the first thing that came into my mind. Even though I was dressed entirely in black clothes and wearing a helmet, it was immediately obvious to the two men that I was just a small female and therefore not a serious threat.

My shout awakened something in the girl, and she finally noticed that two men were holding her arms and dragging her towards a van. She started to struggle against them and then collapsed to the ground making it as difficult as possible for the two abductors.

On hearing my yell, one of them reached into his pocket, pulled out a gravity knife and flicked it open. "Or what, you little puta? You want to go for a ride with us too, Chica?"

I stopped just five feet away from him and assumed a ready stance. It wasn't even conscious; I was on autopilot. "Let the girl go and drive away. I'm not going to tell you again."

"Javier, are you hearing the mouth on this one? She thinks—"

Before he could finish the sentence, I moved into his space. He immediately sliced at my upper body. Without any thought at all, I blocked his descending right hand with my left forearm, swept it to the side, and simultaneously hit him in the face with the heel of my right hand. I felt his nose break and retracted the hand for a second palm strike to the same area.

He was hurt but not disabled and still retained the knife. He slashed at me a second time before I could hit him again. I blocked him again and, in the process also deflected the knife to the ground. He was wide open for a second, and instead of going for a second palm strike, I kicked him hard in the balls. He folded over in agony which gave me the perfect opportunity to grab his head with both hands and introduce him to my knee. I kneed him hard in the middle of his face three times. He fell to the ground, out and done.

I sensed his co-conspirator coming up behind me and wheeled to the new threat. He looked as though he'd planned on wrapping his arms around me. I ducked my head in a downwards direction and simultaneously started my right leg up and out into a spinning back kick which caught him squarely on the side of his face. I was suddenly glad for all the painful stretching and training Eva had forced me to do. He stumbled backwards, reeling, but he was still not out, so I punched him with a closed fist in the throat and then seeing an opportunity, side kicked his undefended knee. It folded in at an unnatural angle and he fell to the ground like an aerobatic plane in a flat spin, the cartilage in his knee destroyed.

I reached out to the young girl. "Quick, come with me! There's another one in the truck!"

I could see the third man through the open sliding door of the van. He was a much larger opponent. I got a close look at his face and wished I hadn't. He looked like he was out of some bad prison movie; bald, every square inch of his face tattooed, red eyes and crazy ear lobes that hung down several inches below normal with big black hole expanders in them. He was about the scariest looking human being I'd ever seen, and I watched as he reached behind the seat, grabbed a machete, and turned to open the driver's door.

"Come on girl! We need to go now!" I shouted and pulled the girl towards my motorcycle. I had no desire at all to fight the third man. Somehow, I knew that I was no match for him and that he could absorb my hardest blows and shrug them off like they were nothing and then he would likely simply chop both of us up, where we stood. The girl finally got my urgency and stumbled after me towards my bike. Thankfully Velocitá was still idling and hadn't stalled.

"Jump on behind me and hold on as tight as you can. Hurry!" I directed her.

The second I felt her weight behind me and one of her hands around my waist, I wound Velocitá up to 6,000 rpm, leaned forward as far as I could and eased my clutch out as fast as I could but avoiding popping a wheelie and going over backwards. I could see the third man with the machete raised above his head as he ran up behind us in my rearview mirror. It would be extremely close. The machete started its downward arc just as I took off. I raced away, braked at the far corner of the building, wheeled around the backside of the building to the alley on the other end, accelerated through that alley and then through the front parking lot and prepared to turn right onto Cleveland.

***

Esteban wanted to go after them right away but knew it would be foolish. He looked at Javier and Darian in disgust and then scraped them up off the pavement and got them into the back of the van. The little girl on the bike had gotten a very good look at his face and also at the van and caught them right in the middle of an abduction. He needed to get the van off the street right away. The police would have a description of both him and their vehicle within minutes. "Fuck!" he shouted. How could a tiny little girl have taken out two guys so quickly? He'd watched the whole thing and in just seconds she had completely destroyed his two boys.

***

I watched anxiously behind us to see if the van would appear in my rearview mirror as I waited to pull into traffic on Cleveland. Eva's dojo was just one block further down Cleveland on the other side of the street, but I didn't want to go there yet. I knew the girl and I would be safe there, but I didn't want to inadvertently lead the men in the van there.

"What's your name," I shouted to the girl behind me.

"Karen."

"I'm Callie, Karen. Hold on tight. I don't know who those people were, but I'm going to put some distance between us and them before I pull over and stop. We'll talk then." I accelerated onto Cleveland and looked up the side of the parking lot where we'd left the van, as we passed. It was no longer there. They only way out of the area for them was the same way we'd left the parking lot and I accelerated up to 80mph weaving in and out of traffic until we reached Boy Scout Drive. I roared around that and then leaned right again and took us up Summerlin Road until we reached Colonial again. Once on Colonial we went back to the speed limit and turned down South Cleveland back towards where the incident had happened. I saw no sign of the van as we passed the parking lot we'd just left and after traveling another block, turned left into the Dicks Sporting Goods strip mall where Eva's dojo was. I went to the far end of Dick's and drove around the back of the building and then to Eva's back door on the service road. Once there I parked behind the dumpster, shut down the engine, took off my helmet and just sat for several seconds. My heart was pounding.

"Karen, we'll be safe here. This is a friend of mine's martial arts studio."

"Thanks for helping me out back there."

"You're welcome. Do you know who those men were?"

Karen shook her head. "No idea." She swung her leg off the bike and took off her knapsack. "Shit!"

"What is it?"

"Everything that was in my knapsack is gone!"

She held her knapsack up for me to see. There was a slash down the back of it. I thought back to the tattooed man and his upraised arm with the machete that I'd seen in my rearview mirror right before we took off.

"I think we're both really lucky we didn't get our heads cut off back there. Why don't you come inside with me?"

She shook her head. "No, I've got to get going."

"Karen, we really should call the police and report them."

She shook her head again.

"Where're you going to go?" I asked. "Aren't you scared you'll run into them again? I think those might be the men who've been snatching teenage girls. We really need to report this."

"No, I'm really sorry but I can't get involved with the police."

I put my hands on her shoulders and tried to get her attention. "It's important."

She shook her head, not looking me in the eye. "Sorry, no police."

I was frustrated and guessed she likely had either warrants or a need to get high; maybe both.

"Can I at least drop you somewhere? I hate the idea of you just going back out on the same street that they just tried to snatch you on."

Karen thought for a second. "Can you run me up to Winkler? I've got some friends there that I can crash with."

I looked at my watch. I knew I should file a police report as soon as possible if the police were going to have any chance of getting the men in the van, but I really didn't want to abandon Karen on the street. "Hop on. I'm going to be late to class anyway."

I restarted Velocitá and put my helmet back on. After Karen got back on, I took the service road back to Cleveland, turned North and then accelerated to 50mph, keeping an eye out for the van.

"Take a left on Winkler once you get to it," she instructed me.

I nodded. Winkler was only ten blocks North. Once I got there, I turned. "Where to now?"

"I'm up about five blocks."

I looked on both sides of the road. There was a boxing club on the right and several other commercial looking buildings on the left. I accelerated back up to just 20mph taking in the neighborhood. It wasn't a bad one judging by the cars in the driveways; not rich, but comfortable. "Where do you sleep most nights?"

"Here and there."

Obviously, she wasn't going to tell me much about her life or her circumstance. We traveled about five blocks.

"This is good."

We were on a corner and not directly in front of any house. "Are you sure?"

She nodded. "This is good, really."

Karen got off.

She still wouldn't look me in the eye but asked, "Listen, can you spare twenty dollars? Everything I owned was in my knapsack."

She probably meant "her fix" was in there. Reluctantly I took off my own knapsack, pulled out my wallet and gave her a twenty-dollar bill.

"I doubt this will be much help but listen, if you see that white van again or feel unsafe you can go to my friend Eva's dojo. The woman who owns it teaches martial arts. It would be a safe place."

"What's your name again?"

"Callie."

"Thanks, Callie, I appreciate you helping me out. You probably saved my life."

"I might have saved you from something worse. You need to get off the street, Karen. You're going to die out here if you keep doing what you're doing."

"Yea, well, it is what it is. I've got to go." She bumped fists with me and started walking east. I did a U-turn and slowly started back towards Cleveland Ave. I watched in my rearview mirror to see if I could tell which house she went to, but as if sensing my intention, she waited till I was almost out of site before crossing the road and disappearing from my view.

I drove modestly back to Eva's wishing I'd been able to do more for her. I knew the police report was important and immediately after getting back to the dojo and briefly explaining to Eva what had happened, I called the police. The dispatcher sent a cruiser and within ten minutes a patrolman and a patrolwoman pulled up outside and took my report. I hadn't thought to look at the license plate on the van but after describing it and the three occupants they put out a BOLO for all white vans within city limits being driven by a suspected MS-13 gangbanger. I agreed to go in the next day to look at mug shots in the police gang book to see if I could identify any of the men. By the time I finished my report, Eva was done with her class.

"Eva, can I talk to you?"

"Sure, Callie."

I repeated all the details of the confrontation with Esteban and the other two gang members. She'd missed most of the details that I'd reported to the police simply because she'd been teaching her class.

"Sounds like you did a great job of protecting yourself and that girl."

"I did, but I made some mistakes too. I knew I had to intervene before they drove off with her and probably should have run into the Italian Ice store and yelled for them to call the police before I went into the back of the parking lot."

"True. At least you'd have known backup was on the way."

"But everything happened so quick."

"Yeah, that's usually the way those things go."

"The reason I wanted to talk to you isn't about the two guys who were dragging Karen towards the van. I don't know whether it was subconscious or conscious, but the second I confronted them, I knew I could handle both of them; even when one of them pulled out a knife."

"That's the threat assessment I talk about. If you're paying attention, you can tell a tremendous amount about an opponent with just a glance-"

I interrupted. "But when the really big guy with the tattoos all over his face and head got out of the van and came towards me with a machete, I knew just as quickly that there was no way I could handle him. He had this aura of power surrounding him that made me feel completely helpless. I just knew he could overwhelm any defense or offense I was capable of mounting. Add the machete to the mix and I felt totally powerless. It freaked me out. All my training with you has been empowering, but I felt completely vulnerable to this man. What would you have done with someone like that?"

Eva looked at me for several seconds, then walked across the room to where the coats were hanging. She reached into the pocket of her coat and pulled out what looked like a skinny, black, flashlight. She turned back to me and held it up.

"What, you think I should have shined a light in his eyes?"

"Not at all." Eva threw her hand towards the floor. Instantly the black metal tube telescoped into an eighteen-inch steel baton. She walked over and handed it to me.

I hefted it and felt the weight and then took a couple of swings with it. I could tell it was a formidable weapon the second I had it in my hand.

"This could break some bones."

Eva nodded her head. "It's steel and it's a serious weapon. Try a few strikes on the heavy bag with it."

I did as she suggested and hit the bag hard several times and looked back at her.

"Your training requires you to get close enough to someone to strike him or disarm him which is almost impossible if the assailant is wielding a long reach weapon like a machete. If you're confronting an aggressive, experienced, much larger assailant who knows what he's doing you really need an equalizer. I carry this concealed on my person whenever possible. Remember, Krav Maga isn't about fighting fair; it's about fighting and winning."

I nodded.

"Okay, try it again but hit harder. Strike right through the bag like you do with your palm strikes. If you've gotten to the point where you've pulled that baton out, you know your opponent is going to kill you if he gets the chance. Don't give it to him. Take him out, and don't forget retention of your weapon. If your assailant gets it away from you, you're screwed."

I nodded again and then struck the bag several times with much more force.

"Good but turn your whole body into each strike and keep your left arm and hand up and keep pushing them off with that arm while you strike them with the baton with the other. You don't want them to get a hand anywhere near the base of the baton. Same thing as hand strikes; overwhelm them with repeated strikes until they are down and out. Knees, hands, throat, face, head."

"Where'd you get it?"

"Amazon. Police are trained to use them to get people to submit without causing permanent, lasting injury and generally aim for meaty muscle groups like thighs and upper arms. If someone is coming at you with a knife or a machete though, don't hesitate to target wrists, hands, knees, elbows, head, throat, and neck. The police may have to fight fair, but we don't. If someone is trying to hurt you, hurt them back worse, before they do you." Eva smiled at me. "You keep this one; I've got several."

"Thanks." I grabbed the end of the baton and tried telescoping it back into itself. It didn't move. I looked at Eva with a questioning expression and held it out to her. She took it and simple punched the end into floor. The baton retracted and she handed it back to me. After changing back into my leathers I slid the baton into an inside pocket of my leather jacket.

"See you tomorrow, Callie?"

"You will, and thanks for the baton."

I finally got home at 10:30 pm and was grateful to find that my whole family had already gone to sleep. I hadn't been anxious to explain my lateness out of fear that my parents might not want me going into downtown at night anymore.

***

After Esteban pulled the van into the the clubhouse, he had Javier and Darian follow him into Diego's office. They were both limping painfully and had dried blood on their faces. They sat down on the front edge of Diego's couch, Esteban remained standing and explained to Diego what had happened during the disrupted abduction.

"And these two got taken by some little girl?" Diego asked with disgust.

"Sí, es verdad (Yes, it's true.)"

Diego shook his head.

"You want me to disappear the van, or do you think we can just paint it?" Esteban asked.

"Just paint it and put a different plate on it."

"What should I do with these two?" He pointed to Darien and Javier.

"I should probably bust a cap into them but for now just get them out of my sight and don't take them to a hospital. The policia might be looking for two 'little girls' with injuries like these two fucks have. What useless pieces of shit!" Diego kicked Darian's bad leg.

"Si, Jefe. Come 'on you two." Javier and Darian started to get up off the couch.

"Esteban."

He turned back. "What?"

"You say the girl on the motorcycle was young and good looking?"

"Sí, from what I could see. She was dressed in motorcycle gear and wearing a helmet but yea, I'd say she was cute."

"Spread the word. If anyone sees her out on the street, I want her brought here. We'll see how tough she is after we run a train on her for a couple of days."

"Sí."

"What kind of bike was she driving?"

"I never seen one like it before. It was like a red ninja bike. It said something on the tank like Ducat or something."

"Ducati. Italian bike. Should make her easier to find."

Diego's cell phone rang. He looked at the face on the screen and held up his finger for Esteban to wait while he answered. "Hello, mama. How are you feeling?" He listened for almost a minute before speaking again. "No, don't you worry about it. I'll go to the pharmacy now and pick it up. Did you eat anything for supper?"

He listened for a moment again before responding. "I'll stop at Taqueria San Julian on the way home and bring you some ceviche and warm corn tortillas. Would you like that?"

He listened again. "You have to eat. I know it's hard, but if you don't eat, you'll get weak. You know what the doctors say." He listened for a few seconds. "Okay, love you too, Momma."

Diego pressed the end button on his phone and then slammed it down on the desk in front of him. "Fuck, Fuck, Fuck!" He started pacing maniacally behind his desk, walking one way, then wheeling and walking the other. Esteban watched, saying nothing. Diego suddenly stopped, opened the right-hand drawer of his desk, took out a Colt 1911, racked a shell into the chamber, turned, and shot both Darian and Javier in the chest, one right after the other. The gun was very loud in the small room. Esteban watched the smoke from the shots drift lazily through the air, saying nothing.

Diego pointed to Javier and Darien. "Chop these two worthless fucks up and throw them in the river and tell everyone else that if they let themselves get beat on by some girl, then they damned well better best her or they'll deal with me. And move the two little putas to the stash house. If the motorcycle girl is able to identify you, the police might come by here looking for you."

"Sí, Jefe." What Diego said made sense about the police possibly coming by the clubhouse to look for him and it wouldn't do at all for them to find the two kidnapped middle-school girls.

"And give them a shot before you go. They haven't had one since this morning. It will make them easier to handle. I don't know what's wrong with those two anyway. What's with all the crying they do?"

Esteban shrugged his answer, went out into the main part of the warehouse, looked over the assembled faces, and picked two of the younger gang members. Whenever possible he liked to "lock in" the younger gang members and make them participate in as many crimes as possible. "Danny, you and Omar help me. We got some trash that needs hauling."

RIP CONVERSE

Chapter 15

I skipped the first of my online classes the next morning and went straight to the Fort Myers police station on Widman Way to look at mug shots. I went up to the bulletproof glass in the lobby and gave the desk sergeant my name, explained why I was there, and then took a seat. A detective had yet to be assigned to my case and I sat in the waiting area as the desk sergeant called up to the detective's section to find out how to proceed with me. Ten minutes later an attractive Hispanic looking woman in her late twenties came out from behind the secure area and addressed me. She was wearing a blue pantsuit.

"Miss Babich?"

"Hi, yes I'm she. Just call me Callie."

"I'm Detective Camila Sanchez. I handle all cases related to Hispanic gangs." She looked at the helmet in my hand.

"What're you riding?" she asked in a sociable way.

"A Ducati Monster."

"Which one?"

"Velocitá is a 796."

"Cute name; that's a lot of bike and under 400 lbs. if I remember correctly. What will she do, about 125?"

I prudently avoided her question. "That's what the manufacturer says."

"You wouldn't personally know, though?"

"Respectfully, ma'am, I wouldn't personally say."

"Right...Well, it sounds from the report I read that you had a pretty close call last night."

"Yeah, it got pretty scary."

Camila looked me up and down. "The report says you fought three gang members and took two of them out. I don't mean to insult or doubt you, but you're a lot smaller than I expected. MS-13 has a deserved reputation for being very violent. You want to tell me how someone your size can fight off three male MS-13 gang members?"

I was nervous. It was my first time in a police station and Detective Sanchez's question felt skeptical and confrontational. "I didn't fight three of them, just two." I shrugged. "I'm stronger than I look I guess, and I've had some self-defense training, ma'am. Maybe I just got lucky; I'm not sure. I don't think I would've done so well against the third man who came out of the van after I'd put the other two down. He was older, much bigger and armed with a machete. Honestly, I think he'd have eaten my lunch if he'd been able to get his hands on me."

"I'm impressed; (if it's true)," she added under her breath. "How old are you anyway?"

"I'm sixteen, ma'am. What do you mean, 'If it's true'?"

"Do you use drugs, Callie?"

I shook my head, confused. "No, ma'am, absolutely not. Why would you even think that? If you don't believe me talk to my employer from this summer. I was part of a mandatory drug testing program all summer as part of my employment."

"Court-ordered?"

I was getting really pissed at that point. "No, ma'am. I work on a commercial passenger ferry and it's a U.S. Coast Guard requirement to be enrolled in a random drug testing program. I'm working at becoming a licensed captain and honestly, I'm offended at your questions and what you're suggesting."

"Well, that was this summer, wasn't it? Easy does it, girl. I'm just making sure you're on the up and up. It's not every day I get a runt of a girl like you claiming to have put down two violent male gang members and saving a girl from getting kidnapped."

"A 'runt of a girl'! Ma'am, if you weren't a police officer, I do believe I'd put you on the ground for a comment like that. I risked my life to save that girl and I expected a little more civility and professionalism from you. Perhaps there's someone else I should be speaking with."

"No, I'm the gang person. I apologize; I don't guess my calling you a runt was very professional. What say we start over?"

"_We?_ There's only one of us that needs to start over."

She stood there with her hands on her hips, looking me pointedly in the eye.

"Point taken, Miss Babich. I apologize. Let's go upstairs to my desk. I'll show you our gang books. You said in your report that all of them were Hispanic, correct?"

I nodded, cooling off a little. "Yes, they appeared that way to me."

"That narrows things down a lot. MS-13 has only been in Fort Myers for two years now and the only other gang we deal with here is the Lake Boyz and they're all black. Follow me."

I followed her to the lobby elevator.

"Ma'am, do you always treat the public this way? I've never even gotten a parking ticket and you're making me feel like I did something wrong by helping that girl out."

"We get all kinds in here, Callie." I followed her past several cubicles. She eventually stopped at an empty desk in an open area with two chairs in front. "Have a seat. You got any ID on you, Callie?"

I nodded, took out my wallet and handed her my license. She looked at it, wrote down my info and then asked if I had a cell phone number."

I nodded again, recited it to her and then watched as she turned in her chair and reached into the bookcase behind her desk and pulled out two three ring binders. Both of them were full of glassine covered pages. She hesitated before sliding them across the desk to me. "Are you up on what's going on with the gangs in Fort Myers right now?"

I shrugged. "No, ma'am, I don't know a thing about them."

"I'll give you the condensed history. The Lake Boyz have been around for years and are based right here in Fort Myers. They're all black and based around Martin Luther King."

I nodded.

"MS-13 is a little more complicated. A lot of people think they originated in El Salvador. That's actually wrong. While most of their members are from El Salvador originally, the gang was set up to protect Salvadoran immigrants from other gangs in the Los Angeles area. Over the years they've grown into a pretty traditional criminal organization like the mafia and engage in prostitution, protection, and drugs. The most notable thing about them over other gangs is their savagery and merciless retribution. They came to Fort Myers just a couple of years ago, but already they're taking market share from the Lake Boyz which in turn has precipitated a state of open warfare between the two gangs. They're killing each other on an almost nightly basis. Now, between the two of us, I could care less about them killing each other. But of late both sides are also killing each other's prostitutes, and one or both gangs have started snatching innocent girls off the street. That will not fly."

"I've heard about young girls disappearing on the news and they also warned us about that at a special school assembly."

Camilla opened the first book, turned it around and slid it across the desk to me. "See if you recognize any of the people in here."

I looked at the individual on the first page and then flipped the page, looked at the second and then looked at the third. He was right there, the one with all of the spider webs on his face; the one who had come out of the van last with the machete. I inadvertently shivered and then pointed. "This is the third man, the one who got out of the van last."

Detective Sanchez was leaning back in her chair. She knew the two books well and didn't even have to pull the book back and read the data on the third individual. The book was loosely organized in descending order of hierarchy with Diego Alturaz on page one, as the leader of the gang, to lesser members at the back of the book.

"Esteban Pérez, numero two or three in their illustrious organization. Esta es muy mal."

I looked up. "I don't speak Spanish."

"Sorry. Esteban Pérez, the man you pointed to, is number three, maybe number two. He's not a nice man." Camila drummed her pencil on the desk blotter in front of her, a nervous tick. "You're sure?"

"Yea, I'm sure."

"Look through the rest of the book please. See if you can identify either of the other two men. With all the ink they put on their faces, sometimes they can look alike."

"I'm certain. This guy has the same weird, stretched out earlobes and the same eyes, I got a very good look at him."

I kept looking at pictures, finished the first book and was halfway into the second book when I recognized another one of the men. I pointed at the page.

"This is the one who first attacked me. He had a knife. I broke his nose with a palm strike then kicked him in the balls and kneed him in the face three times before he went down for good."

Camila listened silently to my description of taking down the first man and then looked at me as though there was something wrong with me. "Weren't you scared of this individual, Miss Babich? Most women get terrified when confronting a man with a knife."

I thought for a moment before answering and replayed the fight in my head and then my description of my actions to her and shook my head. "I guess I was scared after, when I started thinking about what could have happened to both of us. But at the time I'd have to say no, I just saw someone who had to be put down." I realized how that must have sounded. "That's a little weird, isn't it?"

Camila nodded, continuing to stare at me and touching the eraser on her pencil to her lower lip. "Yup." She agreed and pointed back at the book. "Keep going, see if you can find the third."

I stopped on the second to last page of the second book. "This was the third man. I took him out with a punch to his throat, a spinning side kick to his face and a kick to one of his knees. He won't be walking right for a long time if you ever find him."

Camila made another note on her pad, then summarized. "So, we've got Esteban Pérez, Darian Lopez and Javier Flores. That's actually quite helpful, Callie. Given what these three were trying to do it's not a stretch to wonder if these fine young men might also have had something to do with the disappearance of some or all of the other girls that've been reported missing in recent weeks."

"When I saw them following that girl into the back of the parking lot, it's the first thing that came into my mind."

"Do you know what happens to these girls?"

I shook my head. "No idea, what?"

"You sure you want to know? It's pretty rough."

I nodded.

Camilla let out a frustrated breath before continuing. "MS-13 has been getting heavy into the sex trade business of late and almost always they hold these girls they take somewhere for a few days so the gang can break them in. Often the entire gang will sexually abuse the victims. Sometimes, it's several gang members at once. They try to totally break the women psychologically and make them feel powerless. They also addict them to drugs which makes them more dependent. All of this plus the shame these girls feel makes them less likely to try and escape. Once they break them in, they're put to work here and in various other metropolitan areas around the country until they either commit suicide, overdose, or die of a disease. Believe it or not they also do a similar thing to their own women."

"Prostitution?"

"No, for initiation."

"I don't understand."

"Cliques of the gang here in the U.S. tend to be a little more progressive than their counterparts in El Salvador. Here, women are sometimes allowed to join. They get to choose between either gang rape or an incredibly rough beating for initiation."

I was appalled. "What woman would ever willingly choose either of those? And what's their reason for wanting to join? It doesn't make any sense to me."

"Doesn't make any sense to me either. I guess there's some level of protection that they benefit from once they're members, but honestly, I think it has more to do with the women wanting to be a part of something. The women who do join usually do so at an incredibly impressionable time in their lives. They're young, stupid, and poor, and all the people they see who have power and money and respect, are gang members. Everybody wants those things. You heard of those girls who go to the Mideast and join ISIS?"

I nodded.

"It's kind of the same thing."

"What sorts of things do the women do once they're in the gang?"

"Good question. The gang derives most of its income from extortion, prostitution, and drugs. The more 'progressive' U.S. gangs realized that women were more disposable and also good at collecting extortion money, working as drug mules, and for intelligence gathering against marks or rivals. Without all the tattoos that the men have an affinity for, these women also tended to float under everyone's radar, for a while. That's been changing as authorities have seen more and more cases around the country where these women are present or participants in some of the murders. Some of these girls are really dangerous."

"Where do the women gang members fit in on the prostitution side of things?"

"I'm not sure, Callie. You'd think women would be appalled seeing their sisters abused. These people have gone so far off the spectrum you and I are used to for civilized behavior that I can't even guess at what motivates them."

I was speechless as I tried to imagine the horror of what Camila had just related and immediately thought of the two thirteen-year-old girls that were missing. "How many of these animals have you arrested this year?"

"Six or seven."

"How much time did they get?"

Camila held up her hand and made a big zero with her thumb and index finger. "When trial time came, our witnesses disappeared, every single time. The gang is exceptionally good at intimidation. Which leads me to my next question. If we find these three, would you be willing to identify them in a lineup and also be willing to testify against them if we were able to charge them?"

I nodded but wondered if that was true. "Why wouldn't you be able to charge them?"

"Well, first we'd have to find this Karen girl. Without her, there's no crime except perhaps your assault and battery of the two men."

"You're joking, right?"

"Actually, I'm not. It would be the word of three against one. And from what I can gather there's a strong likelihood Karen may be a drug addict. If that's the case I'm going to guess she won't want to get involved."

I knew Detective Sanchez was right. Karen hadn't even been willing to hang around long enough to file the initial complaint.

"This whole thing sucks."

"Well said, young lady, but let's try and look at this from a positive angle. At least we have some specific subjects to focus our attention on now thanks to your reporting this. We'll also try and locate Karen, although

I'm not hopeful about that. We don't know her last name, we don't know where she lives, and I'd be surprised if she was willing to bring charges against MS-13 gang members. She's vulnerable living on the street and as I already said, they're famous for going after witnesses. She'll know that."

I'd have to give this a lot more thought. Would I be willing to become a target of MS-13 in order to help bring a case against them?

"Would you be willing to help me try and locate Karen."

I nodded. "I've got online classes till 3:30 this afternoon but after, sure."

"Great. Come back here around 4:00 this afternoon and you and I will go out and have a look around the neighborhood you dropped her off in."

I went home after leaving the police station, attended two of my on-line classes, had lunch, then skipped my last class and drove back downtown to Eva's dojo. She always seemed to have good advice and before I proceeded any further with tracking down Karen and getting involved with MS-13 and the police, I wanted to see what she thought.

"Hi, Callie. What's up?" she asked as I walked in.

"I went in this morning and identified the three men in the van from the police mug books."

"That's great! That gives the police solid leads, I'm sure. Maybe they'll actually catch and charge whoever's abducting girls around town."

"It does give them a lead for sure, but there's a catch."

"What's that?"

"Unless the police can also find that girl Karen and get her to agree to testify, they won't charge anyone."

"Why not? You saw what they tried to do."

"I did, but that's just my word against three others and if there's no victim then there's no crime."

"I see the problem."

"What's really on my mind is whether I should get any further involved."

"Why? What's your reservation?"

"Camila, the detective, told me that MS-13 is notorious for intimidating witnesses into not testifying against them. My inclination is to do whatever I can to help the police stop what's been going on and not worry about them coming after me because I believe what they're doing is wrong. Am I being naïve? Is it the right thing to do?"

Eva was silent for a long time thinking and then spoke. "Callie, perhaps some of this is because I'm Jewish and biased, but so be it, it doesn't make what I have to say any less true. I would say this to you. No one really knows where this quote comes from, but it's frequently attributed to a guy named Edmund Burke."

"What is it?" I asked.

"Supposedly he said, 'All that is necessary for the forces of evil to triumph, is for enough good men to do nothing.' Does that make any sense to you?"

I thought about the words for a few seconds and nodded. It made a great deal of sense to me. In my own life I couldn't begin to count the number of times that I or other kids I knew were bullied at school by an aggressive few. Other kids that I knew to be perfectly good kids didn't want to draw attention to themselves and risk retaliatory bullying so frequently stayed quite about the bullies.

I nodded. "Yes, it does, Eva, more than you know."

She smiled at me. "I figured it would."

RIP CONVERSE

Chapter 16

I put on my jacket as I walked out to my bike, deep in thought. I briefly put my hand into the inside pocket and felt the reassuring presence of the collapsible steel baton. I zipped up the jacket, put on my helmet and then lovingly petted Velocitá's gas tank before firing her up. What Eva had said resonated with me and sounded like good advice. I think her reminding me of her Jewishness was an obvious allusion to the fact that the holocaust had only been possible because so many good Germans had ignored the German State's antisemitism and remained silent in the face of it. I was not and would not be that silent person.

I arrived back at Fort Myers Police Department right at 4:00. Detective Sanchez was on the front steps and came down off the steps and pointed across the street to the jury-duty parking lot.

"Callie, park in there and we'll go in my car."

I nodded, parked, and then crossed Broadway on foot back to her. She was unlocking an ugly brown Crown Victoria that had seen better days.

"Nice ride," I said sarcastically.

"Beats walking. Why, you think maybe we should go on your bike?"

"No."

"Didn't think so. So, where're we headed?"

I got into the passenger seat. "Head over to Cleveland and Winkler. I dropped her off about five blocks East on Winkler. I didn't actually see her go into a specific building or house though. She was jiggy and acted like she didn't want me to know where she was going."

"Sounds like a druggie trying to protect her source." Camila started driving. "You told me you were sixteen. What does that make you, a sophomore in high school?"

"I'm a senior. I was young for my first-grade class and then I skipped 6th grade."

"You some kind of a brain or something?"

"Something like that."

"What about this ferry job you mentioned? What's that about?"

"I want to be a ship captain and I need 360 days at sea for my first license. I got a job as a deckhand on the Boca Grande ferry that runs back and forth to Marco Island."

Camila seemed to be trying to have a normal conversation with me. "That's cool, I guess. I don't know much about boats. What do you do for fun?"

"Krav Maga, run, and swim."

"What the heck is Krav Maga?"

"It's a martial art discipline. The Israelis teach it to all their soldiers in the IDF."

"You any good?"

I shrugged. "I guess, but I've still got a lot to learn. I have a fantastic teacher."

"You must be pretty good if you can take down two eighteen-year-old guys and one of them with a knife.

We drove for several minutes more, silently. I saw that we were approaching the spot that I'd dropped Karen.

"Pull over here. This is where I dropped her."

Camila pulled to the side of the road and looked at the houses around us. Most of them had well maintained yards and just one, or no cars in the driveways. "Not really the bad neighborhood I expected. You really think she was trying to score?"

"I'm pretty sure. The last thing she did was borrow twenty dollars from me."

Camila turned off the car and then turned to me. "Stay here. I'll knock on a couple of doors and see if anyone feels like one of their neighbors might be up to questionable activities. Tell me again what this girl Karen looks like."

"She's about five foot three, skinny, and has short black hair with purple streaks. She was wearing dirty jeans and a black tee shirt last night. Sure, you don't want me to come with you? She might be more willing to talk to you if I'm with you. That's if you can even find her."

Camila shook her head. "You're a minor. If something were to happen to you, I'd be in a world of trouble. Just stay in the car. If I find her, I'll bring her out to the car."

I nodded and then watched Camila walk to the first house. There was a Lexus in the driveway. She rang the bell. After a few seconds, the door opened, she showed her ID, and then chatted with a middle-aged woman in the doorway for several minutes. She walked back to the car and got in. "That was pretty easy."

"What was? No way Karen was going to a house like that. The lady you were speaking to looked like June Cleaver from *Leave It To Beaver*."

"How do you know *Leave It To Beaver*? You're way too young to have seen that show."

I smiled. "My Aunt Nancy has all these cable channels and she showed me an episode one night."

Camila chuckled out loud. "You know what the dirtiest line in television history is?"

"No, I don't even watch TV normally."

"Loosen up, don't be so serious. It was when June Cleaver, the mother, said to her husband, "Ward; don't you think you were a little hard on the Beaver last night?"

I looked at her blankly without a clue as to why that was funny.

She sat there for several seconds waiting for me to "get it." I didn't. "You're kidding me. You really don't get it, do you?"

I was annoyed. "No. What's to get? Beaver was the son, right?"

Camila shook her head. "You're a piece of work. What else does beaver mean? How about cooch, hoo haw, cha cha, lady business, poon; no? What about bearded clam or vajayjay?"

I suddenly understood and turned crimson.

Camila looked at me with a stunned look on her face. "I'll be damned. You're for real, aren't you? You actually are a bright, hardworking, innocent, principled, young lady. I didn't think there was such a thing. I was trying to figure out your angle from the moment you came into the station. I just realized; you don't have one."

"No, ma'am, I don't think I do."

Camila started the car. "Listen, Callie, while I appreciate your efforts to afford me respect by using the word ma'am, it's starting to grate. What say when it's just the two of us you call me Camila?"

"I can do that."

"Good. Okay, the woman in the house knew right away what we're looking for. She doesn't know anyone named Karen and can't recall seeing her walking on the street, but she did say that there's only one house within two blocks likely fitting our bill. She said it's a blue house down the street about five houses on the other side and that we'd know it when we see it."

Camila put the car in drive, looked quickly into her rear-view mirror and pulled out going just 10mph. We went up the street three houses and as soon as we could see the blue house ahead, she pulled to the side of the road again and turned off the car.

"How come you're stopping here?" I asked.

"I want to prudently surveil the premises."

"Don't you mean 'prudently surveil the aforementioned premises.'"

"Are you getting smart with me, Miss Babich?"

I smiled. "A little."

"Wisenheimer." Camila reached into the backseat, pulled out a pair of binoculars, and looked through them for a minute.

"Oh yeah, this must be the place. This is definitely a suspect-rich environment." She passed me the binoculars. "See the beater car in the driveway and the one parked on the grass?"

I nodded.

"And a nasty, Harley hog also on the grass?"

"Yup."

"And two guys smoking a joint on the steps and another doing lines of some powdery white substance on the porch?"

"I do."

"In my world, we call what you're looking at, 'probable cause.'" Camila picked up the microphone off the dash radio set. "Central, this is 16 requesting backup at...."

As she gave our location a second bike came up the street from behind us, slowed and the driver gave us a long, slow, look-over before pulling into the driveway we were watching.

"Shit, he made us." Camila opened her door and got out. "Callie, don't get out of the car." She slammed her door and then started to walk rapidly towards the house. The biker who'd arrived last was talking with the two guys on the porch steps and pointing back at the Crown Victoria. The one on the porch who'd been snorting lines, quickly gathered up his paraphernalia and turned to go into the house.

"Sir! You on the porch. Stay right where you are," Camila shouted as she walked up the short driveway.

I watched as the biker who'd sounded the alarm turned to Camila and obstructed her from following the man on the porch into the house. Camila tried simply walking around him, but he reached out and grabbed her with both hands on her biceps. He was big and doughy, maybe 275 but I discounted him as being slow and overly confident of his size.

"Lady, this is private property. Unless you've got a search warrant you aren't going a step further."

"Sir, I'm a police officer engaged in lawful business and you're impeding me. You've got exactly three seconds to take your hands off my person or you will be placed under arrest."

"Yeah? You and what army? You need to haul your little gash back to wherever the hell it was you came from."

Camila kneed him hard in the groin. He released her arms and went down like the first drink of the day for a chronic alcoholic. The two other men responded by tackling her to the ground. I watched in disbelief and couldn't help but think Camila's first mistake was not putting the biker away while she had the chance. She should have kneed him repeatedly in the groin and then followed up with a knee to the face. As it was, he'd be back in the fight shortly and now he'd also be pissed.

Camila got several good punches in against the other two, but ultimately, they overwhelmed her. They dragged her to her feet and then while one held her arms behind her back, the second man punched her several times in the stomach and then once in the face. I wasn't exactly sure what I'd do once I got there, but I leapt from the car and started to run the short distance into the melee. When I reached the driveway, I slowed my pace to a walk and yelled to get everyone's attention and. "Hello! Excuse me! Can you guys help me?"

The biker who she'd kneed first was slowly getting up off the ground, red faced and still trying to recover from the knee to his groin. But the pain was starting to fade, and I knew he'd be a player in what was about to happen next. The man who'd been punching Camila stopped and turned to face me. My focus was on him and the biker. The man holding Camila's arms behind her back was no threat and could wait.

"You're kidding me. What the fuck is going on today, boys? We're being besieged by mouthy, little, cunts."

I decided I would take the "puncher" first. He was everything I despised; loud, obnoxious, stupid, and a batterer of women. I could almost taste the blood in my mouth from the day Christopher had punched me.

Camila yelled at me, "Callie, get out of here! Don't worry about me, I've got backup coming. Just run!"

I shook my head ignoring her and keeping my attention on the biker and the man who'd been punching her. "Sorry, Camila, can't do that."

The puncher leered at me, casually reached into his boot, and pulled out an ugly looking hunting knife. I thought to myself, *what are the odds of coming up against two guys in a row who are carrying knives?* His stance was sloppy, however, and he was exuding overconfidence. I put my hands up into the air and continued walking towards them as if appealing for calm.

"Callie, please, get the hell out of here! These guys aren't messing around."

"Relax, Camila. I'm sure this is all a big misunderstanding; I just need to talk to these gentlemen and get things straightened out."

I was playing to the "puncher's" overconfidence and also trying to buy a little time for the cavalry to get there. My attention was focused primarily on the man with the knife.

The biker suddenly came up behind me, wrapped his arms around me and picked me up off my feet in a bear hug. He smelled of sweat and stale beer.

"Let's take this little spinner into the house and have us a time, boys. I owe the bigger one some special attention."

I made eye contact with Camila and mouthed a three count. She had blood dripping down her face from where the puncher had hit her in the nose. Initially she was confused by what I was miming, but when I mouthed the words a second time, she got it and blinked once acknowledging me.

"One, two, three." When I hit three, I snapped my head back into the biker's face smashing his teeth and nose with the back of my head. He immediately dropped me. Then I leaned all the way forward, reached back between my legs, grabbed one of his legs and pulled him off his feet onto his back. Then I spun around and dropped onto the middle of his sternum with all my weight using my knee as the focal point.

Simultaneously, Camila raised one of her feet and stomped down as hard as she could on the bony protuberance on the side of the man's ankle who'd been holding her from behind. He screamed out in agony and let her go.

I got to my feet prepared to meet the next threat. The "puncher" was looking back and forth between me and Camila suddenly unsure of who represented the most threat and which one of us he should attack first. Camila continued her offensive against the man who'd been holding her, drew back and got a good solid punch into the center of his face breaking his nose, but hurt her hand in the process. With her fully engaged, the "puncher" shifted his focus to me, but with more wariness. He approached me in a crouch waving the knife from side to side.

I'd lost the earlier advantage I'd enjoyed of appearing defenseless by virtue of my sex and size and no longer expected that I could get inside his perimeter without getting cut. I made an instant, split-second decision, cross-drew my metal baton from inside my jacket, snapped it open with a wrist flick, then struck the "puncher" on his collarbone right where it met his neck. I put all my weight into the strike and heard his collarbone crack. He was hurt and screamed out but retained the knife. I feinted right, then using both arm moment and the weight of my body, dropped to one knee and brought the baton down hard again, this time on the wrist of the hand holding the knife. My strike broke another bone and the knife fell harmlessly to the ground. I struck him one more time, in the knee, just hard enough to bring him to the ground, but not hard enough to permanently disable him.

"Callie, enough!" Camila shouted. She'd pulled her Glock and was pointing it at the three men. "All of you, face down! Now!" She spit some of the blood out of her mouth. "Goddammit! I said now!"

Camila's shout was like a shade snapping open in a dark bedroom and my awareness of self, started to return to me. When I'd been engaged in active combat with the two men I'd taken on, my focus had become tunnel-like and autonomic. I hadn't thought about anything, I'd gone on autopilot again and every single thing around me that _wasn't_ directly related to those two men and the threat they represented, had disappeared from my consciousness.

Once all three men were down and no longer a threat, the aperture of my consciousness slowly opened back up to wide-angle and I became aware, once again, of my thoughts and surroundings, the groans of the men, the sound of approaching sirens, the porch, the driveway, and Camila.

In the middle of the fight, my focus on the threats around me had been total and everything else had become muted and irrelevant. My assessments, actions, and reactions had all been automatic, reflexive, and somewhat autistic. I'd known intuitively how to respond and what every next right move was at every moment of the confrontation. I'd felt no fear, or uncertainty, or indecision at any time. It was freaky, and after tapping my baton on the ground to collapse it, I slid it back into my pocket and then looked down at my hands. They were steady and hadn't yet started to shake. I replayed the entire incident in my head thinking of all the things that could have happened but didn't.

"Are you hurt at all, Callie?"

I finished my quick self-assessment and looked up. "No, Detective. How about you? Are you all right?"

"I'll be okay; just a few bruises."

The first of two cruisers responding to Camila's request for backup accelerated up the street and then skidded to a stop at the end of the driveway. Two patrolmen jumped out and seeing Camila with her gun drawn, also drew their weapons.

"What have we got here, Cammy?"

Two more officers joined the group after parking their cruiser.

"These three dirtbags lost their minds and thought it would be a good idea to jump a police officer. There are one or more other individuals in the house. I haven't cleared it, yet."

She paused for a second to collect her thoughts. "I was pursuing a suspect who I saw using a controlled substance in plain view. When I started after him these three yabos jumped me."

"You hurt? You're bleeding from the mouth." one of the cops asked.

"I'm all right, Neil."

"Which one hit you?"

"The one in the middle. Can you and Sam get these three restrained and in a radio car?"

"It would be my pleasure."

"Chris and Jean, you come with me and help me clear the house. We're looking for the male who was snorting drugs on the porch and a young girl with short black hair with purple streaks in it. She answers to the name of Karen and we're looking for her on another case."

"What's up with Evil Knievel here?" The one named Jean asked nodding her head at me no doubt referring to my black leathers.

"That's Callie. She's helping me find Karen. Callie, wait in the car please. And I mean it," she added.

"Will do, Detective Sanchez."

I started back for the car and turned several times to watch. Camila and officers Chris and Jean entered the house with guns drawn. Neil and the other officer put the fat biker and the man who'd been holding Camila, in cuffs after patting them down. The biker required two pairs of cuffs strung together to accommodate his girth. They called an ambulance to transport the "puncher" in light of the seriousness of his injuries. He was whining.

"The little one over there did this to me. She's got like a piece of pipe or something in her jacket. Aren't you going to arrest her?"

"Sir, please have a seat on the ground while we wait for the ambulance."

"You need to arrest the little ninja girl!"

Neil took a quick look around to make sure that there were no concerned citizens filming and then put his foot behind the "puncher's" leg, pushed him in the chest, and tripped him to the ground. Then in a loud voice he said, "Sir, I told you to be careful! This is rough ground and if you don't watch where you're going you can trip."

I smiled at the whole scene as I got into the car. Cops hate it when civilians strike them. I expected the "puncher" might well have several more "accidents" before the day was done. While I sat there waiting, a third cruiser with "Supervisor" printed on the side arrived and then an ambulance.

Camila came out of the house after five minutes. Karen was not with her. After one of the paramedics looked her over, she got into a ten-minute conversation with the Supervisor on the porch. Finally, she returned to the car.

"What a clusterfuck."

"Any sign of Karen?"

"No, she wasn't in there and neither was the guy I was trying to detain. He must have gone out the back. If Karen was there, she beat feet too. The only thing that went our way is that there was a shit ton of drugs in there so I expect my coming uninvited onto their property without a warrant will become mute."

Camila paused for a few seconds while she pulled away in the car, then launched into me. "What the hell were you thinking, Callie? You could have been killed back there! And what was all that kung fu shit?" Camila reached over and patted my jacket from the outside, identified the baton by its shape, then reached into my jacket and pulled it out.

"Hey, that's mine!"

"Callie, you're a sixteen-year-old teenager, not Chuck Norris."

"Those men might have killed you, Camila! What was I supposed to do, just sit there and watch?"

Camila hit the wheel with her hand. "Callie, me getting killed would have been far preferable to what would have happened to me if you were hurt. I can't even begin to imagine the trouble I'd be in. The department would pull my badge and likely prosecute me for reckless endangerment. The news media would crucify me. I would be in so much trouble right now that dying at the hands of those yabos would have felt like a vacation."

"I'm sorry, but I couldn't just stand there and watch three guys beat you up!"

Camila shook her head and then handed me back my baton. "You're forgiven and you can have this back for now, but this might not be the end of things. I'll have to fill out a detailed report later. I don't think you'll get into any trouble for your Good Samaritan behavior, but my lieutenant might have my ass for having had you in the car in the first place. I'm going to just put out a bolo for Karen and see if any of our other units can turn her up. Right now, I'm going to drop you off, get cleaned up, and then get some ice on my face."

Camila returned me to the parking lot across the street from the police station.

"I'll call you if we make any progress finding Karen."

"Don't you think she might be a dead end? I really doubt you could talk her into testifying."

Camila shrugged. "Maybe, maybe not. Who knows, maybe we pick her up on a drug charge and she agrees to testify in exchange for us dropping the charges."

"Maybe. Okay then, see you, I guess."

"Callie."

"What?"

"Thanks for saving my ass back there. Those guys were going to work me over for sure. If you ever do it again though, I'll arrest you for something."

"You're welcome, I guess. What would you arrest me for?"

"I'd think of something. Maybe use of excessive force."

"You're weird, Camila."

"There's too much potential liability in having underage citizens getting involved in police business. You're a good kid; don't get yourself involved in this."

I nodded.

"I mean it, Callie!"

I got home for dinner fifteen minutes later.

"Hey, Mam, I'm home." I announced as the screen door slapped shut behind me.

"Hi, Callie. I wish you wouldn't let that door slam like that. Did you have a good day?"

"Sorry about the door. No, nothing special, just my regular outstanding work at school and then coming to the aid and comfort of local law enforcement in our beleaguered city using my superpowers."

Mam looked at me funny. I'm not sure she'd really heard a word I'd said. "That's nice. Dinner won't be for another half hour. I put the roast in late."

I hung my jacket on a hook in the mudroom. "Where're Daddy and the two bozos?"

"They're doing something down on the dock."

"Okay. Well just yell when it's ready. I'm going to make a phone call." I went down the hall to my room, closed the door and dialed Nancy."

"Liddell residence, may I help you?"

"Hi, Rosario, it's Callie. It's good to hear your voice. I've missed you."

"Miss Callie. It's good to hear your voice also. I can't believe how quiet it is here with you gone. Are you doing well?"

"The only thing that could make my life better is if I were sitting there with you in the kitchen about to eat one of your incredible meals. How're Aunt Nancy, Jesús and John?"

"Everyone is good. Would you like to speak with your aunt?"

"Yes, please.... And, Rosario?" I added, as an afterthought hoping she'd heard me and would come back on.

"Yes?"

"Please say 'hi' to Jesús and John and tell them I miss them also."

"I will, Callie. Nancy's in the study; just wait uno momento."

Nancy came on the phone moments later. "Catherine."

"Hi, Nancy."

"How pleasant to hear your voice, it's like a cool drink of water with all that I've got going on."

"Why, what's going on?"

"Last week I was catching up with one of my old college friends and she mentioned an interesting business concept that I was unfamiliar with. Since then, I did some research, came up with a very clever hybrid version of my own, and took the first steps in bringing my vision to birth. I think it will make me pot-loads of money."

I couldn't remember Nancy so animated about a subject in the time I'd known her and forgot about my own problems for the moment.

"You sound really excited about it. Tell me more."

"Have you ever heard of business incubators?"

I thought about her question quickly. The two words together rang absolutely no bells in my head. "I have not," I admitted.

"Don't feel bad, neither had I. In any case, the concept is that you put a bunch of different kinds of companies and brains together into the same building, facilitate interaction, then they all feed off of one another and produce brilliant breakthroughs."

"That sounds like an interesting idea," I mused out loud. "You mentioned a 'hybrid version' and 'pot-loads of money.' What would you do differently?"

"Well, the unique part of my concept is that I, acting as the real estate developer, would offer space in my buildings to various start-up companies for no-rent or reduced-rent in exchange for ten percent equity in all of them and the right of first refusal on purchasing additional equity at a pre-determined rate for the really promising ones. It's brilliant actually because it would also afford me ongoing access and insight into all of their operations as a stockholder and position me ahead of VC companies and other future investors when much of the stock dilution typically occurs."

I thought about what she'd said for a few seconds before responding.

"What are VC companies?"

"Venture Capital; high-tech start-ups frequently get investment money from VC companies although it's frequently at predatory rates."

"Okay." Was all I could manage at first as I tossed all the unfamiliar terms she'd just used around in my head and thought of my next question.

"You said start-up companies, right? Does that mean companies that aren't making any money yet?"

"Yes, that's almost always true."

"So, you're going to buy buildings and then you're going to either give away free or cheap space to a bunch of companies that have ideas but aren't making any money yet, in exchange for partial ownership in each of them. Do I have that right?"

"Essentially. What do think? It's brilliant, right?"

I was hesitant to respond as I really knew absolutely nothing about business or what she was talking about. I also didn't want to be critical of her or throw any cold water on the first thing I'd seen her really excited about.

"Go ahead, you can tell me what you think, Catherine. I'm curious what your analytical mind has as a gut reaction."

"Nancy, you know I don't know the first thing about business, but I'm not sure how good an idea that is. How can you know if any of them will be successful?"

"Dear girl, that's where my vast knowledge comes in. I can't know if any of them will be home runs, of course, but if I choose my tenants wisely, a certain percentage of them will be successes. The challenge will be in identifying the best ideas and what the ideal mix of companies will be in each incubator."

"You were a publisher, right?"

"I was."

"How does your knowledge and experience with books, authors and magazines help you evaluate a concept for a new type of software or a breakthrough pharmaceutical or some new piece of mechanical hardware. You don't know anything about those types of businesses."

"Who says I don't? They may all be different, but they're also all the same."

What I was, was incredibly confused. "Aunt Nancy, I feel like I did the other night when we were talking. You just told me that you don't know anything about any of those high-tech businesses and in the same breath made it seem as though if I could understand your lack of knowledge in those areas, I would suddenly understand something much bigger. You're speaking in riddles."

"That is entirely accurate." She paused for a moment. "My process is very similar to the one you are presently going through as you attempt to decide what you will do next. How's that going, by the way?"

I felt like pulling out my hair in frustration. I didn't get her parallel at all. "It's not!" I said in frustration. "Can't you just tell me? Why does it have to be a guessing game?"

"Because, Callie, when you get it, if you get it, it will become a transformational moment for you. Every one of us tends to throw ourselves more completely into something when we believe absolutely in the rightness of it."

"But, Nancy, I'm not getting it! I'm going in circles. That's why I called you. I've got to get my applications in for next year within the next two weeks and I'm completely stuck."

"I've got faith in you, Callie. You'll figure it out."

"I'm glad you think so." I was tired of going in mental circles. I was used to being able to formulate goals and then simply doing whatever was necessary to reach them. This whole college thing and what to do next felt beyond me.

"I've got an idea," Nancy said.

"There's a news flash."

"Don't be sarcastic, Callie, live in the solution. What are you doing the week of November 8th – 15th?"

Nancy was right; my comment had been sarcastic and making sideways comments to her wasn't going to help. I took a breath. "I'm sorry, you're right. I'm just frustrated at my inability to come up with a plan. I suppose I'll probably be doing my regular things that week like going to online classes, sparring at Eva's, and running; nothing special, why?"

"You want to do something with me?"

"I love doing stuff with you. What do you have in mind?"

"I'm hoping to finalize the first incubator building in Boston that week. Why don't you fly up there with me? I can show you the building I'm buying and let you read some of the business plans I'm considering for tenants. I'm also going to meet with my Boston attorney and a building contractor. While we're up there maybe we can look at a couple of colleges and kill two or three birds with one stone. Besides, we'd have a blast while we're doing it."

I didn't have to think about her offer at all. "I'd love to do something like that. Maybe it will help me break out of this mind-freeze I'm in. By the way, I've been meaning to ask you, where did you go to college?"

"I went to a business school in Wellesley, MA called Babson."

I wasn't familiar with the name. "I can't imagine going to a business school. I guess I expected that you'd tell me you went to some school that specialized in journalism or printing."

"Nope. I went to a school that specializes in thinking."

"Before we go, I'll look at some Boston area schools online. Maybe I can find a couple that interest me."

"Do you think you could take that whole week off?"

"I think so, especially if I'm looking at schools. I've got to talk to my parents first and then my guidance counselor."

"Do you want me to speak to your parents?"

"No. I should that. Will you make the plane reservations?"

"Of course."

Mam called all of us into dinner twenty minutes later. The pot roast and mashed potatoes she'd prepared were delicious, and no one said anything for several minutes as four of us shoveled food into our mouths. My brother Harley was the exception. He seemed distracted and focused on something else and was pushing food around his plate instead of eating it. I found out why a few seconds later.

"I joined the Marines today," he announced to the table.

Everyone stopped eating and there was silence for a several seconds until my father's fork clanked loudly as it fell to the plate. "You did *what*, Harley?"

"I joined the Marines."

"Did you actually sign on the line son, or did you just tell them you were interested in joining?"

"Signed on the line."

"Damn." My father nodded at my other brother. "Did you know anything about this, Damon?"

"No, sir, it's news to me."

Damon looked over at Harley and gave him a stink-eye, obviously pissed off that his brother had made such a major decision without discussing it with him first.

"I thought we had a plan that the two of you were both going to continue working on the Damon & Harley this year," my father said.

Harley shrugged his shoulders. "I guess we did, but I just got to thinking that I wanted to have some other options going forward. I'm not exactly college boy material and I figured I might learn some other skills in the service."

"That's true enough, son, but I wish you'd discussed it with us first because what you do affects your brother and me too."

"I expected you'd want to talk me out of it. It's just four years though; It's not forever."

"When would you be leaving?" Mam asked.

"In a month."

She nodded, but I could tell she was thinking hard about it. Politics was not discussed much in our family as so much of what goes on in Washington is simply incomprehensible to all of us. Our military presence in Iraq and Afghanistan was a good example.

My parents were both big supporters of the military, but they felt that we'd really lost our way once we'd displaced Al Qaeda and Saddam Hussein. They no longer felt that we had any business in either country, and the steady stream of local boys who'd been either killed or maimed in the twenty years since, underscored this point.

"Well at least we're not seeing as many boys getting hurt in the Mideast," Mam offered.

"Thought you all might be a little prouder of me for joining up."

"We are, son. It's just that you surprised us is all. It's a big step to take without discussing something like that; especially with you being half the crew on Damon & Harley. I am proud of you. Service in the military is an honorable thing. I just hope you don't get hurt fighting all those crazy Muslims (Daddy pronounced the word as moos-lims). Those people have been fighting each other for thousands of years and I don't expect they plan on stopping anytime soon."

"I don't think it's likely I'll end up over there. There's just a few thousand troops left, and I also picked an MOS of motor transport."

"What's an MOS, Harley?" I asked.

"It's the area of specialty that you receive extra training in. All marines are riflemen first, but you can pick an area that you receive special training in. I picked motor transport just because I've always been good with engines and it wouldn't be a bad trade to go into when I get out. They'll probably just put me in a motor-pool somewhere."

I knew that in fact Harley was _not_ particularly "good with engines," but I sensed what a big deal Harley's decision to join the military was and didn't want to say anything that would take away from that.

"That makes sense, Harley. I'll bet you would be good with engines." I was surprised at his independence. I'd never thought of Harley doing anything but shrimping with my father and brother and was really surprised that he'd taken such a big, bold step on his own into the outside world and not even discussed it with Damon.

No one seemed to know what to say next, so I figured now would be as good time as any to announce my college plans.

"I've got an announcement too."

Everyone turned to me.

"What's your announcement, Callie?" my mother asked.

"I'm pregnant."

"You're what! Goddamnit to hell!" my father shouted, dropping his fork again.

I bobbed my head up and down a few times. "That's right, I'm seriously preggers and I don't even know who the father is."

Mam put her hand to her mouth and looked like she was going to cry. "Callie! How on earth did that happen?"

Everyone had stopped eating at this point and all of them were staring at me with open mouths.

Damon muttered out loud. "Probably the same way it usually happens."

Mam slapped his arm.

I said nothing for a few seconds.

"Actually, I'm _not_ pregnant; I was just messing with y'all."

I was next to get a Mam scolding and she slapped me on the shoulder. "Callie, what on earth is wrong with you? You shouldn't joke about something like that. You near gave me a heart attack. What's wrong with you?"

"Actually, I do have an announcement and I figured you'd all be so happy that I wasn't pregnant that you'd all give me your blessings for what I'm thinking of. I'm not sure where yet, but I've decided I want to go on to college."

My father spoke after thinking for several seconds. "Well that makes a hell of a lot more sense than trying to be a shrimp boat captain."

"I haven't given up on getting my captain's license, Daddy. I'm going to keep working on that, but kind of like Harley, I want to have a few more options and I think college makes sense."

"I think that's a great idea, Callie." My mother put a reassuring hand on my forearm. "Would you go to Florida Gulf Coast?"

"I'm not sure yet, Mam. FGCU would be convenient and affordable, but Aunt Nancy has offered to help me out with tuition if I decided I wanted to go to an even better college. I'm going to look at some other schools before making up my mind."

Daddy didn't say anything, and Mam pushed her food around the plate without looking up at me. I knew what was going through their heads.

"You thinking of going to go to one of those 'liberal' schools up North?" Damon asked. "Seems like the type of place Aunt Nancy would like."

Damon's resentment of Aunt Nancy and her wealth was awkward. I decided not to get into it with him. "Like I said, I don't know yet. She's going up to Boston the second week of November on business and asked me if I wanted to come with her and look at some schools. I'm trying to keep an open mind. One thing I've thought of is possibly going the maritime route and going to a place like Kings Point or Mass Maritime."

"Not sure how I feel about us being beholden to her," Daddy said.

"You wouldn't be, I would."

"You're still a minor, girl."

"I know that, Daddy. Don't make it a pride thing. She's got plenty of money and she wants to do it. I'm just going to look."

Mam and Daddy exchanged a look and I decided not to say more for the moment.

RIP CONVERSE

Chapter 17

After I finished my online classes the next day I went downtown to have another look for Karen. I'm not exactly sure why it felt so important to me to find her, but it was. I also kept thinking about the two missing girls from the middle school and what Camila had told me happens to girls who are kidnapped and brought into the sex trade. It made sense that the two separate incidents were connected. If I could find Karen and convince her to cooperate with the police, that might in turn give them enough leverage over the gang to turn up the two missing schoolgirls.

I returned to the cross streets where I'd dropped Karen and drove a grid pattern that extended five blocks north, south, east, and west of there. I drove the area twice, quite slowly, and stopped whenever I saw a pedestrian or someone in their front yard and gave Karen's description in the hope that one of them might have seen her. No one could recall her and frustrated I gave up after an hour and started home again.

I changed direction and headed out of the residential neighborhood towards the main road. After just one block I pulled up behind a light green El-Camino that was stopped at a stop sign. There was no cross traffic and after waiting four or five seconds I realized that the driver was thinking about something besides his driving and gave him a short beep on my horn. He looked up, startled, and after acknowledging me with a little apology wave, he proceeded through the stop sign and then through the intersection. Even though I wasn't in any particular hurry, the driver seemed distracted and was driving below the speed limit. I looked in my rearview mirror and seeing no traffic behind or ahead pulled out and started to pass him. I gave him a polite head nod as I came abreast of him, continued past, signaled, then pulled back into the lane in front of him.

***

Gino Cruz was headed back to the auto body shop from the stash-house. He'd made several trips that day running product around town from the stash house to dealers on the street and as he drove, he kept thinking about his friends Darian and Javier. The three of them had been friends since they were in diapers and it just didn't seem fair that Diego had killed them and then had them chopped up and thrown in the river like garbage. Their families didn't even have bodies to bury and that just wasn't right. And all because some girl had bested them in a fight and screwed up a snatch. No, it just wasn't right.

The two young middle schoolers had been moved from the body shop to the stash house the night before. Diego had ordered it in case the police came by the clubhouse looking for Esteban. Gino had a problem with that end of the business too. He had eight- and ten-year-old sisters at home that he adored and couldn't imagine what he would do if they were abused like the two thirteen-year-old kidnapped girls, Laura and Heather, had been.

He'd brought them meals on several occasions at the clubhouse since they'd become captives. The first time he'd gone in to feed them, they'd cowered and cried in each other's arms and begged him not to hurt them despite the crystal meth that Diego was having administered to them on a daily basis. He couldn't imagine touching them let alone hurting them. They reminded him too much of his sisters. After he'd reassured them and given them food, they'd told him their names. Diego just called them puta one and puta two.

Gino's father had been in the gang. He'd also died in the gang when Gino was just six. The few memories he had of his father were good ones and he wondered if his father would like him and approve of the man he was becoming. He stopped at a stop sign lost in his thoughts and sat there without proceeding until someone beeped at him from behind. He briefly held up his hand in apology and looked into the rearview mirror as he pulled away from the stop sign and through the intersection. There was a motorcycle behind him. The driver was dressed in black leathers and a full-face black helmet.

Gino nodded back at the driver as she passed and noted the name painted on the side of her red gas tank, Ducati. It stirred something. As the motorcycle continued past, he noted the driver's curly blond hair coming out from under the back of the helmet and her tiny stature. He watched as she leaned right to come back into his lane after passing and then left, to return to upright. The fat rear tire and upswept dual exhaust were prominent. All at once, it clicked. This was the bike and rider that Diego wanted them to find so badly. This was the person that had bested his friends Javier and Darian and indirectly caused their deaths!

Gino accelerated after her and simultaneously picked his phone up off the seat, selected Esteban from his favorites, and dialed. Esteban picked up after two rings.

"Sí."

"Esteban, this is Gino."

Esteban thought for a second. "Gino, yeah, sorry, what is it?"

"You know that girl that you and Diego wanted us to keep an eye out for?"

"I know her, why, have you seen her?"

"I'm following her right now. "

"Where are you?" Esteban asked with uncharacteristic enthusiasm.

"I'm on Edison near that auto salvage place. We'll be coming up on Shoemaker Blvd in a second."

"Shit, I'm nowhere near you. Think you can follow her and find out where she's going?"

"I can try man."

"Good. Put your phone on speaker and stay on the line with me."

"Okay." A few seconds passed. "She just turned right onto Shoemaker and accelerated. She's moving pretty good."

"Stay with her."

The light was red as I approached Shoemaker Blvd in the far-right lane. There was one car in front of me and I slowed and looked in my rearview mirror as was my habit whenever slowing. I always worried about cars coming up behind me and rear-ending me. I noted the green El Camino which I'd passed and pulled away from several blocks before.

The car in front of me turned right on red and after a quick stop I also turned right. As I accelerated, I looked in my rearview mirror again and saw the green car turn after me. I didn't think much of it as he'd been traveling in the same direction, but I stored it away. As I got down to Canal, I noted the green car was still behind me several cars back and when traffic opened up, I quickly accelerated from 45mph to 75mph and traveled at that speed for a block before coming to Hanson. The light was red, and once again I came to a stop. I looked in my rearview. The green car was still just three cars back behind me which meant he'd accelerated when I had and passed all the cars I had. Something was up.

"She just went from forty to like seventy-five! She might be onto me, man."

"Fall back a little but keep following her."

"Okay. Now we're stopped at Hanson."

"Is she looking back over her shoulder or acting like she sees you?"

"Not that I can see."

"Good, she might not be on to you yet."

When the light turned green, I wound up Velocitá, leaned forward and accelerated from 0-80mph in just six seconds leaving everyone at the light far behind. When I got to Winkler, I caught the green and continued through that light keeping my speed over 60mph and chanced a quick look in my rearview. Although a quarter mile behind me, the El Camino was still on my tail and closing.

"Esteban! She's on to me for sure. The bitch took off from the light like she was at a drag race. She's already got a half mile on me."

"Keep on her." Esteban thought for a second. "Listen, I don't know if you can catch her before Colonial, but if you can, see if you can't come alongside her and crowd her off the road. She'll get fucked up if she goes down, but Diego really wants her."

"I'll do my best man, but I think that bike of hers is a lot faster than my car."

I decided it was time to put an end to the car following me and put the hammer back down as I went into the smooth corners of Shoemaker approaching Colonial. I got up over 100mph and leaned into the corners like I'd seen the professional racers do on the Isle of Man races I'd watched on TV. I easily kept my distance from the El Camino and once I got to Colonial lucked out one more time with a green right arrow and leaned into the turn and accelerated away once again. The El Camino didn't make the light. Despite my significant advantage at that point I pushed Velocitá all the way down Colonial till we hit 75N and once on that, I pushed both Velocitá and myself to our limits all the way home. What on earth had the car following me been all about. Was the driver simply pissed because I'd honked at him and then passed? Was he MS-13, or was he just some perv trying to stalk me?

"She's history, Esteban. Sorry, man, nothing I could do; that bike of hers is a rocket ship. I didn't even get close. Then she got the light on Colonial, and I didn't."

"That's too bad. At least we know she either lives or works at that end of the city. She'll turn up again. When she does, we'll get her. Make sure everyone knows that you saw her and where you were at the time. I also don't care at this point if she gets a little damaged if we can get our hands on her."

I pulled into my driveway fifteen minutes later and took one last anxious look over my shoulder to be certain that no cars had followed me. The road behind remained dark. I put Velocitá up on her stand and after turning off the engine and taking my helmet off, leaned down and gave her a little kiss on the tank. I listened for several seconds for the sound of a car on the road, but all I heard was the sound of Velocitá's exhaust cooling and contracting in the cool night air.

RIP CONVERSE

Chapter 18

On Wednesday afternoon the following week I went by the Dojo earlier than usual. I'd skipped practice the day before doing college research and getting my paperwork together for admission applications and simply wanted to spend time with Eva and work out. She was sparring with a private student that I'd never met, when I walked in. After noticing me, she took a quick look at the clock on the wall and dropped her defensive hand position which signaled a "stop" to her student.

"Let's end there, Stuart, I know you have to go meet your father. Keep working on your non-dominant leg sidekicks. They're still a little weak."

He nodded. "I will, Eva."

"Good. I also think that you're more than ready to start sparring with some of my regular students instead of just me."

"Are you sure?"

Eva nodded. "You're ready for sure. I don't put orange belts against brown or black belts. You'll do fine."

Eva turned to me. "Callie, I'd like you to meet Stuart Alexander. Stuart, this is Callie Babich."

Stuart turned to me and briefly lit up like a Christmas tree after making eye contact, then averted his eyes and looked down as if he'd somehow done something wrong. "Hi, Callie, it's a pleasure to meet you," he muttered shyly.

I looked at him for a second before responding. He was about 5'10", had angular facial features with a few pimples, a skinny body and black hair that seemed to grow out of his head in twenty different directions. I could tell he was close to my age but for some reason painfully shy. "Hi, Stuart. It's really nice to meet you." I held out my hand where it remained untouched for two or three seconds. Stuart finally noticed the silence in the room and raised his eyes a few inches.

"Oh, sorry." He reached out and grabbed my much smaller hand in his and pumped it a little too enthusiastically as if that would make up for his failure to notice my gesture. Then he let it go, just as quickly. "Sorry, I'm not terribly good at meeting new people."

I smiled broadly at him. His modesty was a refreshing change from the false bravado and snarky remarks that so many of the guys at school overcompensated with. I tamped down my normal directness and assuredness in empathy with him. "I know what you mean. Meeting new people can be difficult. I'm not a biter, though, I promise."

Stuart didn't look as though he knew how to respond. He seemed sweet and genuine, however. Before I could think of anything else to say he spoke again.

"Well, I better get going. I don't want to interrupt you two. I've got to meet my father, don't want to be late."

Eva spoke. "You're not interrupting us, Stuart. I see this shishka every day. We're good friends. Maybe you and Callie could spar some time. She's small in stature, but she's also one of the best students I have."

Stuart got a panicked look on his face. "I'm sure she's very good. I'm worried I wouldn't be enough of a challenge for her."

Now I was getting embarrassed. "I'd love to spar with you, Stuart. Sparring with Eva is great, of course, but I'm weakest trying to fight with guys that have a big height advantage over me, especially when I'm trying to do arm bars and tie up their shoulder and elbow joints. Eva's a shrimp like me, so you'd be a great practice partner."

He turned bright red. "Sure, anytime, Callie."

I surprised myself. "Why don't you give me your number and we'll figure out some mat time that would work for both of us." I noticed a glint in Eva's eye as I made the offer to him. He tripped over himself going to his workout bag to get his phone. "Sure, that would be great, Callie; let me get my phone," he said over his shoulder.

Eva and I exchanged knowing smiles as he rushed to get his phone. Once he got back, we exchanged numbers. He looked down at his phone probably wondering if the number I'd given him was real.

"Thanks, Callie! I'll call you for sure and we'll get together." He rushed from the room and out to his car, leaving Eva and me staring at each other. We both laughed at the sound of the outer door closing.

"Wow. I don't think I've ever met anyone so shy."

Eva started taunting me in a sing-song voice. "Callie's got a boyfriend; Callie's got a boyfriend."

"Shush, you terrible woman. That poor boy can barely talk he's so shy. Have you no heart!"

"I know he's shy, but you're sure as hell not! At the rate you were going with him I thought you were going to wrap that boy up and take him home to momma."

I turned red. "Don't be silly. He seems like a very nice boy, but he's not my type. I was just trying to be nice. Don't make something out of nothing."

"Uh huh, whatever you say, Catherine."

I feinted left, then quickly turned right and did an arm-bar maneuver wrapping up Eva's left arm and elbow. I hugged her left shoulder tight to my chest under my chin and her lower arm extended with her elbow joint tightly wrapped. Simultaneously I started pushing her hand up into the air behind her back and her shoulder further downwards towards the mat.

"You brat! You can't waylay your instructor like that." Eva pretended to yield and then in a sudden explosive countermove spun counterclockwise ninety degrees, freeing her arm, put the same hold on me and took me to the floor.

"You should have broken my elbow, my wrist or at least given me a femoral strike with your knee while you had the chance."

I smiled up at her. "I didn't want to embarrass you."

"Fat chance! So, what did you come by for at this time of the day; something on your mind?"

I sat up on the mat and faced her. "I really needed a workout, but I also keep thinking about those two missing thirteen-year-old girls and what the detective told me happens to the girls that get abducted and brought into the sex trade business. I'm also still nervous about testifying against this gang."

Eva nodded. "What did the detective tell you?"

"It's pretty brutal. Are you sure you want to know?"

"If it's bothering you, get it off your shoulders."

"She said that the entire gang rapes the girls they take. They call it 'breaking them in.' Then they addict them to drugs and move them from city to city renting them out as prostitutes until they're worn out or die from an overdose or kill themselves. And I keep thinking about how young those two missing girls are and how terrified they must be."

When I'd started, Eva had been looking right into my eyes. Once I started giving her the details, however, I noticed that she'd shifted her gaze towards the floor, avoiding eye contact.

I continued. "Can you imagine? I know I keep thinking back to how horrible it was when that boy I was dating tried to rape me and I still think about that, all the time."

Eva continued to pointedly stare at the floor. All at once her shoulders started to tremble, and I realized that she was silently crying, and I watched as tears started to run down her face and fall to the mat.

I leaned forward and put my hand on her shoulder. "What's going on, Eva? Are you alright? What did I say that made you so sad?" I asked gently.

She completely broke down at that point and started sobbing. I was heartbroken. "Eva, talk to me." I moved closer and put my arm around her shoulders.

"Oh, Callie, I guess I just haven't been paying attention to what's been going on around us and what you're telling me hits very close to home."

"Why, what happened? Tell me."

She shook her head. "I've never told anyone. I'm so ashamed."

"What, Eva? I can't imagine you doing anything so wrong or shameful that you would be so heartbroken."

She continued to shake and sob before speaking again.

"Several months after I finished basic training with the IDF I was patrolling the northern border with another female soldier one night. We were the same age and had a great deal in common and were laughing and telling each other stories as we patrolled. At the time we were in the demilitarized zone between Israel and Lebanon. One of the remote sensors tripped and we were sent to the area to investigate. Once we got there, we thought we saw some movement in a gully to the side of the road, so we called in our position and indicated we were leaving our Plasan Sand Cat to investigate on foot. We got out with our rifles and flashlights and started doing a foot search. Back then we had to constantly watch for Arab infiltrators who wanted to get into the settlements to either kidnap or kill Israelis and our job was to try and find and capture these infiltrators before any of them got too far into Israel or into any of the settlements."

She paused, collecting her thoughts. "Five heavily armed terrorists ambushed us. Ronny, my friend, took a round right in the throat when they first opened fire and was killed immediately. I lasted long enough to call in to our base that we were taking fire and was able to hold out for several minutes longer, but ultimately I was hit in the leg and also went down, and they overran my position."

"That's terrible! I can't imagine getting shot and also losing a close friend at the same time."

"It was awful, but unfortunately for me, that was just the beginning of something far worse."

"What's worse than getting shot?"

Eva hesitated obviously collecting her thoughts. "The five Arabs took me hostage. They used the Plasan we'd been patrolling in and immediately retreated back into the blue zone before other soldiers from my unit could get to me. You have to understand, Callie, that this is the nightmare of every Israeli soldier and why units never, ever give up trying to find a fellow soldier when one is lost or taken."

I sensed it was best to let Eva continue with her story at her own pace and simply sat, facing her, with her hands in mine, staring into her haunted eyes.

"The Arabs had me for three days, Callie, three days. Do you know what that means?"

I had my suspicions where her story was going but shook my head.

"These terrorists are not like you and me. They do not believe in things like the Geneva Convention or humane treatment of prisoners. Israelis are not humans to them, you see. The hatred these religious fanatics feel towards us is so evil that it's difficult to comprehend. I was raped by all of them, multiple times over the days they had me. They moved me every night to different safe houses as they tried to avoid the hundreds of Israeli soldiers searching for me, but every moment we were stopped I would be raped again, beaten, humiliated; anything they could think of to demean and degrade me. These animals even defecated on me."

I was stunned and couldn't say anything.

"I have so much hate in my soul now, Callie. I know that none of it was my fault, but I still blame myself for not being able to escape or kill them. They took my soul, Callie, and I was helpless to do anything about it. No one will ever want the person you see here. I am too broken."

I started crying also. "Eva, I can't even conceive of this. I feel ashamed myself right now for even being of the same species as those men. Oh, God, what can I do? I would do anything for you. I adore you and look up to you. I want to be like you. Please tell me how I can help."

"You can't, Callie, no one can. What they took is no longer in me; I don't think it can ever be regained. I feel as though my only purpose for living is to keep what happened a secret. Even at that, I am failing."

I hugged her again and then simply moved my head forward until my forehead was gently resting against hers. I flashed back to the night that Nancy and I'd first had dinner with Eva and how she'd avoided Nancy's question about why she'd become a Krav Maga instructor. I suspected I now knew the answer.

"Were these men ever caught?"

She shook her head. "My brothers and sisters in arms took them out when they finally found me. The terrorists lived only seconds once my fellow soldiers saw what had been done to me."

"Good, I'm glad. They deserved worse!"

"It did not end there, I'm afraid. As a result of what happened to me, I am an outcast." She paused and then quickly added, "Not officially of course; officially I was a hero. But on an unspoken level, I felt as though everyone blamed me. I don't know what more they expected I could have done. I would certainly have killed those men if I could have. I was even ready to kill myself simply to deny myself to them, but I never had the opportunity to do either and committed the sin of surviving."

I kept silent, but I knew exactly what Eva was talking about because I had felt some of the same scorn from my peers after Christopher's attempted rape. It wasn't fair and it isn't right, but it happens.

Eva continued. "I am an unwelcome reminder, I suppose, of what no Israeli can accept as even a possibility. The implications of what happened to me are so vast I think that they are incomprehensible to my countrymen. For them to acknowledge that these things happened to me would be to admit that such things still exist in the world we live in and that these things could also happen to them as well. If I am not there to remind them, people can avoid having to think about it."

"Eva, your thoughts are so sad. I think I understand from my own experience how things can get so twisted around that the victim can feel guilty and end up the outsider. It isn't fair. No one should have to feel so alone. What about your parents? Surely they haven't abandoned you?"

"They say they want me to come home, but I don't really believe that. My father can't even look me in the eye. What happened to me, Callie, was truly evil, and it cannot be ignored or tolerated in any way, or it grows."

"What are you suggesting?"

"That the girls who have been kidnapped must be found. If what you say is true, then these MS-13 gang people are no different than the men who stole my soul and my life. You wanted my advice. I think finding this girl Karen would be a start. Perhaps that will in some way help lead the police to those missing girls. And if your testimony would in any way help to make these men pay a price for the things they have done, then I would do that also."

I hugged her tightly again and then the two of us sat silently for several minutes sharing our bond and slowly returning to the world.

I looked into her eyes. "Thank you for sharing your story. You're right. The only way something like that can be stopped is if each of us is willing to do the right thing, even if it's dangerous."

Eva nodded her agreement.

Two of Eva's students walked into the dojo at that point and both of us looked up at the clock.

"I've got another private lesson to teach with those two." She nodded in their direction. "Are you going to stay and work out?"

"No, I don't think so. I've lost my enthusiasm. Will you be all right?"

She smiled at me. "Yes, Callie, of course. I will survive. I've lived with this for eight years; what's another day?

****

That same evening just after sunset, but before night's darkness, Rory Markle was running his twenty-seven-foot Boston Whaler Dauntless North on the Caloosahatchee. He was returning home with two friends after a long and unsuccessful day of fishing in the Gulf. They'd worked the shore between Manasota Key and Sanibel Island using live blue crabs hoping to get Snook or Permit. Despite getting onto several small groups of Permit and following them down the shore and casting into them, none would take the delectable bait, and his fish box was annoyingly empty. His mind eventually wandered to the upcoming monthly payment coming due on his boat. He'd bought it on impulse at the Miami Boat Show earlier that year, sucked in by the supposedly low monthly payment that he'd be paying for the next fifteen years. The two Yamaha 250's on the stern had sucked up $300 of fuel over the course of the day.

"Hey, I hope you two yabos are going to kick in for the fuel we burned today."

"Shoot, Rory, I didn't bring my wallet," his friend Neil said. "I'll have to catch you on the backside."

His other friend Wayne said, "I've got about fifty dollars on me. You're welcome to that."

"Great." Rory muttered under his breath.

"Hey, Rory. What's that caught up in the mangroves over there?" Neil asked.

Rory looked where he was pointing in the fading light. "Don't know, might be a manatee. Listen, guys, running a boat like this is expensive. The least you two could do is pay for some damned fuel when I take you out for the day."

Wayne and Neil ignored him and continued to look over at the mangroves. Neil spoke. "Seriously, Rory; go closer, I want to see what that is." He pointed again to the object in the mangroves.

Rory backed his throttles down to an idle and angled his course to the mangroves. "Don't think getting me distracted by some crap in the bushes is going to get you two off the hook. I'm serious, I want you guys to split the fuel costs."

"What the hell? Rory, I think it might be a body!" Neil said.

Those words got his full attention and he shifted both his engines into neutral and coasted up to the edge of the mangroves where the object that had their attention was floating. Rory tried to put the pieces of the puzzle he was looking at together and reconcile them with what his brain was expecting. Something wasn't quite right. He could see what looked like an arm and a leg and the trunk of a body, but there was no head where one would normally be. He pulled a flashlight out of the console and turned it on. The light lit up the dark mangroves and he attempted to process what he was looking at, but his brain could not reconcile his expectations with what he was seeing for several more seconds.

Once his brain finished analyzing the unidentified object and delivered its conclusion, Rory lunged for the side of the boat and projectile-vomited five beers, a bag of pretzels and a tuna sandwich into the water. Despite his horror, he refocused the light on the body hoping the head would magically appear. It didn't and he stared open mouthed at the blue and white bloated stump of a neck and the crabs feasting on it.

"Jesus Christ!" He turned the wheel, kicked his engines into forward and grabbed for his VHF mike simultaneously. "Mayday, Mayday, Mayday! This is the *Knotty Boy* calling the U.S. Coast Guard, *Knotty Boy* calling the U.S. Coast Guard, over!"

"This is United States Coast Guard Fort Myers Beach on 16, *Knotty Boy*. What's the nature of your emergency, over?"

"I've found a headless corpse! Over."

"Say again, *Knotty Boy*."

"A body, as in human body. It's got no head!"

"Roger that, *Knotty Boy*. What's your location, over?"

"I'm on the Caloosahatchee. The body's caught up in the mangroves on Marsh Point, about one to one and a half miles north of the Edison Bridge, over."

****

Later that evening after dinner, I was reading quietly in bed when my phone rang. I looked down at my phone and saw that it was Stuart the boy I'd met earlier at the dojo calling. I didn't really feel like talking with anyone but remembering his shyness and insecurity pressed the "Accept" button.

"Hi, Stuart."

"Oh hi, Callie, I guess you know it's me calling."

I smiled. "Yup, remember we exchanged phone numbers earlier today?"

"Oh right. Listen, you probably have plans and everything, but I just wondered if maybe you might, you know, maybe want to spar with me on Saturday? I'm sure you're really busy doing other things, but I thought I'd ask."

God, he was shy. "Hold a second, let me check my really busy social calendar."

"I understand if you've got plans..."

"Stuart, stop! I'm only kidding. I'd love to, that would be fun. About the only things I normally do are go to school, run and go to the dojo."

"Really!"

"Yes, really. Would 10:30 or 11:00 work?"

"Absolutely! I mean yes."

"Great, I'll see you then."

Chapter 19

I woke up Saturday morning at 6:00. The temperature was a perfect sixty-eight degrees for a long run, and I threw on a pair of shorts, tank top and sneakers and went out to the kitchen for a glass of juice before stretching out in the front yard. Crab Claw followed me outside, did his business at the edge of the woods and then watched from a distance as I did my upper body stretches. The moment I sat down on the lawn for some toe touches, he bounded over and started whining at me. I looked up at him from my bent over position.

"Don't start on me."

He lunged in and started nuzzling my neck and licking my face.

"No, Crab Claw!" I tried with my sternest tone of voice.

He stopped and cocked his head at me briefly. He knew the meaning of the word "no" but decided that I didn't really mean it and kept lunging in, nuzzling and licking my face.

"No!" I tried again. But my heart wasn't in it, and I started to giggle.

"Bad dog, Crab Claw!" I tried with an even deeper tone of voice, but I couldn't pull it off. He knew I wasn't serious and lunged in once again and caught me full on the mouth with a wet tongue. I gave up, pushed him away playfully and jumped to my feet wiping his slobber off my face with the back of my wrist.

"You're like a 'bad Lassie.' Why don't you go harass some squirrels or eat something nasty?"

He snorted twice, cocked his head at me again, and went down into an expectant ready position with his forelegs out in front of him. I playfully swiped my hand at his face, first one way and then the other, which he dodged effortlessly and then he growled at me. I growled back.

"Okay, you win, but I've got some important human stuff to do. You can come if you want, but it's going to be a long run."

He barked twice at me as I started running up the driveway and then followed, passed me, and started zig zagging back and forth across the road and into the woods in front of me with his nose down.

I decided at that moment to do a ten-mile run and looked down at my watch to note the exact time. I expected that I would end up running the ten miles averaging about 7:30 minutes per mile. It was always fun to see how close I came to my estimated pace at the end of each run.

Once I got to the main road, Crab Claw stopped, looked at me, and seemed to sense on some level that I was going on a serious run and that the opportunity for more play had come and gone. He decided against continuing with me, barked one last time at me, then turned around and starting walking back towards our property. I understood; I couldn't imagine running in a fur coat.

There was a lot going on in my life to think about, both positive and negative. On the positive side I'd accrued almost two months of sea time towards my captain's license over the summer and learned quite a bit about mechanics, ship-handling, and navigation in the process. My people skills had also improved from having to deal with the general public daily and I enjoyed the feelings of being engaged with the world instead of always being alone and in my own head. Most of all, I was grateful for the relationships I'd formed with Aunt Nancy, Melissa, and Eva and the effect all these strong women were having on me and my life trajectory. Each one was an amazing gift.

I also thought about the negative things that had suddenly popped up in my life. Any youthful innocence and naïveté that I might have enjoyed had been shattered in recent weeks by what I'd been exposed to and become aware of; MS-13, the sex trade, barbaric and senseless violence, life without purpose, and the people like Detective Sanchez who have to deal with all these things on a daily basis. One of the things that bothered me most was the fear and powerlessness I'd felt when I'd faced Esteban. I had expected that learning Krav Maga would equalize me and empower me. It had helped for sure, but I still had vulnerabilities and I decided at that moment that improving my self-defense capabilities would remain a priority going forward. I also reaffirmed in my head the rightness of being willing to do the right thing, even if I was fearful of something and everyone around me was doing nothing.

At the end of my run, I looked down at my watch and smiled. My pace had averaged 7:10 per mile. When I got to my room, I did 100 crunches and 100 pushups, then jumped in the shower. Fifteen minutes later as I put on my clothes for the day, my cell phone rang.

"Hello."

"Callie, it's Detective Sanchez."

"Hi, Camila, what's up?"

"A couple of things. Wednesday night, a couple of fishermen coming home on the Caloosahatchee found the bodies of those two boys you beat up when you saved Karen. They were hung up and floating in the mangroves."

I was quiet for a moment, disturbed by her news. "I'm sorry to hear that."

"Well, bad things happen to bad people. They'd both been shot and, how can I put this delicately, they were also both missing their heads which leaves little doubt in my mind that they were killed by their own gang."

I was appalled. "That's terrible, Camila!"

"Live by the sword, die by the sword."

"Doesn't any of this bother you at all? You sound so casual about it."

"Of course it does, Callie, sorry. That's a 'cop' thing; sometimes we make jokes out of serious things simply because taking everything seriously is too depressing."

"You said you called for a couple of things. What else is going on?"

"I was wondering if you could come by the Lee County Jail this morning and look at some men in a lineup?"

I was suddenly apprehensive. "Who would I be identifying?"

"Esteban, the man you identified last week out of the mug shot book."

"Did you find Karen?" I asked excitedly, drawing a false conclusion.

"No, I'm sorry. We haven't located her yet."

"I didn't think my word alone was enough to charge him with attempted kidnapping?"

"It's not, and we're probably going to have to let him go in a couple of hours, but your positive identification will help us nail down that we're looking at the right people. We're also trying to ramp up the pressure on the gang in every possible way hoping that something or someone breaks free. There's incredible pressure on us to find those two missing middle-schoolers. Will you do it?"

I thought back to my discussion with Eva and what I'd decided while running and didn't hesitate. "Yes, I'll do it."

"Good; and Callie don't worry about him seeing you. You'll be behind one-way glass and he won't be able to see you or hear you."

"Where will the lineup be done?"

"At the Lee County Jail. It's almost directly across Martin Luther from the main station where you and I met."

I thought about my morning and my date to spar with Stuart. "I've got to meet someone at 10:30 this morning? Can we do it at 9:00 or 9:30?"

"Works for me."

"I'm really sad about those two thirteen-year-olds. I think about them all the time and what they must be going through."

"I know. I think about them too. We're doing our best."

"I know you are. Okay, Camila, I'll see you just after 9:00. Should I meet you at the station or the jail?"

"The jail. I'll go over there now and get things set up, so we take as little of your time as possible."

I pushed "end" on my phone and sat on the edge of my bed for a few seconds thinking about going to the jail. When Esteban had come out of the van with that machete in his hand, that had been the first time in my life I'd ever experienced an instinctual, visceral fear of someone. I thought about my reaction for a few moments, aware on a cerebral level that identifying him would likely be safe for me, but uncomfortable with the fact that I'd be in such close proximity to him again. I wasn't looking forward to it. I knew that my fear of the man was prudent, but it didn't make having that fear any more acceptable. I didn't want to feel fearful of anyone. I looked at the clock on my phone and realized I was starting to get short on time. I finished dressing, packed my knapsack for the day and stopped in the kitchen for some fruit and yogurt before heading out.

"What are you up to today?" Mam asked, as I hurriedly ate.

"I'm going downtown first and then I'm going to spar with a boy from the dojo."

"What ever happened to dinner and a movie?" Mam asked whimsically.

"What do you mean?"

"That's what young boys and girls used to do in my day when they had a date."

"Oh, it's not a date, date. We're going to meet up to punch and kick each other."

Mam cocked her head at me lovingly and in an unusual display of affection slid her fingers through my hair on both sides of my head and tucked it back behind my ears.

"Listen, Callie, I know I didn't say much the other night when you told us about your decision to go to college, but I want to tell you how proud I am of you for making that decision. That also goes for whatever school you decide on. I know I have some issues with my sister, but I also know she cares about you. Your father and I will just have to stuff our pride on this one. I'm glad you're going to have some of the chances I didn't have. You going to a good college would be a wonderful thing."

I slid my hand alongside hers and gave it a squeeze. "Thanks, Mam. I'm not sure I can find what I'm looking for at any regular college, but I'm trying to keep an open mind. With school ending this spring, I've got to do something." I leaned over and gave her a peck on the cheek. "Love you."

I went outside and started Velocitá. While she warmed up, I attached my cell phone to the bracket next to my tach and put on my helmet. I took the slightly longer, slower route over the Edison Bridge continuing to examine my anxiety over the prospect of seeing the MS-13 gangbanger Esteban again. I think one of the reasons I felt anxious then, and downright scared when I'd first confronted him, was that I'd never before been in the presence of another human being that had the capacity or mind-set to kidnap a defenseless minor to sell into the sex trade or attack someone with a machete with the intention of killing them. Those behaviors were antithetical to every value and behavior I'd ever known or been exposed to. Who is that way? Who does things like that? How could a human spirit become so deformed that brutality, slavery, rape, and domination replaced empathy, freedom, love, creativity, and individual freedom? Esteban's mindset was so incomprehensible to me that it made predicting his other behaviors impossible. That was where I think a lot of my fear of him came from.

As I crossed the Edison bridge, I stopped reflecting on the darkness of MS-13 and their horrific values and lifestyle long enough to appreciate what was around me. The morning was one of those incredibly soft Florida days, and with Velocitá purring between my legs I simply soaked up the sun on my face and shoulders and watched the boats going by beneath me as I crossed the bridge. I was aware of feeling grateful for the day and all the many blessings I enjoyed. I was also in touch with delicious feelings of freedom I always felt when riding Velocitá. I accelerated from forty up to eighty for several seconds for no other reason than I could, smiled, and then downshifted back to the speed limit, came off the bridge, and drove the few remaining blocks to the Lee County Jail.

I parked on Cottage, across the street from the jail, aware once again of my anxiousness. I got off Velocitá, unclipped my cell phone, took off my helmet, and started across the street.

****

Gino and Pedro had been sitting in the public parking lot across the street from the jail for several hours. They were in Gino's El-Camino waiting to see if Esteban made bail or not.

Gino watched as Callie got off her Ducati and crossed the street to the jailhouse door. "Hey, Pedro! There's the girl I followed yesterday!"

"Where? You sure?"

Gino pointed excitedly across the street at Callie's back as she pulled open the doors leading into the jail.

"I'm sure. I wonder if she's the witness that fingered Esteban."

"I'll call Diego." Pedro pulled out his phone and waited as it rang.

"Diego, it's Pedro."

"Si, what is it?"

"Gino and I are still across the street from the jail. We just saw the little motorcycle bitch. She just went into the jail complex."

"Any way you can grab her when she comes out?"

Pedro shrugged even though Diego couldn't see him. "I don't know man. There are police everywhere around here. That would be really risky."

"Ok, listen; when she comes out, follow her, and don't lose her. I'm going to send another car to help you. Don't fuck it up."

****

Once I entered the complex, I identified myself to the desk person and told her I was there to meet Detective Sanchez. Camila came out several minutes later. She looked serious as she approached.

"Hi, Callie. Thanks for coming down to do this."

I shrugged. "I'd be lying if I told you that I didn't have reservations."

"I understand, believe me. This guy Esteban gives even me the creeps. He's part of the sewer I was talking about last week and why I don't want you playing policewoman. Leave finding Karen to us and just stay alert. I don't know if what happened to those boys has anything to do with the attempted abduction you witnessed, but you need to stay as far away from this as possible."

I thought about what she'd just said and where I was. "Isn't me being here about to identify one of them a little contrary to that advice?"

"Yes and no. Identifying Esteban in a lineup is safe because you'll be behind one-way glass. I was thinking more about direct involvement like being out there on the street looking for Karen."

I immediately thought back to the green El Camino that had followed me Wednesday evening and wondered if the car and driver had been connected to MS-13. I didn't know and decided to keep that incident to myself.

"Even with your identification of Esteban, there isn't much we can do beyond hold him for another few hours without Karen's identification and willingness to prosecute. The prosecutor has already told me that he won't bring charges against him without her. As far as the two murdered boys go, we don't have any evidence that points towards a specific suspect. The beheadings are classic MS-13, but we can't arrest a whole gang just because a crime fits a pattern."

I nodded my head understanding her problem, but it did nothing to alleviate the personal anxiety I was feeling. "Esteban won't be able to see me through the glass during this line-up, right?"

Camila shook her head. "No, absolutely not." She put her hand on my shoulder. "Let's go get it over with."

****

Outside, a chopped, electric blue, Monte Carlo pulled slowly into the parking lot and then up alongside Pedro and Gino. There were two men inside. The passenger window rolled down. "Que pasa, Gino. Where's she parked?"

Gino nodded at Boyko and Benicio in recognition and pointed to Callie's bike. "Right there."

"How long's she been inside?"

"Ten minutes or so."

"Listen, we'll drive down Cottage a block and park on the side. Once you see her come out call my phone and stay on the line. You start following her and once you both go by us; we'll start following you about a block back."

"How do we know she'll go that way?"

"We don't. Just follow her. Let us know where you are, and we'll catch up. If she's going far, we can switch out who stays close to her to keep her from getting suspicious. When she stops, we'll box her in if we can and grab her."

Gino nodded.

After Boyko and Benicio left, Pedro turned to Gino. "Gino, you already blew it once following this puta. I'm gonna drive this piece of shit."

"Pedro, I'd rather you didn't, man. This is my ride, I know her."

"You know her like your momma. Fuck that; I'm driving."

Gino gave up the driver's seat without further pushback. As Diego's enforcer and right-hand man, Pedro had been responsible for dozens of beatings and brutal slayings over his years with Diego, and Gino had no desire to go head-to-head with him. Pedro was also the one that had cut up his friends Javier and Darian after Diego shot them.

****

I sat nervously in the viewing room waiting for the five males to be brought in.

"This guy creeps me out," I admitted out loud to Camila.

"You haven't even seen him yet. Hang in there. Once they do come out, take your time, tell us which one he is, if you see him, and I'll take care of the rest. You won't have any direct interaction of any kind with him. He won't even hear your voice."

There was another man sitting silently in the viewing room who kept looking over at me. He was in his fifties, overweight, wore a shiny suit and had a greasy combover. He held a pen in his hand and was resting his arm on a legal pad. He didn't look like a policeman.

"Who's that?" I whispered to Camila and nodded my head in the man's direction.

She moved her body between me and the man. "That's Quirk. He's the illustrious attorney who represents all of the gentlemen connected with MS-13. Don't pay any attention to him. He's just here to witness the lineup and your identification and to make sure we do it by the book. Just ignore him."

I nodded my head in understanding but was uncomfortable with his presence. Esteban might not be able to see me behind the glass but what would prevent his attorney from describing me to the gang members?

Five men were brought into the room on the other side of the glass several moments later and lined up under the numbers 1-5. Camila pressed a button and spoke into a mic. "Everyone, face to your right." She waited a few seconds and then spoke again. "Now, everyone turn back towards the glass." She waited a few more seconds. "Turn left now." She took her finger off the mic button and turned to me. "Do any of these men look like the man who assaulted you the other evening?"

I didn't say anything right away. I'd recognized Esteban the second he'd walked into the room in the number two position. Only one of the other men had facial tattoos, but it wasn't even close; I knew it was him.

"It's number two." I continued to stare at him validating my earlier threat assessment when I'd first confronted him. Had I built him up too much in my mind? No, I had not. He was fearsome-looking; not in a big, bouncer sort of way, but in a hard boned, hard-to-hurt sort of way. The surface veins visible on his head, chest and biceps made him look as though he was suffused with steroids and about to explode. He radiated strength, speed, and a focus I recognized. I would not want that focus directed at me.

"Are you certain? Do you want me to have him face right or left again?"

"No, I'm certain; number two was the man driving the van and the one that came after Karen and me with a machete when we fled."

Camila nodded at me once. "Let the record reflect that the witness positively identified Mr. Esteban Cordilla."

The attorney Camila had identified as Quirk looked pointedly at me and made some sort of note on his legal pad.

Camila pressed the mic button again. "Okay, thank you, gentlemen; you can file out."

She turned to me and spoke quietly so Quirk could not overhear us. "Thank you, Callie. I know that wasn't easy. We've got extra units out in the neighborhood where you dropped Karen and we're doing everything we can to find her. If we're able to locate her, I'll let you know. In the meantime I don't want you to do anything more. Just go about your business."

Quirk got up out of his seat and after one last pointed look at me, left the room.

"Callie. At this point the gang doesn't know that your identification pointed us towards Esteban, so I doubt you're any kind of a target, but just to be safe, stay alert and call me right away if you see any gang members. This case is a big deal right now and we've got a lot of resources looking for both Karen and the two missing girls."

All I could think to myself at that moment was that although the gang might not be aware of my identification of Esteban, his attorney certainly was.

"What are the missing girl's names, do you know, Camila?"

"Laura and Heather."

"I really hope you find them."

I couldn't imagine being kidnapped and abused by gang members. The ages of the girls made it all the more horrific. Camila escorted me back to the lobby.

"Thanks for doing that, Callie. It was good to see you again." She smiled.

I reached out and shook her hand. "Nice seeing you again as well, Camila. I really hope you're able to find those girls and arrest whoever's responsible for the deaths of those boys. Just because they're gang members doesn't mean they should get chopped up."

Camila walked me to the door leading out to the and then held it open as I exited.

RIP CONVERSE

Chapter 20

Attorney Quirk went out to the public waiting area after the lineup and over to the vending machines. He got a Diet Coke and two packages of Ding Dongs, and then looked around for an unoccupied bench to sit on. There was nothing free. He picked a bench already occupied by a timid looking elderly woman wearing a mask, nodded at her in apology for crowding her on the small bench, and then lowered his corpulent derrière onto the bench next to her. Once seated, he loudly passed wind and then watched her disgusted reaction with amusement. He chuckled as she fled the bench.

"What a fucking Karen," he muttered out loud and then proceeded to eat one of the packages of Ding Dongs and open the second. He took a long sip from his Diet Coke, belched, and then watched as Callie emerged from the line-up room and departed the building. In no hurry of any sort, he consumed the second package of Ding Dongs and then dialed Diego's number.

"Que?"

"The young girl just positively identified Esteban as the driver of the van which the police allege was used in the attempted kidnapping of that teener you didn't get."

"Yes, I'd heard she was in the building from several of my men. How big a problem is that going to be?"

"I'm not concerned. They still haven't found the alleged kidnap victim; no victim, no crime." Quirk loudly slurped his Diet Coke with the phone still to his face. "They'll try and hold him a while longer, but I've already told them that if they don't charge him in the next couple of hours that he walks. They know they don't have a case."

"Get him out of there as quickly as you can."

"I'm on it."

"Yeah, you sound 'on it' you fat fuck. Just get it done."

****

I emerged from the building distracted and walked across the street to Velocitá; my earlier sunny mood gone. Simply seeing Esteban again left me feeling dark and empty inside. I put on my helmet, put the key in the ignition, and cranked Velocitá. She started right up. I put my cell phone in the bracket, briefly checked to make sure it paired with my helmet, and then, after looking both ways, pulled out onto Broadway South. I didn't notice the green El Camino as it pulled out behind me and started following about 200 yards back. I took a right on Victoria after a quick look to both sides. It wasn't until I shifted into 2nd that I caught a green flash in my rear view and focused. The same car as yesterday was behind me again. *Shit!* I thought to myself.

Before I shifted into 3^{rd,} I held the Bluetooth button on the side of my helmet long enough for Siri to come on.

"Call Camila Sanchez, cell." I spoke out loud into my helmet mic. While I waited for the call to complete, I got on the accelerator and rapidly accelerated away from the El Camino. I kept hitting stop signs every block, however, and couldn't really put any distance between me and the car. I could easily out accelerate most cars but with stop signs every 300 feet or so, each time I'd get going I had to stop again almost immediately which gave my pursuers an opportunity to catch up. I needed bigger roads.

Pedro hit the steering wheel with the heel of his hand and floored it as Callie took off ahead of him. "Boyko, this is Pedro. The little bitch made me already!"

"I can see that, Bro. I'm going to shoot down to Edison and turn right there. I'll wait at Cleveland. Let me know which way she goes once she gets there, then you back off."

Camila answered. "Hey, Callie, what's going on?"

"When I left, someone started following me right away. I think it's MS-13. I saw the same car yesterday and it tried to follow me then."

"They must have been outside the jail watching! What color and kind of car is it?" As Camilla spoke, she snapped her fingers several times to get her partner's attention and put Callie on speakerphone.

"It's a green El Camino. You know those older two door cars that have a truck bed in the back?"

"I know the car. Can you stay away from them?"

"I think so. I'm on Victoria right now, coming up to Cleveland. If I can get onto Cleveland, I think I can stay out in front of them."

"Stay on the phone with me. I'm with my partner Dan and we're on our way down to my car. We'll try and get other radio cars to your general area. The main thing is to get you safe somewhere. Any way you can head back towards the jail? I don't think they'd try anything right in front of the jail."

"I'll try. Give me a couple of minutes."

"You bet."

I got to Cleveland quickly. The light was red, but I wasn't about to stop and let them hit me from behind, so as I downshifted down into 1st gear, I veered sharply around two mini-vans and a landscaping truck that were stopped at the light, just barely avoiding the trailer behind the landscaping truck. Despite the El Camino having gotten to the intersection right behind me I expected that my unplanned jog around the two mini vans and the truck would give me some extra time to put some distance between us once I turned North. He'd have to wait at the light until the traffic blocking him turned right. I was barely successful at merging between two northbound cars in the far-right lane and accelerated as quickly as I could to their speed. The driver of the second car had to stomp on his breaks to avoid hitting me and lay on his horn for several seconds as I pulled away from him. I stole a quick look into my rear-view mirror.

"Crap!" I said out loud.

"What is it, Callie?" Camila asked in a panicked voice.

"The driver of the El Camino didn't stop at the light. He just drove up on the curb and then around all the stopped cars. He's coming up behind me again!"

I'd watched in my rearview as the El Camino had made the turn and attempted to merge into the Northbound traffic. Several cars skidded to a stop attempting to avoid hitting him. Those cars were now sideways in the road and the El Camino accelerated away and was now just several hundred yards behind me again. I had an idea.

"Camila, I'm northbound on Cleveland and he's coming up on me again. If I just circle back towards the jail on Martin Luther, he could catch up and just run me down before I have a chance to bail and I don't think you have time to set up any kind of a roadblock there. I really need some open road to put some distance on this guy and you'll need some time to get some sort of barrier in place for me to shelter behind."

"So, what are you thinking?"

"I'll stay on Cleveland and go right over the river. Once I get to the other side I'll circle back and come back over the river on the Edison bridge. That will let me put some distance between us and also give you a chance to set up in front of the jail. No way he knows I'm talking to you right now so he might fall for the trap."

"I wish I had a better idea, but what you're saying makes sense, Callie. Be careful. I'll get things set up here."

"Thanks, Camila." I was already going ninety, but I could see that the El Camino was getting closer. I twisted the throttle to the stops as I got to the straightaway crossing the Caloosahatchee and briefly caught air as I launched off a hump in the road and watched my tachometer as it climbed past 6,500 to 7,000 to 7,500 and finally to 8,600 where the engine started to complain. I looked at the speedometer. I was going 128mph and the El Camino was no longer visible in my tiny rearview mirror. "Good girl, Velocitá." I wasn't aware that I'd spoken out loud until I heard Camila's voice in my helmet again.

"What's that, Callie? Are you okay?"

"Just praising my girl here; 128 mph! Didn't know she had it in her!"

She shouted back at me. "Christ, Callie, that's too damned fast!"

"Girl's gotta do what a girl's gotta do, Camila. Okay, I'm coming down the other side of the bridge and starting to slow now. I'll be turning onto Pondella and then coming back at you on 41/Edison. Will you be ready?"

"We'll be ready. We're still letting cars through right now, but as soon as you get close, we'll stop traffic right here in front of the jail. We've got three cars to block the road and three more on side streets near here. All of them are ready to close up the back door once the two of you get to the blockade. You just veer around us and get behind the roadblock then run into the jail complex. We'll take care of the people in the car. Do you know how many there are?"

"Not sure, Camila. I think two, but it's hard to make out detail through this little rearview mirror. Gotta focus now. I'm just about to turn onto 41 and I'll be starting over the Edison Bridge in fifteen seconds or so. I've still got a lead on him, but he's coming up behind me again. Get ready."

"We'll be ready."

I changed up through the gears again and by the time I started over the Edison Street Bridge I was once again traveling over 100. I wanted some distance on the car following, but not so much that he'd lose sight of me once I got back to Martin Luther and approached the jail complex. I ran the last few blocks through my head. As I came off the bridge the road turned into Fowler and I would have three sets of lights I'd have to contend with before turning right onto Martin Luther and the final stretch. I decided more distance between me and the car following would be prudent so before slowing I briefly accelerated again to about 120.

I got both the First and Second Street lights but didn't make the Thompson Street light and had to come to a complete stop with five cars ahead of me. The El Camino appeared in my rear view again like a tired apparition from an old horror movie. I carefully idled up between the two lanes of stopped of traffic so that I wouldn't be exposed to the El Camino as it came up behind me and edged between the stopped cars with just inches to spare. Drivers on both sides of me honked their horns and gave me the finger thinking I was trying jump the line. Once I was at the stop line, I put all my attention on the traffic crossing ahead of me hoping for a good enough gap between cars so that I could blow the intersection and get some distance on the following car. I saw a break, leaned as far forward as I could, and smoked the rear tire as I accelerated out into traffic.

I still had the Martin Luther light to get through, but I didn't expect difficulty there as it was a wider road and Saturday traffic was lighter than usual. I got that light with no traffic obstructing me and accelerated away, but before I could even get into 3rd gear, I had to stop again where Martin Luther crosses Thompson, Lee, and Central. He was still right behind me!

"Gino, where are you now?" Boyko asked.

"We're on the other side of the river coming back towards the city on the Edison Bridge still trying to catch up to her. Where are you?"

"We're in the Burger King parking lot near Martin Luther and Cleveland. Both of you totally blew past us."

"Okay we're back on the city side of the bridge and she's making a right onto Martin Luther. Looks like she's headed your way but there's no way anyone's going to be able to follow this girl without her knowing. She's totally amped and driving crazy."

"We'll watch for her. Maybe if she sees you drop off, she'll let her guard down and we can follow her."

"Maybe. Listen, I gotta focus right now. She's just in front of us stopped at the Central light. Damn! Scratch that. She blew the light and is headed your way. A block before I get to you guys, I'll turn off. Maybe you'll have better luck than me."

"K, bro; we're ready. Feed her to us."

I screamed up the next two blocks in about six seconds and started downshifting. I could see traffic stopped ahead at Camila's roadblock. I looked into my rearview again as I slowed. They were just a few hundred feet behind me and still hauling. They were obviously going to slam into me from behind. My only safety would be within the stopped cars, and I started weaving through them ahead of the El Camino.

Pedro skidded to a stop behind the stopped traffic and watched with frustration as Callie wove between stopped cars and alluded them again. He hit the wheel with his hand and spoke out loud so Boyko in the other car could hear.

214

"Boyko, traffic's backed up here for some reason and she just drove into the stopped cars. No way I can get her. Can you guys pick her up once she gets through all these cars on the other side?"

"I'm looking down the block towards you now. It looks like the police set up a roadblock. You two better get the hell out of there."

When Pedro heard the word "roadblock" it suddenly dawned on him that they were driving right into a trap.

"Gino, this is bad man!"

"What's bad?"

"All these cars are backed up because there's a roadblock up ahead. No way I can get caught up in something like that. I got all kinds of warrants out on me and ICE has a "hold" on me. If I get picked up, I'm facing life in prison or extradition. Fuck!"

Pedro jacked the shift into reverse. He turned his head backwards in time to watch two patrol cars skid to halt right behind him. He had nowhere to go! He threw the shift into Park, reached behind his back, and pulled out a Glock 9mm.

"Gotta go, bro, you're on your own." Pedro bailed out of the car.

Gino knew there were two cruisers right behind them and when Pedro pulled his gun, he suddenly wanted nothing to do with him and what was about to happen. He put his hands up as Pedro jumped out of the car and then, thinking again, quickly rolled down the passenger side window and put both of his hands out of the window praying that the cops wouldn't shoot him.

The moment Pedro was clear of the car he brought his pistol up, aimed at one of the officers, and pulled the trigger. Nothing happened; he didn't have a round chambered. He swore at his mistake, ducked around and then below the frame of his door long enough to pull the slide on his Glock and chamber a round. But, having made his intention clear when he'd first aimed and misfired, the cops were ready when he stood back up and started to take aim again. All three officers opened up on him at the same time and fired a total of forty-three rounds in less time than it took for the first brass to hit the ground. Seventeen of the rounds hit him. Gino looked on in terror as the bullets impacted his friend's body sounding like meat hitting a slab at a butcher's. Pedro looked as though he were dancing the jitterbug as the bullets tore into him from three slightly divergent angles. One of the last rounds impacted his forehead and blew the back of his skull out. He collapsed to the ground in a ragged heap.

I heard the unmistakable crackle of gunfire behind me. Even though I didn't know much about guns I knew that an incredible number of rounds had been fired in a very short amount of time. Obviously, the car that had been following me had engaged with the officers tasked with "closing the back door." I slowed my frenzied weaving through the stopped cars as I approached the roadblock. Camila came out to meet me with her firearm pulled, but at her side.

"You okay, Callie?"

I stopped, took off my helmet and nodded. "I'm good."

"Can you hang here? I've got to check and make sure the situation behind you is stable and under control."

"Like I said, I'm good."

Camila nodded then ran back towards where I'd come from in time to watch Gino with his hands on his head backing towards the officers who'd shot Pedro. They were predictably on edge from having already fired their weapons. The front of Gino's jeans were suddenly wet with urine reflecting his fear of being cut down like Pedro.

I got off Velocitá, put her up on the stand and looked behind me. Many of the stopped drivers I'd just weaved through had abandoned their cars at the sound of the gunfire and were running past me to the perceived safety of the roadblock. My heart was still racing, and I flashed on the two very different trips I'd made across the bridge that morning: one at 45mph soaking up the sun and watching the boats moving under the bridge with my heart full of gratitude. On the second and third bridge crossings I'd been traveling at speeds up to 128mph, laser-focused on traffic, the road, and a car behind me that was doing its absolute best to kill me.

I walked halfway back towards the El Camino. Despite there being a crowd of almost twenty police officers present and milling about, I got glimpses of Pedro's torn and bleeding body which was still laying in the street uncovered.

I'm not sure what I expected to see or feel, but seeing the young man ripped up by gunfire, was traumatic. The police had certainly been justified in their use of lethal force, but that didn't make it any easier to see. The lifestyle and life choices that the members of MS-13 made on a daily basis seemed absolutely pointless. Had the young man on the ground ever done or produced anything of value? Had he ever had any aspirations of creativity or tried to help another human being?

I looked over at the three officers who'd fired their weapons. All of them looked shell shocked. One was openly crying and the other two had lost, vacant expressions on their faces. Clearly reality was very different from the paper bad guys that they were used to shooting on the range.

I overheard a supervisor order the three of them to separate from each other, to make their weapons safe, and to then turn them in. I knew that separating the officers was to prevent them from coordinating a specific version of what had just happened in advance of the inevitable inquiry they would face. While I knew this was standard police procedure, it was sad because I could sense from the lost expressions on their faces that these same officers probably needed one another at that moment to process what had just occurred.

The adrenalin was still leaching out of me. I'd been fine during the most dangerous parts of the pursuit; focused, clear headed and sure of myself. The aftermath was very different though. Tears ran down my face and my hands were shaking.

"Callie."

I looked up into Camila's eyes. She instinctually knew I needed someone to lean on and put her arm around my shoulders. "What a stupid waste."

She nodded. "Let's you and I go back to the station. I need to get your statement. We can talk there."

"Okay." We started walking back in the direction of Velocitá.

"What just happened?" I asked her. "In a matter of seconds this whole morning went from being a beautiful, sunny day, to insanity!"

"The sewer overflowed. It happens. I honestly don't know, Callie. Half of these gangbangers never live to the age of thirty."

"It's just so sad."

"Yes, it is. You want to ride to the station with me? You're probably not in any condition to drive. I can get your bike transported over there."

"No, that doesn't make any sense. I'll drive it back. It's just three blocks."

"Okay. I'm glad you're all right. I'll meet you there."

My phone rang. Before answering it, I nodded my agreement to Camila and then after looking down at the caller ID, I answered.

"Hi, Stuart."

"Hi, Callie. I was just wondering if you still planned on coming by the dojo?"

I looked at the time and realized that I was likely to be tied up for hours answering questions and giving Camila my statement. Sparring was the last thing on my mind but knowing Stuart's shyness and insecurity I knew if I canceled, I'd probably shatter what little confidence he had.

"Yes, I'm still planning on it. Listen, Stuart, I can't really talk right now. I'm in the middle of something that I don't understand, and I might be tied up for an hour or more. Do you want to wait for me, or would you rather we just reschedule?"

"No, no; I'll wait. Are you okay?"

"I think so, but some really sad stuff just went down. I'll tell you all about it when I see you. And, Stuart…?"

"Yes."

"Thanks for understanding. I'm really looking forward to getting together with you."

I climbed onto Velocitá, did up my helmet, started her, and drove up on the curb to avoid all the stopped cars still choking Martin Luther and idled down Monroe towards the Widman Way Station. I passed a little parking lot on my left on the other side of the triangle formed by Monroe and Broadway.

"Do you know what happened to Pedro and Gino?" Diego asked.

"No, sorry. The girl saw them early on and they chased her over the river and back. They were going to feed her to Benicio and me and we were waiting at Cleveland and Martin Luther to follow her. Next thing we know they ended up stopped at a roadblock and then we heard gunfire. We're too far away to see anything, but I've tried calling both of their phones and I'm not getting an answer on either one. They just ring through to voicemail."

"Can you walk up there and see if you can see anything?"

"Yea, we can do that. Wait! Diego?"

"What?"

"The girl on the motorcycle just drove by us." As he spoke, Boyko started his car again, turned out of the parking lot and started to follow Callie.

"That fucking girl! What's she doing?" Diego screamed into his phone.

"Hang on, we're following her." Boyko kept his distance and watched as Callie idled up the street.

"She just parked on the side of the Widman Street Police Station, and it looks like she's walking in."

"Goddammit! Send Benicio up the street to see if he can find out what happened to Pedro and Gino. You stay right where you are until she comes out again. I want that girl! I don't care what you have to do but bring me that fucking girl!"

"Si, Jefe, we'll do our best."

"Your 'best' sucks!"

It took me over an hour to give a formal statement to Camila about what I'd observed and how the two men in the El Camino had followed me at reckless speeds likely trying to either kill or capture me. Pedro's criminal history, the warrants out against him and the fact that he'd actually fired a gun at police provided adequate cause for their use of deadly force, but just to be safe I think Camila also wanted reckless driving and attempted manslaughter on the record. The phone on her desk rang while I was still sitting in front of her.

"This is Camila." She nodded silently in agreement as she listened. "What about the one you have in custody, what's his name?" She scribbled on the pad in front of her and listened some more. "I get that, but I'm not the prosecutor. You'd have to run that by him. Put more pressure on him. Tell him you'll put him away for twenty years for being an accessory to the attempted murder of my witness. Okay!" She slammed down the phone.

"What happened?"

"Gino, the second man in the car, just lawyered up."

"That was quick."

"Quirk was still here and latched onto him as soon as they brought him into the jail."

"Did they ask whether he knows anything about the two missing thirteen-year-old girls?"

"They did. Mr. Quirk said that his client might have some information related to the missing girls, but that his client would require some 'consideration,' as he put it, before saying anything more. He's being very coy. I think Gino does know something about those girls, but he also knows if he rats out the gang, he'll need to completely disappear. Very few are willing to do that. These guys have no salable skills to survive outside the gang and they'd never see family or friends again. They'll also be marked for life. If they ever end up in custody again, they wouldn't last ten minutes inside. It makes it almost impossible to turn one of these people."

"Anything I can do?"

"I don't think so. You've got to be very careful though. We know these people are interested in shutting you up, so be extremely careful. If anything looks out of whack, call me immediately just like you did this morning. Can I give you a ride home or do you want me to call your family?"

"No, I'm good, Camila. I'm going to my friend Eva's dojo right now. I'll be safe there. Would you please call me if you hear anything more about the two schoolgirls?"

She nodded her assent. "Be careful."

Chapter 21

I felt burnt out and shaky as I drove the four minutes to Eva's dojo. I kept thinking about the dead gangbanger's body on the ground bleeding out onto the pavement and failed to note the electric blue Monte Carlo that followed me from a discreet distance. It never occurred to me that MS-13 would already have another car following me so quickly after what had happened to the green El Camino. When I got to Dick's Sporting Goods plaza, I parked off the service road in back and went into the Dojo through the back door.

Boyko followed, giving Callie plenty of room. He watched as she entered the parking lot at Dick's, stayed left and then turned right onto the service road behind all the stores. He waited a few seconds before following her around to the backside of the building. She seemed in no particular hurry and was driving as though this were her destination. He expected to see her taillight once he made the turn and was surprised when he looked down the access road. She was nowhere in sight. "Mierda (shit)! Where has the little puta gone?"

"No way she could have made it all the way to the end of this road in the short time we waited. She must be somewhere along here. You look ahead, I'll watch the side," Benicio suggested.

Boyko didn't have to drive far. As they passed the rear entrance doors at the southern end of Dick's, Benicio called out. "Right there! She's parked behind the dumpster right over there. I just saw her going in the back door."

"You think she works here?"

"I don't know. The door she went in didn't have a sign on it, but it didn't look like Dick's. Let's drive around front, look through the windows and see what business is next to Dick's."

Boyko drove around to the front of the building and then slowly past the commercial space abutting Dick's. The printing on the glass said, "Pilates by Laurie and Eva's Krav Maga."

"What the heck are Pilates and Krav Maga?" Benicio asked.

"Fuck if I know. Let's park and look in the window. She doesn't know us."

Boyko parked and the two of them slowly walked by the windows and peered in. There were ten women on mats, all in spandex, doing some sort of isometric pose while facing a mirrored rear wall.

"I guess it's some sort of women's fitness place. Let's just go in the back door she went through and snatch her. We've got masks and these women don't look like they'll be any kind of problem."

Benicio nodded and smiled. "Diego and Esteban will be very pleased if we bring the little puta back to the clubhouse."

They returned to the car, drove around back again, and parked their car on the side of the building next to the dumpster Callie was parked behind.

Eva's half of the space was in the rear half of the shared unit behind the mirrored wall, and not visible from the front. It did not appear nearly as benign as Laurie's space. If Boyko and Benicio had been equipped with X-ray vision when they'd looked in the front windows, they would have seen four pairs of very fit students in full MMA fighting gear all sparring one another and grappling or throwing each other to the floor as they worked on their fighting styles. They also would have seen three sparring dummies, racks of wooden fighting staffs, and very realistic looking rubber guns and knives used in simulated attacks.

When I came in the back door at Eva's, I saw her and Stuart talking in the corner. There were also six of my fellow students out in the middle of the floor working on their throws and holds. I put my helmet down and hung up my coat before joining Stuart and Eva.

"Hi, guys. What a day."

Eva reached out to me as I approached. "Stuart told me that something bad happened to you, but he didn't know what it was. Are you okay?"

"Yeh, I'm okay, but there's some really screwed-up stuff going on right now. That detective called me this morning to come down and identify the guy with the machete who almost got Karen and me. She also told me that the two boys I put down saving Karen were found by some fishermen Wednesday night in the river. Both had been shot and had their heads cut off."

"What!"

"Then, when I left the police station earlier to come here, a car started following me. I'd seen it yesterday and ditched them, but today they got way more aggressive. They were going to either run me down or at least run me off the road."

"What'd you do?" Stuart asked.

"I called the detective back using my Bluetooth phone and then led this car on a crazy chase through downtown and then twice over the river going over 120mph to give Detective Sanchez enough time to get a roadblock set up. Then I suckered the car into following me into the trap they'd set up on Martin Luther."

"Callie, that's crazy!"

"There's more. Once I suckered them into the roadblock there was a gun battle and one of the men in the car was killed by the police."

Neither said a word for several seconds. It all sounded so unlikely. A few tears leaked out of my eyes and Eva leaned in and wrapped me up in a big hug and Stuart put his hand on my shoulder.

After a few seconds of their sympathy I started to feel ridiculous, like I was some sort of crybaby, and disentangled myself. I wiped my face. "Sorry, it freaked me out is all."

Boyko parked next to the dumpster in back blocking the little girl's motorcycle in. Benicio reached in the glove compartment and pulled out two tubular, cloth, sun masks. Boyko's was a colorful, caricatured clown face with monstrous teeth. Benicio's resembled the face of a black and white tiger sticking an oversize tongue out. They pulled them over their heads onto their necks and then pulled them back up so that the masks covered their mouths and noses. Boyko reached behind his back and withdrew a chrome 1911, .45. Benicio reached under the seat and took out a short, ugly, eighteen-inch machete.

"Boo!" Boyko joked.

Benicio held up the machete in mock surrender. "Oh, you're scaring me, man." They both laughed. "Vamanos, my scary friend. This should be muy fácil (very easy). I can't wait to see Diego's face when we bring the girl back tied up like a little piglet in the backseat."

The rear fire door slammed shut.

"What the hell!" Eva said after turning towards the sound of the fire-door slamming.

Stuart and I turned as well. "You're kidding me," I mumbled.

The other six students in the room also sensed the intrusion, stopped their sparring, and also turned towards the two masked characters with weapons at the rear of the room.

Boyko was sharper than people gave him credit for and quickly took in the fact that everyone in the room (with the exception of the little girl) were wearing black cotton Gi's with different-colored belts. Half of the eight people were men and all but three were also wearing either headgear and/or MMA fighting gloves. He looked around the room and took in the fighting staffs, the life-size, flesh-colored, anatomically correct sparring dummies, and the heavy bags hanging from the ceiling. "What the fuck?" he said out loud.

Benicio started to get it also. They had both expected to find a group of scantily clad women in an exercise class. He held the machete aloft in a threatening manner. "Everybody down on the floor!"

None of Eva's students moved at first, looked towards her for guidance. She made several "down" gestures with her hand and started to walk towards the two intruders in a non-threatening manner. The six students all got down on the floor. Stuart and I remained standing and stationary on the side of the room.

In as non-threatening a voice as she could muster, Eva asked, "What's going on here, guys? If this a robbery of some sort I think you came in the wrong door. Dick's is one door down. We don't sell anything here. I don't even have a cash register."

The one with the gun pointed it at her head. "Sit the fuck down on the floor now, you perra estúpida (stupid bitch)! This isn't a robbery. A certain man is anxious to meet the little motorcycle girl over there." He nodded his head towards me. "None of you need to get hurt if the little bitch comes with us."

Eva stopped advancing towards them and held her hands up. "Easy, I'm just saying I think you might have made a mistake." She advanced a little bit more to within six feet of him. I knew what was about to happen if she got just a little closer. I'd watched her do it 100 times. Her right hand would start moving from right to left and her left hand would move from left to right, but it would happen at blinding speed. She would simultaneously slap his wrist with her right hand while grabbing the gun barrel with her left. Then she would twist the gun inwards towards him, break his trigger finger and take control of the weapon.

If she weren't able to get close enough to do that, I expected she would feign compliance with his order to get down on the floor and then launch from a half crouch, sweep his gun hand outwards with her left hand and palm strike him in the face with her right. After, there was no telling what she would do to the man. But she had to get a little closer.

He surprised us all when he fired his gun into the mat at her feet. The concussive sound of the .45 was terrifying in the small space and Eva stopped her advance.

I didn't know how or when, but I'd watched Eva for long enough to know that this was not over yet. She would never just lie down on the floor and comply. Somehow, in some way, she was going to take offensive action in the next few seconds, and I started to plan the moves I would make to back her up and neutralize the second man with the machete, while she dealt with the gunman. I knew the fighting-staff rack was three feet behind me.

In the background I heard the women on the other side of the wall cry out at the sound of the gunshot and flee into the parking lot. I was certain they'd call the cops, but it would take them several minutes to respond.

"Bitch, I told you to get down on the floor."

"Eva pretended to cower and shrink as if she were going to comply and actually moved her feet another eight inches forward as she started down towards a crouch. She raised her hands higher from shoulder height which effectively got them closer to the gunman. I turned my head ever so slightly verifying my distance and angle to the fighting staffs.

225

Eva spoke again as she started downwards. "I'm sorry, I'm sorry. Please don't hurt me."

The gunman started moving towards her, assuming abeyance. He was likely planning on standing over her with the gun which would free the other to control the rest of the room with his machete.

I got ready.

With her headed towards the floor, the one with the gun let his eyes move briefly towards Stuart and me. The gun remained pointed at Eva.

I had absolute confidence that once Eva moved, the gunman would no longer be in play. The challenge would be to neutralize machete man before he could strike her. The instant I saw Eva's muscles bunch, I started my turn for the staff rack. The one variable I had not factored into my plan, however, was Stuart, and at the same instant I started my turn and step towards the rack, Stuart did exactly the same thing and the two of us crashed into one another.

Eva came up from the floor like a heat seeking missile at the precise moment Stuart and I started our respective turns. Her timing and her aim were flawless. She wasn't quite close enough to take the gunman's gun from him on her first strike, but she did manage to get inside his gun arm before he could fire, swept it to the side, and she got in two forearm strikes: one to his nose and the second to his trachea.

Stuart and I quickly recovered from our collision. I grabbed one staff, he grabbed another and the two of us wheeled simultaneously towards "machete man" with upraised staffs. We each then took two steps. If someone had been filming us, it would have looked like we'd practiced together for years and were following a precise, choreographed script.

After her disabling strikes to the gunman's face and neck Eva grabbed the barrel of the gun and violently twisted it free, breaking his trigger finger. He fell to the floor unable to breathe from the throat strike.

The man wielding the machete raised it into the air in advance of taking a swing at Eva. She was still disarming the gunman as Stuart and I both swung downwards simultaneously with our heavy, hardwood staffs on either side of machete man's head from behind, fracturing both of his collar bones. The sound the staffs made as they made contact was a loud and distinct crack and he fell to the mat howling in pain.

With both men on the floor and incapacitated, Eva casually picked up the gun, press-checked it for a round, and then held it on the two of them while we waited for the police to arrive. Stuart and I looked at each other a little shellshocked at our role in the violence and then down at the gang member we'd taken out. He was writhing in agony on the floor but pointedly took the time to look up at both of us with visceral hate in his eyes. Without thinking I put my arm around Stuart's waist, and he put his arm around mine.

"Enjoy your time together while you can," the gangster taunted. "Diego will not rest until both of you are dead and in pieces."

RIP CONVERSE

Chapter 22

The police started to arrive three minutes later in response to the panicked calls of the Pilates students. Eva took the lead in answering their questions after both gang members were taken away in ambulances. I took a moment to call Detective Sanchez.

"Camila, it's Callie."

"Hi, what's up?"

"They came after me again. Two more men followed me from the jail and then tried to kidnap me from my friend Eva's dojo."

"I heard a call about shots fired somewhere on South Cleveland. That was you?"

"It was them. I don't know what they were thinking, but several other gang members must have followed me from the jail and then in through the back door of Eva's dojo. They had masks, a gun, and a machete. Who would be stupid enough to try and kidnap someone from a studio full of martial arts people?"

"MS-13 is bold for sure, but they've never been known for their brilliance. I take it from the fact that I'm talking to you that it didn't go so well for them."

"No, Eva my teacher, took the gun from one of them, broke his finger, his nose and almost crushed his trachea. My friend Stuart and I took out the other one out and broke both his collar bones. The reason I called is that I figured you'd probably want to question them once they get released from the hospital and are brought to the jail. They might know something about the missing girls."

"They might. Once they're booked, I'll go over and have a chat with them. The one we have in custody who chased you earlier, Gino, is going to be easier to pressure though because he's got 'accessory to attempted murder of a police officer' hanging over his head."

"Any progress on getting him to talk?"

"Not yet. He's meeting with that lawyer Quirk again now. Dammit!"

"Why're they so hot on getting me?"

"I suspect a big part of it is that you've caused them to lose face. Even though we can't prosecute Esteban on your word alone for trying to kidnap Karen, you did beat two of them up when they tried to kidnap her, Gino's in custody, and another one is dead as a direct result of going after you. And now, two more are under arrest for trying to kidnap you at your friends' dojo. Damn!"

"You said that already."

"I know, I'm frustrated. You've stirred up the whole hive and just because we have a couple of them locked up doesn't mean they're going to stop coming after you. I'm so sorry that this is happening to you Callie."

I was silent for a few seconds as I thought. "I am too. I was just trying to do the right thing. I never thought it would become such a big thing."

"Listen, we're going to have to release Esteban later today unless Karen magically turns up and agrees to testify against him, and that's looking less and less likely. I hate to say it, but I think you need to stay close to home and avoid downtown and places like the dojo for a few days."

I thought about her suggestion. What she was saying made sense. "Yes, I can skip coming to the dojo for a few days. I've got a ton of college-related stuff to do this week anyway and the following week I'm going to Boston to look at colleges."

"That's all good. These attempts the gang has been making on you have a reckless almost desperate feel to them and I've got a feeling that things are coming to a head. If we can get Gino or one of the others to flip, we might be able to break the back of the entire gang."

"I hope you can; I don't like being a target."

"Stay out of downtown and other places you normally frequent and call me anytime, especially if you are threatened again."

"I will, Camila, thanks." I pressed "End" disturbed at the whole idea of being a target.

"Who was that?" Stuart asked after I ended the call.

"The detective I've been working with. Hey, Stuart?" I asked wanting to change the subject.

"What?"

"That was pretty cool that you gamed out what Eva was going to do and when she was going to do it and how we both grabbed staffs and went after the one with the machete at the same time. You're good!"

Stuart smiled broadly at me. "You're not so bad yourself."

I smiled back and touched his arm. "Thanks."

There was a slightly uncomfortable pause before he spoke again. "Callie, can I ask you something a little weird?"

I thought about his question for a second dreading whatever it was that he expected I'd find weird. What had just happened was weird enough and I was hoping he wasn't going to ask me some off the wall personal question.

"What?" I asked tentatively.

"Do you like flying?"

I cocked my head to the side wondering what on earth he was thinking. "You're right, that is a weird question, especially considering what just happened."

"I'm sorry, I knew I shouldn't have asked."

I waited, but he didn't say anything. "You can't *not* ask now. What is it?"

"I'm a pilot is all and when I've got a lot on my mind and simply want to check out and unwind, I go flying. I was wondering if you'd like to go up with me."

I didn't say anything for a few seconds wondering if he was pulling my leg. "For real?" I finally managed. "You're a real pilot?"

"Yes, for real. My dad's a flight instructor and I've been flying since I was fourteen. I soloed when I was fifteen and got my license a year ago."

"You're not just messing with me?"

He nodded his head and then quickly shook it, taking back the first gesture.

"I mean 'no', I'm not messing with you and 'yes', I'm serious about being a pilot."

"That is so cool. I'd love to! When?"

Stuart pointed towards the rear wall. "Right now, right here, from Page Field. We could literally jump the fence out back, but my father's flight school is on the other side of the airport, so we should drive. They wouldn't like us walking across the runways."

I punched his arm lightly. "I'm in, let's do it!"

"I'm never sure what planes are available, but I'm checked out in the Cessna 150s, 172s and also the Citabria. My dad owns all of them. I can take any of them as long as they aren't booked. I just have to pay for the gas."

"I don't want to leave Velocitá here with all that's happened. Can I follow you?"

Stuart nodded. "Sure."

"What are you driving?"

"A red Jeep." He pointed towards the front of the building. "I'm parked in front."

"I'll meet you at the end of the access road."

He nodded and walked away towards the front of the building and turned back once and looked at me as I quickly gathered up my helmet, jacket, and knapsack.

Eva was still talking with a policeman, but I caught her attention and held a closed fist up to the side of my face simulating a telephone. She got what I was trying to tell her and mirrored my gesture back at me, then quickly turned back to the officer questioning her.

I went out the back door wondering if what I was about to do was a little crazy. It was, but I didn't care. Before getting on Velocitá I looked over the electric blue Monte Carlo closely, memorizing it. The police hadn't yet towed it. I took Velocitá off the stand, walked her back clear of the car and the dumpster, and started her up. Before leaving I carefully looked over the surrounding area for any other signs of surveillance. Seeing none, I accelerated up the service road to the corner of the building. Stuart was already there and after giving me a little wave, he pulled away. I followed him onto Fowler and then Airport Road. His father's flight school was just two minutes from there.

CALLIE AWAKENS

After parking, I followed Stuart inside to meet his father who was seated at the front desk. He smiled warmly at me as we approached and stood up. "Hi, Stuart, who's this?"

"Hi, Dad. This is Callie. She's a friend of mine from Eva's school. Callie, this is my father Court."

Court was slightly taller than Stuart, had dark black hair with some grey coming in on the sides and looked quite fit. Stuart and he shared a lot of the same features and I realized that once Stuart finished growing and was out of his awkward teenage phase, that he would likely turn into as attractive man as his father.

"Hello, Mr. Alexander, it's a pleasure to meet you, sir." I looked him in the eye, held out my hand and shook his.

"You can call me Court if you're comfortable with that. I know I'm getting older, but I don't feel as old as I look."

"You don't look old, you look experienced."

He laughed. "I'll have to remember that one, Callie."

"I have an aunt your age that I'm close to. She straightened me out about using terms like Sir and Ma'am. She says that people in their forties are at a 'delicate' age, as she puts it, and often don't like to be reminded of their advancing years."

"I bet I'd like her. She sounds very astute." He turned back towards Stuart. "What's going on with you two?"

"I asked Callie if she'd like to go flying, Dad. Is anything available?"

Court looked down at the schedule on the desktop. "It's pretty open. You can take 78November, 97Juliet or WhiskyPappa3. 89Hotel, SamSam40 and your favorite, are all flying."

"We'll take 78November if that's okay."

"That's fine; just have her back by 5:00. I've got a lesson in her then."

"I will, I'll make sure we're back in plenty of time."

Court handed Stuart a clipboard and a key, then turned to me. "Callie, it was a pleasure meeting you. I hope we'll see you again."

"Thanks, Court. Nice meeting you as well. Would it be all right if I left my helmet with you? I'm hoping I won't need it with Stuart flying."

He laughed. "No, you won't need it, Stuart's a great pilot. Just put it back here behind the desk."

I did as he suggested and then followed Stuart out onto the tarmac, and then over to a small red and white, two-door, high-wing airplane. It had N5978N written on the tail. I figured this was 78November. "How come your father and you called it 78November and not 78N?"

"Pilots use a phonetic alphabet. It helps avoid miscommunication. The letter 'N' sounds a lot like 'M', so we say November instead of N."

"What do you say for the letter M?"

"Mike."

"How about A and B?"

"Alpha and Bravo. You learn them pretty quick."

Stuart pointed to the two lines tied to the wings. Can you undo this one? I'll get the one on the other side."

I nodded and untied the line from the ring on the bottom of the wing. Stuart undid the one on his side and then came back over, opened the right-hand door, put the key in the ignition and checked some gauges on the dashboard. Then he turned the key back off and climbed down.

"What were you doing?" I asked.

"Checking the fuel gauges."

Then he got a small ladder off the side of a fuel truck parked nearby, removed what I assumed was the gas cap on the top of the wing and peered inside. He put the cap back on and then repeated the same thing on the other side of the plane.

"Aren't you curious what I'm doing now?" he asked.

"Nope, I think I figured it out already."

"Really."

"Yup. I do the same thing on the ferry I work on."

"What ferry?"

"I work on the commercial ferry that runs between Boca Grande and Marco Island. One of my responsibilities is engine maintenance and my boss Melissa always says, 'trust but verify.' Gauges are nice, but they aren't infallible so it's always a good idea to verify your fuel. I stick the tanks on the ferry every morning before we leave."

Stuart smiled. "You're full of surprises. Do you ever get to drive the ferry?"

"I do, but I don't have my license yet so Melissa or another captain still has to be on the boat when I'm driving. I need more sea time to qualify for the license I want to get."

"How much more?"

"You need a total of 360 four-hour or more days at sea to get an inland ticket. It's good to ten miles offshore and all inland waters."

"Wow, that's a lot of time. You only need forty hours to get a pilot's license. I soloed an airplane after just eight hours."

I was surprised by his statement. "You're kidding."

"No, serious."

I thought about what he'd said and watched as he walked around the entire airplane touching and moving surfaces and then he opened the engine compartment, looked it over carefully and checked the oil level.

"The engine's really clean," I noted.

"It is. It gets completely torn down every 100 hours of engine time."

"We keep the engines on the ferry really clean too. It's easier to spot oil leaks."

"Same with these."

"Mine are bigger than yours though." I smiled at him when I said it.

"Oh yeah? How big?"

"Turbocharged twelve cylinders; they produce about 900 hp apiece."

"Monsters! This little engine is only four cylinders and it's just 160 hp. I bet your ferry doesn't fly though."

"About as well as your plane floats."

"Okay, you win. Despite my horsepower deficiency, I've got a feeling you're really going to like this. You've never been up in any kind of a plane?"

"Nope."

"Nervous?"

"Not yet."

"Okay then, climb in and we'll go flying."

"Where do I sit?"

"Co-pilots sit on the right side of the plane. The pilot sits in the left seat."

It really was my first time flying, and I didn't feel scared; just excited. From the moment we'd gotten to the plane, Stuart had been like a different person; serious, knowledgeable, and confident; his painful shyness forgotten. This was obviously his element and something he was extremely comfortable with. That in turn gave me confidence.

We got in and after putting on our seatbelts he handed me a headset with a built-in microphone. "Go ahead and put these on. This will enable you to hear everything I hear and also make it possible for us to talk back and forth over the sound of the engine."

I nodded, put them on, and then watched as he started the airplane. There were various knobs he pushed in and pulled out before actually turning the key. Right before he did, he opened the window on his side and loudly called out, "Clear prop!" and then turned the key.
The engine started right up.

As it warmed up, he checked the fuel gauges again, oil pressure, altimeter, and a host of other things. Then he tuned one of the radios to 123.725 and we listened to something call ATIS which had the local weather for Page Field and other information. He listened twice and then changed the frequency of the radio to 121.7 and pressed a button on the wheel.

"Page field ground, this is Skyhawk 5978November at Left Coast Aviation. We'd like to taxi to the active. We have information hotel and will be Eastbound."

"78November, Page Field Ground. You are cleared to taxi to runway 5 via taxiway alpha. Contact Tower on 119.0 for departure clearance."

"Page Field Ground, 78November, taxi to 5 via taxiway alpha, will contact tower on 119.0 for departure clearance."

Stuart briefly pressed down on the tops of the foot pedals and then advanced the throttle knob on the dash forward. The engine speed increased, and we started moving forward. Once he was going about 10mph he pulled the throttle back a little and the engine rpm decreased slightly. I noticed he kept us lined up with the yellow line and as we made our first turn, that the plane turned without him ever touching the wheel.

"How did you do that?" I asked over the headset. "You never touched the wheel."

"When you're on the ground you steer using the rudder pedals and the brakes. The brakes for the airplane are also in the same pedals. If you press down on the tops of the pedals you can activate one or both brakes simultaneously. Turning the wheel controls the ailerons which control the bank of the airplane and pushing the wheel in or out controls the elevators which make to plane head up or down. Once we're in the air I'll let you try all these things, so you can feel what each of them does. You can put your feet lightly on the pedals right now if you like. Feel how much I have to move them as we taxi to the runway."

I did as he suggested marveling at all the information he seemed to process at once. We stopped short of the runway, he turned the plane into the wind, set the parking brakes with his feet, then pushed the throttle in until the rpm indicator read 1,800 rpm. The plane buffeted from the wind coming off the propellor. He looked at the checklist in his hand and then turned the ignition key two clicks left from the "Both" position, to "Right Mag," watched the rpm gauge and listened to the engine, then briefly turned it back to "Both" and then turned it back just one click left to the "Left Mag" position and once again listened to the engine and watched our tachometer. After a few seconds he returned the key to the "Both" position and scanned all his instruments again checking oil pressure, vacuum pressure, amperes, fuel flow, artificial horizon and heading indicator. Then he moved the throttle back to idle and checked control surfaces for freedom of movement by turning the wheel from side and pushing it in and out. The last thing he did was adjust a little wheel between our seats to "Takeoff position."

"What was all that business turning the key and listening to the engine?" I asked.

"Each cylinder has two spark plugs and two magnetos. Car engines just have one. I was checking to make sure that both were functioning properly."

"Why are there two?"

"Redundancy; if one fails for any reason, you have a backup."

I pointed to the small wheel he'd rotated. "What does that one do?"

"That's a trim tab control. It controls the attitude of the plane, so I don't have to pull or push the wheel too hard when we initially leave the runway."

"How do you remember all this stuff, Stuart?"

He shrugged. "Repetition I guess." Then he held up his checklist, "And this," he added. "Even if you're an experienced pilot it helps a lot to have a checklist to remind you to do everything, every time, and in the proper order."

I knew what he meant about repetition, and I thought back to the first few times I'd taken *Gulf Runner* off the dock. I was amazed at the similarities between the two very different conveyances shared. He was operating in air. I operated in water. Despite that, the two craft were similar in many ways.

Stuart taxied forward to a line just short of the runway, adjusted the frequency on his radio to 119.0, and called the tower.

"Page Field Tower, Skyhawk 5978November holding short of runway 5 ready for takeoff."

"Cessna 78November, Page Field Tower, you are cleared for takeoff. Fly runway heading."

"Roger tower, 78November cleared for takeoff runway 5 flying runway heading."

Stuart taxied out onto the runway, lined the plane up with the centerline, and then pushed the throttle in to the max setting. I watched closely as our speed down the runway built. He had one hand on the throttle and the other loosely on the wheel. His attention seemed to go back and forth between the runway center line and his airspeed indicator. When our speed reached sixty knots on the airspeed indicator, he started applying light back pressure on the wheel, the nose lifted, and we were suddenly flying! I was ecstatic. I looked out over one wing and then the other not really believing what was happening. We were in the sky, flying!

"Stuart, this is so cool!"

He smiled broadly but still kept his attention on the airspeed indicator. I noticed that he seemed to have settled on a speed of 65-70 knots as we continued to climb. Several times he reached over to the trim tab wheel without even looking down and made several adjustments. He still seemed very intensely focused on what he was doing, and I didn't want to distract him. Once we'd gained several thousand feet of altitude, he reduced the engine rpm, trimmed the nose down to straight and level and spoke with the tower again several times.

Within minutes were away from congested, densely populated Fort Myers and over an endless green savannah that stretched east, as far as we could see. There were occasional houses visible, but it was almost entirely cultivated fields and cattle ranches.

I sat, looking out the window at the ground below. "I had no idea how empty of people it is just ten miles east of town. It's beautiful."

I didn't say anything for several minutes, blown away by the fact that we were floating thousands of feet above the ground. I looked over at Stuart several times. He was incredibly relaxed and made flying the airplane look very simple; a sharp contrast to the shy, seemingly insecure teen he was on the ground. Who would ever have guessed that this confident side of him existed?

"What a surprise you are, Stuart."

"Thanks, Callie. I'm glad you were willing to try this; not everyone would have been willing."

"It's like there's this other person living in you. It's a nice surprise."

He was quiet for a few moments. "I'm thinking that we might fly to Immokalee Regional Airport which is southeast of here and do a couple of touch-and-go landings there. Sound good?"

I nodded.

"Aren't you curious what a 'touch-and-go' is?"

I smiled knowingly recalling Mellissa using the same phrase when she described what we would be doing the day she'd taught me how to dock Gulf Runner.

"I think I know. Is it where we land the airplane, but don't actually stop?"

Stuart nodded. "As soon as all three wheels are on the ground, we'll increase speed and take off again. How'd you guess?"

"When my boss taught me how to land the ferry, we did the same thing."

"Before I teach you to land though, I've got to teach you to fly. Would you like to try it?"

"Absolutely!"

"Great. The first thing I want to show you and have you get comfortable at are simple turns and ascending and descending. Put your hands on the wheel and your feet on the rudder pedals. We'll do a nice gentle left hand turn first. You want to try and maintain a consistent altitude when you turn. I'll show you first; then you do each thing I just did. Before turning the airplane always look around the plane before you start turning to make sure there aren't any other planes in the area." He looked left and then the right before beginning the maneuver then started by banking the airplane to the left using the wheel. I could feel it in my feet as he also added some left rudder using the rudder pedal. I also noted that he added backpressure on the yoke as our turn progressed. Then he returned the wings to level and did the same thing to the right. I noticed that the sharper we banked on each side, he also had to pull back on the wheel more. Throughout his demonstration the altimeter never varied more than fifty feet up or down.

"You try it now."

I looked out both sides of the plane to check for other traffic then started turning the wheel gently to the left. The plane responded instantly and once I felt like I was at the same angle of bank as he'd been, I held the wheel steady. "How's this?"

"Your angle of bank is good, but see how your altitude is starting to drop?"

I nodded after looking at the altimeter.

"You need to add more backpressure on the wheel. When you turn an airplane, you increase its drag through the air. The steeper the bank the more you have to pull back on the wheel."

I added more back pressure on the wheel, as he'd suggested, and maintained my bank. The altimeter started to climb back towards 5,000 feet.

"Excellent. Now add a little more left rudder to get the ball back in the center of the turn and slip indicator. Whatever side of the instrument the ball goes to indicates you need to add more rudder on that side. So, if the ball is left of center, add left rudder till it comes back to the center. If it's to the right, add right rudder."

I did as he instructed totally absorbed in the process of coordinating a turn in three dimensions instead of the two, I was accustomed to. My eyes danced back and forth between the horizon, the altimeter and the turn and slip indicator.

"Okay, you're doing great, Callie. Now bring it back straight and level and then try a right-hand turn."

He had me do a few more turns and then got me used to ascending and descending at constant rates by pushing the wheel inwards or pulling it out and adding or taking away power. I also got used to using the trim tab and coordinating the throttle with the pitch of my nose. It was intense and I found myself sweating from trying to do so many things at once and keeping everything in balance. It was difficult, but I totally loved it. I got frustrated a few times because I couldn't do something perfectly, but even in that first hour I could sense improvement and knew absolutely that I wanted to get a flying license.

"How much does it cost to take lessons, Stuart?"

"It depends on what plane you're using."

"Let's say it's this one."

"My dad charges $240/hour for this plane. That includes the plane rental, instructor and fuel."

"And how many of your forty hours have to be with an instructor?"

"It varies slightly from student to student, but I'd guess about twenty of the forty hours."

"So about $4,800 for instructed time. How much is it to just rent the plane per hour?"

"This plane is $175/hour."

"So total, it costs what, maybe $8,000 to get a license?"

"That's about right. You'll probably want to do a ground school course for $600 and the actual flight exam with the FAA inspector runs $400. Everybody's different. I can tell already that you'll be at the low end of the cost range by how quickly you're absorbing this."

I smiled at the compliment. I didn't have $8,000 but I'd find a way.

"Ready to try some takeoffs and landings?" he asked.

I nodded, absolutely beaming. I couldn't remember a time, ever, that I had had so much fun doing something with another person. Stuart had a lot more going for him that I'd originally thought. The process of learning something new was a key of sorts to my heart.

He talked to the tower at Immokalee and set us up for our first touch-and-go, then coached me all the way through three approaches and three touch-and-go landings. He had to take the controls from me on the first landing because I flared too early, but I was able to touch the plane down on my own for the next two, without killing us.

After we finished there, we flew back to Fort Myers. He coached me through a landing there too. By the time we taxied to his father's hanger, set the parking brakes, and turned off the engine, I was completely hooked.

As we walked from the plane to the front desk, I almost skipped across the tarmac.

"You really liked it didn't you?"

"Oh, you think?"

As we walked back to the flight center, I realized that not once during our flight had I thought about MS-13 and all the negative things that had transpired over the past few days. I was really grateful to Stuart for having taken me away from it all to the other magical world that this shy, nervous boy had surprised me with.

I stopped outside before we went into the office, turned, and looked up at him. "Thank you so much for that, Stuart. That was one of the most exciting things I've ever done." Then I reached up, pulled his head down towards mine, and gave him a chaste kiss on the cheek. We maintained eye contact after, and I watched him turn bright red. "You're a very sweet guy and I'm grateful."

"Would you like to go up again soon?"

I think he'd surprised himself with his question. "I mean if you're not doing something else more important of course."

There was that shy, insecure kid again. "I'll fly with you anytime, Stuart. You call and I'll be here before you can hang up the phone."

Court looked up as we walked back into the flight center. "Well… what'd you think, Callie?"

"I've decided to marry your son. Are you free next weekend?"

Court laughed out loud. Stuart looked like he was going to burst into flames he was blushing so hard.

"You hated it; I knew you would."

"It was so awful that I'm thinking of taking flying lessons! How can you not be permanently excited about what you do, Court? If I could afford it, I don't think I'd walk on the ground again!"

"Well you've certainly got the right attitude to be a pilot. How'd she do, Stuart?"

"She's a natural, Dad. Never met someone who picked up coordinated turns so quickly. And her landings at Immokalee were great except for the first one which was more like an arrival than a landing, but we've all had those."

I gave Stuart a playful punch on the arm. He shrank back with a smile.

"I mean, they were all perfect. She's a natural, really. In the summer Callie works on a ferry and does engine maintenance and also gets to drive it sometimes."

"I'm impressed, Callie."

"I was actually serious about taking lessons, Court. Do you have some sort of beginner's book I can buy on flying that particular plane?"

"I sure do, and friends of Stuart's get the fifty-percent family discount."

That was a huge discount. "You don't have to do that, sir. I can afford full price."

"I want to. Sometimes I meet people that I just know have the right attitude to be good pilots and I'm guessing you're one of those people. If I'm lucky maybe, you'll choose me to be your instructor."

I walked around behind the counter, reached into my knapsack, and took out my wallet. "How much is it?"

"Were you serious about taking lessons?"

I nodded. "Totally."

"Then I would suggest you buy this beginner's course. It's a little more expensive than just a book on the plane, but you'd have to get it for ground school anyway. It includes a flight bag, 5 cd roms, flight computer and logbook, and includes classes on everything from communications and flight to sample tests for your exam."

"That's the one."

"It's $200," then he quickly added, "but with your discount it comes to $100."

I hadn't intended to spend that much, but I realized if it really had everything I needed to get a license in it, that it was a deal. I looked in my wallet dismayed to see only $80. "I'll have to pick it up another time; I've only got $80 on me."

He handed it across the counter to me. Don't be silly. Just give me the $20 difference next time you're in.

"Are you sure?"

"Absolutely."

I took the package off the counter with my left hand and reached over with my right hand to shake his. "Thanks, Court, see you soon I hope."

Outside, after I put the student flight package in my knapsack, I turned to Stuart again. "I'm going to be around the next couple of weeks, but Detective Sanchez suggested I avoid downtown and the dojo for a while since MS-13 knows I frequent there. I'm also trying to get applications in and set-up some college interviews for the week of the 9th through the 17th. I'm going up to Boston that week with my Aunt Nancy and want to look at some schools up there while we're up there. I'm telling you all this just because I don't want you thinking I'm avoiding you if you don't see much of me for the next couple of weeks. I would love to go flying again with you and maybe take my first lesson with your dad, but the next couple of weeks are going to be busy."

I could see the disappointment on his face over what I'd just told him. "I had a really nice time with you today, Callie."

"It was really special for me as well, thanks for asking me."

I liked his choice of words and squeezed his hand. "Later."

I pulled on my helmet, started Velocitá, and took off across the parking lot with a little more speed than was necessary.

Stuart watched me disappear down the main road before walking back into the flight school. His father was standing just inside the door. He'd been watching the two of us.

"That is some girl, son."

"Yeah, no kidding."

Chapter 23

S unday morning, Diego set a glass of ice water with a straw in it on his mother's bedside table, then pulled the sheet up farther and tucked it under her chin. He gently swept a stray strand of hair off her face and tucked it behind her ear. When he withdrew his hand, the hair came away in it. Most of her hair was gone from the chemo she'd been going through.

He'd been nursing her and cleaning her up for days. She'd gotten sick to her stomach and had diarrhea the previous night and he'd had to change the sheets twice. After brushing the hair off on his pant leg, he looked down into her face. Her skin was a whitish/blue and hung listlessly. She had sores on her tongue and inside her lips from the chemo and because it was so painful for her to eat and take pills, he'd been giving her anti-nausea suppositories. When it was first suggested to him by the visiting nurse, he'd had a difficult time imagining himself performing such an intimate act on his mother, but after seeing the pain she was in when she vomited, he would have done anything to alleviate her pain. The worst seemed to be over, and he hoped she'd be able to sleep peacefully for a few hours.

He walked out into the living room leaving her door open in case she called for him and walked out onto the front porch. There was a gangly puppy sleeping in the sun at the top of the steps. He'd given the mutt a bowl of food the day before feeling sorry for him, but now the dog wouldn't leave. The puppy rolled onto his back in the sun and watched innocently as Diego came out onto the porch. Diego looked down at him and with no warning at all, kicked him, off the steps and onto the ground. The puppy yelped out in shock and pain and looked back up at him with eyes like his mother. If he'd had his gun on him, he would have shot him. "Go on; get out of here!"

The dog stared back up at him not moving or understanding. Diego was filled with rage and looked around the front porch for something to throw at the pathetic little dog. There was a dying geranium in a pot on the porch railing. He picked it up and cocked his arm. The dog understood the gesture and quickly limped away yelping pathetically with each step.

"Fuck!" he yelled, and sat down in a wicker chair, put his head in his hands, and wept for several minutes.

After he got his composure back, he wiped his eyes, sat back in the chair, and thought about his mother and all that she'd suffered and done for him and his brother over the years.

Diego's mother had entered the U.S. with him in her arms, penniless, twenty-one years before; led by a blood-sucking coyote. She'd been illiterate and unskilled and had worked endless hours doing stoop labor in the fields for five years before eventually getting a job with a house-cleaning service. She'd done that for three years. Then she'd worked as a maid in a cheap motel scrubbing toilets, making beds, and picking up used condoms. After that she worked in a convenience store until he was finally making enough from gang activities to support her. She'd enjoyed just six short months of relative ease before being diagnosed with pancreatic cancer. Most people died within six months of diagnosis. She'd lived a whole year but at such a heavy price he couldn't really conceive of it. She didn't have much longer left.

His cell phone rang. "Que?"

"It's Quirk."

"I know who it fucking is, pendejo. What?"

"You've got me very busy today. The cops now have Boyko and Benicio also."

Diego thought back to his last conversation with Boyko the day before and realized that he'd never heard back from him after he'd sighted the little motorcycle girl again. He'd simply been too distracted taking care of his mother. "How, why? Tell me what happened."

"I don't have all the details yet. Somehow, they both got beat up after they followed that little girl that you're so hot for. Benicio's got some broken bones and is under guard at the hospital and Boyko's already here at Lee County Jail.

"Mother-fucker! How does one little girl take out six of my men!"

"I can't answer you that. They do the crime, you spend the dime, I get them out. That's all I know. One bit of good news I can share is that I finally got them to release Esteban. I'm sure you'll hear from him shortly if you haven't already."

"What are Boyko and Benicio being charged with?"

"All kinds of things; assault and battery, carrying a concealed weapon without a permit, attempted kidnapping; all the regular, wholesome, activities that your boys seem so fond of."

Diego was silent for a few seconds as he thought. "Listen, I've got some shit going on here at home. I can't leave right now or really process all of this. Just do what you can for them."

"I always do. Oh, one other thing, Diego."

"What?"

"Gino's going to be a problem for you. He wants to exchange all sorts of information on various things that he alleges you've done for a lighter sentence. He's putting the finger on you for the two dead boys found floating in the mangroves without their heads and for the kidnapping and rape of two underage young ladies that the police are very motivated to find. I'm sure you don't know anything about either of these crimes, but I thought you should know that he's saying some terrible things about you behind your back." Quirk looked down at his dirty fingernails waiting for the explosion he knew would come shortly from the other end of the line. He really didn't like his gang-clients, especially Diego. He had his standards, after all. He would miss the regular revenue if Diego went down, but he'd never liked the spic, or the way Diego treated him.

Diego exploded as expected. "You tell Gino that if he says one fucking word to the police, he is dead! Do you hear me? Dead!"

Quirk smiled, pleased that he'd gotten such a strong reaction from his client. "I did mention to him that you were likely to be disappointed."

Diego pressed the "End" button on his phone and almost threw it against the side of the house, but he needed to call Esteban.

He went inside, snorted some cocaine, and then dialed him.

"Sí, Jefe," Esteban answered.

"Where are you now?"

"I'm at the clubhouse. I was just going to call you."

"Gino, Boyko and Benicio are all in custody right now because of that same little girl and Quirk says that Gino's going to turn on us."

"I knew Gino was in there when I was, but I never saw him. Are you sure about this?"

"Well, Quirk says he is. If he tells them about the stash house and the two little putas, you and I are fucked. I need you to head over there now and get the two girls and our drugs out of there. Bring them here to my mother's. Gino's never been to the house here, so he can't tell the police where it is. We'll put the putas down in the basement until you and I figure out what to do with him."

"Sí, Jefe, whatever you say."

"Wait! And stop at a hardware store on your way and pick up four padlocks. I've got some chain in the basement, but no locks."

"Sí, Jefe."

Diego went back into his mother's room and read to her in Spanish from the dog-eared Bible that she'd had for as long as he could remember.

Ninety minutes later Esteban knocked quietly on Diego's front door with one hand. He had a suitcase in the other. Diego answered after several minutes, looking like shit, and ushered him into the house.

"How much is in there?" Diego asked, pointing to the suitcase.

"Two kilos of blow, mas o menos (more or less), about a pound of crystal, and six pounds of weed."

"Bueno; and the girls?"

"In the van."

"Park it on the side of the house next to the kitchen door and we'll get our little friends comfortable in the basement. I'll open the door for you."

"Si, Jefe."

Esteban returned to the van outside, turned it around and then backed it alongside the house until the sliding door in the side was adjacent to the kitchen door. He shut off the van, got out, slid open the side door, reached in and untied the feet of one of the girls. Both of them were crying, terrified as to what might happen to them next. He cuffed the one he'd untied on the side of the head.

"Shut up! No sound."

Diego opened the kitchen door and Esteban passed the blindfolded girl to him. Then he turned back to the van for the second girl and after untying her feet and giving her the same warning as the other, led her into the house and followed Diego down the basement stairs.

Once in the basement, Diego pulled an old milk crate off a dusty shelf on the rear wall. It contained several lengths of light chain that had last been used to chain two pit bulls he'd had growing up.

"You got the locks?"

Esteban nodded and held out a plastic bag with the ACE logo on the side. "I got four locks that all use the same key."

"Bueno, chain them to the Lally columns there and there." He pointed to the ones he meant. "And bring me one of the keys. I'm going back upstairs to check on my mother."

Esteban nodded without saying anything and went to work chaining each girl and then untying their hands and removing their blindfolds. Both girls cowered silently on the floor scared to say or do anything that would draw his ire.

"You're both lucky you're still alive. If you want to stay that way, keep silent. Comprende?"

They both nodded their heads.

Esteban turned, went up the stairs, walked into the living room and watched silently as Diego inhaled several fat lines of coke off the coffee table. The suitcase was open on the floor next to him.

"Jefe, you look very tired. Perhaps you should ease up on the blow."

"Did I ask you for your thoughts, Esteban? If I want your opinion, I'll give it to you."

Esteban silently absorbed the insult. "How is tu madre?"

Diego leaned back on the couch savoring the sweet rush of the chemical before answering.

"She is better. I was just about to make her some breakfast."

"That's good to hear. Listen, if what you told me about Gino is true, then we need to take him out."

Diego spoke as if he hadn't heard Esteban. "It's not right, my friend. My mother's a saint. Why has God put this on her?"

"I don't know, Jefe. I'm sorry for you. Please let Adriela and I know if there is anything either of us can do for you."

"I will, thank you. I'm sorry I've been out of action for the last few days."

"Familia first, bro, I understand. Listen, we can't take a chance on Gino. He knows too much."

"I agree. He needs to be dead. He was at the clubhouse the night I shot Javier and Darian and he can also testify against all of us for sexually abusing the young girls and a thousand other crimes." He stood up and started pacing. "Motherfucker! That one little shit could take all of us down. And all of this, all of it, started with that girl on the bike! You haven't found her yet, have you?"

Esteban shook his head. "No, nothing, Jefe. She's like a ghost. We're watching that exercise studio that Boyko and Benicio followed her to, but she knows for certain that we're after her and I expect she's laying low somewhere. I don't know where else to look."

Diego broke out into a cold sweat thinking through all the implications of someone like Gino turning on the gang and continued pacing around the room for several more moments. With no warning, he picked up a heavy glass ashtray off the coffee table, turned, and threw it through the front of his mother's glass-doored hutch that housed her treasured collection of porcelain chihuahuas.

Esteban shrunk at the explosion of sound. "Jefe, tu madre! You're going to wake her."

"Fuck my mother! I never liked those stupid little dogs anyway. I want Gino dead and you need to make sure he dies badly, as an example."

"Si, Jefe. Cesar is in the same area of the jail right now, but I don't know if he could take Gino. He's a pretty tiny guy. Also, they might have moved Gino to segregation to keep him from us."

"Who is Cesar?"

"Marko's brother."

Diego turned and grabbed Esteban by the throat with both hands. "Stop telling me what you can't do, maricon! Poison the fucker if he's in seg, make it an open contract and offer $5,000. Drop a hand grenade in there if you have to! I don't care who kills him as long as it gets done. If you have to, get yourself arrested and do it yourself, but make sure it happens. I'm a prisoner here until he's taken care of. And at the same time, I also want that girl, the little one on the Ducati. Do whatever you have to but find out where she lives. Someone must know where she lives." He paused and took his hands away from Esteban's throat as a thought came to him.

"Remember Matèo?"

"Si. I think he's working as a landscaper now; what good is he?"

"Doesn't his wife work for a janitorial company?"

"I don't know. Why's that important?"

"I think they clean the offices at the police department."

Esteban thought about that for a few seconds. "And you're thinking maybe she can find something in Camila Sanchez's office about the girl?"

Diego nodded. "We've followed her twice from there and that whore Sanchez is their gang expert."

"My wife knows Matèo's wife. I'll put her on it."

Diego drifted away momentarily from the combination of the cocaine and lack of sleep. "I really can't wait to meet that little girl and lick the tears from her face as she begs me to stop the train. When she can't take anymore, I think I will beat her to death."

"Si, Jefe. I'll take care of things."

"Best you do, Esteban, best you do. Find that girl and kill Gino. Nothing else matters."

When Esteban got home, he sat down with his wife Adriella and asked her about Gabriela. "Do you still run into Matèo's wife Gabriela?"

"Here and there. Why?"

"Diego wants that girl on the motorcycle in the worst way. He's crazy right now. With Gino turning and his mother dying Diego's losing it."

"How can Gabriela help?"

"She works as a janitor at the police department, right?"

"I think that's one of their accounts."

"Diego wants her to go through Detective Sanchez's files and find out where that girl lives."

Adriella thought about it for several seconds. "I don't know. I can ask her, but she and Matèo are really trying to make it on their own, outside the gang. I doubt she'd agree. I don't really have any influence over her."

Esteban thought about it. "I see what you mean. Okay, I'll speak to both of them. You know their address these days?"

"They live over on Maria Street."

Esteban drove to Matèo and Gabriela's next. It was early evening and he found them on their front porch watching their two young children kicking a soccer ball back and forth in the mostly dirt front yard. He got out of the van, held up his hand in a greeting gesture, and then walked up to the edge of the porch.

"Matèo, Gabriela."

"Hey, Esteban," Matèo responded. "Long way from the clubhouse; what can we do for you?"

"Are things well with you both?"

"No complaints."

"Good, glad to hear it. It's really Gabriela that I need to speak to. Diego wants her to do him a favor."

Matèo spoke. "Why would we want to do a favor for Diego? We're not a part of his whole thing anymore."

Matèo's lack of respect annoyed Esteban. "It's a small thing he wants. You know how crazy he can get when he doesn't get what he wants."

"Yeah, well that's one of the reasons we're doing our own thing now. We keep to ourselves. No offense, but we'd like to keep it that way."

"Hang on now, before you get all offended, let me tell me tell you what he wants."

"Go ahead, but the answer will still be no."

Esteban had expected some push back from them but not an outright "no." Their seven-year-old boy and nine-year-old girl had stopped kicking the ball back and forth when he'd gotten out of the van. He walked over to the young boy, reached out, and rubbed his head. "You any good with that?"

The young boy shyly withdrew from his hand. "I play okay."

"Your boy's a little shy, Matèo." He turned to the girl.

"What about you, Hermana? You shy too?"

She kept her head down and also stepped back from him without responding.

Esteban looked back up at the porch and moved his eyes back and forth between Matèo and Gabriela. "You know, I'm probably not going to be telling you anything you don't know, but this world we're all living in can be a dangerous place. All kinds of bad things are happening to people. Did you read about those two boys that were found in the Caloosahatchee missing their heads? Terrible thing."

The threat was not lost on Matèo. He knew perfectly well from friends he still had in the gang what had happened to Javier and Darian. He stood up, reached behind his chair, and pulled out an aluminum bat. "How dare you come onto our property and threaten harm to our children."

"Settle down, Matèo, settle down. No need to go loco on me." Esteban reached behind his back and slowly drew a long barrel Colt Python .357 from his waistband. He let it hang alongside his leg.

Gabriela motioned to her two children. "Niños, aqui, ahora (children, get over here now)!" Both children ran up the steps and then behind her. Matèo walked down the steps and stopped several feet in front of Esteban.

"You need to go now, Esteban."

"Not going to happen, bro." Esteban thumbed back the hammer on the colt but still kept it alongside his leg pointed at the ground. "You and your wife need to listen to me first."

"Matèo! Listen to him," Gabriela begged.

Matèo said nothing with hate burning in his eyes, but eventually took a step backwards.

Esteban continued. "What I want is very simple. Gabriela, you know that gang detective, Camila Sanchez?"

"Sí, I know her," Gabriela reluctantly agreed.

"Diego wants the address of the little puta on the motorcycle that beat up Javier and Darian. She's responsible for Pedro getting shot and Boyko, Benicio, and Gino being in the jail. You know Diego; if he doesn't get what he wants he'll personally come over here and chop up both your little ones and make you watch. Es verdad (it's true)." Esteban shrugged as if he had no control over the outcome. "It's your choice; I'm just the messenger."

Gabriela was furious but also knew what Esteban said was true. Diego would, absolutely do something like that and she didn't have any choice. "What is it that he wants exactly?" Gabriela asked.

"Just what I said, he wants the address of the little girl, and he wants you to get it. You still clean the police department with that crew you work with, right?"

Gabriela nodded. "Sí, we do them on Friday nights."

Esteban smiled. "And you clean the detective's offices as well?"

"Sí."

"Bueno. See, this is simple, just like I told you. When you clean Detective Sanchez's cubicle I want you to go through her files and find out the name and address of the little girl. Do you think you could do that for Diego, Gabriela?"

She nodded "yes" knowing it would be a small price to pay for the safety of her children.

"I knew I could count on you; I even told Diego that."

Matèo spoke next. "I won't forget this, Esteban. You can't come to a man's home and threaten his children."

"I just did, Matèo, I just did." Esteban opened his car door with his left hand and continued to hold the gun in his right, got in and slowly backed out of the driveway keeping eye contact with Matèo.

The next morning Esteban set out to solve the "Gino" problem. He'd thought about it quite a bit and thought he had a solution. Two months previous, Gino had ridden along with him several times in the snatch-van before Javier and Darian had joined his kidnapping-crew full-time. As a result, he knew something that few other people knew about Gino.

The solution he'd thought of involved Cesar, the gang member who'd been arrested when the police had raided the stash house looking for the two young, middle school girls. He was in the general population of the jail, where Gino was being held. He didn't expect that the smaller Cesar could take out Gino because Gino was bigger and would be watching for a frontal assault, but he knew a weakness of Gino's that would be every bit as fatal, if he could simply gain Cesar's cooperation.

Esteban knew Cesar's brother Marko well and the next morning he went by the glass shop where he worked.

"Marko, que pasa?"

"Nada, Esteban; how are you?"

Asi que, asi que (so, so). Listen, how's your brother Cesar doing? I'd go by and visit him but me going by the jail might not be such a good idea; know what I'm sayin?"

"For sure, bro. Cesar's okay, but he's looking at a long stretch. The lawyer you guys got in to see him says there's not much to work with to defend him."

"I understand, for sure. I was thinking though that maybe one thing we could do to make his time a little easier is to get some money into him, you know, for the commissary or for a little weed when the day is getting long. If I give you some, will you take it in?"

"For sure, Esteban; Cesar'd appreciate that for sure."

"Also, when you go in to visit him, I'm going to give you something else. I want him to do something for Diego and me. In exchange we'll keep the bread coming into him."

"Sure, no problem."

"Can you get in to see him tomorrow?"

"Yea, I can do that. Afternoon would be best for me with my job."

"Great; meet me at the clubhouse at 4:30 tomorrow. I'll have some bread and something else."

"Not drugs, I hope. They've usually got a drug dog that sniffs us before we head in. We also have to go through a metal detector."

"No, no drugs or weapons. See you tomorrow."

"K, bro. See you then."

Esteban got on his phone next and ordered a couple of glass test tubes with stoppers from Amazon and selected overnight delivery for the next morning. Then he drove to Walmart and bought a couple of Ball canning jars and a squeeze bottle of honey. He loved it when a plan came together and turned up the volume in the van blaring Central American hip hop and banged his hand on the dashboard to the beat of the music. He was getting it done and Diego was sure to be pleased. Next stop after Walmart would be his tía (aunt) Espinosa's garden.

RIP CONVERSE

Chapter 24

Esteban met Marko at the clubhouse at 4:30 the next afternoon, as promised. He was standing in the parking lot sharing a joint with another gang member as he drove in. Esteban picked up a small paper bag off the seat next to him and got out of the van. Marko held out the joint as he approached.

"This is some good shit, Jefe, try some."

Esteban seldom did drugs but accepted the joint and took a polite hit. "Thanks."

"Hey, what happened to your lip, man? It looks sore."

Esteban reflexively touched his swollen lip. "Oh, it's nothing. I was in mi Tia Espinosa's garden yesterday and got a bee sting."

Marko laughed and shook his hand snapping his fingers. "Ayee, that must have hurt." Marko adjusted himself. "Suppose it could have been worse though. At least it wasn't your Johnson, Holmes."

Esteban cracked a forced smile. "Es verdad." In truth his lip hurt like hell. He'd gotten stung by three wasps in nearly the same place. He'd been catching wasps and putting them in the Ball jars. He'd mistakenly thought that one Ball jar was empty and had inadvertently put the lid up to his mouth as he'd walked through the garden. Three wasps had been clinging to the underside of the lid and had stung him simultaneously. He held out the paper bag to Marko. "Here's $500 to give to Cesar. There's also something else in there."

Marko took the bag and peered into it. There was a folded wad of twenty-dollar bills and also a large glass test tube with a cork stopper in the top. He withdrew the test tube. It was full of live wasps crawling over each other.

"What the hell?"

"Give that to Cesar along with the money. Tell him to throw it into Gino's cell when he's locked in there. The glass will break on the floor of the cell, the wasps will take care of the rest."

Marko looked at him quizzically.

"Gino needs to go down. He's working with the police. He's got a bee allergy."

Marko suddenly understood. "I don't know, man. Cesar might not want to do that."

Esteban reached out and wrapped one of his massive hands around Marko's neck and squeezed his thumb against his trachea. "It's not a request. Diego ordered it; comprende, tonto (fool)?"

Marko nodded his head like a wooden dummy. "Sí, Esteban. I'll tell him. How do I get this in?"

"Carry it in, you moron. Stuff it down your pants or put it in your shirt, I don't give a shit. The dogs won't alert on it and the metal detector won't go off. Even if you get caught it's no big deal. What are they going to charge you with? Just do it and make sure Cesar knows this needs to get done as soon as possible." Esteban released his neck, slapped his cheek a few times, turned and got back in the van. Before leaving he rolled down the window and motioned him over to the side of the van.

Marko reluctantly came over, staying just out of arm's reach. "Que?"

"This needs to get done, no mistakes. Both Diego and I will be very disappointed if this doesn't happen. You don't want that."

Marko swallowed hard and then nodded.

Chapter 25

amila's suggestion that I avoid the dojo for a while was a good one. I really needed to get more conscientious about all the college stuff and planned on staying home for the entire week collecting transcripts and recommendations, trying to arrange tours and interviews, and filling out applications. I quickly discovered that you can't just call major colleges and schedule an interview with one week's notice without first going through their online application process, sending each one fifty to seventy-five dollars -$75, submitting academic records, teacher evaluation forms and standardized test scores. Covid-19 further confused things as many schools had stopped in-person-tours altogether. Thankfully, the three schools I was registering with in the Boston area all accepted the Commonapp application which saved me from having to fill out three different applications. I was able to schedule a group campus tour at Harvard and an orientation presentation at Mass Maritime for the week that Nancy and I would be in Boston. I'd also decided that I wanted to look at Babson. Partly this was a tip of the hat to Nancy, but I'd also spent some time on their website after talking with her and had really liked the independent feel of the school and their emphasis on entrepreneurship. Babson didn't have any campus tours available that week. I called Nancy on Wednesday.

"Nancy, it's Callie."

"Hi, Callie. Are you making progress with your applications?"

"I am. I've got tours scheduled at both Harvard and Mass Maritime next week, but I haven't been able to arrange anything at Babson."

"You've put Babson on your list!" Nancy noted with surprise. "That's delightful; I'm so pleased. Any particular reason? I didn't think you were interested in business."

"I've been thinking a lot about our past conversations. One thing you said to me keeps bouncing around in my brain."

"What's that?"

"That Babson 'taught you how to think.' I've been thinking about that a lot and even though I'm much more attracted to operating big, complex pieces of machinery than I am business, I also realized that if I had money, then I'd be able to do or study anything I wanted."

"Sounds like you're connecting some dots up there in that teenage head of yours, although generally speaking, doing something just so you can make a lot of money usually doesn't work out; you still have to have a passion for whatever it is you do."

"I get that and that's why I'm still not sure that studying business is the route for me. I just can't see myself at a desk all day long working as an accountant. I realized though, thinking about what you're doing and what you've done, that there must be some sort of evaluative process involved in what you do. That sounds more interesting to me. Can't hurt to look, right?"

"That's my girl. Don't worry about scheduling a tour at Babson. As an alumnus and a Whale, I've got some pull there."

"What do you mean 'Whale'? I've never heard of that before."

"It just means that I'm a big-bucks contributor to the school. What days are you scheduled at Harvard and Mass Maritime?"

"Wednesday morning the 11th at Harvard and Thursday morning the 12th at Mass Maritime. Is that alright? I don't want to mess up any of your business meetings."

"Don't worry about those. All the people we'll be meeting with want something from me, so they'll take whatever time I give them. I'll schedule Babson for Friday morning. That way we can keep the afternoons free all week for me to do my business. Does that sound good?"

I smiled. I really missed Nancy and her "can do" attitude. "I've missed you, Nancy."

There was a pause before she spoke again. "Yes, I've missed you as well."

"Where are we going to fly out of, Naples or Sarasota?"

"Wherever you like. What's the most convenient for you?"

"What, did you charter a plane?" I asked excitedly.

"I don't imagine the pilot would be terribly impressed with your description of his aircraft as simply a plane. But yes, I generally fly private. I believe the aircraft we're flying up on is called an Embraer Phenom 300."

"Oh, Nancy, you've got to be kidding me; that's so cool! I didn't even tell you this yet, but I went flying with my friend Stuart a few days ago. It was incredible and he even let me fly and do some landings." While I was talking, I looked up the Embraer Phenom 300 on my phone. It was an awesome looking jet. Telling Stuart was the first thing I thought of and how this jet would blow him away.

"Stuart would be a young boy?" Nancy inferred.

I blushed, grateful that she couldn't see me. "He's very nice."

"Oh, dearie; they all are. Next you'll probably tell me that he's not your type and he doesn't have the slightest interest in you."

"Well, I wouldn't say that." I suddenly had a thought and interrupted myself. "Wait, what if you had the jet pick us up right at Page Field here in downtown Fort Myers? His father owns a flight school there."

"What's it called?"

"Alexander aviation. I'll call his dad and see if we can leave our vehicles there for the week."

"Let me know; otherwise I'll have to have Jesús drop me and then come back and pick me up. I have no intention of riding in one of those Uber cars with a total stranger."

"Of course not, Aunt Nancy; I would never ask you to do something as plebeian as that."

"Did Callie learn a new word?"

"You dreadful woman."

She laughed. "Okay, if I don't talk to you again, I'll see you Monday at 9:00 am at Alexander Aviation at Page Field. Call me if there will be a problem with me leaving my car there for several days. And, Callie...?"

"What?"

"I'm really looking forward to our trip. It's been too damned quiet around here since you left."

The second I hung up the phone with Nancy, I called Stuart. "Stuart, you won't believe this!"

"What?"

"You know how I'm going to Boston next week with my aunt to look at colleges?"

"Yes."

"I just talked to her to find out what airport we're flying out of, and she said we can have them pick us up wherever we want. We're flying up in a private jet! So I told her Alexander Aviation of course. We're flying in an Embraer Phenom 300." I held my breath wondering if he even knew what one was."

"Oh, you're kidding, they're incredible! That's one of the coolest, small, private jets made!"

I chuckled at his response. "Listen, the other reason I'm calling is I wondered if there was any way that my aunt and I could leave our vehicles at your place while we're up in Boston?"

"I don't see why not. I'll ask my dad, he's right here."

I listened as Stuart asked Court.

"My dad says sure, not a problem. I'll see if I can find a place inside the hangar for your bike. Given what's been going on with those gang people it'd probably be a good idea to keep it out of sight."

"The jet's picking us up at 9:00 a.m., Monday morning. Any way you can blow off your online classes and meet us at your father's hanger? I really want you to see this jet too."

"I'll just bring my laptop to the airport." He paused. "Of course, seeing you would be the main attraction. So, see you just before 9:00?"

"Stuart, are you saying that you think I'm better than a private jet?" I couldn't see his face, but I was sure it was probably red.

"You are, Callie."

I found myself liking that analogy but still wasn't 100% certain where I wanted my relationship with him to go so, I played it safe. "Brilliant, see you then."

I hung up thinking about it. Not counting that dirtbag Christopher, who'd tried to rape me, I'd never really had a real boyfriend. Stuart's adoration was flattering, and he did seem to have a lot more going on than all the yabos my age at school. But even recognizing all that, I felt like I was right on the cusp of moving forward in big and important ways in so many areas of my life and I wasn't at all certain I wanted the responsibility of a boyfriend who might have too many expectations.

****

Cesar had been carrying the glass test tube of wasps in the waistband of his pants since receiving it from Matèo the day before. Saying "no" to Matèo would have been like saying "no" directly to Diego, which was unthinkable. The cash he'd received and accepted when Matèo had given him the wasps, removed any lingering doubt. It would make his time inside much easier and he was grateful for it. The fact that he was going to kill a fellow gang member didn't trouble him at all. Fucking Gino had been stupid to agree to testify for the cops and he deserved what he was about to get.

Gino had been given the option of segregation by the police but hated solitary and figured if he kept alert and didn't put himself in vulnerable places like alone in the restroom, he could stay safe. Camila had told the guards to accommodate him as best they could and when he wasn't out in the common area with the rest of the population. they'd agreed to lock his cell door whenever he was in there alone.

Cesar watched him during lunch. When he left the protection of the group to go back to his cell, Cesar was behind him, just out of sight. Once the guard locked his door and went off down the hall, he casually walked up to Gino's cell, paused at the closed cell door, and looked in through the bars at him.

"Gino, que pasa?"

Gino was sitting on the edge of his bunk with his head down thinking about what lay ahead for him. He was screwed, either way. He was an accessory to kidnapping the two girls and then acting as one of their jailors. He was also an accessory to the attempted murder of the cops when Pablo had shot at them. Either charge was easily worth ten years with his prior record. The deal he'd struck with the prosecutor was that he'd serve just two years in one of the lower security prisons usually reserved for white collar criminals if he testified against Diego.

He briefly looked up at the sound of Cesar's greeting and then back at the floor. He wasn't afraid for his life with the cell door closed and Cesar on the outside, but he was mortified at what Cesar was no doubt thinking of him. "Cesar, I got nothing to say to you. Just that I'm not going to give up twenty years of my life for Diego. What he did to Javier and Darian wasn't right, man. He didn't stand by them; why should I stand by him?"

"Gino, I don't know what to say. We all have choices. You went against the gang and…" He shrugged without finishing his sentence, looked both ways up and down the cellblock, and then reached into his waistband and pulled out the fat test tube filled with wasps. He tapped the tube lightly against the bars which stirred the wasps and got Gino's attention.

"What?"

"Got a little present here from Diego. He wanted me to be sure you knew it came from him."

Gino looked up at the glass tube Cesar was gently tapping against the steel bars. He could see what it was, but not what was in it. Cesar unwrapped his fist from around the tube and held it by the top with just two fingers. There was some sort of movement inside it. Just before Cesar casually flipped it into his cell, the contents became clear to Gino. He started screaming before it hit the floor and broke at his feet. His most personal nightmare was happening in the light of day, and he started wind milling his arms before the wasps even attacked. "No, fuck no!"

It took the wasps a second or two to realize that they were no longer confined. Three or four then took flight trying to sense what was going on around them while the balance of them seemed to walk harmlessly and aimlessly around on the floor. Then, sensing Gino's rapid movements and the waterfall of fear pheromones shedding off him, all of them suddenly remembered that they were really pissed off at having been taken out of their habitat and confined in a strange glass tube for two days, and they attacked. They followed him about the cell darting in and out with incredible speed and started stinging him. Gino swatted at his clothes as they stung him. He was successful at killing several, but not before every single one of them had stung him. Near the end, three got onto the back of his bare neck and simultaneously stung him there. At that point he was hanging onto the bars and shrieking in abject terror, his eyes bugging out with fear.

Cesar backed away from the bars, watching the execution like a slow-motion train wreck. He had intended to continue walking on after breaking the test tube, but Gino's absolute terror was fascinating. He couldn't take his eyes off him and even after other inmates and guards started responding to Gino's screams, Cesar stayed nearby and watched things play out. Sobbing, Gino tried explaining to the guards that he'd been stung by multiple wasps and that if they didn't get an EpiPen, he would die. One of the guards ran off towards the infirmary understanding the urgency of the situation. Two other guards unlocked his cell, came in and got him to lie down on his bunk.

Almost immediately, the swelling started in his hands and face, but especially around his neck. His breathing became more and more rapid as his face and throat started swelling.

The guard who had run off to get the EpiPen returned out of breath carrying an AED emergency defibrillator. "The med locker was locked, and I couldn't find the damned doctor with a key; so no EpiPen, but I brought the defibrillator. Shit, Gino doesn't look so good."

It took less than twelve minutes from the time of the first sting, until Gino's entire system crashed. His blood pressure fell from 200/120 to 70/30 as his vascular system dilated in response to the venom coursing through his bloodstream. His heart briefly ramped up to an impossible 240 beats per minute as it attempted to fill the void caused by the vascular dilation. Then his breathing stopped, not due to the swelling around his trachea but simply due to massive anaphylactic shock. His heart stopped, started, and pumped a few strokes, then stopped again going into fibrillation.

The guard who had gotten the defibrillator quickly opened his shirt and stuck the two pads from the emergency AED defibrillator on his chest. "Clear!" he shouted, then energized the pads. Gino's back briefly arched up before returning to the mattress. The guard placed his fingers alongside his carotid artery and felt for a pulse. Nothing. They hit him three more times, but Gino's heart muscles couldn't be persuaded to restart in a cohesive, coordinated way. He was dead.

RIP CONVERSE

Chapter 26

Diego was only managing to sleep an hour or two a night as he continued to care for his worsening mother. In addition to her care he now also had the two girls in the basement to deal with and was in the basement bringing them bowls of cold cereal when his mother cried out loudly for him from upstairs.

After two days of respite from her pain, she'd gotten worse again and cried and begged him to relieve her of the near constant agony that she was in. It ripped him up inside and he could no longer stand it. The doctor had prescribed Fentanyl patches for her pain several weeks previous but had warned him that once she started needing them that she would not likely live long after that. He'd also warned him that she would sleep more, lose her appetite, and might not even recognize him from the effects of the powerful synthetic narcotic. He'd held off as long as he could but couldn't stand to listen to her crying for a moment longer. He ignored the pleas of the two girls to "please let them use the bathroom," stomped up the stairs, and slammed the door behind him.

"Diego, please! I cannot deal with this pain. Isn't there something you can give me?" she pleaded.

"Sí, Madre. I do have something," he said gently. Several tears rolled down his face as he went to the bathroom and then returned with the box of Fentanyl patches. He tore the protective foil off of one and removed the backing on it. He paused thinking of what the doctor had said about it being close to the end once the Fentanyl was needed.

"Diego, please. It hurts so much."

He pressed the patch against her upper arm. "This should help, Madre."

"Bless you, my son."

"De nada (it's nothing), Madre. Just let me know if you need more."

He got up, went into the living room, and snorted several fat lines of coke, then put his feet up on the sofa and lay back. He was almost asleep when his phone rang in his back pocket. He reluctantly took it out and answered.

"Que?"

"It's Esteban. Gino's no longer a problem."

Despite being high as a kite and exhausted, the significance of that was not lost on Diego.

"Bueno. How?"

"He was allergic to bees and somehow some got into his cell and stung him."

Diego smiled for the first time in weeks. "The poor fucking baby, I hope he passed peacefully."

Esteban smiled on his end of the phone. "As I understand it, Jefe, he was very scared, blew up like a balloon, and then his heart stopped."

Diego chuckled. "Bueno; and the girl, have you—?"

Diego's mother cried out for him from the other room interrupting him. "Not yet, but I'm working on it."

"Bring her to me, Esteban. Don't fail me on this. Right now, I've got to go."

"I won't. Go to your mother, Jefe, I can hear her calling in the background."

Diego walked back into his mother's room. She was tossing and turning on the bed, still in agony.

"Madre?"

"Diego, please. The pain will not stop. Please give me another patch!"

Diego sat down on the edge of her bed for a few seconds looking at her, then silently nodded, reached for the box of Fentanyl patches, took one out, took it out of the foil pack and peeled the backing. Then he put it on her arm right above the one he'd applied just fifteen minutes earlier.

"See if that doesn't help, Madre."

"Bless you, my son," she said, as earlier.

Chapter 27

B y Friday morning I felt like pulling my hair out from boredom. On a whim, I picked up my phone and dialed Stuart's number.

"Hi, Callie."

"Hi, Stuart. Listen, this is a little impulsive of me, but I'm going crazy here at the house. I haven't done anything all week except college stuff, and I was wondering if by any chance my very good friend Stuart might maybe, possibly, have the tiniest bit of interest in taking his friend Callie flying again today?"

Stuart was silent for a second or two pondering my question. "I don't know. I'll ask him. Can you hold?"

He had me confused for a second and I wondered if maybe Court had answered his phone. Then I thought about his voice. It was definitely him and I smiled and let him play out his little one-man skit. I listened as he carried on his imaginary little conversation with himself on the other end of the line.

"Stuart, Callie's on the phone and she's wondering if maybe, possibly, you might be willing to take her flying again today?"

"Callie? Oh that Callie, the one that rides the motorcycle. Let me think about it for a minute."

"She's on the line right now."

"I know that. I'm just checking my really busy social calendar."

I got it; he was going to torture me like I'd done to him when he'd first called. I listened to him as he loudly flipped the pages of a magazine into the phone.

"Okay, I give up." I interrupted. "You had your little game. You're very talented and likely have a big future on Broadway."

"You think?" he asked excitedly and then caught himself and said it again with a deeper tone to his voice. "You think?"

"Yes, really."

"How about 3:00 o'clock?"

I smiled. "3:00 would be wonderful, Stuart, thanks."

"You're welcome."

As I thought about our exchange it seemed as though Stuart was losing some of his shyness.

I got to Alexander Aviation at 2:45 and went right into the flight desk. Court was on the phone and Stuart was looking at something on his laptop. They both looked up and smiled at me as I walked in which felt good. Stuart closed his laptop and Court wrapped up his phone call as I approached the desk.

"Hi, Callie." Stuart offered with a smile.

Court spoke next. "Nice to see you again, Callie. Stuart tells me that he's taking you up in the Citabria today. I hope you have a strong stomach with not much in it," Court said.

I cocked my head at them wondering what they were talking about.

"Why's that?" I asked, confused.

Court looked at Stuart. "You didn't tell her about the Citabria son?"

"She'll be fine, Dad. I doubt she'll get sick."

"What? What's a Citabria and why would I get sick?" I asked, honestly confused.

Stuart looked at his father instead of me. "I'll be gentle, Dad, don't worry. Callie's a trooper, she'll do fine."

"Okay, if you say so." Court reached into a compartment on the top of the desk and pulled out a folded paper bag and held it out to me. "Just in case." He added as he handed it to me.

"What's this?" I asked.

"It's a sick bag. You should probably take it, you know, just in case." Stuart suggested.

"What's going to happen to me up there that I might need this?"

"Nothing. Don't worry about it. If you feel queasy, I'll just bring you down again."

"Alright you two, what have I signed up for?"

Court and Stuart both laughed at their private little joke.

"It's not that big a deal, Callie, really. I just thought it would be fun to take you up in our aerobatic plane and do a few maneuvers," Stuart said in a perfectly reasonable way.

"Maneuvers? You mean like coordinated turns, ascents and descents?"

"Yes, exactly," Stuart confirmed a bit too quickly.

Court chuckled behind a raised fist.

I knew they were setting me up for something but wasn't about to give the two of them the satisfaction of playing the role of 'worried little girl.'

"Excellent, I can hardly wait! Let's get this party started!"

"You've got the chutes in the plane right, son?"

"I do indeed, Father," Stuart said with a straight face while looking me in the eye.

"Chutes? You mean like parachutes?" I asked aghast.

Court nodded. "You know, in case the wings fall off or something. But I doubt you'll need them," he added.

I knew intuitively that neither Stuart or his father would ever do something that was really dangerous with me and decided to play along.

"Parachutes are cool. I like parachutes. In fact I love parachutes and just this morning thought to myself, 'maybe I should go parachuting' I just hope that the one you have for me is pink. I always insist on pink when I'm parachuting you know; me being a girl and all. It is, right?"

They both burst out laughing and I joined them after a few seconds although I honestly had no idea exactly what I was laughing about.

Stuart and I walked out on the tarmac in front of the school, and I followed him until we were alongside a bright red single-engine plane. It was different than the one we'd first flown mainly because the tail of the plane was resting on a tiny wheel under the rudder. The other thing I noticed right away was that the plane wasn't made out of metal like the first one we'd flown. This one was made out of some sort of canvas which was stretched over a tubular frame beneath. I put my hand on it feeling the skin of the plane.

"You've got to be kidding me, Stuart! Is this plane really made out of some sort of fabric?"

Stuart nodded. "It's very light."

"We're actually going flying in this thing?'"

Stuart nodded again. "Trust me, you'll like it. And Sid probably doesn't appreciate being called a 'thing.' She can be sensitive."

"Sid? Why is your plane named that?"

"I'm glad you asked. Svetlana Kapanina may be the best pilot flying in the world today. She's won the World Aerobatic Champion title more times than any other human being. My dad and I love watching her YouTube videos and named the Citabria after her in tribute."

"Fair enough," I replied. "Is Svetlana still alive or did she go down in her aerobatic plane?"

"Oh, she's alive and well. Look her up and watch some of her performances. She's incredible."

I followed him around the plane to the right-hand side. He opened the door and leaned in to turn the ignition on for a second and check the fuel gauges. I looked over his shoulder.

"We sit one in front and one in back?" I asked somewhat surprised as I pointed to the two single seats, one in front of the other.

Stuart nodded.

"Where's the wheel, I mean yoke?" I asked completely confused. I'd spent quite a few hours over the past week reading about the Cessna we'd flown in on my first flight and the cockpit of "Sid" had almost nothing in common with the Cessna.

"Doesn't have one. You steer Sid with a stick."

"A stick? That's reassuring. Wonder why I didn't think of that. And how does this stick work?"

"It's similar to the yoke you got used to in the other plane. You push it forward to go down, pull it back to go up, and move it from side to side to bank and turn the airplane."

"And do the pedals work the same?"

"Sort of."

"And the throttle?"

He pointed to black knobs in both the front and back, recessed into the left side of the plane.

"How come this plane has a sunroof and none of the other planes do?" I asked, noting the glass ceiling.

He chuckled. "The glass ceiling enables you to keep an eye on reference points like the horizon in the middle of maneuvers so you can stay oriented."

I was confused again. "Explain."

"You know, when you're upside down and such," he muttered under his breath.

"What was that?"

"Nothing. I was just saying that it adds a lot of visibility."

I realized that flying Sid was going to be completely different than our first flight together in the Cessna and decided that rather than question everything, I'd just watch him and see if I couldn't absorb it.

"Okay, let's do this!" I said with a confidence I didn't feel. "I'll just watch for now because I'm so confused at this point that we'll never get flying if I ask all the questions in my head."

"You'll pick it up quickly, Callie. Just follow me around while I do the preflight. Sid's very similar to the Cessna in that way."

Five minutes later we climbed in, with me in the back and Stuart in the front. He yelled, "clear prop," engaged the starter, listened to the airport advisory and then spoke to ground control. He turned his head and looked back to make sure both my seatbelt and shoulder harnesses were tight.

"Ready?"

"Ready, Freddy. Let's see what this bad-girl can do."

Stuart advanced the throttle and we started to taxi. With the tail on the ground I couldn't see anything over the dashboard.

"How can you see anything, Stuart?" I asked over the mic.

"I look out the side windows mostly and occasionally zig zag the plane so I can see what's directly in front of us. Once we start our takeoff roll, our tail will come up off the ground and you'll be able to see fine out of the windshield."

I nodded but didn't really understand why a plane would be designed that way.

After he did his run-up and got clearance, we taxied out onto the runway, he gave Sid full power, and within 100' or so her tail came up off the ground and her nose dropped, allowing me to finally see what was directly ahead of us.

He came over the headphones. "Keep your hands and feet lightly on the controls, Callie, so you can feel what I'm doing." I clicked the mic button twice to let him know I'd heard.

For the first ten minutes after we got clear of the airport, he got me used to using the stick to ascend and descend and also had me try a few coordinated turns. It was easier than I'd anticipated although having to look over Stuart's shoulder to see the instruments was less than ideal.

"Want to see why Sid is my favorite plane, Callie?"

"I do, Stuart. I'm positively on the edge of my seat. Just don't kill us, please."

He chuckled. "My dad was just messing with you. I think you'll like this."

"I'm totally in your hands."

Stuart nodded. "Okay, I'm going to start out by clearing the area just like we did in the other plane to make sure there's no traffic around."

This time, however, instead of doing gentle turns to both sides he snapped Sid over into a tight bank to the right, came straight again, and then did the same thing on the left looking intently out the windows both times. I felt myself sink down in the seat both times.

"How come I get pushed down into my seat when you turn like that?" I asked.

"Those are called G's, or gravities. In those turns we were pulling two G's or two times your body weight. In some of the maneuvers we'll try, you'll feel quite a bit more. If you feel yourself starting to get lightheaded try flexing your stomach and thigh muscles as tight as you can."

I wasn't sure I'd heard him right. "Why?"

"It will help to keep some blood in your head instead of all of it going down into your legs and feet. It will also help prevent tunnel-vision."

What on earth was he talking about? I wondered to myself.

"Ready?"

"I think so."

He pushed the stick forward and we started to dive towards the ground. As our speed built, I noticed he came back on the throttle some. Despite his reduction in power, our speed continued to increase as we hurtled towards the ground. I have to admit, it was disconcerting, looking through the propeller and seeing nothing but ground ahead of us. I looked over his shoulder at the airspeed indicator, and noted we were entering the yellow zone. All at once he pulled back sharply on the stick and we arced away from the ground and started to head back upwards towards the open sky. I was immediately pressed down into my seat and when I tried to lift my arm it seemed to weight four or five times its normal weight. My eyelids got heavy and then then my vision tunneled, and my peripheral vision disappeared. I dimly heard him add power at some point and then all at once I became lighter and lighter and lighter, until I finally became weightless. I looked up through the glass ceiling of the plane and I realized that I was now looking at the ground through the ceiling. The checklist Stuart had been using on the ground floated by me in midair and my body came out of the seat upwards, or was it downwards?

"Holy crap, Stuart!" I yelled through the mic. "This is incredible!"

"You okay back there?"

"I think so, but did you know your airplane is upside down?"

"Hang on, we've still got to go through the last part of the loop."

As he said that, the engine speed started to increase again as we flew down the backside of the circle he was describing in the air. As we got to the bottom, he pulled back on the stick again and I got another rush as I was pushed into the seat at several times my body weight. After several seconds of that he straightened the plane out to straight and level flight with the horizon straight ahead and our wings parallel to it.

I tried to understand in my head what we'd just done but had difficulty. "Tell me what we just did!" I asked excitedly.

"That's called a loop. If I did it correctly, we just did a perfect circle in the sky. Sometimes I hook my loops a bit at the top, but that wasn't bad. Did you like it?"

"I loved it! How many G's did we pull?"

"About five when we were coming out of it on the bottom."

"That was intense. When you were pulling out on the bottom, I almost passed out."

He nodded his head. "That's where we pulled four or five Gs. Did you remember to squeeze thighs together?"

"I didn't, but I will next time. What else can we do?" I asked excitedly.

"How about a four-turn spin?"

"Only four?" I shouted, giddily. "Wouldn't six be better? I've got my pink parachute."

"You're crazy, Callie!"

"I know!" I shouted back deliriously happy. "I love this!"

Stuart checked the area again for traffic, then pulled the nose up and started climbing. I could hear the engine straining, but despite its best efforts our airspeed got lower and lower as we headed straight up into the sky. Stuart kept the stick all the way back and Sid started to lose speed and go slower and slower as we climbed. Right when it felt as though she was going to stop altogether, the audible stall warning started to shriek, and Sid started to buffet and buck, warning us, I suppose, of our imminent demise.

Stuart ignored the stall warning and kept the stick back. Then right at the moment where Sid transitioned from flying airplane into falling object, Stuart chopped the throttle, and kicked in sharp left rudder.

Sid stopped flying, her nose dropped sharply, and Stuart and I started to spin towards earth in a counterclockwise direction. It was unreal! I tried to count the revolutions, but I was too disoriented watching the ground spin towards us through the propellor. At some point he released the hard left rudder, let the stick come back to neutral, and added power. Once we regained sufficient airspeed, we were able once again to return to straight and level flight with the horizon where it belonged.

"More, more!" I shouted, feeling crazy as a loon.

"Still not feeling sick?" he asked.

"Not a bit. How many was that?"

"Six; you told me to do six."

"And what, you just automatically do whatever I tell you? What else can we do?"

"We could try a snap-roll."

He'd said "try a snap-roll" a bit tentatively.

"What do you mean, *try* a snap roll? That doesn't sound very confident. Don't they tell you in 'airplane trick school' not to use words like that with your passengers?"

"Well, my snap rolls aren't the best," Stuart admitted.

"There, you did it again. What does 'not the best' mean exactly when you're in an airplane full of gasoline hurtling towards the ground?"

"They aren't that bad! It just means I don't always end up on the same heading I started out at, which is what you want."

That wasn't exactly a ringing endorsement, but for some reason I still trusted him implicitly.

"What the heck, Stuart. Nobody's perfect. Give it a shot."

"You asked for it!" Stuart rolled Sid over onto her side, upside down, up on the opposite side, and then finally upright again. I tried to watch the stick as he articulated it but once again became slightly disoriented. We did finish the maneuver, however, still headed in the same general direction with both wings still attached.

Over the next half hour he gave me some instruction and got me used to stalling the Citabria and doing what he called "some simple wing-overs." During that maneuver he would have me climb the plane in much the same way as we'd done in the first part of the loop, but once the plane reached the top of loop, instead of continuing around upside down and doing a circle, he would have me continue upwards a little farther until our airspeed had fallen to a level that would no long support aerodynamic flight. Then, as the airplane stalled, he'd have me bank the wing over to one side or the other and we would fall on our wing for a brief period, before regaining airspeed and returning to straight and level flight.

"That was completely awesome! Thank you so much for trusting me enough to try those." I said after we'd done three or four.

"You're amazing, Callie. I'm so glad you enjoyed it."

"I did. I truly did. I'm almost scared to ask what's next. Do you and your dad have jets in the hangar you haven't told me about?" We headed back to the airport after that.

Without question I was going to learn to fly, I thought as I drove home. Velocitá was still my true love on the ground, but being in flight, away from the earth and corkscrewing through the sky was like being in another world. After talking with Stuart at the end of our flight I added aerobatics to my growing list of things I wanted to learn. I'd asked him how he'd gotten into it. His answer had surprised me, but it also made perfect sense.

Apparently, someone he'd gone through ground school with had gotten too low and too slow on an approach with two passengers in the plane with him. He'd stalled and then inverted his plane with just 300 feet of altitude.

His friend, who had never been inverted (upside down) before, did exactly the wrong thing. He'd applied full power and pulled back on the stick and as a result nosed into the ground at full throttle killing all three of them.

As Stuart explained the accident, he said that flight training no longer includes mandatory spin recovery training or inverted flight of any kind, just stall recovery. At the time of the accident Stuart realized that he might have made the same mistake as his friend if he'd been in the same situation. It was with that realization that he'd decided he wanted to be as comfortable upside down in a plane as he was right-side up and signed up that day for some aerobatic lessons. Once he'd started, he'd enjoyed it so much that he continued to fly the aerobatic plane as often as possible. That made tremendous sense to me, and it also gave me more respect for Stuart. Many people would have been freaked out to lose a friend that way and I expect that many might have given up flying altogether or become super-timid pilots. Stuart had instead confronted the logical fear, learned from his friend's mistake, and become a better pilot.

****

Saturday morning, Esteban called Matèo to see if his wife, Gabriela, had gotten the girl's address from Camila Sanchez's office. "Matèo, did Gabriela get the information I asked for?"

"Esteban, listen, she tried, but…"

Esteban cut him off. "But nothing. You're telling me she didn't get the information. I told you what would happen if she didn't do this. Sounds like you need to be *incentivized*, pendejo. You really think I can't get to your kids?"

"No, wait, wait! She tried, but there was always someone else with her! What was she supposed to do?"

"That's not my problem. I gave you a job and you're telling me that it didn't get done, right? Now I've got to do what I've got to do. Do you think your son will still be able to play soccer with just one leg? How about your daughter? I expect she might have difficulty brushing her hair with no arms. Es verdad, no?

"Esteban, please, I'm begging you! Gabriela will get the girl's name and address, I promise you! We just need a little more time."

Esteban let his threat sink in for a few moments. "When? When will she get it?"

"Next time, next time she cleans there, I promise man!"

"When!"

"Next Friday, I promise you she'll get it. Just don't go near my kids, I'm begging you."

"You better not be fucking with me, Matèo. She's got one more chance, but no more."

"Gracias, thank you. I'll make sure she gets it next week."

Esteban hung up the phone.

Matèo hung up, relieved at the reprieve. When he'd first joined the gang in El Salvador it had been out of a desire to simply survive. Without gang affiliation he had no options. Had he known that he was going to end up living in the United States, with children of his own and the limitless opportunities available there, he might have reached a different decision. As it was, he and his family were trapped and lived at the whim of his old gang, and he hated it.

RIP CONVERSE

Chapter 28

Monday morning, I struggled to get everything I was bringing to Boston, into my knapsack. Despite it being full, I wasn't at all sure I had the appropriate clothes for looking at colleges. Jeans were too casual and the few dresses I had seemed too girly. I was hoping Nancy could offer some insight and if what I'd brought was wrong that we might have time to shop for an outfit somewhere. I finally got my knapsack closed and after putting on my leather jacket, went out into the kitchen. Mam was sitting alone at the kitchen table working on a bracelet. Daddy and my two brothers were off shrimping.

"Well, I'm off."

Mam had all of her jewelry tools in front of her and was just starting a new bracelet. Next to her on the table was an incredibly intricate finished bracelet with what appeared to be thousands of links.

She took off the inexpensive 4X power Walmart readers she used as a substitute for an expensive jeweler's loupe and looked up at me. She had to close her eyes for a second and pinch the corners and reopen them and then blink repeatedly before I came into focus. She smiled as my features sharpened. "There you are."

I smiled back. "You're going to ruin your eyes, Mam, if you don't get a proper magnifier of some sort."

She swiped her hand sideways. "These are fine. Those fancy jeweler magnifiers are expensive; I can make do."

I hadn't really paid much attention to her work for a long time. The detail in the piece lying on the table was extraordinary. "Can I see that one, Mam?"

"Sure." She handed it to me. "I made it for you."

I looked at her with a stunned expression on my face and picked it up and examined it closely in the light. It was exquisite. I normally don't wear jewelry of any kind but thought I would wear this bracelet.

"Mam, this is incredible! It's one of the most beautiful things I've ever seen."

When I used to help her as a little girl, we would string her tiny stones on nylon or cotton thread. I noted that she was now stringing on a gossamer silver thread and that the stones had gotten even smaller. The result resembled super-fine chainmail. The bracelet I held in my hand was comprised of six, one-inch by one-inch sections, and within each horizontal section there were perhaps forty longitudinal rows of blue sapphires. Each inch-long strand held perhaps sixty tiny stones. Because of their size I knew the sapphires weren't expensive. They were industrial grade chips, likely the same rough grade that is glued to industrial abrasive bits. I did a rough calculation in my head multiplying the number of rows by the number of stones in a row by the approximate length of the bracelet, "Mam, there must be 10,000 stones in this bracelet! How long did you spend stringing this one?"

"Not that long, about a month. I think it has 14,000 stones."

"You're kidding; this is unbelievable! Show me how to put it on, will you?"

She glowed at my obvious reverence for her work and nodded. "Give me your wrist."

I handed her the bracelet and then put my wrist under her work light. At both ends of the bracelet there were five tiny silver barrels. She lined the round, offset barrels up, then meshed them together so that all the holes lined up, then inserted a silver wire about 1/16" of an inch in diameter. The wire was threaded on one end and had a small fitting on the other. She slid the wire through all the barrels. The last one was threaded, and she gently turned the wire into it until it was secure. "There."

I turned my wrist under the work light. Thousands of random facets caught the light and winked back at me. It was stunning. I raised my eyes to hers. "I don't know what to say."

"You don't need to say one word. The look in your eyes said all I need to hear. You're one of a kind and you should have something that says that."

I walked around the table, leaned down to hug her, kissed her on the forehead, and then pulled back so I could look into her eyes. We were both teary. She was wearing a simple, well worn, cotton dress. It was reflective of the almost monastic life she led. I noticed that the few strands of grey I remembered in her hair now made up the lion's share of her mane. I also noted the crow's feet at the corners of her eyes for the first time. Mam was getting older. Despite her flaws, she was no less attractive. I cocked my head a little realizing that the lines in her face actually added to her attractiveness.

"You're a gorgeous woman."

"Callie, don't be ridiculous. I'm a tired *old* woman. You better get a hustle on, girl, or you're going to be late for your flight. I'm excited for you and what you're doing this week."

"I know, me too. Thanks again for the bracelet, it's beautiful."

"Shoo, get going."

I got to Alexander Aviation at Page field by 8:30. It was a peerless fall Florida morning with the temperature a moderate seventy-eight and unlimited visibility beneath an azure-blue sky. Aunt Nancy was already there parked in her Bentley. I pulled up alongside her on Velocitá.

She was wearing a Hermes silk scarf over her head and had on big designer sunglasses. The top was down in the Bentley, and she was putting on lipstick in the visor mirror.

I turned off Velocitá, pushed my sun visor up and raised the hinged chin bar on my helmet. Nancy had never met Velocitá or seen me on her.

"Hey, lady; nice wheels," I offered.

Nancy kept looking into the vanity mirror and finished applying her lipstick. "Nice wheels, indeed. Obviously, there's no security at this establishment; they'll let anyone in here." She slowly turned her head and once we made eye contact, she dropped her façade and actually squeaked. "Callie!" She got out of her car and held her arms open. "Come here, you, and give me a hug."

I swung my leg off Velocitá and almost jumped into her arms. I'd no idea that I'd missed her so.

She couldn't wrap her arms around me due to my bulging knapsack. "What on earth is that thing on your back? I can't give you a proper hug with it on."

"Had to bring some clothes to look at schools." I slipped it off and dropped it on the ground and went back for a second try.

"Yes, of course, how silly of me. I'm sure you have your finest garments in that sack that you just heaved to the ground."

"Now, now, don't be a snob. It's the only way I can transport anything on Velocitá."

"I assume that Velocitá is this...?" She paused, looking for the right word. "Conveyance?" She took off her scarf and put it in her purse.

"It is. Velocitá is the fastest, sexiest, Italian I know."

"Dear girl; I assure you, if I wanted an exciting Italian, he wouldn't be made out of metal and smell like motor oil and gasoline."

"Don't be so sure. Have you ever been on a true racing motorcycle and traveled at 129 miles per hour with an engine turning 8,600 rpm?"

"I can't say as I have, and please don't tell me that you're being serious, or I'll never sleep again."

"Serious as Crab Claw gets with a bone."

Nancy scrunched an eyebrow. "And who, pray tell, is Crab Claw?"

"My dog."

"Oh, I see, some sort of a rural idiom. Callie, don't you know that motorcycles are very dangerous? You could be killed or maimed on this. What if I forbid it?"

"Oh, I'm sure that will work out for you about as well as it did for my parents."

Stuart came around the side of the building, interrupting us.

"Hi, Stuart." I said in a slightly more reserved way than I customarily greeted him. "I'd like you to meet my Aunt Nancy Liddell. Nancy, this is my friend Stuart Alexander."

Stuart turned his gaze to Nancy. "Hello, Mrs. Liddell. It's a pleasure to meet you."

Nancy held out her hand to him and turned to me. "Well I can see he's got the Eddie Haskell thing down to a tee."

Here we go, I thought to myself having forgotten momentarily Nancy's directness and occasional sarcasm. I was worried she'd run roughshod over Stuart's shy nature.

"Aunt Nancy, Stuart's a very nice boy. I was so hoping you'd be on your absolute best behavior this week."

"Did I say something wrong?" Stuart asked.

"You're fine, Stuart. I'll explain later."

He turned back to Nancy. "Do you have a bag I can get for you, Mrs. Liddell?"

I think Nancy was finally starting to get it; that Stuart was in fact as nice a boy as he appeared to be and that his politeness was genuine and not contrived.

"That would be lovely, Stuart. It's in the trunk." Nancy pressed the trunk release button on her key fob and the lid rose.

He went around to the rear and pulled out her two matching Bentayga bags and a hanging garment bag.

Nancy looked at me while he was out of site, made her hand into a gun shape, and mimicked shooting herself in the head.

"This is a really nice automobile, Mrs. Liddell."

"Thank you, Stuart, that's kind of you to say. Listen, I may have gotten off on the wrong foot here. First of all, there is no Mr. Liddell. I roll alone these days. A friend once told me that I'm a minister of fun in the church of one. Just call me Nancy if you would."

"Oh, sure, whatever you like. I didn't mean to suggest anything. I was just trying to be polite."

"I know that now, Stuart. I apologize if I came off sarcastic."

"No problem. Listen; let's get the bags inside, talk to my dad, then figure out where to put the vehicles."

"That's very thoughtful of you, Stuart. I'm sure my car will be fine here if I just put the top up and lock it."

"No, we wouldn't hear of it. Let's go in, I'll introduce you to my dad, and then Callie and I can come back and figure out space for the bike and the car."

I slung my knapsack over my shoulder and started towards the door at Stuart's side.

He leaned over and whispered, "Who's Eddie Haskell?"

I whispered back, "I'll tell you some other time."

Court was in his normal spot at the front desk talking on the phone as we approached. Nancy was slightly behind Stuart and me. After he hung up, he smiled at me and then stood. "Hi, Callie. How's my favorite new student pilot?"

"Hello, Court. I'm fine thanks." I turned sideways and tipped my hand towards Nancy. "I'd like you to meet my aunt, Nancy Liddell. Nancy, this is Court Alexander."

Nancy came out from behind Stuart and me and looked at Court. The two of them stared opened mouthed at one other. Neither spoke for a second or two. Then they both spoke at once.

"Nancy?" "Court? Oh my God."

Obviously, they knew each other. I looked closely at Nancy and saw something pass across her face that I'd never seen before, softness and vulnerability. *What's going on here?* I asked myself.

Stuart spoke next. "Dad, Nancy has a really nice car. Do you think we could move some of the planes around in the hangar and find space for it also?"

Court was non-responsive.

"Dad?"

Court's eyes shifted to his son for just long enough to suffice as acknowledgement and then went back to staring at Nancy. "What is it, Stuart?"

"Can I shift some of the planes around in the hangar so that we can make room for Nancy's car?"

"Sure, just put 99Juliet out on the line and tie her down. Frank isn't going to be able to get to her 100hr inspection this week anyway." He turned back to my aunt. "Nancy, do you have time to sit and catch me up on your life?"

She nodded. Court came around the side of the desk, took her elbow in his hand and led her over to one of the couches, both of them completely absorbed in one another and oblivious to Stuart and me.

I looked at Stuart and laughed. "Okay then, I guess they don't need us to break any ice."

"I've never seen my dad act like that before."

"Same thing with Nancy. It's a little scary. I'm not sure your mother would approve though."

"Oh, I guess I never mentioned it; they're divorced."

"Ah ha, the plot thickens."

There was a VHF scanner behind the desk monitoring both tower and ground communications and Stuart and I both listened as the tower spoke with what I imagined was our jet.

"Page Field tower, Embraer Phenom 56893Hotel at the outer marker. We have information Lima."

"Roger, 93Hotel at the outer marker with information Lima, you are cleared for long final on runway 23. Once off the active contact ground on 121.7."

"Page Field tower, Embraer Phenom 93Hotel; cleared for long final on runway 23, contact ground on 121.7 when off the active. Thank you, tower."

"We better get cracking, Stuart. Sounds like our ride's about to land."

"Want to help me move some planes around?"

"Sure." I put my knapsack down next to Nancy's bags and followed Stuart through the door leading out, into the hangar. There were seven aircraft in the cavernous space all parked in seemingly random ways; a twin engine and two single engine planes were close to the wall we'd come through. All three planes had their engine covers off and two mechanics were in conference in front of the twin.

Stuart spoke to one of them.

"Roger, we're going to move 99Juliet outside onto the line to make room for a car and a motorcycle for the week. Any particular place you want us to put the vehicles?"

"Not really; just put them where 99Juliet is right now and make sure we have the keys to both of them in case we need to move them."

"Thanks, will do. Come on, Callie, we'll use the tug."

I figured correctly that a tug must be some sort of towing vehicle and after Stuart hooked it up to the nose wheel of 99Juliet I climbed on and sat beside him as he carefully backed the little Cessna out of the hangar and onto flight line.

"Help me tie her, would you, Callie?"

"Sure."

The Embraer Phenom 300 came off the taxiway and held short of the Alexander Aviation parking area as we finished tying down the wings and the tail of 99Juliet. Stuart rushed out to a large open area and using arm gestures got the jet moving towards him. I just stood next to the tug, out of the way, catching bugs in my open mouth. If an inanimate object could be called "sexy" my vote would definitely go to the purring machine that idled into the parking area. Everything about the jet, from the sound of the purring turbine engines to the almost predatory design and perfect complementary paint scheme, was exciting.

The Embraer was a flat dark grey; similar to the color of a B2 Stealth Bomber, but three shades lighter. It had shiny silver/chrome trim accents on the leading edges of the wings, around the cockpit windows, cabin windows, doorway, and engines. I couldn't wait to see the inside.

Once he had the jet parked where he wanted it, Stuart drew a finger across his throat and the pilot of the Embraer shut down the turbines. Before the fan blades came to a stop, the primary cabin door came away from the top of the fuselage and swung slowly downwards, the first step coming to rest just twelve inches off the ground.

An attractive uniformed young man in his mid-twenties came down the steps and stood at the bottom. Stuart finished blocking the wheels of the aircraft, said something to the young man at the bottom of the steps, then joined me next to the tug.

"You better close your mouth, or something might fly in there," Stuart jibed me. "Pretty sweet aircraft, isn't it?"

"I can't believe I'm actually going to get to ride in it; it's totally awesome."

"I told the crew that your aunt will be right out. Should we go get the bags?"

I nodded my head like a dummy, unable to take my eyes off the Embraer. As we walked back into the terminal office, I looked over my shoulder several times afraid it might disappear."

Court and Nancy were standing, facing each other, and speaking quietly as we approached. I rolled my eyes for Stuart's benefit. They didn't acknowledge us. I wanted to get aboard the jet.

"The jet's here, Nancy."

Nancy reluctantly broke her eye-lock with Court and turned to me.

"Court and I were just catching up. We went to high school together."

"That's nice, but don't you think we should be getting going?"

Both Court and Nancy burst out laughing and Nancy put her hand on my shoulder.

"Callie has a thing for machinery in case you failed to notice, Court. I suppose we should get going before she has some sort of a stroke. I've got to park my car first though."

"Just leave the keys with me. Stuart and I will take care of everything."

"The top's still down."

"Not a problem, don't worry about a thing. We'll take good care of your vehicles. What day will you be back?"

"Tuesday, late afternoon. Are you sure the car's not an imposition?"

"It's no trouble at all. I'll be here when you return, and we'll catch up more then."

Nancy smiled warmly, put her hand on Court's shoulders, then leaned in and gently kissed him on the lips. I couldn't wait to get the backstory on this.

All four of us walked out together, Nancy and Court with theirs arms loosely linked. The captain and the 1st officer of the Embraer Phenom greeted the four of us at the bottom of the airstairs before taking us aboard and offering seats in the cockpit to Court and Stuart once he found out they were both pilots.

The steward stowed Nancy's large bag in one of the exterior luggage bins and then brought Nancy and me into the jet and invited us to sit wherever we liked. I, of course, wanted to be as near as possible to the cockpit. Captain Sheren was leaning into the cockpit doorway explaining the high-tech instrumentation screens, flight controls, and the plane's flight characteristics to Stuart and Court. I wanted to be part of that but the flight deck didn't have enough room so I strained to hear his every word and hoped that later in the day I might get my own tour.

Ten minutes later Stuart and Court vacated their seats on the flight deck, came into the main cabin to say goodbye to Nancy and me.

"I hope you have a good week looking at schools, Callie. I'll take good care of Velocitá for you."

"Thanks, Stuart. I can't wait to find out more about those two." I nodded my head towards Court and Nancy."

Stuart nodded. "I know. What's the deal with your aunt? Is she single? I don't think my dad's been out with anyone since my mom and he split."

"Nancy's been single a couple of years. I've never seen her so engaged with a guy. She's normally one of those 'a woman needs a man like a fish needs a chainsaw' types."

Stuart smiled. "Have a good trip. I'm looking forward to flying with you again when you get back."

I gave him a quick kiss on the cheek and smiled back. I did like him and was curious as to what more was underneath his shy exterior.

Chapter 29

After the steward closed the main cabin door, I watched closely through the open cabin door as Captain Sheren and 1st Officer Hickey went through their checklists, fired up the engines, and spoke with ground control over the radio. The instrument panel was nothing like the ones in the Cessna or the Citabria that I'd flown in with Stuart. While the Cessna did have a single GPS nav screen, most of the other instruments were analog. The Citabria hadn't even had a built in GPS. There wasn't a single analog instrument that I could see in the Embraer except for a tiny old-fashioned compass that was mounted above the dash. I immediately thought of Melissa and *Gulf Runner* and how she would have likely approved of the old school compass.

The pilots obviously got all their information from five different video monitor screens. I watched their fingers dance with remarkable speed over the two, bottom middle, touch sensitive menu screens which in turn changed what was displayed on the three primary screens. I didn't recognize much of the information displayed but knew with certainty that familiarity and understanding would simply be a matter of training and repetition. Once we were airborne Chris the flight attendant got up out of his seat and checked to see if there was anything Nancy needed and then sat down across from me.

"Callie, can I get you anything?"

I smiled politely. "Thanks, Chris, I'm fine for now." I turned my attention back to what was going on in the cockpit.

"I can't help but notice your interest in what's going on in the cockpit. Would you like to get a closer look once we're at our cruising altitude?"

I turned back to my suddenly new best friend. "Really? That would be great, Chris. I just started flying a couple of weeks ago, but I've already decided that I'm going to get my license."

"I'll see what I can do."

Chris got up and leaned into the cockpit and chatted with the Captain Sheren and 1st Officer Hickey.

I'd surprised myself a little when I'd confidently told Chris that I was going to get my pilot's license. Looking at the bigger picture, I realized that if I could be distracted so easily from my primary end-goal of getting a ship-captain's license, then there were bound to be any number of distractions out there. Deciding what I was going to do next, what I'd study, and where I'd do it was becoming more complex by the minute.

"What's going through your head, young lady?" Nancy asked. "And I use that term lightly," she added playfully.

I immediately thought of Stuart's father and the closeness the two of them had shown one another. "Look who's talking, gentle Aunt. If I'm not mistaken it was someone else, whose name shall not be spoken, that was observed falling into the arms of a man she'd just met just minutes before."

"What a brat you are to mention it. Not that it's any of your business, but years ago Court and I were an item. Nothing untoward took place back there."

"Not how it looked to this young lady, ma'am. I was starting to wonder if we'd even still be going on our trip and whether you and Mr. Alexander would still be there when Stuart and I came back in."

"What's that sound I hear?" Nancy looked pointedly around the air near her head and swiped her hand a few times. "It sounds a little like a mosquito, only more annoying."

"Very funny."

"There's that buzzing sound again," she muttered absently, wetting her fingertip, turning a page in the magazine she'd been reading, and pointedly ignoring me. While she was turned in profile to me, I noticed a Band-Aid on the side of her neck.

"What's the deal with you two? Obviously, you knew him from sometime before. I'm sure you'd feel better if you got it off your chest."

"Why, Callie, you're too funny. I think that's the first time I've seen an interest in gossip from you."

"I'm just watching out for you."

"How adorable." She patted my cheek in a condescending manner. "Okay, here's the deal. Court and I were pretty serious our senior year in high school and when he found out I was serious about moving to Boston and going to Babson, he got a little possessive. I, in turn, got defensive and before we knew it, we were on a break. It was kid stuff. Going to college was really important to me and Court was just thinking about our relationship.

"Anyway, while we were on our 'break,' Stuart's mother, who'd been lurking in the background for years, saw her opportunity and bedded him, the little trollop, and before you could say preggers, she was. Court was quite Catholic and decided the best and right thing to do was to marry the harlot, and off I went to Boston. That's it, that's the story."

"And you hadn't seen him or spoken to him since?"

She nodded.

"Wow, that's quite a story. You still like him, obviously?"

"I do, he's my one that got away. I've thought about him often over the years."

"Are you two gonna see each other again?"

"As soon as possible."

"Well don't throw yourself at him; you might scare him away."

"Aren't you sweet to give me relationship advice. Oh, by the way, what I just shared with you is obviously between us. I wouldn't want you saying anything to your boyfriend about his loose mother and how he came into the world."

"Of course not, and he's not my 'boyfriend,' he's just a friend right now."

"Uh huh."

"What happened to your neck?" I asked and gently touched the Band-aid I'd noticed.

"It's nothing, just a little freckle that the dermatologist didn't like. He froze it off."

Fifteen minutes later, 1st Officer Hickey got up out of his seat in the cockpit and came aft. "Would you like to go up into the cockpit and joint the captain, Callie? Chris tells me that you're working on your license."

I blushed slightly at his comment; he'd probably spent more time aloft today than I'd spent over the course of my entire life. "I'm really just starting, but yes, if it would be possible."

"I imagine Captain Sheren can keep us all safely aloft for a few minutes without my assistance."

I unbuckled, walked up to the cockpit, and poked my head in. "Would it be all right if I joined you, Captain Sheren?"

"Absolutely, Callie, just buckle in after you're seated."

I slid into the vacant right-seat making sure not to hit anything as I sat, looked around, then put on the lap-belt. I noticed that the captain was also wearing shoulder restraints. "Should I put those on also?" I asked.

"No need but do put on the second headset. That way you and I can talk, and I can monitor radio traffic at the same time."

I did as he suggested.

"You read me, Callie?"

"Yes, sir." I looked around the cockpit and the first thing I was startled to notice was that there was no wheel or yoke as Stuart called it or even a stick like was in the Citabria. Instead, I surmised, the elevator and ailerons were likely actuated by two joysticks, one on either side of the aircraft, mounted in the armrests. I looked over all the screens and what they were displaying next. I could see our position as we moved over the digital map in front of him. The center screen was displaying data on the jet, fuel, engine temps, rpms, and several other things I didn't recognize. Captain Sheren put his right-hand down on one of the two smaller displays between us and cycled through various display options.

"Using these visual keypads, either one of us can change what's displayed on the three primary screens, Callie, see?" He cycled thru a number of the displays while I watched, mesmerized.

"And you steer her with these joysticks?" I asked pointing to the one in my armrest.

"Sometimes. To be honest we don't have occasion to do a lot of flying in the traditional sense. More often than not, I program in rates of climb, descents, even turns, and the computer executes it. Most days I feel like more of a programmer than a pilot."

I nodded.

"What's our current speed, sir?"

"Our air speed is currently 520 knots. With the twenty-knot tailwind we've got helping us along that would give us a ground speed of about 540. Most of the time, I try and maintain an airspeed of about 500 which gives us the best fuel burn at this altitude, but she can get up and go when you need her to."

"How fast?"

"The manufacturers listed top speed is 598 knots."

I nodded my head again thinking about how fast 129mph had seemed on Velocitá.

"So, you're on auto pilot most of the time?"

"Unfortunately, yes. The bigger and fancier the aircraft the less actual piloting you do. I spent three summers up in Alaska flying a bush plane for a fishing camp and really loved it. I miss that type of hands-on flying. This is much more technical and procedural. I guess that's the price you pay for a good salary."

"I think I'd miss the flying too."

I spent about fifteen minutes asking him questions about the Embraer's flight characteristics, procedures, and handling, and then asked what the cost per hour was to take lessons in an aircraft like it.

"There's no simple answer to that. Before you can even seek a rating in an aircraft like this you need to first get your private license, then a multi-engine rating, and then an instrument rating. The private license is probably the cheapest part. Once you get all of those ratings there are a number of programs you can choose from to get certified in a high-performance aircraft like this. But assuming you got all of those ratings first I would say it will cost you an additional $15,000-$19,000 on top of that for a weeklong certification program. And like any plane you get certified in, if you don't fly it on a regular basis then there's really no point."

I nodded my head. "So, I'd either have to own one or operate one for someone else?"

"Exactly."

"What does one of these cost, new?"

"This one, equipped as it is, was about $10.5 million."

I nodded realizing that I currently had about $900 in the bank. What was I even thinking? Conscious of the amount of time I'd spent bending his ear,

I started to unbuckle my seat belt. "Thank you for all the information, Captain Sheren. It sure is a beautiful piece of machinery."

"You're welcome, Callie. One thing…"

I stopped getting up and gave him my attention. "Yes?"

"There are almost 5,000 private jets like this one operating around the world. Some of them are flown by wealthy owner-operators who have a ton of money, but most of them are operated by guys like me. I didn't have two nickels to rub together when I started flying. I set some goals for myself, studied hard, worked hard, and eventually I got to sit in this seat."

"Yes, sir, I know exactly what you're saying. Well, thanks again for your time."

"You're entirely welcome."

I returned to the main cabin and sat down, deep in thought. I'd intuitively known that everything he'd told me was true. I also knew that I could learn to fly a plane like the Embraer by simply deciding that was what I was going to do. But that realization put me back on the same hamster wheel that I'd been spinning on for weeks. I knew with absolute certainty that I was capable of learning and doing anything I set my mind to. I could be a brain surgeon or an astronaut, but I didn't see how I could be all of them.

"What are you reading?" I asked Nancy.

"It's a business plan for a new startup company called Interact-IV. I'm considering them as a tenant and also thinking about investing in them."

"What do they do?"

"They develop interactive training aids for workers in industry."

"What sorts of training aids?"

"All kinds, everything from how to respond during a fire and what type of fire extinguisher to use, to hazards and protection from particulate matter and toxic fumes, to how to properly lift something and avoid back injury. There's really no limit to the things that can be taught using their system."

"I thought most of your prospective tenants were going to be high tech. What's so high tech about teaching classes on those subjects? There must be hundreds of companies already doing that."

"There are. Good question though. The problem with teaching people technical, complicated, or boring things in a traditional classroom setting is that a significant percentage of those people either don't learn the material because it's tedious or they weren't paying attention. And generally they don't retain the information for any length of time. As a result, companies continue to be faced with high levels of workplace injury and liability lawsuits. That's expensive. What makes this company different is the way in which they teach the material."

"How do they do it?"

"They do it using a unique interactive, computer, system that dramatically improves comprehension, understanding and retention."

"What, do they shock them or something when they aren't paying attention?"

Nancy smiled. "No, it's much more sophisticated. Their platform consists of a computer, a touch sensitive computer screen, and software that forces the student to constantly respond to multiple-choice questions as the material is being taught. One of the really clever things they also do is show what happens when someone makes the wrong choice. When people can see the consequences of a wrong decision, that also tends to reinforce correct decisions."

"What do you mean?"

"Take the ferry you work on, for example, I imagine you have several ways of fighting fires. There are right ways and wrong ways depending on the type of fire, right?"

"Yes, we use water on wood and trash type fires and dry chemical extinguishers for most everything else."

"You wouldn't use water on electrical or grease fires, right?"

"Right."

"Well, this company has a production studio, and they film people using the right kind of extinguisher on different types of fires. Then, they also film what happens when the wrong type of extinguishing agent is used. The trainee gets to see what happens when they make both the right and the wrong choice. In addition to that they also reinforce what they're teaching by looping."

"What's looping?"

"A trainee can't advance to the next section of the course material until they correctly answer every test question. If they answer something wrong the system loops them back through that module of the training until they get it right. It's brilliant, really.

Everyone learns at different speeds. A teacher or professor can't possibly teach at one speed, using one technique without losing half the class. If she teaches too fast, she loses the slower students. If she teaches too slow, the bright students stop paying attention. With this system, everyone eventually learns 100% of the material, 100% of the time and they can go through the material as quickly or as slowly as they like. It also tracks every employee's participation and course completion which frees the company from most liability law suits."

"That sounds pretty cool. Why couldn't a system like that be used to teach academics or technical skills? I'll bet most of the kids at my school only learn and retain about twenty-five percent of what they're taught?"

Nancy thought for a moment. "That's actually quite a good idea, Callie. I know the military has had some really good success teaching soldiers how to do complex things with interactive technology. Why couldn't traditional education be replaced with this? There'd obviously be some resistance from teacher unions that would have to be overcome, but that would be a huge market to go after! That's going to be one of the questions I'll ask the principles of the company later this week." Nancy scribbled a note inside the front of the business plan.

"Can I read it after you?"

Nancy smiled and then nodded.

My mind wandered back to deciding about a school, and for the next several minutes I ran the old, familiar arguments through my head again. Should I just pursue a general knowledge-based education, a specialized degree program or more of a trade-based education like a maritime program? Could one of the maritime schools offer me both a logical route to a captain's license and a useful college degree at the same time?

Nancy looked over at me. "What are you thinking, Callie?"

I looked up at her. "That choice, is a pain. I can be anything or do anything I want, thanks to your generous offer, but I can't make up my mind. I'm still lost as to what I should do next."

"Well, what's your process for making difficult decisions in other areas of your life? How do you decide what's best?"

I thought about it for a few seconds. "I do research first and try to look at both sides of an issue."

"Okay, how?

"By talking to or reading the opinions of others."

"Why are other people's opinions important?"

"On their own, they're not. Everybody's full of opinions, but you already know what your own opinions are and sometimes people with an opposing view came by theirs by thinking of or knowing something you've never thought of or were never exposed to."

"That's very healthy, what next?"

"Then I look at what my options are, think of the plusses and minuses of each course of action and then assign a likelihood of success to each one. Lastly, I ask myself whether my decision is consistent with my values, and does it broadly advance me in the direction I want to go or is it just a diversion."

Nancy was giving me her full attention now. "That's actually pretty sophisticated; I'm impressed. Most people just wonder if something will make them feel good, right now."

"Nancy, I really respect your opinion and the decisions you made in your life. You know me better than anyone. Can't you just tell me what I should do."

"Nope. What I did was right for me and might not be for you. One of the biggest reasons I was successful was because of my self-determination, not someone else's." She looked over at my wrist. "Callie?"

"What."

"Where did you get that bracelet? It's very interesting." She held out her hand. "May I see it?"

I extended my arm to her and let her look more closely. "Mam made it for me."

Nancy raised her eyebrows. "Frances, my sister made that!"

"Yup."

"I had no idea she had this kind of talent. She was always stringing something when we were growing up, but I had no idea that her work had gotten to this level. What are the stones?"

"Sapphires."

"Wow. This is some of the finest and most detailed handwork I've ever seen. There must be thousands of stones in it."

"Mam said about 14,000. I'm a little scared to wear it. What if I hit it on something and it broke?"

"You do have a pretty active lifestyle. Anyway, it's gorgeous. Tell Frances I really think she has a rare talent. Actually, give it here, dear girl. It's a bit much for you to wear to college interviews. It would probably look much more appropriate on me. Don't worry, I'll take good care of it, and I promise to give it back."

I unscrewed the wire going through the barrel clasp and pulled it out freeing the bracelet from my wrist, wrapped it around Nancy's, and tightened the wire. I felt a little strange as I did it, realizing that Nancy saw the bracelet as a unique object to be coveted. For sure, she appreciated the workmanship, but she also seemed to like it in the same way someone would like a much simpler but very expensive diamond bracelet or necklace for the associative value it might confer on her in the eyes of others. I didn't care at all whether someone else saw me wearing my mother's bracelet. I wore it simply because it reminded me of Mam and the fact that she had given me something that had taken so long to complete.

"You'll be careful with it, right?"

"Of course, you silly fool. Why would you even think you needed to say that?"

"I just realized when I was fastening it onto your wrist how valuable it is to me; not as a piece of jewelry but simply because Mam made it for me."

"Of course. Don't worry, I'll be incredibly careful with it. There's someone I want to show it to in Boston who's a specialist in fine pieces like this and I expect I'm as proud of my sister for making it as you are as her daughter."

Nancy's words made me feel instantly better and I let the subject lie as we continued towards Boston. I reclined my seat some and reengaged my mind on the conundrum I was facing regarding schools and trying to evaluate pros and cons of the three schools I planned on visiting again. I'd been over this same ground hundreds of times and kept coming up with the same non-answers.

Suddenly, a lightbulb started flickering on somewhere in my mind and I recalled Einstein's definition of insanity as "doing the same thing over and over again and expecting different results." That's what I'd been doing! Perhaps I needed to be asking entirely different questions. In one of my earlier conversations with Nancy she'd suggested that I look at my strengths and my weaknesses and try to envision what I wanted my life to look like ten, twenty and thirty years out. I had yet to do that and had instead remained focused on simply picking a career and then identifying the best higher education source to realize that career. Was that even the right question? What were my strengths? I knew I was bright and could master the knowledge part of virtually anything. I also knew I had a unique ability to focus on something and do whatever was necessary to realize a goal. I was also principled, physically fit, and high-energy.

What were my weaknesses, though? I'd never once in my life asked that question. As I began thinking about the subject, I quickly realized that rather than just having one or two, I was loaded with them! How could I have gone through sixteen years of life without addressing this?

"Nancy?"

She looked up. "Yes."

"Do you have a pencil and paper I could use?"

"Certainly." She reached into her briefcase on the seat next to her and took out a fresh legal pad and a mechanical pencil and handed them to me.

"What are you working on?"

I blushed, embarrassed. "I feel like an idiot for saying this, but I just realized that I've never, not once asked myself what my weaknesses are."

"And that's important to you, why?"

"I'm not certain yet, but I suspect it might have something to do with why I'm struggling so hard to decide what my next step will be."

She smiled at me. "Weaknesses are hard to acknowledge." She held up the business plan she was reading. "That's one of the first things I look for as I read business plans. People as a rule are exceptionally good at identifying and bringing to your attention their strengths, but not so much their weaknesses. Sometimes they're in touch with them and try and hide them, but just as frequently, they have no idea. It's a big part of evaluating an opportunity and the likelihood of its success."

I bent to my task and spent the next twenty minutes writing. I was appalled at the end of the exercise as I looked at how long my list of weaknesses was.

"Nancy?"

She looked up again.

"This isn't good. I honestly had no idea. I don't know if I'm equipped to do any of the things I've been considering."

She laughed. "What, you've discovered you're human?"

"Oh, I'm human all right. I can't believe this."

"Read me a couple."

"Well a biggie is number one, right at the top of my list; *I don't play well with others.* I'm really uncomfortable doing anything where I'm forced to rely on other people's contributions. As a result, I almost always do things where I'm the sole decision-maker and contributor."

"Give me a couple more."

"That I'm, *callous and don't empathize well*, that I'm, *impatient and unforgiving, opinionated, stubborn, overly blunt, intolerant, manipulative, reckless, overly serious, close-minded, judgmental.*"

"Is that all?"

"No, I've got two pages here!"

"You're funny. We all have pages of flaws and anyone who doesn't, is either delusional or lying."

"What organization would ever want to hire a person like me?"

"Perhaps none."

"How can you say that? I thought you believed in me and thought I could do anything."

"I do. Do another list now; one with all your character strengths. Cogitate on both of them and let's have the same discussion tomorrow."

I was more perturbed than I let on to Nancy but followed her suggestion for the next twenty minutes. About the same time I finished my lists Nancy passed me the business plan she'd been reading, and I spent the balance of the flight reading it. The interactive video training company was more interesting than I'd expected, and I quickly thought of a number of additional uses for the technology. I read the executive summaries of the principals last. One had a background in finance and accounting, the other had expertise in video production and writing software code. Both had extensive experience in public health. Those skills seemed positive. What I didn't see, however, was any experience on either's part actually running a company. I wondered if that was important.

Chris interrupted my thoughts to let us know we needed to fasten our seat belts and prepare to land in Boston.

RIP CONVERSE

Chapter 30

W e thanked Captain Sheren, 1st Officer Hickey and Chris as we deplaned and then Nancy and I made our way to the rental car center where Nancy selected a Mercedes Benz G550 from Hertz's "Ultimate Collection." As we drove into the city via the old Sumner Tunnel, I couldn't resist ribbing her about the SUV.

"Is there something you're not telling me, Nancy?" I asked with a straight face.

"Not sure to what you're referring, dear niece."

"Just curious, but why did you rent a car with rhino-bars?"

"Rhino-bars? What on earth are they?"

"They're the metal bars surrounding our grill and headlights. They afford protection to the front ends of safari vehicles should they encounter charging rhinoceri."

"Is that what those things are? I always wondered. Well, better to be safe than sorry I always say."

"Are you expecting we might encounter a herd of wild rhinos in downtown Boston?"

"Don't be silly, Callie, of course not."

I loved pulling her chain.

"I don't believe I've ever heard you use that expression, 'better to be safe than sorry.'"

"Well, you simply haven't been listening to me then. One can't be too careful."

"Another phrase that you no doubt live by."

"Callie?"

"Yes, Aunt Nancy?"

"Are you trifling with me?"

"Of course not. I would never do that."

"My ass."

"Tsk, tsk, language, Nancy."

"You're impossible!"

"Temper, temper."

Nancy reached over and gave me a loving pinch in the side. "How on earth did I ever get hooked up with you?"

We drove through Sumner Tunnel and emerged in the downtown financial district. After, we drove over Beacon Hill and past the statehouse via Beacon Street.

"Wow, the city's bigger and older than I expected."

Nancy nodded. "Actually it's quite small and manageable compared to New York and Chicago. You can easily walk anywhere in Boston proper."

"Where are we staying?"

"We're staying at the Ritz Carlton in an Executive Suite."

"Fancy."

"Indeed. I selected it simply because they have a separate room with a sofa bed that I can lock you in. I didn't want to share a room with you and be kept awake by your snoring."

"I don't snore. Older people snore."

"I distinctly remember this past summer when we both fell asleep on my bed one afternoon that I was rudely awakened by the sound of snoring."

"That wasn't me, gentle Aunt."

"Don't be absurd. Ladies don't snore."

We pulled up in front of the Ritz two minutes later and followed our bags into the lobby behind the bellhop. Nancy went to the counter and addressed one of the women behind it by her first name.

"Hello, Dianne."

"Miss Liddell, so nice to see you back. I saw you were in the system when I came on duty earlier this morning."

Nancy took an American Express card out of her purse and handed it to Dianne. "I'd like you to meet my niece, Catherine. She's a bit of a troublemaker, but you can't pick your relatives. Somehow I put up with her."

Dianne turned to me. "It's a pleasure to meet you, Catherine. If there's anything I can do to make your stay more comfortable here at the Ritz or answer any questions about Boston, please don't hesitate to ask."

I offered Dianne my hand. "Nice meeting you as well, Dianne."

Nancy took her credit card back after an imprint was taken and passed something to Dianne at the same time. Then, after putting her card back into her purse, reached back in, turned to our bellhop, and passed him some folded money. "Arthur, could you take our things up to our room? I think we'll go into the bar and get some lunch before coming up."

"Certainly. Thank you, Miss Liddell."

"Are you hungry, Callie?"

I nodded and followed Nancy into the Artisan Bistro. "You must spend quite a bit of time here. Everyone is so nice and helpful."

"Just once or twice a year."

"Why do they all recognize you?"

Nancy smiled and rubbed her thumb and her index finger together. "Money."

"How much did you tip?"

"I gave Dianne $100 and Arthur fifty. They'll take good care of us for the remainder of our stay. I also make a point of remembering other people's names, especially staff. So many of the people who stay at places like this are stiffs and they talk down to the employees. Nobody likes that. Treat people like people and they'll go out of their way to help you."

The maître d' at the restaurant also greeted Nancy by name and after showing us to our table and seating us, placed our napkins into our laps. I found that made me a bit uncomfortable and was glad he'd done Nancy's napkin first. If I'd been alone the first time that had happened to me, I might well have broken one of his fingers for reaching into my lap without permission. As it was, I acted as though that happened to me at every meal and thanked him politely. *Rich people are strange,* I thought to myself. Nancy tipped him also.

Once seated, I looked around the room and became increasingly self-conscious as I noticed how everyone was dressed. I was wearing a clean, white, button down shirt and a clean pair of jeans, but I still had on my black leather jacket.

"I'm underdressed, aren't I?"

"A little. Did you bring anything more…"? She struggled for the right word. "Upscale?"

"Like what?"

"Like a dress or a pant suit or perhaps a nice pair of slacks and a fashionable top."

I shook my head. "I brought one of the dresses that you got me in Boca Grande, but I don't own anything at all fashionable like the women in here are wearing. Sorry I'm so pathetic."

Nancy put her hand over mine. "Not to worry, dear girl. Pathetic you are not. You are simply without the appropriate costume for the situation that we find ourselves in. There's a Brooks Brothers on Newbury Street just a few blocks from here and we can easily rectify the situation after e a spot of lunch."

Despite her kind words I felt like a rube and made a note to self to think situations like the one I was in through better. I'd brought one of the dresses that Nancy had bought for me over the summer thinking I could wear that as we went to her meetings and looked at colleges, but after seeing the way the women were dressed in the Ritz Carlton bar, I realized that it would make me look like a young kid. That wasn't the image I wanted to project as I interviewed.

When you walk into the bar at the Ritz Carlton it's like walking into a parallel world. Both sound and light are designed and controlled to mute the harsh outside world. The tablecloths are spotless, the service attentive and the food and beverages delicious. Yet you turn your head and just feet away through the glass, are dirty streets, people rushing to their destinations, bums trying to hustle change, and all the noise and tension of a busy city. Even though I'd traveled to Boston on a private jet, I had still felt comfortable being me. The second I'd walked into the Ritz, however, I'd felt self-conscious and less-than. I wasn't used to being out of my element and didn't like the feelings that arose in me.

I thought about it for a few moments and realized that one of the reasons that I felt uncomfortable was that I was in a world where I didn't understand any of the rules. I liked feeling competent and special. I liked excelling and being the best, whether in the classroom, on *Gulf Runner*, on the mats at Eva's dojo or even on my motorcycle. Doing all of those things, I was in control. It was unsettling to find myself somewhere where virtually everyone around me were experts in things I knew absolutely nothing about and all I could do was just quietly observe.

"You're very quiet, Callie."

"Sorry, I was just doing a little introspection."

"And what was revealed by this self-analysis?"

"I feel like a fish out of water. Normally I go through my day confident and self-assured. Here, I have no idea how to be or who to be. I guess I feel a little stupid, and I don't like it.

Nancy tapped a perfectly enameled fingernail on her Lillet cocktail, thinking for a moment. "You like being the best at everything you do."

I nodded.

"And here you have yet to even identify what's prized, let alone become the best at it."

I nodded again, embarrassed. "Is that vain?"

"No, I don't think so. Appearance means nothing to you. You're the real deal. You don't want to just look a certain way; you want to actually be that way. All this is simply new and unfamiliar. Once you get the lay of the land, you'll figure out your place in it. It's one of the things I respect and like most about you." She chuckled.

"What?"

"I was just thinking that if I were to suddenly disappear and you were stuck here, penniless, and with no way home that you'd probably have a custodial job folding sheets down in the basement before the end of the day, and within six months be the general manager of this place. Two years later you'd probably control the largest hedge fund in the city. I'll bet there isn't another person in this room that could do that."

"What's a hedge fund?"

"It's a pot of money."

I took the last bite of my chicken & duck club sandwich and smiled at her. "Thanks for the vote of confidence. It makes me feel better."

"Are you ready to go shopping?"

We took a cab to Brooks Brothers on the corner of Newbury and Berkley Streets and found two lovely pairs of cashmere wool slacks, two blouses, a sport coat, shoes, and a belt. When I tried on the slacks the tailor had to pin up the unfinished hems.

"Do you have any already hemmed?" I asked.

"No, sorry, miss, and we're about a week out on alterations."

"Any way we could get them done today?" Nancy asked hopefully. "I'd be quite willing to pay a rush fee."

The tailor just shook his head. "We send everything out to be done these days and no longer have the flexibility we once had. I'm terribly sorry."

Nancy thought for just a moment. "Just pin them and mark them as you normally would. We'll still take them."

I was confused. I couldn't wear them with just pins holding up the hems and I'd never touched a sewing needle in my life. "What are you thinking, Nancy?"

"You'll see."

I carried the bags as we left Brooks Brothers and Nancy took a right instead of a left out the door and then a right on Newbury."

"Where are we headed?" I asked.

"I'd like to stop in at Firestorm & Perkins on the way back."

"What are they?"

"A little jewelry store I know. I've bought quite a few pieces from them over the years, and I want to ask David, the owner, something."

We walked just a few hundred feet. Nancy stopped, cupped her hand to the side of her face and peered in through a glass door.

There was another glass door right next to it and standing in front of it was a man wearing a long, dark grey, wool overcoat, wool watch cap, and a mask in deference to the pandemic. He was pointedly staring at his cell phone. I found it odd that he didn't turn or acknowledge us in any way when we stopped just inches from him as Nancy looked through the door next to him. Nancy pressed the doorbell on the wall next to the door she'd been peering into and then waited, I guessed, for access.

I continued to focus on the man. Why was he standing where he was so pointedly ignoring us?

I heard a key turn in the lock and then Nancy stepped back and smiled as the door was opened by an armed, middle aged, black security guard. He held the door for her. "Good afternoon, welcome to Firestorm & Perkins." I took my eyes off the man in the overcoat, turned, smiled at the guard, and followed Nancy as she walked into a tiny foyer with a second security door which then led into the actual store. There was a buzzing sound as the magnetic lock in the second door was unlocked by a clerk inside, behind the counter. Nancy opened that door and walked into the store. The guard and I followed her in.

A man in his fifties smiled broadly at Nancy as she entered, rushed around the counter, and took both of her hands in his. "What a pleasant surprise! And looking like a million dollars if I do say so myself."

"David, you're sweet, but I'm not here to purchase anything today. I just want your opinion on something."

David pouted. "Nonsense, a woman such as yourself can never have too much jewelry."

"Callie, I'd like you to meet David Firestorm. David is perhaps the most knowledgeable jeweler in the city of Boston. It's rumored that he can tell paste from gem quality from 1,000 yards. But, fair warning, he's also a master salesman. The last time I was in, he assured me that the world would stop spinning if I didn't purchase the diamond earrings that I'm wearing now. David, this is my niece, Catherine."

I put down the two bags from Brooks Brothers and shook his hand. "Very nice to meet you, Mr. Firestorm. I should tell you, while my aunt may have unlimited resources, mine are non-existent. It's all I can do to keep gas in my motorcycle. You do have a beautiful store though."

"Thank you, Callie. You obviously have your aunt's discerning eye."

"Callie, see how he's softening you up as a future client already? David's like the Chinese; his memory and his sales game are patient and quite long. You must remain extremely vigilant around him, otherwise you'll find yourself in here ten years from now shopping for an engagement ring that you could have bought in Florida for half the price."

I was quite used to Nancy's outrageousness when we were alone but not so comfortable with it when we were with others.

"Nancy, you know I offer an incomparable level of service and knowledge that simply isn't available anywhere else."

"I imagine a location like this is quite expensive," I mused out loud trying to soften Nancy's jab.

"What a perceptive young lady." David reached over and touched my shoulder as he said it. He turned back to Nancy. "So tell me. If you didn't come in to purchase anything from my modest little bauble shop, why did you stop?"

Nancy pulled up the sleeve on her long leather coat and held her wrist out to him. "Believe it or not, Callie's mother, my sister, made this piece and I'm quite taken with it. I simply wanted you to look at it and give me your considered opinion as to its retail value."

A loupe appeared in David's eye as if by magic. I honestly hadn't seen him put it in his eye, it just appeared there. He took Nancy's wrist into his hands and bent down to better see it.

"What an interesting, lovely piece! Would you mind bringing your wrist over to the counter so I can get a better look at it in the light?"

"Not at all, it is lovely though, isn't it?"

While David looked closely at my mother's work, I took a moment to look at some of the pieces he had on display in his cases. I knew nothing about jewelry or gems as I'd never been able to see any practical use for them, but even to my untrained eye I could tell that what he had to sell in his cases was of extremely good quality and beautifully crafted. After looking at several of the tiny price tags I was stunned. Many of the pieces were hundreds of thousands of dollars. I moved over to the counter where David continued to examine Mam's bracelet.

"Would you mind taking it off for a second, Nancy? I want to see how that clasp works." David asked. Nancy rolled her wrist and I leaned in between them and twisted the solid wire bar that threaded through the intricate hinge, withdrew it, and handed the bracelet to David. He brought the bracelet back up to his face and spent a good solid minute rotating it and looking closely at it through his loupe.

"Extraordinary. I don't think I've ever seen as much fine handwork in a single piece."

"What sort of retail value do you suppose a piece like this would bring in your store, David?"

"Well, the stones are almost worthless and the clasp, while lovely, isn't quite strong enough so that would need to be redone...."

"David, please, this isn't a negotiation. This particular piece isn't for sale. Just answer the question. What sort of retail price would this command as it is?"

David took the loupe out of his eye and nervously scratched his head. "Well, considering as the artist is unknown, the stones practically worthless and the issues I mentioned with the clasp…"

"David! Just answer or I'll take it down to the bandits at the Jewelers Exchange in Downtown Crossing," Nancy pushed.

David moved his hand from the top of his head to his chest looking as though he might have a cardiac arrest at any moment. "Okay, okay, I'm thinking." He brought his hand back up and scratched his head one last time. "I would retail it at about seventy-five."

I hadn't said a word to that point and started by firmly inserting my foot into my mouth. "Seventy-five! My mother spent over a month stringing that piece."

"Okay! Maybe ninety."

Nancy looked over at me knowing what I was thinking and spoke without looking at David. "You mean thousands of course."

"Yes, of course, $90,000 dollars."

"And what would you offer her wholesale, if she were to make another?" Nancy added.

"Not a penny over $70,000. Not one penny!" David blustered back. "Do you have any idea of the expenses I have here on Newbury Street and the value of my clientele?"

Nancy reached up and patted him condescendingly on the side of his face. "I know, I know David. You poor baby. It's terribly expensive. Now that wasn't so hard, was it?"

David looked at me. "Can your mother make other bracelets like this Callie?"

"Yes, sir, I imagine she could."

I was stunned at the price, and barely heard the sound of the buzzer as David's sales associate Marguerite pressed the button for the inner door release. The guard got up off his stool behind me and walked into the foyer to let another customer in from outside the store.

I finally looked up when Marguerite pressed the button a second time to allow the guard and the new customer back through the inner door. Things suddenly went very bad from there.

My elation at the value of my mother's bracelet was replaced by dread as the guard collapsed unconscious in the inner doorway and a masked man stepped over his body and trained a shotgun on us all. It was the same man who had been hanging out near the entrance when Nancy and I had first entered.

"Hands up, everyone!" he shouted. "If anyone reaches under the counter, I *will* shoot you."

I complied, quickly raising my arms, and looked down at the guard who was bleeding from the forehead and unconscious. I surmised that the robber had hit him in the head with the butt of the shotgun.

David spoke next. "Whatever you want sir, it's yours. Please, just stay calm and don't hurt anyone."

The robber reached into his pocket, pulled out a folded shopping bag and threw it towards David while still keeping the gun trained in our direction. As I'd raised my hands, I'd also instinctively taken two steps away from Nancy and the counter hoping to split the gunman's attention and to remove some of the threat to Nancy. There was no sense in staying in a tight cluster with Nancy, David and Marguerite and making the gunman's job any easier. He obviously didn't perceive me as a threat as he allowed me to stay out in the middle of the floor.

I knew right away that I was close enough to the robber to get inside his perimeter without getting shot, but I didn't move because I didn't want to take a chance that the gun would go off while it was pointed anywhere near Nancy and the other two.

A plan started coming together in my head and I began to feign fear and played the part of the shaking, scared little girl about to break down or pass out. I averted my eyes from him, cowered inwards and brought my hands down with my palms extended towards him as if I were trying to ward him off. I let my shoulders start to shake as if I were sobbing and moved my feet several inches apart and brought by right foot back ever so slightly. If I'd been in Eva's studio at the time, she might well have pointed me out to the rest of the class as exhibiting a perfect, Krav Maga, ready stance. "Please.... don't shoot us. We'll do anything you ask."

"Shut up, you daft twit! No one's going to shoot anybody if you just do what I say."

CALLIE AWAKENS

His attention turned more fully to me and with it the gun, away from Nancy and the rest of the group. I still knew with absolute certainty that I could get inside the arc of his gun before he could pull the trigger and without any further thought, I launched.

Inside his perimeter, I grabbed the barrel of his gun in my left hand and pushed it upwards towards the ceiling and swung into the middle of his chest with my back. The gun immediately went off into the ceiling and scared the heck out of me, but I kept my momentum and never stopped throwing the weight of my back into his chest. Then I grabbed the butt of the shotgun with my right hand and pulled the barrel down to the floor with my left and jacked the butt up, right under his chin. That stunned him and he staggered backwards. But he was not out.

I reversed the gun and trained it on him. "Get on your knees!" I yelled.

I expected that he would comply, faced with imminent death. He didn't, started laughing and walked closer to me. It was not at all what I'd expected.

"I mean it!" I shouted.

He reached towards me and grabbed the barrel of the gun. "Idiot." And then he started to pull it out of my hands. I really didn't want to shoot this guy, but I couldn't let him get the gun back.

I pulled the trigger expecting the gun to roar again. Nothing happened, not even a click. He pulled the gun away from me, reversed it, and then racked the pump under the barrel.

"You need to have a shell in the chamber, you moron. Now it will fire."

Note to self, I thought. *Learn more about guns.*

He started to bring the barrel back down towards me and it was at that moment that Nancy swung her $15,000 Tom Ford Alligator handbag, squarely into his face from the right side. I expect there were probably five pounds of essentials in that bag, and it got his immediate attention. Simultaneously I reached into his perimeter again with my left hand, grabbed the barrel of the shotgun for a second time and with my right-hand, cross drew my steel baton from the inside pocket of my jacket with my left, snapped it open, and backhanded him as hard as I could across the left side of his face with it. He went down like an express elevator in a high rise. Just to be certain that he stayed down I went to my knees, grabbed his left arm and shoulder in a brutal wrestling/Krav Maga hold and twisted it up

315

behind his back at an unnatural angle in case he woke up. If he did, I would tear it out of the socket and break his wrist.

"Nancy, would you be so kind as to pass me the guard's handcuffs?"

Everyone in the store was staring at me silently with astonished looks on their faces.

I tried again. "Nancy? Cuffs?"

She came out of her trance. "Of course, gentle niece." She reached into a leather holster on the guard's waist, pulled them out and dangled them awkwardly in midair. "I assume you mean these bracelets?"

"Yes, Aunt, those would be the ones."

She passed them to me and then turned to David.

"You know, David, you really need to improve the quality of your clientele. This," and she gestured to the unconscious gunmen, "is simply unacceptable. I wouldn't be surprised if Callie never returns to this hovel."

David had been speechless since the moment before I'd engaged with the gunman and laughed out loud for a few seconds. I suppose he was just releasing pent up tension. Just as quickly he stopped.

"Marguerite, please call the police and tell them we require an ambulance." Then he rushed around the counter and gently took the guard's head into his lap. "God, I hope Willy will be all right."

I looked down more closely at the gunman and pulled the ski mask up and off his head. He was bleeding badly from his mouth and there were several broken teeth on the floor and a deep gash in the side of his face where my baton had made contact. I hit the tip of my baton on the floor collapsing it, and then slid it back into the inside pocket of my jacket in a single, fluid, movement. Nancy watched me as I did this.

"Callie."

I looked up at her.

"You and I really need to have a talk." Then she smiled and started to laugh. The police and ambulance arrived just minutes later, and we patiently answered all their questions for the next hour while they filled out their report.

It was four o'clock when we finally walked back into the Ritz Carlton on Avery Street. Nancy walked up to the desk and approached Dianne.

"I trust you had a nice afternoon out?" Dianne inquired.

"It was interesting; thank you for asking." Nancy looked back at me and then into the two bags that I still carried. She grabbed the one with the two pairs of slacks in it and passed it over the counter to Dianne. "Could you see to it that these two pairs of pants are properly hemmed by 7:00 am tomorrow morning and then have them brought to our room?"

"Of course, Miss Liddell. Are they already marked?"

Nancy nodded. "That's very kind of you, Dianne."

"Is there anything else I can do, Miss Liddell? Would you like me to make dinner reservations for you and Catherine in the dining room for later or somewhere else perhaps?"

"Not right now, thank you. We're going up to our room for a little rest and we'll decide later. Shopping can be so exhausting."

"May I send up some tea?"

"That would be nice, yes, please do. Come along, Catherine."

RIP CONVERSE

Chapter 31

As soon as we got up to the room and the door was closed Nancy read me the riot act.

"Callie, what on earth were you thinking in David's store? You could have been killed by that man!"

I was surprised at her attack and immediately became defensive. "I wasn't."

"You weren't what?"

"I wasn't really thinking. When I get into situations like that, I don't think at all; everything I do is reflexive."

"What do you mean 'situations like that'? Have there been others?"

I suddenly felt guilty. Despite several opportunities, I hadn't mentioned any of what had taken place between me and MS-13 over the previous two weeks.

"I've had a couple of situations with MS-13 over the last couple of weeks. Honestly, I just forgot to mention them."

"MS-13! Callie, what the hell's been going on? And I'm not buying that 'you forgot.' One does not have violent confrontations with gangs and then forget about it."

"It wasn't intentional. I wasn't hiding it; I just hadn't thought of mentioning it." I'd never felt Nancy's anger before and didn't like it. "A little more than a week ago, I interrupted some gang people trying to kidnap a teenage girl. I wasn't looking for trouble or anything. I was just going to Eva's dojo one evening and saw several men trying to snatch a girl off the street. I stopped them and saved the girl. Anyone would have done what I did."

"How did you stop them?"

"I put two of them down; kind of like what I did to that robber at David's store."

Nancy moved over to the couch I was sitting on and sat down next to me and picked up one of my hands in hers.

"Callie, you're sixteen years old and you've got an incredible life ahead of you. People your age don't 'put down' armed robbers and MS-13 gangbangers. You could have been killed or seriously injured both times. I'm really starting to wonder if this Krav Maga was a good idea. You're supposed to be enjoying your last year of high school; dating and going to proms and singing in the glee club."

I looked at her with a dubious expression on my face. "Are you serious, glee club?"

She blew out a frustrated sounding breath. "Yes well, I suppose glee club might be a bit of a stretch, but you get my point, right? Any kind of wholesome activities would be a damned site better than what you've apparently been up to. Why didn't you mention this to me before?"

"I don't know." I really didn't. "It just didn't seem relevant to our relationship and this trip. Once it was over, it was over. This trip and our relationship are completely unrelated. I honestly didn't even think about it. I'm sorry for not mentioning it."

"Christ, I'm not sure what to do with you."

"There's nothing 'to do' about me. Stuff happens and I respond. I'm sorry if I didn't think to mention it, but it was honestly out of my mind once it was over. And about what happened with that robber in David's store; I had it totally under control. Same thing with the bangers; once it was over, it was over. I'm on to the next thing now."

"How can you be so casual about all this? It's not normal!"

"Whoever said I was normal?" Nancy's opinion was incredibly important to me, and I felt close to tears. I wanted to please her. "I thought you liked me because I wasn't normal?"

Neither one of us said anything for a few moments, cooling down.

"Do you think there's something wrong with me, Nancy? I'm not talking about my propensity to get into physical altercations with bad people but more how I deal or don't deal with things. Maybe I'm missing something. It's like there's some sort of emotional cutoff switch in me that suddenly turns off. I know I don't feel fear until something is over."

"I don't know, Callie. I suppose maybe you could talk to someone about that. Right now, I'm just concerned you won't see your seventeenth birthday at the rate you're going. Is that all? Is there anything else you haven't told me?"

I looked down at my hand to avoid her eyes. "Maybe one or two more things." I muttered.

"What! There's more!"

I nodded still not making eye contact. "After I put down those two gang members and saved that girl I got chased by the gang in a car."

"Oh, Callie!"

"Twice." I added quietly.

"What? Do the police know?"

I nodded. "The second time they chased me I was able to lure them into a police trap. One of them got shot and killed by the police and the other is in jail now."

Nancy was suddenly furious and got up off the couch. "People were shot! I'll sue them, every single one of them! What were they thinking using a sixteen-year-old girl as bait to trap a bunch of gangbangers?"

"No! That's not what happened. They didn't use me at all. They rescued me. The gang was already after me and I called the detective I know while they were chasing me. She set it up so I could get to a place of safety."

"Callie, do you have any idea how crazy all that sounds."

"It's not that big a deal, Nancy! It's over, I think." I added as an afterthought.

"'Not that big a deal', and 'you think!'"

"Well, all or most of the people involved in the kidnappings are either dead, in jail, or in the hospital."

"What do you mean kidnapping<u>s</u>? There, you fucking did it again; you're minimizing! I'm sorry for my language, but I'm mad. You only mentioned one attempted kidnapping and I thought you interrupted that?"

"I did, but apparently the gang has been kidnapping young girls for the sex trade for a while."

"Oh, this is beautiful, just beautiful! And what makes you think it's over? You said once it's over, it's over. Well, is it? Are you telling me that the police caught the leader of the gang and locked up all the other gang members?"

"Not yet." I muttered. "But I'm sure they will."

"Not yet. Oh, that's perfect, just perfect."

I'd never seen Nancy so angry, and I could tell she was really frustrated with me.

"Callie, don't you get how much danger you're in? You're being incredibly naïve. These people are dangerous, and they have long memories. I know because I read about them all the time in Chicago."

"I'll be careful, Nancy. I can take care of myself; there's no need to insult me."

She shook her head probably giving up on me, sat back down and put her arm around me. "I don't mean to insult you; I just care about you. I don't want to see anything bad happen to you."

"Can we talk about something else then? You're mad about something that happened in the past that I'm no longer in control of. It's over. I'm sorry I didn't think to tell you all about it and I'll try not to do that again. Could we go over our schedule for the next four days?"

Nancy reluctantly gave in to my suggestion and later she took me out to a really good Asian/Fusion restaurant on Washington Street called Myers & Chang where we must have tried over half the menu. She didn't mention MS-13 again that evening, to me.

****

Later that evening, after saying "goodnight" to Callie, Nancy made a phone call from her bedroom to a private detective named Kevin Grainger in Chicago. She'd employed Kevin several years previous to investigate and plug an intellectual property leak in one of her divisions that was costing her a fortune in lost revenues. She called him on his cell.

"Hello."

"Kevin, it's Nancy Liddell. Sorry for calling so late."

"No worries, I'm just sitting at my desk staring at a computer screen and getting nowhere on a tricky case. How can I help you? I thought you'd sold your company and moved to FL."

"I did. This is about something else. What I'm looking for may not be in your purview, but I'm hoping that maybe you can give me a referral. Over the past year I've gotten extremely attached to a sixteen-year-old niece of mine. We're actually in Boston right now looking at colleges. Long story short, she's an incredibly gifted girl and she's gotten involved on the wrong side of MS-13 down near where I live in Fort Myers. She's disrupted their business and several of them are now in prison as a result of her involvement. This girl has no idea of the danger she's in."

"Go on."

"When she was living with me this past summer, I introduced her to and encouraged a relationship with an Israeli self-defense instructor who teaches Krav Maga, which may have complicated things. Callie, that's my niece, is actually exceptionally good at it, but she's just sixteen, only five feet tall and maybe ninety pounds. I'm worried that she's gotten falsely confident in her ability to defend herself and she seems to be totally clueless as to how much danger she might be in as a result of her actions. I know these animals from the time I spent in Chicago and watching what they did up there."

"I've heard of Krav Maga but don't know much about it other than it's a supposedly brutal form of self-defense. How can I help?"

"I don't know if you can. I don't want to smother the girl or scare her, but I'm trying to figure out a way of providing real protection for her and her family in Fort Myers and was hoping you had some ideas or know someone in our area who could help me."

"When would this start?"

"As soon as possible. We won't be back for a week, but I wanted to see if I could arrange for some discreet protection for her family. Once we're back, the focus can be on Callie."

"I'll make a few calls and see if I can't get a referral for someone in that area. It would be a specialized thing and would have to be someone who understands and doesn't mind the real physical threat of those punks."

"I would expect so."

"This might take a couple of days."

"As soon as possible."

"I'll do my best. And, Nancy?"

"What?"

323

"I just want to warn you, it could get very expensive, especially if you want real twenty-four-hour protection for the girl and her family."

"I'm not worried about the expense, but it has to be discreet. My sister in-law and her husband would freak out if they knew what was going on and Callie would be really pissed at me if she found out. Will you call me as soon as possible? Evenings would be best."

"I'll do my best."

"Thanks, Kevin."

Chapter 32

Tuesday, I woke up at 6:00 and went down to the indoor pool at the fitness center. It was only half the length of Nancy's pool in Boca Grande, but it was warm and wet, and I got in 100 laps and then my regular sit-ups and pushups before heading back to the room. It was 7:00 when I finished my exercise routine. As I walked down the hallway to our room, I could see my newly hemmed trousers, as promised, hanging on the outside of the door. They'd even pressed them for me. After showering I tried them on. They fit perfectly. I knocked on Nancy's half open door.

"Enter."

"What do you think?" I asked turning around so she could see.

"Very nice, Callie, you look great."

"I'm still blown away that Dianne could get them done on such short notice."

"That's the Ritz for you and its why they're worth a little extra. They actually teach employees that when a customer asks for something they are supposed to personally address and solve customer service challenges. There's none of that passing-the-buck stuff where someone says, 'It's not my department' or 'It's not my job.' For all we know Dianne sewed them herself when she got home last night."

"Pretty cool. I'm really looking forward to seeing what you do today and getting a better feel for all the elements of your idea."

"Don't give me too much credit. I didn't think of the incubator concept. There are probably a dozen of them here in Boston already. I'm just trying to put my own spin on it by taking equity positions in all my tenants and using more care in selecting them."

"Can I read some of the other business plans?"

"Absolutely; read them all. Right now we need to get ready to go. The Realtor I'm working with is picking us up at 9:00. Let's finish dressing and head down to the dining room for some coffee and croissant before she gets here."

Dianne was once again at the front desk when we came downstairs, and I went over to thank her for having taken care of my pants while Nancy went to speak with the maître d' and get us a table.

"Good morning, Catherine."

I smiled at her. "Please, Callie's fine. I just wanted to thank you for getting my pants done. Now at least I won't embarrass my aunt."

"Well, you look very chic in your new outfit."

I colored slightly at her compliment. I wasn't accustomed to compliments on my appearance. Besides the tailored slacks, I was wearing a loose-fitting silk blouse, a cashmere wool sport coat, and a pair of leather-soled loafers. Nancy had tried to talk me into a pair of heels that would have added several inches to my height, but I'd felt ridiculous in them and couldn't imagine walking fast let alone running in them. I was used to sneakers, and the leather soles on the loafers in combination with the one-inch heel left me feeling much less confident on my feet. I'd also been forced to abandon the steel baton that I'd gotten quite used to carrying in my leather jacket. When I tried putting it in the inside pocket of the sport coat it made the jacket sag on that side and looked wrong.

"Thanks, Dianne, we'll see you later. I'm going to join my aunt for breakfast and then we're off for the day."

"Oh, Callie."

I turned back. "What?"

"I almost forgot; someone left a package for you last night. It was late so the person on the desk didn't bring it up." Dianne reached down into a cabinet beneath the check-in desk and then handed me a small rectangular box about two inches wide, one inch thick and six inches long with a tiny bow on it, and a card.

"Wonder who this could be from?"

"No idea. I'm sure the card will probably answer your question. Have a good day."

CALLIE AWAKENS

I opened the card as I walked to the dining room. It was from David Firestorm and it said, "To a scintillating young woman; thanks for all you did yesterday. Your brave action saved not just my store inventory but perhaps even our lives. Please wear this in gratitude and don't hesitate to get in touch if I can ever be of future service. Kind regards, David Firestorm."

I unwrapped the box and then sat down at the table with Nancy and handed her the card before removing the wrapping paper from the outside of the box.

"Well, open it. I can't wait to see what David sent you. He's very tight as a rule, but you really did save him a pile of money yesterday so I'm curious."

I took the lid off the box. There was a layer of royal blue velour hiding what was in the box and I folded it back. Resting in the bottom, on top of cream-colored silk, was a very fancy diamond bracelet with about sixteen stones in a nice white-gold setting. They sparkled in the light cast by the halogen spots recessed into the ceiling above. I passed the box to Nancy.

"My my, David *is* appreciative! That's not some inconsequential bit of costume jewelry. That's a really nice, and I might add, expensive tennis-bracelet. What do you think?"

I didn't know what to think let alone say. "I don't play tennis."

"You don't have to, silly. The only reason it's called that is because a famous tennis player back in the 80's had her diamond bracelet fall off during the U.S. Open.

For sure the bracelet was a nice sparkly object, and it did have some really nice-looking diamonds in it, but I could see absolutely no practical use for it in my life. "What would I ever do with something like this?"

"Wear it, you dummy."

"Where? At the gym, running, swimming, on the ferry! This looks like something Princess Diana would have worn. I can't accept this; it must be worth a fortune."

"You like your mother's bracelet, and you wear that."

"But that's because she made it; not because it sparkles or is worth a lot of money."

"Callie, you're too funny. I think you might be the first and only woman in history who doesn't like diamonds."

"They're nice, don't get me wrong and I can see why someone would be attracted to them, but to me it would just be something else I'd have to worry about, and I don't care about looking flashy."

Nancy put her hand over mine. "You are different; I'll give you that. That's one of the things I like most about you, you don't get all mollified over shiny objects."

"What should I do with it?"

"Send David a nice note thanking him for it and say how you'll treasure it always, blah blah blah and then next time you want a new car or a motorcycle or a down payment on a house, sell it. You can put it in a safety deposit box or, if you like, I can hang on to it for you and put it in my safe at home."

"That sounds like a good idea. That way I wouldn't have to worry about it. Would you mind?"

"Not at all."

I took one more look at it and then closed the lid and handed Nancy the box. Immediately I felt relief rather than loss.

"Thank you."

We planned to tour Harvard Wednesday morning, Mass Maritime on Thursday morning and Babson on Friday morning. Today, we were going to first look at the building Nancy planned on buying and then in the afternoon we had a meeting with the men who had the interactive video training company.

After a light breakfast, Nancy's commercial Realtor picked us up in front of the Ritz and we drove to Dorchester Avenue in Southie to meet with the developer who would oversee the renovation of the building. The Realtor's name was Anna Ruiz.

"Good trip?" she asked.

"So far; we've got a busy week though." Nancy then introduced me to Anna.

"What can you tell me about the developer we're meeting with this morning?"

"His name is Dudley Norgen. I've done a number of projects like this with him. He's a straight-shooter, knows the city code enforcers and is used to negotiating with the unions."

"Are the unions problematic here in Boston?"

"They can be, but I don't think they're any worse here than other cities. I think you'll like him and be able to work with him."

We rolled up in front of an old four-story textile building several minutes later and parked behind a dark green Toyota Tacoma pickup truck. As we got out of Anna's Mercedes the two front doors on the pickup opened and two people got out. The driver was huge; about 6'3". He appeared to be in his mid-forties and was dressed in chinos, work boots and had on a worn canvas car coat. He had a hard-boned look about him as if he were no stranger to physical labor. The passenger who got out on the other side was as opposite in appearance as a person could be. She was my age, maybe 5'5" with long straight blond hair and looked like some sort of young debutante. She was wearing jeans and a foul weather gear jacket over a thick wool sweater but would have looked more at home in a pleated tartan skirt and blue school blazer. I was suddenly aware of how dressed up I was in comparison and felt like an imposter of some sort.

"Nancy, I'd like you to meet Dudley Norgen. Dudley, this is Nancy Liddell and her niece Callie."

Dudley put out his hand and looked Nancy in the eye. "It's a pleasure to meet you, Nancy. This is my daughter Meredith. She's doing remote learning like just about everyone else these days and tagging along if that's okay."

"A pleasure; not a problem at all. This is my niece, Callie. In addition to moving this project forward we're also looking at colleges this week. I'm looking forward to hearing your ideas and getting a rough idea of the costs I'll face in renovating this dinosaur of a building. Anna gives you high praise."

"I've done a few buildings over the years."

"How many." Nancy asked in her confrontational style.

"Over 150."

"So, you know a little bit about construction. That's good." Nancy offered with a smile.

"Yes, ma'am."

Meredith and I were walking behind the three adults. I lightly elbowed her when her father called Nancy 'ma'am' calling her attention to the conversation ahead of us.

"Dudley?"

"Yes, ma'am."

"Are you a married man?"

"No longer, why?"

"Figures."

"What figures, ma'am?"

"That you're no longer married. Do you know what images 'ma'am' conjures in the mind of most women?"

"Apparently not."

"Old and boring to name just two. Do I look old and boring to you, Mr. Norgen?"

Meredith and I burst out laughing behind them and Dudley turned bright red.

"Dad, I think Miss Liddell is offended by your use of that term." Meredith correctly deduced and chuckled.

He recovered quickly. "I'm sorry, I didn't mean to offend. What would you prefer?"

"Smoking hot," I whispered to Meredith.

Dudley didn't hear me, but Nancy had. "Callie, you're skating on very thin ice right now."

"Yes, ma'am." I smiled at Meredith as I said it. I think I was showing off to her.

Nancy turned back to Dudley. "Children today can be so…. cheeky."

"They can." Dudley nodded in agreement.

"I, for one, think they should bring back corporal punishment. When I was Callie's age, if I even thought the way she sometimes speaks, my mother would have washed my mouth out with soap."

"My mother would sometimes do that to me preemptively."

"You're not serious?"

"Actually, no, I'm not." Dudley said while nodding his head up and down. "What would you prefer I call you?"

"Nancy, would be just fine."

"Consider it done."

CALLIE AWAKENS

We started in the basement of the 30,000 square foot building. Dudley had thought to bring a flashlight. There were cobwebs throughout and puddles of standing water in several places. Dudley started by walking over to the out-of-date electrical service panels and shone the light over them.

"The existing power won't come close to passing code. You'll need to run in a new 3-Phase electrical service. It will have to be engineered to support new 125-amp panels for each of the ten new tenant spaces." He then shined his light over the massive old ceiling joists above our heads and the vertical supports for them that ran the length of the basement. "Originally, this building was built to accommodate large textile looms which were quite heavy. Obviously, they're now gone and since you'll just be putting up lightweight dividing walls and ceilings on the floors above, I don't anticipate the need for any structural changes."

Nancy nodded her understanding. "What about fire suppression? That would be expensive to add, wouldn't it?"

"Believe it or not you're good on that. It's already been built in. We just need to change out some of the sprinkler heads in the retail foodservice space above on the first floor." He showed his light into the far corner from where we started. "The only other notable expense you'll have on this level will be your sewer hookup. You currently have a four-inch connection. You'll need to upgrade to an eight-inch one for all the planned restrooms. And the city has scheduled a moratorium on new hookups after April 15th, so we need to keep that deadline in mind."

Meredith and I listened as we followed them up the stairs to the first floor. The sunlight coming in through the windows was a welcome change after the dank basement.

"As I understand it you are planning a 3,000 square foot foodservice space here on the ground floor, right?" Dudley asked.

"That's correct. It will be cafeteria style serving and they will offer a menu that includes both breakfast and lunch fare. There will also be a good size coffee bar." Nancy swept her hand around in an arc. "Instead of four-top tables and booths I'm envisioning larger harvest type tables and comfortable nook type sitting areas where small groups can congregate, eat, and share ideas. The space will be open except for the kitchen and hood areas."

Meredith and I continued to chat and get to know each other as the five of us made our way from floor to floor.

"Your dad really seems to know his business."

"Yup, he's a construction machine."

"What's he like to work for?"

Meredith shrugged her shoulders. "I don't work with him, but I know he's super-organized and from what I hear in the background, he gets stuff done on time. One thing he's not really good at is dealing with lazy union workers. He doesn't have a lot of patience with incompetence or laziness. I'm like him that way at school. It drives me crazy when I know how to do something better than a teacher and I have to do it their way just to get a good grade."

I smiled at Meredith. "I thought I was the only one who had to deal with teachers like that. What grade are you in?"

"I'm a junior. What about you?"

"Senior. I started early and skipped a grade."

"My dad said you and your aunt were also up here to look at colleges.

I nodded. "Harvard, Mass Maritime and Babson."

"How come Mass Maritime? That's like totally different than the other two."

"I worked on a ferry this past summer and I want to get my captain's license."

"That's pretty cool. How'd you get interested in that?"

"My dad's a shrimper." I shrugged. "I grew up on the water and I've wanted to be a captain since I was about six. My dad doesn't want me to. He thinks it would be a waste of time. Told me it's no place for a woman."

"I'll bet you took that real well." Meredith smiled at me. "What else are you into?"

"I run and swim, a lot, and I'm also really into something called Krav Maga."

"What's that?"

"It's a type of martial arts invented by the Israelis."

"That's super interesting. What about boyfriends?"

I had to think about that for a few seconds. "Sort of, kinda, maybe?"

"How so?"

"I guess I'm trying to figure that out. He's super shy and he's not a hunk or anything. He's just a really nice guy and he keeps surprising me. I met him at my Krav Maga studio and the other day he asks me out of the blue if I want to go flying with him. He's got his pilot's license."

"That's awesome! How old is he?"

"Seventeen."

"Sounds like a keeper to me. Does he treat you well?"

"Like you wouldn't believe, he's super polite and considerate."

"I'll take him if you don't want him." Meredith elbowed me.

As we'd talked, we continued through the building and would alternately listen to the discussion between Dudley, Nancy, and the realtor. Eventually we got to the 4th floor.

"What do you want to do about exterior windows?" Dudley asked.

Nancy replied. "Replace them I guess; these don't look very efficient."

"They aren't, but if you wanted to keep the look of the building the city would probably let you keep them due to the age and historic nature of the building."

"Why don't you give me a number both with and without. The old windows are distinctive. What about the roof?"

"It's a pretty standard pebble covered ballasted roof. It's in good shape. I think we can leave that. The only other thing I'd add besides what we've already discussed is I'd reseal the entire rear parking area and have it relined."

"What are we looking at for a final number?"

"This isn't a firm; but I'd say about $2,500,000 if we leave the old windows and $3,000,000 if we upgrade them."

"Timing?"

"Figure six months."

"Any way of getting that down some?"

Dudley thought for a few seconds. "If we did the foodservice improvements on the first floor last, you could probably start getting tenants in after four months."

We all started walking back downstairs. Meredith and I continued our own conversation. "Tell me about yourself."

"Not much to tell. I go to school, hang with friends, ski in the winter, and go boating in the summer. Oh, and I play golf."

"Golf! I've never met anyone who plays golf. Don't you get bored walking around hitting that stupid little ball?"

"You're kidding right? Golf is like the most difficult game on the planet."

"And that makes it fun?"

Meredith nodded. "It's like this incredible game you play against yourself. Very few people can play it well and not because it's too physically demanding but because it's so mentally challenging."

I thought about what she was saying and applied it to my love of running and swimming. Even with Krav Maga I wasn't striving to beat other people as much as I was striving to beat myself. I knew exactly what she was saying. "Okay, you've got me interested. Maybe we could play sometime if I end up coming back here for college in the fall?"

"Absolutely."

I liked Meredith. She was her own person, quietly self-assured, ambitious, and self-directed. She also seemed to have a really good relationship with her father. He seemed very content to let her be whoever she wanted to be, listened to her when she spoke, trusted her judgment, and was outwardly supportive of her independence. I envied her relationship with him.

That afternoon we met with the two partners from Interact IV, back at the Ritz. This was the company that Nancy and I had discussed on the flight up that had developed an interactive training system for better teaching workers about how to deal with hazards in the workplace. Nancy had booked a small conference room, and we arrived slightly early. I wanted to better understand her process and had several questions.

"What is it that you see in this company that makes you interested in them?" I asked Nancy.

"There are a number of things," Nancy responded and then went on to list them in detail.

"I read most of those points in the business plan," I noted. "I understand most of them and taken together they all make it sound like a fantastic business idea. So, what are your reservations? Why not just go for it and negotiate them into your space?"

Nancy thought a few seconds before answering. "Did you read any of the other plans?"

"Yes, I read two of them. The company that manufactures the high-tech cane for blind people with GPS navigation and the company that makes smart eyeglasses with Bluetooth and laser projectors."

"What was your first impression of both?"

"That they were both really cool sounding products with big potential markets."

"So that's your first lesson. You'll never read a business plan that isn't wildly optimistic and upbeat. There are literally millions of great product ideas out there."

"So, how do you determine which ones are good investments and which ones aren't? Obviously, they all can't be winners."

"Okay, write this down in your head. 'You don't buy ideas, they're a dime a dozen; you buy people.' Got that?"

"I heard you, but I'm not certain what you mean."

"Unless *you* personally have the management skills to run a particular company and also the inclination, then ultimately the success or failure of any company is based not on the product as much as it's based on the people running the company. I can't count the number of businesses I've looked at over the years that are run by brilliant inventors with few or no business and management skills. Any company is only as good as the people running it."

"So, you're looking for requisite skill sets in the principals?"

"Or at a minimum the willingness to add people who have those skills which costs equity and money; two things that most start-ups are unwilling or unable to give up."

I nodded my head fascinated with Nancy's process.

The two owners of Interact IV showed up ten minutes later. They started the meeting by giving the "potential investors" a PowerPoint presentation that they'd developed for the company. Not much was revealed in the presentation that Nancy and I hadn't both already read and discussed previous to the meeting, but it was a good opportunity to get a feel for who the principles were. I stayed mostly quiet and watched how Nancy questioned them and how they responded. At one point Nancy mentioned my idea that their technology might also do well in educating students both at home and in the classroom. They agreed enthusiastically that it was in fact a logical market to go after. That made me feel good.

After our meeting Nancy and I decided to get some air and walked through the Boston Commons and the Public Gardens, then up to the State House, and back. It was sunny and about forty degrees although I did note some high thin clouds moving in.

"What did you think about them?" I asked.

"I liked both of them. With their backgrounds in public health policy, video production and software development they check a number of boxes. But they're weak, as I'd expected, on the business management side. Neither of them has actually run a big company."

"But they aren't a big company now."

"True, but they will be if they're as successful as they expect to be."

"So, what will you do?"

"I'll think about it some first and then probably express my reservations to them, see what their response is and go from there."

Chapter 33

Nancy and I took our rented Mercedes to Harvard Square Wednesday morning. I kept a sharp eye out for rhinos. We arrived in Harvard Yard fifteen minutes before the start of the group tour that I had us scheduled in. In preparation I'd read their eighty-five-page Guide to The First Year at Harvard. I wasn't impressed as two thirds of it seemed to be devoted to how woke they were and all the programs they offered for making Harvard a "safe space" for tender snowflakes. Nancy and I were seated on the steps of one of the freshman dorms next to the famous John Harvard statue.

"Nancy."

"Yes."

"I'm reading the first-year guide for students. Do you know what BGLTQ stands for?"

"I haven't a clue. Do I look like someone who goes around memorizing acronyms?"

"Let me read you something."

"Okay."

"It says in here that 'Harvard College has devoted resources to ensure that bisexual, gay, lesbian, transgender, queer, and questioning (BGLTQ) students receive the support they need to feel safe, secure, and connected on campus.' What do you think about that?"

"It really says that? In the first-year student guide?"

I nodded.

"Callie, I'm not really the person to ask; I'm very old fashioned."

"I'm curious."

"Okay then. I believe that whatever two consenting adults choose to do in private is okay and their business, and that none of us should be throwing stones around. I don't believe, however, that just because someone identifies or feels like a member of the opposite sex, that makes it so or that they're entitled to special accommodation or treatment based on their feelings de jour. Sex is a biological fact, not a feeling or a thought.

I don't believe that there's anything wrong with being attracted to a member of the same sex or being attracted to both. What I find objectionable in the current conversation, is that people are trying to change long established definitions of words for their own convenience and trying to tell you and me what we should and should not believe. And how in the hell is sexuality relevant to the type of education I think you're seeking?"

"I don't know," I admitted honestly. "I was trying to figure that out." I shrugged. "I kind of expected it to be about curriculum."

I looked over at the John Harvard statue. There was a young Indian family standing in front of it at that moment. The woman's nose was pierced, and she wore a traditional sari. The man wore pleated Western slacks and a carefully wrapped turban. Their young boy looked to be about twelve. He was rubbing the left foot, as millions before him had, as if it were a talisman. The foot was smooth and golden from repeated human touch, the rest of the statue almost black with patina. I could see from the reverent look on the faces of the family, the great value they assigned to a Harvard Diploma. Perhaps the parents were dreaming of how wondrous their lives might become if their son were to attend Harvard and they'd made their pilgrimage here to wisely incentivize him to work harder and study longer. As I watched the steady progression of tourists filing past the statue, one thing was clear, Harvard was a big deal in the minds of people. I wondered if it would be the holy grail for me also.

Harvard only accepts the brightest from around the world. I was pretty sure that my academics were up to their standards, but their admissions department also assigns great value to outstanding achievement in music, the arts and civic engagement. On that score, I knew I was lacking. Additionally, my gut was telling me that what I was seeking was a far more practical education; one that would recognize, nurture, and support my strongly independent and self-directed nature. I didn't need or depend on the approval of others and didn't much care about their opinions. I also wasn't at all sure that I would be comfortable and thrive in the very liberal, homogenized, safe zone of Harvard.

I've known I was different from my peers since about the age of eight. I'm trying to be honest here. I'm not saying I was better than anyone, but I was different. From that time forward I've been abnormally self-directed, and not relied on the opinions or sought the approval of others as I've gone through school and matured. This tended to exclude me from normal and popular groups. When, on occasion, I compromised myself to "fit in" because I was lonely, that also had felt wrong. People underwhelmed me with the goals and standards they found acceptable. Uniformly, they always seemed to have lower expectations of me, than I had for myself. Eventually I simply decided that loneliness was preferable to feeling dishonest and unproductive.

I knew that Harvard encouraged excellence and principled behavior in their student body and in their applicants. I'd run my life the same way for as long as I can remember, but I got the distinct impression from reading their catalogues that "principled behavior" to them had an invisible footnote that said, "as long as that principled behavior is how *we* define it."

I'd grown up in a very conservative household that prized independence and self-sufficiency above all else and I'd been taught and believed that government was the source of many of our problems, not the solution to them. Harvard believes the opposite and has a decidedly globalist bent to it. I also believe strongly in the rule of law; not just the laws I like. To me, "principled" means without carve outs and exceptions. When making logical decisions for myself I've always tried to listen to both sides of issues and while Harvard gives lip service to both liberal and conservative views of the world, with ninety percent of the faculty progressive liberals, I worried that politics and our respective outlooks would clash and possibly interfere with my education. I wanted an education that was free from politics, one that recognized and prized individuality and one that would encourage my unusual, free, and highly independent spirit. Once again Nancy's comment about "learning how to think," popped into my head. My impression of Harvard and many of the other decidedly liberal colleges that I'd looked at online was that most of them attempted to teach their students "what to think" as opposed to "how to think." There was a big difference, and I didn't want the distraction of the conflict that was bound to occur interfering with my education. I wanted to learn in an apolitical environment.

Despite my reservations, Nancy and I had an incredible tour. The campus and facilities were amazing. Because of the Covid pandemic and remote learning, we were able to poke our heads into many of the facilities that were normally closed to tours. Even with most of the student body off, there was a positive energy that crackled through the air that left me feeling that I was in a special and privileged space.

"It's a pretty amazing place," I commented to Nancy once we were back in our car. "I imagine a degree from there would be a ticket into a very exclusive group and also be a shortcut to a very high income."

"It is and it would."

"What did you think about the place?"

"It's not really important what I think. This is your life. You will excel and do well no matter what school you go to. I would just counsel you to keep an open mind and not pre-judge."

I sighed, frustrated. "I really respect your opinion, Nancy, why won't you give it?"

She reached over and put a hand on my shoulder in sympathy. "I know you're feeling overwhelmed at the enormity of the decision you're trying to make right now. You don't want to make the wrong one. Deciding what your life's work will be is huge and likely one of the biggest things you've been asked to decide so far in your young life. I would say two things, knowing you as I do.

The first is that you don't have to decide what you're going to do for the rest of your life today or this month. With your brain, work ethic, and capacity to learn you will likely change what your life's work will be, several times over the course of your life. What college you will go to and what you will do next is important, but it's not forever. You just have to do the next right thing for you, now.

"The second piece of advice I have for you is to go with your gut. You have really good instincts and an unusually well-defined set of personal standards. Most people your age don't. Allow yourself to pick the thing that feels right to you and excites your soul, not that thing that simply ticks off boxes in some mental checklist."

I think I knew what Nancy was suggesting, but I also knew it would be difficult for me to turn off my pragmatic mind.

"I don't know if I can simply turn off my brain and go with my gut."

"I'm not suggesting you do. Your brain is going to slog along in the background whether you like it or not and it will have you doing all sorts of practical things as you go through your process. All I'm suggesting is that if you're patient and are open to it, you will feel what the right thing is and know it when you see it. Be willing to listen to that intuitive side of your head even if it conflicts with your practical side."

I sensed that what she was telling me was valuable and born of experience and wisdom, but I still wasn't at all certain that I'd be able to implement her somewhat "new age" sounding advice.

"Want to grab something to eat?" Nancy asked after we'd given our car back to the valet at the Ritz.

"Sure, what'd you have in mind?"

"Nothing in particular. Let's just walk up Washington Street and peek in some windows until we see something that looks appealing."

Harvard had been impressive for sure, and I knew that a degree from there would automatically convert into a high paying job in whatever field I selected, but I would still have to select a field and all of the fields they offered were decidedly academic and cerebral in nature. Obtaining an undergraduate liberal arts degree would provide few if any practical real-world skills in the same way that attending one of the maritime colleges would. People didn't go to Harvard to learn how to weld. It would certainly give me entrance into an exclusive liberal club, but I wasn't anxious to join any "clubs" and liberal thinking had zero appeal.

"What about this place?" Nancy asked.

I looked up and then into the window of the coffee shop that we'd stopped in front of. It was called Caffè Nero. We walked inside and stood for a minute looking over the inside. It was furnished with harvest tables, comfy chairs and bookcases overflowing with books. It was full of both students and business professionals many with open laptops in front of them. All, it seemed, were in animated discussions with one another and there was a positive energy present that I found appealing. I tried envisioning myself as a participant. Fort Myers in particular and SW

Florida in general both lacked the intensity and positivity that I could see, hear, and feel. It was exciting and I could see myself in an urban environment like it.

"It looks like a nice place, but I'm not sure we can get a real meal here. It mostly looks like pastries and other baked goods," Nancy observed. "There's a Legal Seafood a few doors down. Have you ever had a proper Boston clam chowder?"

"I'm not sure, when you say it like that."

"They've got lobster rolls too."

I smiled at Nancy's reference to lobster rolls. She knew how much I'd grown to love the one's that Newlin's made on Boca Grande. "Let's go there." I nodded my head enthusiastically.

She reached out and tucked my hair behind my ear in a familiar expression of warmth and closeness.

After a very good lobster roll and a bowl of "proper" Boston clam chowder we walked back towards the Ritz Carlton.

"That was wonderful. Thank you, Nancy."

"You're welcome."

"Can I read a couple more of the business plans when we get back to the room?"

"Absolutely, go wild. Are you able to understand the financials?"

"Some. I get most of the projected income statements, but I'm not really clear on the balance sheets."

"Just focus on the business concepts and the executive summaries. Projected statements are fantasy numbers that have no historical basis. Take that into consideration as you read them. I also look at key ratios of line items. But you don't need to go that deep at this point."

"What are key ratios?"

"Let's say a charity knocks on my door and they want me to give them some money. The very first thing I ask to see is their income statement and I look at what percentage of the money they spend goes to administrative costs and what percentage of their money actually goes to the charitable activities they're purport to fund."

"Why's that important?"

"If the charity/company is spending all of their money on administrative salaries and perks and benefits and not spending much on the people they exist to help then I'm much less likely to give to their cause. Administrative costs should run at about fifteen to twenty percent in a well-run charity. If they're spending sixty-five percent on administrative, then I know the 'charity' is really just a slush fund for the people who run it."

I smiled. "Are there really charities like that?"

"Absolutely. The Clinton Foundation is a good example. In 2014 they spent $5.2 million on charitable grants and $34.8 on administrative salaries, expenses, and benefits. I perform the same types of analyses for for-profit companies but additionally look at lots of other ratios; things like their debt/equity ratio, profitability ratios, liquidity ratios."

"How do you keep all that straight in your head? Don't different companies and industries have different ratios?"

Nancy nodded. "When I was in the publishing industry, I did know all the numbers and ratios by heart, just like you know all of that nautical claptrap on *Gulf Runner* because you work with it every day."

"It's not claptrap, but I know what you mean."

"For other industries I have to use books that tell me in summary form what the ratios are for other companies in the same business. I guess it would be like you getting on another type of ship or flying another type of plane. Many of the principals are the same, but the details are different. Don't get hung up on that level of detail right now. Just read them, see what excites you, what doesn't, and then ask yourself whether you think a particular business has a good chance of success and why. If you've got questions, write them down."

"How did you learn all this stuff?"

"The same way you do; read, study, ask questions and do it over and over again. Over time you get better and better at it. In my case I also had several really good professors at college who had come out of industry and taught from that perspective as opposed to teaching from a book."

At 3:00 that afternoon we walked over Beacon Hill into the financial district to visit Nancy's law firm at 60 State Street.

"What's the name of your law firm?" I asked as we walked through the lobby.

"Doolittle & Steele."

I chuckled. "You're not serious?"

"I should call them Dooless & Steelemore."

"Expensive?"

"A thousand dollars an hour for the partner I use. I think he charges me even when he's in the bathroom."

"That's a lovely thought. I'm not sure I'll ever be able to get that out of my mind."

We got off the elevator on the 30th floor, walked through a pair of tall glass doors and into a large, elegant, open, reception area with gleaming marble floors. Downtown high-rise space is expensive, and the sheer size of the lobby conveyed wealth and extravagance. Small oriental carpets, expensive leather seating enclaves, period antiques, flower arrangements, and large modern art canvasses all said, "money." There was just one person present in the room when we walked in and she was seated behind a large, modern, glass desk and she stood as we entered.

"Hello, Ms. Liddell."

"Hi, Samantha, how have you been?"

"I've been well. Thank you for asking. Who's this with you today?"

"This is my niece Catherine Babich, aka Callie. Is that shark you work for swimming about?"

"Why, whomever do you mean?"

"Cute, very diplomatic; I like that. I'd be referring to my favorite counsel of course—"

"Nancy, what a pleasure!"

We both turned. A handsome older man in his fifties approached us. He had a file folder under his left arm. He was deeply tanned, fit, and had perfectly styled gray hair. He was wearing a dark blue suit and cordovan lace-up wingtips that had been shined to perfection.

"David, speak of the devil. I'd like you to meet my niece, Callie." She turned to me. "Callie, meet David Steele. He's incredibly sharp and a good man to have on your team, even if he does charge a fortune."

"It's a pleasure to meet you, Mr. Steele."

"Shall we go have a seat in one of the conference rooms?" He turned to Samantha. "Sam, is the harbor view conference room available?"

"It is Mr. Steele. Can I bring you all a coffee, some tea or a drink?"

Nancy looked at me. I shook my head.

"Tea for me," Nancy replied.

"Nothing for me, Sam," David responded.

He led the way through the reception area and past the exterior glass wall towards the conference room. As we turned the corner, I paused to look out over the harbor through the fourteen-foot-tall wall of glass. I don't think I'd ever been as high off the ground except for the jet flight up. I inadvertently took a step back after looking down towards the street. The view out over Boston Harbor was stunning. David and Nancy stopped, noticing that I'd paused to look out over the harbor.

"Mr. Steele, why has all the ship-traffic stopped on both sides of the channel?" I inquired.

He looked out before responding. "See that huge ship with the big tanks on deck in the middle of the channel, and the Coast Guard boats in front and behind it?

I nodded.

"That's an LNG carrier. Whenever one comes into the harbor, they shut down all boat traffic ahead, behind and alongside it."

"Why?"

"To avoid a terrorist attack. If there ever was one and the tanks on that ship were breached by gunfire or an RPG, the resulting explosion would supposedly be equal to a small nuclear one. They say it would bring down most of the downtown buildings and that the resulting conflagration would spread to all of the hundreds of fuel and propane storage tanks in the surrounding towns. The chain reaction would be cataclysmic."

"Wow. How often does one of those ships come in?"

"About once a month."

"How many passenger ferries run in the harbor?"

He cocked his head ever so slightly. "There are probably dozens, including the high-speed catamarans and the whale watching boats. Why do you ask?"

Nancy answered for me. "Callie works on a passenger ferry in Florida and is working towards her captain's license. She's fascinated with all things mechanical and dangerous."

"I have a daughter a bit like you, Callie. She's training to be an army combat helicopter pilot of all things. I wanted her to go into banking or law but after she finished college, she joined the army and got into their pilot training program. She wants to drive attack helicopters, but I guess it takes a while to get to that level. She finished the warrant officer training down at Fort Rucker in Alabama and now has fifty-two weeks of flight school ahead of her."

"That's really interesting. I'd like to meet her someday if I'm ever back here and she's around."

"I imagine you two would have lots to talk about. Shall we?" David pointed down the hallway. We followed and then all sat down around the largest table I'd ever seen. David opened the file folder he'd been carrying and then passed Nancy three short, stapled documents.

"Here is the tenancy agreement, the option agreement and the confidentiality agreement that you asked me to prepare."

Nancy looked at the cover pages of all three. "David, could you have someone make copies of all of these so Callie can read along with us? I'm trying to give her a bird's-eye view of what I'm doing up here with this project."

"Absolutely." David dialed an extension on the phone in front of him. "Kim, would you bring in another set of copies of the agreements we prepared for Miss Liddell?" He listened to her response and then hung up the phone.

"Any thoughts on my project off the top of your head, David?"

"Just that you have a ton of financial exposure on this deal. You have the cost of the building, the renovation, the fact that you'll be offering free or under-market rents to tenants and lastly and most importantly, as you well know, seventy-five percent of your tenants are likely to fail or barely reach breakeven and the interest you'll hold in them will be in restricted securities with little or no value. Even with the one in four that might be a success, you have no guarantee that any of them will ever go public."

A sharply dressed, attractive woman with long black hair in her late twenties came into the room, smiled at Nancy and I, and handed David a sheaf of papers.

"Thanks, Kim. I'll let you know if we need anything else." She nodded and left the room. David slid the papers across the table to me.

"I know I'm hanging out there with a lot of upfront costs and a big monthly nut on this one, David. It simply underscores the need for me to pick wisely and identify good synergy between potential tenants."

"May I speak candidly in front of your niece?"

"You may."

David nodded in assent and continued. "Your building cost is $10,700,000 so your monthly debt service just on the building without renovations will run $51,000. Any idea yet of renovation costs?"

"Figure $3,000,000 for now."

"So, $13,700,000; let's call it $14,000,000. Your monthly carrying costs exclusive of taxes, utilities and maintenance will run..." David pecked at a calculator in front of him again. "$66,000 per month. That's a big number. How many square feet is it?"

"30,000 give or take."

"Your breakeven to crack that nut is $27 per sq. ft. If you were to get fully leased up at market it would be a good investment; you'd be clearing $28/sq. ft which would be..." He tapped at his calculator again. "$70,000 per month profit."

"My idea has never been to make my profit off the real estate. I'm looking for exponential returns on my equity."

"I understand that; just making sure you're aware of the personal exposure you'll have every month."

"So, noted." Nancy and I both looked over the agreements he'd drafted. Much of the language was foreign to me. David followed along as we flipped pages.

"As you can see, I've left as many items blank as I could per your instructions giving you maximum flexibility to fill in the blanks with each different tenant as to term, rate and security. I've also included a large blank section for delineating additional terms and conditions. Your initial ten percent stake in each company would be described in the security section giving you various tax advantages.

The option agreement is a bit more complicated since we're trying to lock them in and don't yet know whether any of them will ultimately go public or not, but it should lock them down enough for us to have a well delineated position with whoever takes them public. The confidentiality agreement is self-explanatory."

"Perfect, David; just what I wanted. Do me a favor and have Kim prepare me four or five more copies of all three agreements. We'll be meeting with a couple of the prospective tenants before returning to Florida."

David nodded and called Kim again to request Nancy's copies and then turned to me. "Nancy told me over the phone that you're looking at schools while you're up here?"

"Yes, sir, we are. So far, we've just toured Harvard. Tomorrow we're looking at Mass Maritime and Friday we're looking at Babson."

"Good for you. I've worked with a number of people who went to Harvard and Babson. They're both excellent schools. I don't know much about Mass Maritime. Any idea what you'll major in?

"No, sir, still trying to figure that out."

"How old are you now?"

"Sixteen."

"You've got plenty of time to figure all of that out. It's been a pleasure meeting you, Callie." He turned to Nancy. "If there's nothing more, may I walk you out?"

As we cabbed back to the Ritz Nancy turned to me. "What'd you think of David?"

"He seems like a competent man. Is he a good attorney? I noticed that you gave him a little grief on his rates."

"Don't be silly. David knows he charges an outrageous hourly fee."

"But you pay it so you must see value in it."

Nancy was thoughtfully silent for several moments. "Perhaps you're right. David does save me tens if not hundreds of thousands of dollars every year in taxes. He's a very bright guy."

"There you go. When was the last time you complimented him on his work? I would imagine that even rich attorneys need occasional praise and approval too."

My phone dinged and I pulled it out of my jacket pocket and looked down.

"How's your trip going." Stuart was asking in a text.

I smiled unconsciously at the thought of someone caring what was going on in my life.

I typed a reply. "It's going really well. The Embraer Phenom was a trip."

"Did you get to fly it?" He texted back.

"Not really, we were on auto pilot almost the entire flight, but I did get a chance to spend some time in the second seat."

"I'm jealous."

"Don't be, Mr. Aerobatic Pilot." I chuckled out loud.

Nancy looked over at me. "Your boyfriend?"

Nancy's phone dinged with a text before I could respond. She looked down at her screen and smiled.

"Your boyfriend?" I countered mimicking her query.

She smiled her answer to my question and started pecking an answer back on her phone.

"Where's your dad right now?" I texted back to Stuart.

"Sitting right across the room from me."

"What's he doing?"

"Texting someone."

"My Aunt Nancy."

"You're joking!"

"Not. Looked at Harvard this morning, pretty cool place. Mass Maritime tomorrow and Babson Friday."

"Want to go flying when you get back?"

"I'd love to, although you're going to be hard pressed to beat our last flight."

"Deal. When back?"

"Sunday afternoon sometime. I'll text on the way."

"Okay, have fun. I miss you."

I turned off my phone and sat for a moment thinking. It was nice to be missed by someone. That was a new experience for me. But I wasn't entirely comfortable with it. I thought about it for a few seconds and realized that I hadn't thought about Stuart except for my brief mention of him when Meredith had asked if I had a boyfriend. My thoughts were interrupted by another incoming text. *What's going on?!* I wondered and looked down at the screen.

"Callie; Meredith Norgen here. It was nice meeting you yesterday morning."

I felt the same way. Meredith had been straightforward, self-assured, and interesting but also seemed to have a great sense of humor. I couldn't remember ever meeting another girl my age who I'd immediately felt so comfortable around.

"Same. Was just thinking about you. What's going on?"

"My dad usually hauls his boat out of the water for the winter right before Thanksgiving and I was wondering whether you had any interest in going with me on Saturday to bring his boat from over the near the airport to the boatyard in Hingham where we pull it out?"

"Definitely! What time and where would I meet you? I've got to double check with my aunt though."

"9:00 am and we can pick you up at the Ritz. My dad will drop us at the boat and then drive his truck to Hingham and meet us at the other end."

"Sounds really fun. What kind of boat?"

"It's a thirty-foot, center console, Contender with twin 350 hp engines. It's a beast."

"Sounds like it! Wait 1 while ask my aunt."

I turned to my aunt. "Nancy?"

"Yes?"

"That's Meredith Norgen. She wants to know if I want to go with her and her father Saturday to bring their boat from over near the airport to Hingham. Do we have any plans Saturday morning that would interfere?"

"Nothing right now, although I might schedule in one of my potential tenants."

"I'm sure you could come with us on the boat if you wanted."

"Boats are really your thing, Callie, not mine. It's too cold for me anyway at this time of year. We might even get snow flurries that day. Will you need a ride?"

"No, they're going to pick me up."

"Go for it."

I texted Meredith back. 'You're on! I'll be at the front door of the Ritz at 9:00. Nancy says maybe snow that day. Will that be a problem?"

"No, but it will be cold. I'll bring an extra foul weather gear jacket and some gloves for you."

Chapter 34

Nancy and I toured Mass Maritime Thursday morning. It felt completely different from Harvard. As with Harvard, there were almost no students on campus due to the Covid-19 pandemic, but the students and faculty that we did see and meet, were all wearing uniforms which gave the place a decidedly military feel. I don't mean this as a negative observation; the student who gave us our tour was informative and friendly and clearly proud of both the school and the education she was receiving. Her name was Megan and I liked her right away.

We met up with her in the Admin building and then the three of us walked across the parade field and then down to the shore of the Cape Cod Canal to watch as a massive ship entered the canal and passed just several hundred feet away. There was a thick layer of fog hugging the surface of the water which obscured the lower part of the ship's hull. The ship was so tall that the upper part of it was in bright sunlight while the lower part was hidden in the fog. It looked as though ship was being supported by some ethereal layer.

"Wow, what kind of a ship is that, Megan? It's huge." I nodded towards the incredibly boxlike and unattractive ship going past.

"It's called a RoRo; stands for roll on, roll off. It's a car-carrier," She replied.

"It's not very attractive," I offered tentatively, not wanting to offend.

Megan chuckled. "No, they're not. They're downright ugly if you ask me, but yes, they are large."

"How big are they and many cars can one carry?"

"That one looks about 700' feet long. I think the larger ones can carry 6,000-8,000 cars."

I looked at the current running by the pier, the fog, the bridges, and the turns in the canal. The canal no longer looked so large, and I tried to envision myself driving such a big ship in a waterway that now appeared quite constricted.

"When a ship that size comes through the canal, they often close down traffic coming the other way. There just isn't enough space for two ships that size to safely pass one another with the current we get in here," Megan offered.

"Who controls the traffic?" I asked.

"The Army Corps of Engineers runs the entire canal. See that railroad bridge up the canal?"

I nodded.

"They have a control tower up near the bridge and ships have to coordinate with them before entering."

"The current must make it interesting."

"It runs about five knots depending on where you are in the tide cycle."

I turned to the long black hull of Mass Maritime's training ship the *TS Kennedy* which was gently resting alongside the dock next to us. "I think I'd much rather be driving this one. How long is *Kennedy*?"

"She's five hundred and forty feet. I love her. I've had two semesters aboard her already. Every student who graduates from here has to complete a total of four semesters at sea. During those semesters, in addition to continuing classroom studies, you also cycle through all the various departments on the ship including the engine room, emergency responses, navigation, the bridge and serve watches in each of those departments. Obviously if you're an engineering major you'll spend more time in the engine room. If your goal is a master's license, you'll spend extra time on the bridge. The goal is to expose every cadet to all areas of the ship in a hands-on environment."

"How many students, sorry, cadets, go on *Kennedy* when she's at sea?"

"Six hundred."

"Where did you go on your semesters at sea?"

"I went to the Mediterranean one semester and to Puerto Rico and the Caribbean last year."

"That sounds really fun." I looked over at Nancy as Megan mentioned her two semesters at sea. She appeared to be listening closely.

"It is fun. And you really learn to work together as a team. That's a big part of what you learn here."

"Teamwork?"

Megan nodded. "Large ships require a lot of people working closely together to safely operate. Would you like to see the ship?"

Megan took us through the entire ship; a dizzying array of passages, classrooms, library, hospital, laundry, training facilities and sleeping quarters spread out over 8 decks. Originally, she'd been built as a bulk freighter in 1964 and rebuilt several times over into her current configuration. The berthing areas for cadets were necessarily quite tight and I tried to envision myself living in such close quarters with so many other people for two of the four years I would spend at Mass Maritime if I went there.

After the *Kennedy* we toured the rest of the campus; classrooms, laboratories, the gym, the library, the dining hall and lastly Megan showed us one of their nine, virtual, 360° simulators.

"You guys wait in here. I'm going into the control room. I'll speak to you through the PA."

Nancy and I looked around the room at the full-scale mockup of a large ship's bridge that included joy sticks, engine controls, instruments, radar screens, GPS nav plotters, and dozens of screens and readouts that were all dark. I didn't recognize many of them and was wondering what she was going to show us.

"Can you hear me, Callie?"

I answered. "Loud and clear, Megan."

The entire wrap-around control panel started lighting up and then all the large monitors that surrounded the bridge came to life and we were suddenly transported into a waterway I didn't recognize. I could see the bow of our boat and a skyline of buildings in the distance in front of the helm station, ships off to port and starboard, buoys and even the faint sound of our virtual engines.

"Megan, this is so cool!"

"I know. Okay, Callie, advance your throttles to 1,700 rpm and then, using the joystick, give me starboard rudder and turn from your present course of 30° to 75°. You'll have to anticipate some and start slowing your rate of turn when you are about 10° shy of 75°. She's a big ship and slow to react. As you get near 75° you should see a red and white MOA buoy about two miles ahead off your bow. It will also be visible on both your radar and chart plotter."

I looked at the large virtual compass on the dash in front of me after advancing the throttle. It indicated 30° as Megan had said. I put my hand on the joystick and tilted it to the right and watched as the compass started to change. I looked at both the radar and the plotter. They were both in agreement and sure enough as the ship started to turn, the projected images on the screens of the two instruments changed as real ones would have. Suddenly the display out the windows changed dramatically.

"Callie, from my control panel I can simulate a large number of ships with their specific handling characteristics. I can also load the approaches to over 120 different commercial maritime ports around the world. And...I can change the weather, the tide, the time of day. I can even add ice bergs if you like."

As Megan spoke the view outside our virtual windows changed dramatically. It was suddenly night, rain started to pound our windows, the wind started howling, and the outlines of the ships around us disappeared and were replaced by faint red, green, and white running lights. All my onboard instrument lights went into an infrared, nighttime mode and what had started as relatively straightforward course up a channel in daylight turned into a stormy, disorientating, nighttime approach into a foreign harbor with few visual references. If that weren't challenging enough; the bridge phone started ringing. I was still focusing on my helm change to 75°, and I was going to ignore the phone when I remembered Nancy and turned to her. "Would you get that, please."

Nancy picked up the phone without missing a beat and with a serious sounding voice answered. "Bridge."

I heard Megan laugh in the background and then speak to Nancy in an equally serious voice. "Bridge, engine room. Our port shaft has started to vibrate excessively and I'm going to have to shut down that engine immediately."

Nancy turned briefly to me. I was going to tell her to just acknowledge the order, but she had something else in mind. "Engine room bridge.

Negative, I repeat negative. Do not shut down that engine. I warned you about those counter rotating propellers and the danger they presented. The lives of our passengers and the safety of the free world are at stake here and those things are a damned site more important than some silly old engine. Abaft the beam, shiver my timbers, hard to lee..." Nancy paused for a second. "And keep that goddamned engine running or you'll be keel-hauled." Nancy had apparently run out of nautical sounding expressions and switched to a really bad imitation of the Scottish brogue that Scotty on the Enterprise used to speak with, as a substitute. "Oh, and Megan lassie, you keep that engine running at full power until she kinna take no mooore."

I just stood there with my mouth open seriously impressed with Nancy's impromptu performance. There was a pause and then the overhead lights came on, the virtual screens went dark, and the sounds of the engines went quiet. Megan came in from the other room several seconds later, in tears she was laughing so hard. "You two are a pair."

Nancy smiled at me. "We are, aren't we?"

I looked at Nancy. "That was very impressive."

"Thank you, Callie."

"Shiver my timbers and abaft the beam? You are something, Mrs. Liddell," Megan added.

Nancy reached into her purse and got out a compact and a lipstick and applied some; took one last look in the tiny mirror, then snapped it shut. "Shall we move onward, ladies?"

All in all, I was impressed with Mass Maritime. The facility was amazing, and my sense and impression after spending an hour and half with Megan was that the entire student body was made up of individuals with backgrounds much closer to my own. I had no doubt that I'd be able to acquire the skills and training I'd need to further my maritime career if Mass Maritime were my choice.

I walked away with two other strong impressions. That while they offered business courses and various liberal arts degrees, those really weren't their focus and would not be on a par with what I could get at Harvard. Mass Maritime was primarily a sea-school for training mariners. The other impression that came through strongly was that commercial shipping was not at all an independent trade. If I were going to work in that industry, I would be surrounded by people virtually all the time. It was simply the nature of the profession. Individuals can't operate ships without the assistance of lots of other people. I wasn't at all sure that I wanted to be surrounded by, and dependent on, the actions of so many people and facing far less certain outcomes as result. I was used to relying on myself which among other things provided predictable outcomes. I also thought about the strengths and weaknesses list that I'd made as we'd flown up from Florida. Would going the commercial captain route play to a plurality of my strengths or would I be setting myself up for frustration knowing my weaknesses? I knew for certain that I'd love to acquire the skills to operate big ships, but once I'd acquired those skills would I actually be happy doing it day after day and year after year?

Later that evening as Nancy took off her jewelry and started to get ready for bed, her cell phone rang. The caller ID indicated that it was Kevin Grainger calling her back.

"Kevin."

"Hi, Nancy. Sorry to take so long to get back to you."

"I was starting to wonder if you'd forgotten about me."

'No chance of that but what you asked for is pretty specialized and I had to go through a number of people before finally feeling as though I might have someone who can help you."

"Tell me, what'd you find?"

"Someone who might fit the bill. I spoke to my friend Scott Bond last night and he made a call to this guy and got his permission for me to give you a contact number for him. You need to call him at 8:00 pm Saturday night. It's not his personal number because he's a very private guy, but at least he's willing to talk with you. I gather from Scott he's got a lot going on right now so your biggest challenge will be in getting him to agree to help you."

"Tell me about him."

"I don't know him personally or all of his background, but a close friend of mine has worked with him a number of times doing off-book stuff for DHS and highly recommends him. He lives on an island down in the Keys and is a retired Marine. He still does some consulting for DHS, but he recently got engaged and spends most of his time fishing and working on his island."

"No offense, Kevin, but he sounds a little old and tired. I know quite a bit about MS-13 from when I lived in Chicago and they're young, violent, and ruthless. According to my niece, they've already made several attempts on her life. I'm not sure this is a job for a retiree."

Kevin laughed outright.

"What's so funny? These people are dangerous!"

"What's funny is the conclusion you drew when I said he was retired. He's only retired in the sense that he no longer has to work for money. From what my friend Scott Bond tells me he's an extremely lethal guy and still a long way from using a walker. Scott's a former Navy Lieutenant, SEAL dive-supervisor, and a graduate of Annapolis. His recommendation is like a gold seal. According to him, besides being a top sniper and a special ops guy when he was in the Marines, this guy has also done quite a bit of counterterrorism work since retiring and also put away a lot of drug smugglers and human traffickers. Seriously, from what my friend says this guy is extremely effective. The challenge will be in getting him off his island and convincing him that what you want is a righteous cause. I suggest you try and get him on the phone tomorrow night and lay out what's going on. Just be honest. Tell him about your relationship with your niece and what your fears are. He's got kids of his own. Don't bullshit him. Like I said, he doesn't need the work, but he's a highly principled guy who's gone up against all sorts of bad characters and organizations over the years. Oh, and besides being effective, this guy is the definition of discreet. He doesn't need or want the attention if things go all Western."

"What on earth does 'go all Western' mean?"

"It means, if things go sideways, people could get hurt or killed; MS-13 is a rough bunch."

"I know that; now you've got me wondering if this guy might be like using a sledgehammer instead of a hammer to bang in a nail."

Kevin chuckled. "The cat likes fish but doesn't want to get her paws wet?"

"No, all I care about is that Callie and her family are safe. If MS-13 comes after them, then it's on them if something bad happens. What's his name and number?"

"His name is Jesse McDermitt, and you can reach him at a place called The Rusty Anchor down in the Keys Saturday at 8:00."

"Sounds like a bar."

"It is. I gather he keeps a couple of his boats there and is good friends with the owner. That's the best I could do; what can I say, he's a private guy."

"Okay; give it to me."

Kevin gave her the number.

"Kevin, thanks. I hope I didn't sound ungrateful. I don't mean to be impatient, I'm just terrified that something might happen to her family in our absence and if it did, I'd never forgive myself. I'm really grateful that you were willing to research this for me. I'll buy you dinner next time I'm in Chicago."

"Deal. I hope this guy Jesse McDermitt can help you."

Chapter 35

We left Boston at 8:30 the next morning in our safari vehicle and took the Mass Turnpike to our 9:00 am Babson appointment in Wellesley, MA. We found parking right behind the admissions building on Forest Street and were greeted by the head of admissions and a student volunteer as we entered the building. Nancy's alumni status and the fact that she was a whale-size benefactor, no doubt played into this special treatment.

"Miss Liddell, I'm Patricia Fenway, head of admissions and this is Parker Conway. He's a senior and also a volunteer student tour guide."

Nancy put out her hand and shook with both Patricia and then Parker. "It's a pleasure meeting both of you. This is my niece, Catherine Babich."

I shook hands with both Patricia and Parker. "Nice to meet you both. Please, just call me Callie."

"Callie it is," replied Patricia. "I'm going to let Parker give you a tour of the campus first. After you've done that why don't you come back here, and you and I can sit down and spend a little time talking. I've read over your application, so I've got a bit of feel for who you are, but I've got a few questions and I'm sure you'll have some for me after your tour."

"That would be great, Miss Fenway, thank you."

Parker motioned toward the door. "Ready?"

I looked at Nancy with a querying look. She'd sat down after the introductions and didn't look like she planned on moving.

"I don't need to see the campus, Callie. I already spent four years here. You go, you'll probably feel freer to ask Parker questions if I'm not there. I'll just hang out here with Patricia and talk about alumni stuff."

I turned and smiled at Parker. "All right then. Lead on, Parker."

"We'll probably be an hour or so," Parker said to Patricia. He turned, held the door for me and we walked out of the admissions building onto the street in front."

"Is this the first college you've looked at, Callie?"

"No, the third. I've also toured Harvard and Mass Maritime."

"That's an eclectic mix?"

"Parker, can I ask you something?"

"Of course."

"Before I answer, do you report back to the admissions office on the people that you take on tours?"

"You mean like an assessment?"

I nodded. I was trying to decide how candid to be with him.

He shook his head. "No, not at all unless you ask a question that I don't know the answer to. I mainly do these tours because I love this place. I don't have anything to do with the admissions process."

"I've never heard someone talk about a school like that. You love it?"

He nodded. "Everyone here is highly curious, motivated and excited about the process. I look forward to going to classes every day. When I first applied here, I'd done a few classes at a local community college but really wasn't at all sure of what I wanted to study or what specific benefits going to college would offer me. I graduated young from high school and spent a year building boats first. After that year, I was fairly sure I didn't want to grind fiberglass for the rest of my life, but I just couldn't see myself doing any one thing like banker, builder, accountant, doctor."

"So why did Babson jump out at you?"

"It's kind of a long story. Sure you want to hear it?"

I nodded. "Yes. It sounds as though you had some of the same reservations that I have, so I'm very interested."

"After the summer I worked in that boatyard, I drove across the country in this little sports car I owned trying to see some of the country. Anyway, I was driving along one day wondering why big trucks are designed the way they are. Basically, most long-distance tractor trailer units are incredibly un-aerodynamic boxes. You can really feel all the turbulence they generate when you go by one in a little car. Turbulence is indicative of drag."

I smiled politely. "And?"

"I told you it's a long story. I'll get there. Anyway, I'd done some flying with my father growing up and had a better than average understanding of aerodynamics and when I got home from my trip I wondered if I couldn't design some sort of add-on device that would change the flow of air around these boxy trucks. I knew that completely redesigning the tractor and the trailers was out of the question because they're made by too many independent companies, but I wondered if I couldn't come up with something that could be installed on any truck as an aftermarket product that would make them more aerodynamically slick and as a result decrease fuel consumption. So, I built a small wind tunnel in my parents' garage and then started experimenting with models. It wasn't a real wind tunnel, but it was good enough to visualize the flow of air around scale model trucks using yarn and smoke."

I was starting to become more interested in his story not because I had any personal interest in fuel efficiency or aerodynamics but for the way Parker's mind obviously worked.

"Long story short, I came up with a device that could be added to the roofs of tractor trailer trucks that would cost about $800 to make and would save $40,000/year/truck in fuel costs."

"For every truck?" I asked.

He nodded. "For long distance haulers, anyway. I was able to achieve a nineteen percent reduction in fuel costs."

"Wow! How were you able to prove this?"

"The Titleist Golf Ball company was in a neighboring town and I talked them into giving me some free time in their wind tunnel. They had a real one that could generate 70 mph winds instead of the low-speed flows I was getting in my homebuilt one. Then I used simple spring gauges to measure the differences in drag on my scale models both with and without my device."

"So how did Babson fit in?"

"I'm almost there. So, I knew that I'd designed this really revolutionary product and I'm thinking to myself yay, I'm going to be a millionaire before I'm twenty-one!"

"Are you, did you?" I asked excitedly.

"Not yet."

"What happened?"

"I filed a disclosure document with the Patent Office, but I couldn't afford a real patent at the time."

"What's a disclosure document?"

"It's a document that contains all the information, description, abstract and drawings of a full-on patent. The patent office time-stamps it when they get it, which officially dates your idea, but you aren't afforded patent protection unless you follow it up with a real patent application that's approved within two years."

"Did Babson teach you how to do your disclosure document?"

"No, I'd already filed it."

"You're killing me here. So why did you end up here?"

"After I'd filed my disclosure, I was suddenly faced with all the challenges of bringing a new product to market. How would I finance my new company? How would I get the product into production? How would I market it? What would be the ideal distribution network? I had hundreds of problems to solve before I could sell my first device and absolutely no road map as to how to do any of it. Faced with all this, I realized that what I needed was an entrepreneurial education; one that was specialized for self-starting individuals like myself; something that would give me a logical way of approaching any new business venture."

I swear I heard this 'booiingg' go off in my head as I listened to Parker. Wasn't this in fact what I was looking for?

"How did you get steered to Babson?"

"I was talking with a neighbor of mine who was also a mentor of sorts to me. He's a very wealthy guy who figured out how to make luxury textile products out of recycled plastics. I was telling him about how frustrated I was at having designed this really cool product and not having a clue as to what to do next. He'd studied here at Babson and suggested to me that Babson has the best entrepreneurial program in the world and that it was something I should consider. He also told me that Babson really likes 'retreads' as he called people like me, meaning they like students who have already been out in the real world some and are highly motivated and self-directed."

I hadn't actually been out in the world at all except for my summer job on the ferry, but I certainly was as motivated and self-directed as anyone I knew. Parker's story was stirring me and as he showed me around the rest of the beautiful Ivy League looking campus, I honestly missed a lot of it, I was thinking so hard. My mind was racing as I made a lot of the connections Nancy had been alluding to when she'd talked about "learning how to think." Maybe she hadn't in fact learned to become a "publisher" via her education as much as she'd simply become an entrepreneur who had seen an opportunity that happened to be in the publishing industry. Perhaps her new high-tech business incubator project was just a logical extension of a more generalized love of ferreting out opportunities and improving and adding value to them with a learned entrepreneurial skill set.

Parker interrupted my train of thought. "This is the Elizabeth Morse Swimming Center."

I'd been so busy thinking and connecting various dots that I hadn't even noticed where we were. I looked up and out over the six lanes of the heated indoor pool, and drew in a lungful of moist, chlorine-laden air. And right there, at that moment, during that breathe, I made up my mind. I was going to go to Babson College.

It wasn't the pool that swayed me; both Harvard and Mass Maritime also had pools. It was the entrepreneurial skill set that Parker had spoken of in combination with Nancy's comments about learning "how to think" as opposed to "what to think" and watching her process as she was starting an entirely new business venture that had swayed me. Both concepts were tailor made for someone with my independent nature, thirst for learning, and desire to do many different things. I didn't have to pick just one, which had made the process of picking a college almost impossible. I could do anything and everything and make a living in the process, by acquiring the core skill set of an entrepreneur and it sounded as though Babson was the place to do that.

I knew I'd miss the warm Florida sunshine, but Parker's enthusiasm and explanation somehow brought everything I'd been trying to balance sharply into focus. Was my decision impetuous? Yes. Was I 100% certain that it would be the best thing for me? No. But it felt right enough for me to feel confident that I could do it for four years and learn some incredibly valuable skills.

A plan started to form in my head as we walked back towards Admissions. "Parker?"

"Yes."

"Does Babson offer summer sessions in addition to the regular semesters where you can take full credit courses?"

"It does. Why, are you thinking you need to get up to speed on some particular area like algebra?"

I shook my head. "No, I'm not worried about that. I was just wondering how much I could accelerate the degree process if I also did summers and took a heavy course load during the regular academic year."

"You could certainly do that if you could handle all the work. I'm curious, how old are you, Callie? You seem young yet mature at the same time. Why the hurry?"

"I'm sixteen; I entered first grade a year early and skipped sixth grade. Why not the hurry? When I make up my mind to do something, I totally go for it."

I was thinking that I could get my Bachelor of Science degree before the age of twenty if I did an accelerated program. That left room for a lot of life after, to figure out all the details.

"How's your GPA?"

"I've got a 4.0. It's funny, six months ago, I wasn't even thinking about going to college and then I spent this past summer with my Aunt Nancy. She really encouraged me and even offered to pay for it."

"Wish I had an aunt like that."

"She's very generous and pretty cool too. She's about to start some new business incubator project she thought up. That's another reason we're up here. She's buying a commercial building in South Boston, rehabbing it, and she's going to fill it with high-tech startups."

"You're kidding! I'd love to talk to her about that. I graduate this spring."

"What about your add-on device for tractor trailer trucks?"

"I missed the two-year window on following up my disclosure document with a patent application. I just got so busy here with classes, it took a backseat."

"Couldn't you still make your device?"

"Maybe, but GM snapped it up out of the patent office when it became public knowledge and they're manufacturing a virtual duplicate right now."

"You're kidding! I'd be furious."

"I'm not worried. I've got dozens of ideas just like it and now I have the skills to make some of them a reality."

"What would you say was the best part of your education here?"

Parker thought for a moment, then answered. "When I took those business courses at the State college, I remember feeling bored and uninspired. There was something different about Babson and I wasn't able to put my finger on it until just this year."

"What is it?"

"Here, the faculty teaches from the perspective of upper management and the decision makers, especially in the case-study policy courses. That's been the most valuable part of my education here. Many, if not most, of the professors here ran or still run their own companies and if you're going to be an entrepreneur you want to have the big picture, the long view of things and not be mired in the detail of middle management where you have very little control over your own destiny and even less over that of the company."

I nodded, instantly getting his point about being taught from the perspective of upper management.

"Parker, what you've told me about Babson and why you love it so much has been extremely helpful. I'm grateful."

"You're entirely welcome. You'll love it here if this is where you end up."

We got back to the admissions office several minutes later and after I told Nancy how much I'd enjoyed Parker's tour, I suggested she talk with him about her project. Then I followed Patricia into her office.

"Have a seat, Callie."

"Thank you."

"What did you think?"

"I'm not sure how to do this."

"Do what?"

"Tell you how totally in love I am with your school and the concept of your entrepreneurial program, without sounding like a fool. This is exactly what I've been looking for and I'd really like to go here."

Patricia smiled. "Nothing like playing your cards close to your chest."

I blushed, feeling like I should have played it cooler.

"Don't be embarrassed. That's actually one of the best things you could possibly have said to me as an admissions person. I get really bright people in this office every day trying to guess what I most want to hear. It gets old after a while. I want to know what people are really thinking. I know from your academic records and from talking to your aunt that you wouldn't have any problem with the curriculum side of things here. You're a brain, that's evident from your transcripts. What didn't come through to me from reading over your application was whether what we offer will give you what you're looking for. Your interests are all over the place and a big part of my job is trying to determine whether Babson and an applicant will be a good fit. Neither you nor the school benefits if you aren't happy here or you don't fit in with what we're trying to teach. Your honest enthusiasm for what we teach here, is refreshing. Given that your interests are all over the place, convince me. What specifically do you feel we can offer you that would enable you to make a four-year commitment? Don't overthink it, just gives me whatever pops into your head?"

I really didn't want to blow it at that point. I sensed that I had a really good shot at acceptance if I answered her question well. I'd done pretty well just trying to be honest, so I continued in that spirit.

"You're right, my interests are all over the place and I think that's why I've been struggling to identify the college that would be right for me. I've been trying to identify some narrow specialty to school myself in where perhaps I should have been trying to identify a field of study that would give me the tools to pursue many interests. Your entrepreneur program sounds like it offers that."

I paused for a few seconds then continued. "I think I can learn a way of thinking and problem solving here, that isn't available anywhere else. I also get the feeling from looking at your syllabus and talking with Parker and my aunt, that Babson and the people who go here are less concerned by all the social warrior foolishness I see going on at Harvard and Yale and most of the other liberal arts colleges that I've looked into around the country. Honestly, I'm not looking for guidance in what values I should or shouldn't have or whether I'm sufficiently woke or up to date on whatever groupthink is popular today. I've already figured those things out for myself and I have a well-defined set of personal standards and behaviors that I'm perfectly happy with. I'm simply looking for a school that can teach me unique and different ways of problem solving and I think Babson can do that."

Patricia sat silently looking at me and absently tapping her pencil eraser on the pad in front of her for several seconds before responding, "You're very intense, Callie and quite honestly what you just put into words leaves me wondering if I missed something by not going here myself."

I was surprised. "You didn't go to Babson?"

"No, I went to one of those 'woke,' 'groupthink' schools that you mentioned. I went to Yale."

Shit! I'd totally put my foot in my mouth, I thought to myself. I couldn't think of anything to say that wouldn't compound my mistake, so I sat silently, not sure what to do or say next.

"Do you have any questions for me?"

I shook my head. "I don't think so."

"Well, it's been a pleasure meeting you, and I mean that. We won't make our final decisions on applications till the end of March, but I would say that you have the academic background to get in here and the personality to do well here."

I felt foolish and deflated, certain that I'd just blown my chances for acceptance. What I'd said had been truthful though and backtracking would make me look insincere and weak. I stood up and looked Patricia in the eye.

"Thank you for the tour and the opportunity to interview. I know that my Aunt Nancy pushed a little to arrange all this on such short notice which feels a little awkward, but I really was impressed with the school and I hope you'll give my application serious consideration. I'd love to go here."

Patricia smiled politely but didn't give anything else away. "Let's go out together. I want to say goodbye to your aunt."

"Shit, shit, shit!" I screamed out once we were back in the car.

"Callie, language. What on earth happened to you in there? When you came back from your tour with Parker you looked like you were floating on air. What happened?"

"I totally blew it."

"Blew what?"

"I had an amazing tour and I realized after talking with Parker and hearing his story that Babson is really what I want to do next."

"That's fantastic! I'm so pleased for you. So why are you so upset?"

"I was too honest with Patricia. I think I insulted her."

"Why, what did you say?"

"I just assumed that she was a Babson graduate and after I told her the reasons I wanted to go to Babson, I made the mistake of telling her that I sensed that, and I'm quoting myself here, that 'Babson wasn't as concerned with all the woke groupthink bullshit that's so popular at Harvard, Yale and many of the other liberal arts colleges."

Nancy chuckled.

"Nancy, it's not funny! She went to Yale. She's one of those people I so casually maligned."

Nancy was laughing hysterically at that point and I lightly punched her on the arm.

"Ouch, careful of your delicate aunt."

"I'm sorry, but you don't understand. I really, really want to go to school there, and I just screwed up my chances."

"Settle down. You don't know that. And don't forget that I'm not without influence there."

"No, absolutely not; that's not the way I want to get in. I want to get in on my merits. I worked really hard to do as well as I did in school, and I don't want any special treatment. I just wish I weren't so darned quick to shoot off my mouth."

"Yes, well."

I hit her lightly on the arm again. "Don't agree with me!"

Chapter 36

Saturday morning at 4:00 am, Gabriella returned home at the end of her shift. She hadn't even had to go into the filing cabinets in Camila Sanchez's office to get the information that Diego wanted. The entire file on the gang was right on top of her desk as it had been the last thing Camila had worked on before going home. The report on the attempted kidnapping of a junkie named Karen was part of that file and Callie's name, address and telephone contact info was part of that report although she wasn't listed as "Callie Babich" but rather as "Catherine Babich." She copied all of the information onto a piece of paper.

Matèo awoke when he heard Gabriella return home and come into their bedroom. He rolled over to face her while she undressed and got ready to get into the bed.

"Did you get it?"

"Yeah, I got it. Some white-bread named Catherine Babich. She lives right here in Fort Myers on the edge of town. I'll leave the info on the bedside table. You can call Esteban with it when you get up later. I don't want to talk to him."

"Yeah, okay, baby. I'll call him. Sorry you had to do that."

"Me too. At least it's done for now. Hopefully, they won't want anything more from us."

Matèo didn't respond. He was thinking to himself that there'd always be "something else" that the gang would want and that the only way they'd ever be completely free of them would be to move someplace rural, far away. Where to go, though? As an illegal alien without real citizenship papers and all the tats on his body, his employment options outside of friends and family would be limited. There was also something that bothered him about the name. Why did Catherine Babich sound familiar?

Chapter 37

Saturday morning at 9:00 am I watched from the doorway as Meredith and her father pulled up in front of the Ritz. The sky was a dark gray and the forecast was calling for snow showers. I rushed outside in the thirty-four-degree temperature and climbed into the backseat of their truck, grateful for the warmth and smiled at Meredith. She turned in the front passenger seat to greet me.

"Good morning."

"Good morning," I replied. "Is New England always this cold?"

Meredith looked at me a little strangely and Dudley smiled with his eyes in the rearview mirror.

"This is nothing. Once winter comes it sometimes goes down to zero for weeks at a time. We get northeasters and blizzards too. It's a regular winter wonderland around here; right, Dad?"

"Yup, we even have a little ski resort right on the edge of the city called Blue Hill."

"Have you ever skied, Callie?" Meredith asked.

"I've water skied, but no, no snow skiing. Where I'm from the average year-round temperature is seventy-seven degrees.

"It's going to be cold out on the water today. I brought an extra foul weather gear jacket, a wool hat, and gloves for you. They're in that canvas bag at your feet back there," Meredith offered. "How did your interviews and tours go this week?"

"They were good. I decided that I really want to go to Babson."

"Babson's a great school. So, you'll be here in the fall?"

"I hope, but I might have screwed it up."

"Why, what did you do?"

"I think I insulted the Head of Admissions. I assumed that she was probably a Babson graduate and I basically told her that one of the things that appealed to me most about Babson over the Ivy League schools was that it didn't seem to be so steeped in 'woke BS.' Turns out she went to Yale."

Meredith chuckled. "Way to go, girl. I haven't been on any interviews yet, but I've heard that insulting the interviewer is generally not a good idea."

"No kidding. Thanks for making me feel better."

"Don't worry about it. You're a brain, an athlete, charming, a master mariner, and a kung fu master. They'd be morons not to recognize your awesomeness."

I was flattered and a little embarrassed by Meredith's recall of my skills. "It's Krav Maga, not kung fu, and I'm a long way from being a master."

"What's Krav Maga?" Dudley asked.

"It's this Israeli type of hand-to-hand combat that Callie knows. I looked it up on the Internet after we got home the other day. She's been studying it. She's got this great female Israeli instructor."

I suddenly felt self-conscious.

"I used to box some years ago. What's different about Krav Maga?" Dudley asked.

"Mainly, getting inside your opponent's effective reach range, deflection, and then incapacitating him or her as quickly as possible."

"Doing what?"

I thought about my answer for a second. "By going after their weakest points; eyes, throat, knees, fingers, toes, crotch; and doing it in an explosive, focused manner. You want to cause as much physical damage as possible in the shortest amount of time. It's not a polite form of fighting. It's more like advanced street-fighting where you fight as dirty as possible."

"You're not a very big girl. I would imagine a really big guy would still have quite an advantage over someone your size."

I really didn't want to get into details about using available weapons as equalizers or about the steel baton in my jacket. I liked Meredith and didn't want to scare her father off by telling stories about incapacitating MS-13 gang members and armed robbers. I'd seen Nancy's reaction and didn't want him to think I was a bad influence, so I took a safe approach in my answer.

"I think for sure that really big guys do have an advantage, but my teacher Eva has us spar with people of all sizes. There are various workarounds that can give someone my size an advantage and we practice those."

I changed the subject to get it off me. "How far will we be bringing the boat, Meredith?"

"Not that far as the crow flies; probably just ten miles or so, but if it's okay with my dad I'd like to show you around some of the smaller islands in Boston harbor on our way. There's an Outward-Bound facility on Thompson Island, hiking trails on Spectacle Island, and Peddocks Island is where they filmed parts of that Leonardo DiCaprio movie Shutter Island. Did you ever see that?"

"I don't think so. What's it about?"

"It's like this spooky thriller movie where Leonardo plays the part of a U.S. Marshall investigating the disappearance of a criminally insane patient from this mental hospital on the island. He and his partner get trapped on the island for several days by a big storm. It was a cool movie. The island feels a lot like the movie."

"I'm game."

"Would that be alright with you, Dad, if we poked around some on the way home?"

"Sure; just keep your eye on the weather and plan on getting to Hingham by 2:00. I've got to pick up your brother back in the city by 4:00. I can drop Callie back at her hotel then. If you get in earlier just call me and I'll come down to the boat ramp and pick you up. I'm just going to be messing around the house all day. Text me when you get there. Give yourself plenty of time though. If you get snow showers your visibility will drop and you'll have to go really slow."

"We'll be careful."

"I know you will. I trust your judgment.

We took the old Sumner Tunnel under Boston Harbor and came out near Logan Airport. Traffic was light and after several turns Dudley pulled up to Boston Harbor Shipyard and Marina on Marginal Street and then stopped halfway down the pier. He handed the boat keys to Meredith.

"You two have fun; but not too much."

"I'll be careful, Dad."

"I know you will."

He turned to me. "You're a swimmer right, Callie?"

"Yes, sir. I also worked as a deckhand on a ferry this past summer."

"Meredith told me that. We don't have radar on the Contender, but if you guys lose your visibility you should be alright as long as you follow the GPS, go slow, and stay on your side of the channel. Keep your eyes open. If the weather gets really bad you can always pull off somewhere and tie up until it improves."

He turned back to Meredith. "I filled her up yesterday so you should have plenty of fuel but double check before you leave in case someone siphoned our tank."

"You're paranoid, Dad."

"Just check, okay?"

"I will." Meredith turned to me. "Callie, can you grab that seabag on the floor?"

"Got it." We got out of the truck and after waving goodbye to Meredith's father I followed her down a short gangway to the float where their boat *Sou'wester* was tied.

The thirty-foot Contender with twin 350hp outboards was indeed a "beast" as Meredith had said. "You weren't kidding; this boat is awesome!"

She smiled at me before stepping down into it. "Told you. Here, pass me your seabag."

I did as she asked and then watched as she took the covers off of the instruments, turned on the battery switch and then inserted the key. After lowering the huge outboards into the water using the hydraulic tilts, she started both. They were almost silent compared to the big diesels on *Gulf Runner* that I was used to. I watched as she checked the fuel gauges and turned on the GPS.

"Do you stick the tanks too?" I asked.

She shook her head. "Can't do that with this boat; you have to rely on the gauges. The filler line takes an almost right angle turn before it gets to the tank so there's no way to get a stick into the tank."

I nodded. "I'm going to take you up on your offer of the foul weather gear, I'm freezing." I put on the foul weather gear jacket she'd brought for me. "Do you get to take the boat out on your own often?"

"Actually, this is the first year he's started to let me use it on my own. I've been driving it for years, but I only got around to getting my boater safety certificate at the end of this summer."

"We have to have those in Florida too." I zipped up the jacket that she'd brought for me and then put on the watch cap and gloves. They all fit perfectly.

"Better?"

"Nice and warm; thanks. Ready for me to get the lines?"

Meredith nodded. "Get the spring first, the bow second and I'll get the stern."

"Aye, Cap." I did as she asked, throwing the lines into the boat after untying them from the cleats. Then, after she gave me a head nod, I pushed us slightly off the float and jumped into the boat. Meredith looked behind first and after making sure we were clear, put both engines into reverse, and gently backed us out of the slip. Once clear she pivoted the bow towards the channel by cross controlling both engines. I was impressed and pulled the fenders in once we were clear of the dock. "You drive well."

Meredith blushed as she moved both throttles into forward and started idling past the other tied boats. "What, did you think I was going to do a Rodney Dangerfield and crash into everyone?"

"Not really, but I can't believe how bad some of the drivers are down in Florida."

"It's the same thing here. People just figure if they can drive a car then they can drive a boat. My dad was a good teacher. He always says, 'hope for the best, but plan for the worst.'"

As we cleared the end of the dock and entered the harbor, we heard a car horn and looked back to the end of the dock. Neither one of us had noticed as we'd prepared to leave, but Meredith's father had apparently been watching us the whole time. We both waved. He blinked his lights at us and then started backing off the pier.

"I like your father. He seems like a nice man," I said.

"I like him too. What's your dad like?"

"He makes his living on the ocean and he's a good enough seaman, but I don't know if he'll ever accept my interest in boats. He doesn't think the ocean is any place for a woman."

"That's unfortunate."

"My Aunt Nancy, on the other hand, is very cool. She supports pretty much anything I want to do or learn."

"I liked her. She seems like a powerhouse."

Meredith continued at idle speed past the end of the marina dock until we had traveled several hundred yards past, then turned and smiled at me.

"You want to see what she can do?"

I knew exactly what she meant, smiled, and held my hand up for a high five. Meredith slapped palms with me.

"Hang on." She started slowly advancing both throttles. The Contender stood up on her stern as the propellers dug in. The bow rose and within three or four seconds we were on a plane and continuing to rapidly accelerate. I'd never been in such a fast boat and looked down at the knot meter and watched as our speed quickly rose from eight to twenty, then thirty, forty and finally fifty knots. Meredith had a sick smile on her face and pulled back on the throttles slightly so that we maintained that speed for several seconds. The icy wind tore into my face and I moved inboard closer to Meredith to benefit from the protection of the windscreen. "Woo, hoo!" I shouted. "This thing flies! What's her top speed?"

"About sixty-five if you get her trimmed out right. For now, though, I want to plan out our course so I'm going to back her down some." She started pulling back on the throttles and came back down to just twelve knots or so in order to focus on the GPS screen. She put her finger on Sou'wester's icon on the screen and then traced a course to an island on the right of the screen. "That's Thompson Island over there. We'll stay in the main ships channel to here, and then we'll cut directly over towards the island."

"What's on Thompson Island?"

"It's an Outward-Bound school. It's closed for the winter, but they always have a caretaker there and if we're nice he might let us poke around. They do these coed programs in the summer where students travel and live on these big open thirty-foot rowing boats. They have some sailing capability, but most of the time the students have to row them."

"And what, they stop and camp at different places each night?"

"No, actually, they live, eat, sleep, even go to the bathroom, right on the open boats.

I tried to envision myself doing a trip like Meredith was talking about and basically doing everything I normally did in private, in front of others. "Not sure I'd like that."

"I know, right?"

We idled up to the pier at Thompson Island several minutes later. In addition to a large sixty-foot steel ferry tied to two floating docks, there was a smaller fiberglass Carolina Skiff tied up to another. The skiff had quite a bit of water in it and a dark-haired man with a scruffy goatee, a black wool watch cap, and a canvas coat was in the stern pumping out the bilge with an old-fashioned hand pump. He seemed to be muttering to himself. Meredith put *Sou'wester* into neutral and coasted to a stop alongside the float and close to him.

"Good morning."

He looked up, stopped pumping, and sat on the gunwale of the skiff apparently glad for any excuse to stop bailing.

"What can I do for you?" he asked with a thick Boston accent.

Meredith answered, "I know you're closed for the winter, but I was wondering if there was any way I could show my friend around the island?"

"You connected with the school in some way?" He looked over our fancy Contender with the two gently burbling 350 horse outboards and put out a vibe that he wasn't likely to be inclined to be doing any favors for the two little rich girls in their fancy boat.

"No, I was just telling my friend about the pulling boats and hoped maybe you'd let us tie up for a few minutes and take a look at one of them."

"Sorry, we're closed for the season to visitors, and I've got to head into the city. My electric bilge pump seems to have crapped out. I don't really have the time right now."

When Meredith and I had boarded *Sou'wester*, I'd stowed our seabag in the compartment under the helm seat. I'd noticed a bucket and brush in that same compartment and had an idea. "Can we help you get the water out of your boat, sir? We've got a good-sized bucket and if we took turns, I bet we could get the water out in no time."

I could see he was tempted and was trying to work out in his mind what our help was going to cost him. "That's a nice offer, but I still couldn't let you look around the island unaccompanied."

"I understand, sir. There's no quid pro quo, just one boater helping another," I offered.

"I'd be grateful for your help, then. Just tie up astern of me."

Meredith gave me a side look, smiled, and then spun *Sou'wester* around and started an approach to the float. I flipped the fenders over our starboard side, grabbed the bow line and the aft spring and got ready to jump over to the float. Meredith pulled alongside the float perfectly and after I'd gotten those two lines tied off, she handed me the stern line and I made that fast also. I watched the man watch us as we docked and tied off and knew we'd risen a notch on his respect-meter from the look on his face.

"Can you hand me that bucket under the helm seat, Meredith?" I asked.

She tilted the hinged back-rest aft, reached in, and passed it to me. I walked over to the man's skiff and held out my right hand.

"I'm Callie and that's Meredith."

He nodded at us both and shook my hand. "Nate."

I looked down into the stern of his skiff and figured there was easily 100 gallons of rain and seawater remaining. I was already cold and damp and didn't relish getting my feet wet. I handed Nate the bucket but before getting into his boat nodded at the battery case that was almost underwater. "Mind if I take a look?"

"Go wild."

I lay down on the float, reached into the skiff and undid the strap holding the top of the battery box on, pulled it off and looked at the battery poles. In addition to the thick cables coming off the positive and negative terminals there was a single smaller red wire coming off the positive terminal which provided power to the small electric bilge pump in his stern. There was quite a bit of corrosion around both poles. I looked over at Meredith.

"Do you have a toolbox, Meredith?"

She nodded and opened the small door in the side of her console. She reached in and pulled it out. "What do you need?"

"A small adjustable wrench and a wire brush."

She nodded, pulled out the requested items and handed them to me.

"You mind, Nate?" I pointed to his battery terminals.

"Have at it," he said with an amused expression on his face.

I loosened the negative terminal and wire brushed the pole and the terminal and then put it back on, then took the positive terminal off and wired brushed it also. When I put the positive battery pole back on, it sparked several times and immediately a nice thick stream of water started pouring out of the bilge outlet port in the stern. I tightened the terminal, put the top back on the battery box, redid the strap that held it on, then sat back on my haunches and smiled at Nate as we watched the stream of bilge water shoot out of the stern.

"I was going to do that, you know," Nate offered. "I was just testing you."

I burst out laughing.

"You're pretty handy."

I sensed this was high praise. "Thank you, sir. I work on a commercial ferry in the summer and I'm responsible for doing all the engine room maintenance."

"How's she powered?"

"Twin 1271's."

"Breaux boat?"

I nodded.

"If you ever want a summer job, I'm always looking for good deck hands for that one." He pointed towards the large steel ferry tied up at the next dock. "Course, that one can barely get out of her own way with a single 400hp diesel, but I always tell people if you can learn to dock the *Outward Bound* then you can dock damned-near anything."

"Thank you, Nate. I might hold you to that. I'm up here looking at colleges and hopefully I'll be moving to the Boston area this coming year."

He pulled out his wallet and handed me a business card. "I'm in charge of maritime operations here on the island. Give me a call if you want work."

I stood up, put the wire brush and wrench in the bucket and passed it to Meredith and then got aboard *Sou'wester*.

"I do have to go into the city, but if you girls still want to look at a pulling boat, help yourself. There's one in that shed at the base of the dock that I'm doing some work on. The door's open. You'll have to wait for some other time to see the rest of the island though. And make sure you latch the door behind you when you leave."

Meredith smiled broadly. "Thank you, Nate, that's very kind of you, but you really don't owe us anything for our help."

"I know that, but I'm a good judge of character and I'm just about 100% certain you two aren't going to rip me off."

He started his skiff, threw off the lines, and turned once to wave before jamming the throttle in the Carolina Skiff to the stops and planing off. Meredith and I walked down the dock together to the boat house and watched as he disappeared around the point at Castle Island several minutes later.

"When we first met him, I was thinking, 'no way he'll let us come ashore here.' That's pretty cool how you fixed his bilge pump and got him turned around so quick."

I shrugged. "I try to bring a positive attitude to everything I do. Most times people respond in a like way."

"Well, Nate certainly did. He even offered you a job."

"I know and I might just take him up on it, too."

We spent just ten minutes looking at the pulling boat before agreeing that while the concept of living in an open boat with no bathroom or shower was an interesting idea, neither of us had any desire to do an eight-day trip in one with a group of strangers. When we came out of the boat house, I noticed that the sky had gotten dramatically darker and big, fat, white snowflakes had started to fall. There wasn't much wind and I stuck out my tongue and caught several on the tip.

"Your first snow?" Meredith asked.

I nodded as I looked closely at one of the flakes that had landed on the back of my gloved hand. "They're really detailed; they look just like snowflakes."

"Duh! What'd you think they'd look like?"

I punched Meredith lightly on the arm. "Don't make fun of me. I can't help it if I live in a tropical paradise."

She smiled back and I realized how much I was enjoying spending time with another girl my age who was interesting, competent, curious, and fun.

"Weather's starting to come in some." Meredith pointed towards the middle of the Harbor where we'd originally come from. The far shore was no longer visible and the thick, dark gray/black clouds had descended to within several hundred feet of the surface.

"Time to mosey on towards Hingham. I don't really want to get stuck in a white-out."

We got back aboard *Sou'wester* and after Meredith got the engines started, I undid our lines and pulled the fenders aboard. She turned on the running lights for extra visibility and traced out the route we were going to take to Hingham on the GPS screen with her finger.

"It's almost a straight shot to Hingham once we get back out into the main channel. I'm not worried about finding it if it really starts coming down, but there's quite a bit of high-speed ferry traffic running the same route. Without radar we can't really see them until they're right on top of us, so we'll hug our side of the channel and hopefully they'll be paying attention and watching out for boats like ours. If it gets really bad, we can always stop at Peddock Island and tie up at the dock there for a while."

I nodded my understanding and Meredith bumped our throttles up to about fifteen knots. I stood at her side absolutely mesmerized by the big fluffy white snowflakes hurtling towards us. They were hypnotic. As we approached the main channel the snow started falling faster and Meredith backed our speed back down to about eight knots and gave a prolonged blast on our horn. She also checked the squelch and volume on our VHF radio which was tuned to channel 16. She picked up the microphone.

"Security, security, security. This is motor vessel *Sou'wester*. We are entering the Western Way, westbound from Thompson Island to Hingham harbor. We are not radar equipped. We will be taking Sculpin Ledge Channel to West Gut and then cutting over to Hingham Bay on the South side of Sheep Island. Concerned traffic can contact us on 16."

After a brief silence on radio. "*Sou'wester, Fat Albert.*"

"*Fat Albert,* this is *Sou'wester*, go ahead."

"*Sou'wester*, I'm a small tug with a fuel barge on my hip. Just departed the Valero Terminal in Weymouth. I'll be Northbound in the main channel. Say your position as you approach red #2 on the North End of Nut Island."

"*Fat Albert, Sou'wester*. Will do."

I looked closely at the chart and could clearly see the #2 mark the tug driver was referring to. That would be the last navigational aid we'd get to before driving directly across the main channel. I smiled at Meredith.

"Do you like this half as much as I do?"

"Totally!" Meredith reached over and gave another prolonged blast on our horn. "I love it when I'm completely focused like this and doing something I love."

The visibility continued to degrade as the snow fell faster and Meredith adjusted her speed downward another two knots and gave another blast on her horn.

"It's every two minutes on the horn, right?"

She nodded. "At least every two minutes."

"We don't get much fog down where I am, and even less snow!" I joked.

"Yea, but you've got alligators."

"That's true."

"With the weather like this I think I'm going to skip Spectacle and Peddock Islands. It's cold, the visibility is crap, and it just doesn't seem like a hiking around day."

"I agree. I'm just really enjoying being out on the water."

"You want to take her for a while?"

"I'd love to!"

"Just keep a sharp eye out ahead and keep us pinned to the right side of the channel. If anything comes out of the snow be ready to steer her hard to starboard and goose the throttles if you need to."

"You got it."

A call came over the radio just five minutes later. "Sea Tow, Sea Tow or Boat US, Boat US this is motor vessel *Weather or Knot*, if either of you are out there, please respond." No one responded and the caller repeated his message again. It was a strong signal and the sender sounded close by. Meredith picked up the mic.

"*Weather or Knot*, this is motor vessel *Sou'wester*. Could you switch and answer 13?"

"Sí, switching 13 *Sou'wester*."

Meredith switched frequencies. "What's your location and the nature of your problem *Weather or Knot*?"

"We're a little bit south of Rainsford Island drifting near some rocks. Not sure what's wrong with my engine, but it won't start, over."

"How big are you and where are you headed?"

"We're twenty-two feet. The trailer for our boat is in South Boston."

Meredith looked at me before responding to them. "Want to do a little rescue before we head in? We've got time."

I nodded. "Sure."

"*Weather or Knot*, this is *Sou'wester*. We're headed into Hingham and could give you a tow in there if that would help. We don't have time right now to tow you all the way back into Boston Harbor."

"We'll take it *Sou'wester*. There's hardly anyone else out here right now and my kids are getting cold."

"I'm guessing you're probably drifting right off Quarantine Rocks which is only a half mile from us. Do you have a horn, over?"

Meredith pointed out Rainsford Island and Quarantine Rocks on the GPS screen. "Set a course for there, Callie."

I nodded and turned to Port after checking for traffic behind and to our left.

"*Sou'wester*, this is *Weather or Knot*. We do have a horn, over."

Meredith had them sound it several times and we found them just minutes later. I gave the helm back to her and then rigged a long towing line that I found in the stern lazarette to one of our stern cleats and led it through one of the stern chalks. Then I put two fenders over the side, and we pulled alongside the drifting boat.

Weather or Knot was a dodgy-looking old Sea Ray with what looked like a twenty-year-old outboard on it. There was water sloshing around in the stern, which was covering filthy, out of place looking indoor/outdoor carpeting and four different bottom-fishing rods. Two of the rods had tangled line coming out of the reels. There was also an open, brown cardboard box full of seaweed and long, ugly, sea worms floating on the surface of the bilge water. Besides the operator, there were two young children huddled together in the bow that looked cold and slightly scared. They were both wearing life preservers. Our immaculate Contender with the two Yamaha 350's and bright red and green running lights must have looked like a dream come true as we emerged from the snow squall and came into focus.

"Thank you so much for stopping!" the operator of the Sea Ray said. With both our engines now in neutral and at idle you could almost hear each fat snowflake as it landed. I smiled at the man and handed him several coils and the bitter end of the tow rope. I nodded towards his bow cleat.

"Can you make this off to your bow cleat, sir?"

"Not a problem. Thank you again."

I watched as he made it off to the cleat to make sure that he did it properly and then Meredith slowly pulled ahead until all the slack was out of the line and it came taught. We had about thirty feet of scope out. I looked at the line and then at Meredith.

"Looks good," she responded and then slowly advanced our throttles until we were pulling them behind us at about six knots. I moved out of the stern to the helm station and stood alongside her looking backwards to make sure they tracked properly in our wake. I looked at the GPS screen.

"Are you going to go around the north or the south end of Peddock?" I asked.

"South end. It gets pretty skinny in the channel on the north end to be towing another boat through there with this visibility."

I nodded, agreeing with her choice. "You're pretty good at this, Meredith."

"Thanks, girlfriend; so are you."

Ten minutes later we came to the #2 buoy at the south end of Peddock and Meredith picked up the VHF mic again.

"*Fat Albert, Fat Albert*; *Sou'wester*, over."

"Go ahead *Sou'wester*."

"We're approaching #2 right now and shortly will be crossing the Weymouth Fore River Channel Eastbound, over."

"Roger *Sou'wester*; we're already up at the turn on the north end of Peddock so I'm not concerned. I was listening when that other boat hailed you. I gather you picked up a stray, over."

"We did and we have him in tow."

"Sounds good. You have a good day, *Sou'wester*. *Fat Albert* back to 16."

"You too, *Fat Albert*."

The snow stopped about fifteen minutes later, and the visibility increased to several miles. Meredith picked up her cell phone and called Dudley. I could only hear one side of the conversation.

"Hey, Dad. We'll be at the boat ramp in about a half hour." She listened for a while and then spoke again. "We stopped at Thompson Island for about a half hour, but the vis was terrible and then we stopped to help out a boat that couldn't get his engine started. We're towing them right now."

"No, just a little Sea Ray. We're good. See you in about thirty minutes."

Thirty-two minutes later we pulled up to the public landing in downtown Hingham and got the Sea Ray secured to the dock. The man we'd helped offered to pay us. Meredith declined his offer and we wished them well then drove to the side of the pier and right up onto the trailer that Dudley had already backed into the water. He winched the boat tightly into the bow chalk. Then he pulled the boat up into the parking lot where we cinched down several tie downs and further secured *Sou'wester* to the trailer. From there it was just a short four-minute drive to their house. We dropped the trailer in their backyard and then immediately got back on the road. We got into Boston by 3:30.

I'd watched with interest how Dudley and Meredith had interacted the two times I'd seen them together and was envious. Despite their age difference and their parent/child relationship, they were respectful of each other, worked well together, and in general treated each other as equals. I also noted that he called her Mer for short, and I decided I would do the same.

"Mr. Norgen."

He looked at me in the rearview mirror. "Dudley."

"Sorry, Dudley. I just wanted to say that Mer runs your boat really well."

"That's good to hear, it's a lot of boat."

Meredith was looking out the passenger window pretending not to be listening. I could tell from her expression, however, that she was pleased with my compliment and her father's agreement.

She turned towards her father. "Cat's pretty awesome too, Dad. Every time I started to do something it was like she'd already thought of it and was either on the same step or one ahead of me. We were like Frick and Frack out there."

I hadn't heard that expression since I'd used it when I was trying to describe my relationship with Aunt Nancy to Eva over dinner the first night we'd all sat down together. Nancy and I also tended to know what the other was thinking without saying anything. I felt a similar kinship with Mer and looked up "Frick and Frack" on my phone. The *Urban Dictionary* mentioned "retarded Siamese twins" and I burst out laughing.

"What?" Meredith asked.

"'Retarded Siamese twins'; that's what the *Urban Dictionary* likens us to."

"Yup, sounds about right to me," Dudley offered.

Chapter 38

Diego put another spoonful of soup up to his mother's dry, cracked lips and tried to get as much of it as possible into her mouth. He was grateful that he'd thought to tuck a dishtowel into the top of her nighty as most of each spoonful dribbled out of the sides of her mouth and down her chin. He didn't want to have to undress and wash her again so soon. After each spoonful he would tenderly wipe her chin clean with a damp cloth. He was exhausted from his nursing vigil but also grateful that the Fentanyl patches had worked, and that she was no longer complaining about the pain.

"Madre, you've got to eat a little more. Just a couple of more bites." He gave her several more and was just finishing up when he heard a knock at the door. He got up off the chair, walked to the bedroom door and yelled. "Minuto! I'll be right there." He returned to his mother's bedside, removed the sodden dish towel from her front and then pulled the sheet up to her neck. Then he leaned over and gently kissed her on the forehead. She felt cold to his touch, and he put another blanket on her before going to answer the door.

"I'll be right back, Madre, someone's at the door." He gathered up the empty soup bowl and the wet dish towel, crossed the room to the door and gently closed it behind him. Then he brought the bowl and the dishtowel to the kitchen and put them in the sink before going to the front door.

"Si, quién es."

"Esta Esteban."

He opened the door. "Come in."

Esteban entered. "Jefe, how are you and your mother today?"

"She's better; eating some and no longer in pain."

Esteban looked around the living room. All the shades were drawn, every window closed, and it smelled like rotten food.

"Bueno, that's good to hear. What about you? You look tired. I'm sure if I asked that I could get Adriella or one of the other women to come by and give you a break or maybe make you a meal. Would you like that?"

"Gracias, pero no. This is something that I want to do for my mother on my own. She did everything for me for many years. Now is my time to return her love."

Esteban nodded. "I'm sure she's grateful." Noticing the foul odor again he asked. "Would you like me to pull up the shades and open some windows and let in some fresh air and light? It's a little rank in here."

"Oh, is it? I hadn't noticed. Sure, go ahead."

Esteban let up the shades and opened the windows on either side of the front door. He took several deep breathes of the fresh air before turning back to Diego.

Diego pointed to the couch. "Sit and tell me again about Gino."

Esteban sat and smiled proudly. "I remembered that the little faggot was allergic to bees. Back when I worked with him for a few weeks, we stopped for an ice cream one day and there were these bees hanging around a trash can outside. They were probably attracted by the sugar. Anyway, when a bee flew near him, he got all freaked out and locked himself in the van. When I asked him about it, he told me he was allergic to them.

"Anyway, so I caught a bunch of wasps in my aunt's garden and then got Matèo to bring them into the jail in a glass tube. He gave them to Cesar, and Cesar threw them into his cell when he was locked in. I heard it was a beautiful thing to see. He cried like a little bitch as they stung him. Then he blew up like a balloon with his eyes bugging out of his skull. Then his fucking heart stopped! I would have laughed like a motherfucker if I'd been there."

"That's good, Esteban, very clever. And what about the puta?"

A rare smile crept over Esteban's face. He reached into his pocket and unfolded the notes he'd taken when Matèo had called that morning. He held the piece of paper up. "Her name is Catherine Babich, and she lives out on...."

Chapter 39

Nancy followed Kevin Grainger's instructions and dialed the number he'd given her at exactly 8:00 pm that evening.

"Rusty Anchor."

"Yes, I'm trying to reach Jesse McDermitt."

"Hang on."

Nancy could hear a muffled sound in the background as she waited. "Some woman for you." Then more muffled sounds. "I'll take it."

"This is Jesse McDermitt, speak," a deep voice answered.

"Mr. McDermitt, my name is Nancy Liddell."

"How did you come by my name, Nancy?"

"A private eye who did some work for me back in Chicago named Kevin Grainger found out for me. Kevin used to work for DHS with an associate of yours and that associate gave Kevin your name and where I might reach you."

"The associates name?"

"Scott Bond."

"Fair enough, Scott's a good man and I know him well. How can I help you, ma'am?"

"Please, just call me Nancy."

"Okay, Nancy; how can I help?"

"I'm in Boston right now looking at some colleges with my niece. She's gotten herself into some trouble and I wanted to see if I could contract you to do some personal protection work."

Jesse paused. "That's not something I do. I'm not sure why Scott gave you, my name."

"Part of the reason is that I specified that the person or persons needed to be highly discreet. I don't wish my niece or her family to know that I've arranged this protection."

"Still not ringing any bells on my end, Nancy. I have on occasion done some consulting for DHS, but I've never done any PI or personal protection work. I'm afraid you got some bad info."

Nancy felt like she was pounding on a solid brick wall and sensed she wasn't going to get any further with Jesse on her current tack.

"Mr. McDermitt, I absolutely adore my niece. She's one of the brightest, most ambitious, talented girls I've ever met or known and I'm terrified that she and her family might be targeted and killed by MS-13. I need some help. I'm terrified of what these animals might do to them."

Jesse didn't say anything for several seconds.

"Are you still there, Mr. McDermitt."

"I am. I was thinking. I'm not a big fan of the gang. Tell me a little more about your situation."

"Thank you, thank you!"

"Slow down, Nancy. I'm not telling you I'll help you, but you've piqued my curiosity. What's the story with your niece and why are they after her?"

"I gather from what she told me that she interrupted an attempted kidnapping one evening about ten days ago. In the process she beat up two of the gang members, grabbed the girl from them, and then escaped with her on the back of her motorcycle."

"I thought you said she was sixteen?"

"She is."

"How big is she?" Jesse asked, his voice sounding flummoxed.

"Tiny, maybe five feet if she's lucky."

"I'm missing something here, Nancy, this isn't computing with what I know about the gang."

"I know, I know. I've got the same questions and I would have dismissed what she told me out of hand if I hadn't seen firsthand what she's capable of myself."

"What did you see?"

"As I mentioned, we're in Boston right now looking at colleges. Yesterday we stopped at a jewelry store to have something appraised. While we were in there a masked man wielding a shotgun broke in, disabled the armed guard, and held all of us at gunpoint." Nancy paused then continued. "For about a minute."

"Why just a minute?"

"That's how long it took for my niece to disarm him, knock him out and then get him in cuffs."

"Miss Liddell, no offense but that sounds like what we call a sea story in the Corps. Others might use the term bullshit."

"Swear to God. She disarmed him, hit him in the jaw with the butt of his own gun, and when that wasn't enough, she drew some sort of telescoping pipe out of her jacket and cracked him alongside the head and he went down."

"Sounds like a police baton. Has she had martial arts training or something?"

"Yes. Something happened to her earlier this year. After she told me about the other situation she'd gotten into, I introduced her to an Israeli self-defense teacher and then bought her some lessons. I gather she's gotten quite good at it over the last several months."

"Krav Maga."

"Yes, exactly. How did you know."

"You said the instructor was Israeli. I know a little about it."

"Anyway, since she took down those two gang members the gang has been actively looking for her and has already made three attempts to try and capture or kill her. I'm terrified that they're going to succeed."

"Where do you and she live?"

"I live on Boca Grande and Callie lives just outside Fort Myers on the Caloosahatchee."

"That's about 120 miles from me by boat."

"You'll help me!"

"No, sorry. I was thinking out loud. I need to think about it. You said you're in Boston right now?"

"Yes, we're looking at colleges and we'll be here till Sunday."

"You said your niece was sixteen. Isn't she kind of young to be looking at colleges?"

"Not really. Callie's a high school senior right now. She started school young, and she also skipped a grade."

"So, she's a brain too. Why is it so important to you that she and her family be protected without their knowledge? It's much simpler to protect someone if they're compliant and following some basic rules."

"Is why really important?"

"It is to me. I never work with anyone unless all the cards are on the table."

"The main reason is I'm afraid my sister and her husband will blame me for getting Callie involved with martial arts in the first place and forbid me from seeing her or let her go off to an out of state college. They're prideful people and would resent the rich sister who thinks she can buy their protection. From Callie's point of view, I just don't want to undermine her self-confidence."

"I see. Listen, I need to think about this. Your niece sounds like a good kid and she's likely in considerable danger. I want to do some research on MS-13 in Fort Myers. I'd want to know what I was up against before I gave you an answer."

"What would you typically charge for an assignment like this?"

"I don't *do* assignments like this. I'm sort of retired. If I were to somehow help you out with your problem, I would simply ask that you pay it forward and help someone else who needs it at a later date."

"I can't thank you enough, Mr. McDermitt."

"As I said, I'm not sure I can help you due to some other obligations I have, but I'm not without resources and contacts with others who might be able to help if I can't. Let me make a couple of calls. What's the address of your niece's home in Fort Myers? Also, you and I should exchange phone numbers."

Nancy wrote down Jesse's cell phone number and then gave him Callie's address in Fort Myers.

"Thank you so much, Mr. McDermitt. Call me back as soon as you know whether you can help."

"I will. And just call me Jesse."

Jesse held out the phone to Rusty so he could hang it up. Rusty had a quizzical look on his face as he passed him another Red Stripe. "Who was that?"

"I don't know the woman. Scott Bond put her on to me."

"Scott's a good man. What did she want? You look perplexed."

"She was a nice-sounding woman. She's got a sixteen-year-old niece that she's very worried about. According to her, the niece stumbled onto an attempted MS-13 snatch of another young girl and the niece took out two of the gang members and saved the girl they were trying to kidnap. Now MS-13 wants to put her in the ground or worse."

"There's a story with no happy ending."

"No kidding. I despise that group. Every last one of them is a skin-bag wasting precious oxygen."

"You got that right. So what did the woman want?"

"She wants me to provide protection for the girl and her family."

Rusty put down the glass he'd been polishing and looked up at Jesse. "That's not something you do."

"I know, but it sounds like this young girl has a ton of heart. What teenager puts her own life at risk to save a stranger these days?"

"She must be a big girl."

Jesse shook his head. "Nancy said she's just five feet tall. I gather she's had some Krav Maga training."

"My kind of lady. So what are you going to do?"

"I'm not sure. Her niece is three years younger than my daughter Flo and going off to college next fall. She sounds like a really good kid and I know that if Flo were in the same kind of trouble and someone could help keep her safe, I'd be eternally grateful to that person."

"There are a lot of worthy cases out there, Jesse." Rusty said, putting a glass away and wiping a bar that was already clean as a whistle. "You can't save them all."

"I know. I've got to give it some thought and make a few phone calls. I'm going to head down to the *Dog*."

"You'll figure something out, I'm sure. Oh Jesse, Rufus wanted me to give you a care package for Savannah." Rusty reached under the bar and handed Jesse a small paper bag.

"What's in it?"

"I think it's some of his secret rub that he puts on the fish sandwiches. He won't give anyone the recipe, but he obviously thinks highly enough of Savannah to part with some of it."

Jesse opened the bag and breathed in the incredible combination of allspice, nutmeg, ginger, garlic, cloves, and various other Caribbean spices he couldn't identify. Just the smell made his mouth start to salivate and he suddenly craved a fish sandwich.

"Man does that smell good," he said, closing the bag back up. "Please thank Rufus from the bottom of my heart for his gift to Savannah."

"I will, Jesse. Have a good night."

"You too, brother."

Once outside Jesse walked around to the far side of the canal, the soft night air fragrant and rich with the smells of jasmine, frangipani, oiled deck planks, and exposed mudflats. The complex combination was familiar and unique to the Florida Keys. He stopped at *Sea Biscuit*, his fiancée Savannah's Grand Banks Trawler that they had berthed at the Rusty Anchor. No one was aboard, but he wanted to check her lines to make sure she was secure.

MS-13 gang activity in Fort Myers?

So many changes were taking place. The last thing Jesse needed was another project. He caught himself as he walked back around a barge and continued on down the pier. Since when had helping to save the life of a sixteen-year-old teenager become just another "project"?

"Come on, Jesse, priorities!" he chided himself. As he strolled along the dock, he reviewed the conversation with Nancy. He had a lot going on. He was in the process of renovating several houses on his island to make it more like a home and less like a DHS training facility and was also preparing to take the helm of the research vessel *Ambrosia* with his new wife.

His fiancé Savannah and her daughter Flo had lived on her boat for the past eighteen years, and they'd decided to create a land-based home that felt like a home to both of them.

His tech contact at DHS, Chyrel, might be able to provide some insight into MS-13, but he wanted information about the gang from someone with boots on the ground.

He stepped up onto the deck of his boat *Salty Dog* and unlocked the companionway hatch. After switching on the lights, he then went down to the navigation station, where his laptop was. He remembered a corporal from the Corps named Phil Tucker who'd retired at about the same time he had and gone to work for the Miami-Dade PD. The last time they'd spoken he'd been promoted to detective.

Jesse pulled up his name on his phone's contact list. Phil answered on the first ring.

"Phil, it's Jesse McDermitt."

"Semper Fi, brother. How're they hanging or should I ask *are* they still hanging?"

Jesse chuckled at the dig to his advancing years. "They're hanging like the American flag, brother, with dignity and pride."

"Of course, they are! What can I do for you? Are you in town?"

"Not right now," Jesse replied. "I'm wondering if you can share any intel about MS-13 in Fort Myers?"

"Is this a DHS assignment?"

"You know I haven't worked for the government in years."

"Right, whatever you say, Gunny. Listen, I don't personally know anything, but I'd be happy to make a few calls. Will you be around an hour from now?"

"Sure. I'll listen for the phone."

"Give me an hour."

Jesse sat about doing some boat chores. Owning a boat means constant upkeep and maintenance. Owning several compounded that and Jesse rarely idled away the hours. Phil called back fifty minutes later.

"Found what you're looking for, Jesse. The gang in Fort Myers is run by a banger named Diego Alturaz. His number two is someone who goes by the name of Esteban. They've got about twenty-five regular, full-time members and probably half that again they can call up if they've got something going on. Pretty standard banger shit: they sell Meth and weed and blow, but here's where it gets a little different. Lately, here in Miami, Fort Myers, and the rest of the country for that matter, they're getting more and more into sex trafficking. They've got this horrific new business model where they kidnap young girls, do the gang initiation thing with them, then addict them to drugs and put them to work as prostitutes. The girls don't last long as you'd imagine but they don't care, they just grab more. They used to snatch up primarily young homeless women with drug habits who wouldn't be missed but lately they've also been taking straight girls right off the street."

"What have your gang people been doing to push back?" Jesse asked.

"Not much, I'm afraid. We try, but for all their incompetence as criminals they've proven to be masters at witness intimidation and murders. Every time we put together a good case against one of them our witnesses either die a gruesome death or develop memory problems right before trial. It's incredibly frustrating."

"Must drive you nuts."

"It does," Phil replied. "It's like every one of them knows and accepts that their life-expectancy is around twenty-one years and none of them seem to care about any life outside of the gang. They'd rather go down in a blaze of glory when we back them into a corner. Fort Myers has had a series of incidents lately. The local PD there thought they finally had a really good case against Diego Alturaz for the murders of two young gang members he shot and then chopped up. They also had him cold on the kidnapping and rape of two innocent thirteen-year-old middle schoolers."

Jesse felt the tension in his brow move to his jaw and clamped his teeth tightly together. "What happened?"

"Once again the gang got to the primary witness in the jail. This just happened yesterday and get this, they killed him with a jar of wasps."

"What? How?"

"They must have known he had a severe allergy. Someone walks by his closed cell, throws in the jar of wasps, and bang; he gets stung like twelve times, blows up like a fucking piñata, and he's dead ten minutes later.

In another recent incident in Fort Myers, the gang went after some teenage girl on a motorcycle. The police set a roadblock to catch the guys and just because one of them had an immigration beef he gets out of the car, pulls a cannon, and tries to shoot it out with like ten cops! How can you fight against people who have so little regard for their own life let alone the lives of others?"

Jesse knew the answer, official law enforcement personnel all had very strict rules they had to abide by. He paused a moment before responding. The "teenage girl on a motorcycle" sounded like Nancy's niece.

"The rulebook you guys are forced to play by only works if both parties play by the rules. Obviously, these guys don't."

"What're we going to do, Jesse? You know what it's like out there right now when a cop pulls his piece. He gets totally screwed by the press. Doesn't matter whether his life is in danger or what the perp did. If he's minority, it's hands off. It's like a get out of jail free card for whatever these punks want to do."

"I don't envy you, Phil, with your hands tied the way they are. At some point the media's got to wake up. It's tough to fix stupid. It can be done, but like they say, it's going to hurt."

"You got that, brother."

"Okay, thanks for the information, Phil. It's just what I was looking for."

"Anytime. Keep one on ice for me."

"I will," Jesse replied and ended the call.

It was obvious that Nancy Liddell's niece and her family were all in serious danger. Something like this would take more time than he had. But Jesse wanted to do something, and he had an idea.

He pulled up Billy Rainwater's number. He'd be perfect to discreetly keep an eye on the girl and her family, if he were available. Billy could practically disappear before your eyes. If he didn't want to be seen, he wouldn't be.

The phone rang twice.

"Billy Rainwater, original and authentic American Indian. How may I direct your call?"

"It's Jesse."

"No kidding, Kemosabe. You think I'd actually answer the phone that way if I didn't know it was you?"

Billy and Jesse had been blood brothers since the age of ten. They'd grown up together as kids, hunting and fishing in the Caloosahatchee River and the Ten Thousand Islands area. Later, they'd served side-by-side in the Marine Corps. They'd been covering each other's six; for over forty years.

By blood, Billy was, in fact, the acting chief of the Calusa. Roughly translated Calusa means "fierce people." Few people ever saw that side of Billy. I had.

Since leaving the Corps, Billy had guided hunting trips in the Everglades and also built incredible 4x4s that could go anywhere. Later, he'd received a law degree and helped Jesse's friend Deuce on occasion.

He was an odd mix, but Jesse trusted him implicitly. They'd each put their lives on the line for the other more than once.

"I've got a situation," Jesse began. "And I'm hoping you might be free and willing to help. A woman called me earlier tonight. She sounds like a nice lady and tells me this story about her sixteen-year-old niece whose gotten herself jammed up with MS-13 in Fort Myers."

"Why would that be something you'd get involved in?"

"Couple of reasons," Jesse replied. "From what the aunt tells me the girl sounds like a really good kid, but I also think it's because this gang is so clearly out of control. Apparently, they're going around these days thinking they can kidnap innocent kids off the street, gang-rape them, addict them to drugs, and then run them as prostitutes and do this without fearing retribution of any sort. The police are powerless over them because they're so effective at intimidating and killing anyone willing to testify against them. Apparently, this woman's niece, Callie, interrupted one of their kidnappings and, in the process, took down two members of the gang. That obviously made them look like fools, so they've been going after her hard ever since. The aunt's worried about the girl and her family."

"How did the woman hear about you?"

"A PI she knows up north knows a guy I once worked with. He gave Rusty's number to her. He thought I might be willing to help."

"I don't like MS-13, Jesse. They make the whole human race look bad."

"I was hoping you'd feel that way."

"I've got some time," he offered. "Want me to go down there and scalp a couple of them?"

Jesse explained the situation with as much detail as he knew, including the part about how he would have to basically offer invisible protection to the girl's family for the next few days and then to the girl herself once she got back from Boston on Tuesday.

"And I've got to provide this protection silently, like a ghost?"

"Yup, you'll need your moccasins for sure. But don't put your life in danger over that aspect. I'd much rather the girl and her family find out that her aunt arranged protection than have anything happen to you."

"You said the girl drives a motorcycle?"

"That's what her aunt said."

"I recently treated myself to an Indian and have been looking for an excuse for a road trip."

"Vintage?"

"No, not this time. She's a brand new twelve-hundred-cc, blacked out Indian Roadmaster. She's even got a GPS nav system built into the fairing."

"Jeez, Billy, what happened to *old school*? Your ancestors are probably rolling over in their middens?"

"You forget; I'm chief of the Calusa. It's called executive privilege. Iron horse is heap powerful."

Jesse chuckled. "I supposed it's no worse than the Dehaviland Beaver you fly."

"Text me the address of the girl's parents after we hang up. I can head over to Fort Myers first thing tomorrow. You said the girl will be back on Tuesday?"

"That's what her aunt said. And thanks, Billy, I'll owe you another one. Give me a call once you get settled in and keep track of your expenses. I'll pick up the tab on this."

"You can't afford me, brother. I'll put it on your tab though."

After he hung up with Billy, Jesse texted him the address where Callie lived, as he'd promised, and then picked up the phone one last time that evening.

"Nancy Liddell."

"Hi, Nancy, it's Jesse McDermitt. I spoke to a contact in Miami who made some calls. He was able to get the skinny on the situation in Fort Myers. Then I called a close friend of mine who lives quite near Fort Myers. His name is Billy Rainwater. Billy and I both served together in the Marines and I frequently work with him on various projects. He can be in Fort Myers tomorrow, and will keep an eye on your niece's family till Tuesday and then Callie once you get back to Florida. He's very capable and I highly recommend him."

Nancy was quiet for several seconds. Tears of relief rolled down her cheeks. She wiped them away and cleared her throat.

"Thank you, Jesse. I can't tell you how much I appreciate this."

"I'm sorry that I'm not available to help you personally, but I simply have too much going on right now. Billy's as good as they get, however, you won't be disappointed. If this goes on more than a week, we may have to figure out another solution, but from what I was able to find out she's definitely in their sights and I've got a feeling this whole situation is going to resolve itself over the next few days. Call me if anything new develops on your end that I should know about."

"Absolutely. And thank you, Jesse."

"You're welcome. I'd enjoy meeting your niece one day. She sounds like quite a character."

"She is and thank you again."

"Goodbye, Nancy."

Chapter 40

B illy hung up and several seconds later his phone pinged with the address from Jesse. He opened up Google Earth on his computer, entered the address that Jesse had sent, and switched to satellite view. He could immediately see that the location where Callie and her family lived was rural, surrounded by woods on three sides with the Caloosahatchee River in the back. Their closest neighbor appeared to be about a quarter mile away and there was just one road in, which appeared to end several hundred yards past the house. The location was ideal for covert surveillance.

He would take up residence somewhere in the woods surrounding the house and spent the next few minutes thinking through the equipment he would bring; lightweight camping hammock, collapsible entrenching tool, hydration bladder, jerky, and energy bars, twelve-inch K-bar knife, small SOG throwing axe, third generation night vision goggles, Sig Sauer P226 in 9mm with three extra clips, and two hundred feet of one-eighth inch paracord. The three luggage boxes on his Indian Roadmaster would easily swallow all his gear. He would need to carry his primary weapon in a backpack on his back, however, a custom seventy-pound compound, recurve bow which broke down into three twenty-two-inch pieces, and eight, thirty-inch carbon-fiber, Broadhead arrows.

The next morning Billy dressed in lightweight woods camo, filled his hydration bladder with spring water, then shouldered his backpack, locked the house, and mounted his trusty steed for the brief one-hour trip to Fort Myers. It was Wednesday and once he reached Callie's neighborhood, he drove slowly past her house, just once. He knew from studying the satellite image on Google Earth that there were no other houses past theirs and also that the best likely place of concealment for his motorcycle would be several hundred yards past the house where the pavement ended. He looked the woods over closely for a good spot that he could easily cache his big Indian motorcycle out of site but also leave it available for a quick getaway if the need arose. Nothing jumped out at him, so he put the bike up on its stand at the end of the road, got his SOG throwing axe out of his saddlebags, and went to work clearing a small area in the thick scrub brush right at the end of the road. The ground was dry and after fifteen minutes of work he had a big enough area cut out to back his Indian into. It was almost invisible to a casual observer. After unpacking the rest of his gear and laying it to the side he gathered up several of the larger limbs and some of the brush that he'd cut, covered over the entrance to the little copse he'd created, and stepped out into the road again. The bike was now invisible.

He consolidated everything he'd brought in his backpack, assembled his bow, and moved into the woods on the side of the road farthest from Callie's parent's house. He wanted to thoroughly surveil the entire area on both sides of the house before settling in. As he'd ridden down, he'd thought about how he would infiltrate and approach the girl's home if he were the aggressor and wanted to leave as little evidence as possible. A nighttime water assault was the obvious best choice for someone who knew what they were doing. He knew with absolute certainty, however, that if MS-13 were going to attack the girl or her family, that these child/men gangsters would likely roll up in some loud, tricked out, lowrider, park a short distance from the house and then stumble through the woods talking tough, full of righteous blood lust and overconfidence from the weapons they would no doubt be carrying. Dealing with them would be simple, but Billy wanted to do it in a way that wouldn't alert the people in the house to what was going on outside. That would be the real challenge.

He settled down into a natural hide directly across the street from the house and using his binoculars watched Callie's parents and brothers for almost an hour getting a feel for all of them. He watched as a man and two teenage boys unloaded crab pots out of a skiff onto a dock at the rear of the house and as a woman his age, swept the front porch and then watered the outdoor plants. The family looked like simple, hardworking people who shared values similar to his own; people who didn't mind putting sweat equity into what they were doing. Watching them as they went about their daily business told him quite a bit about Callie, too. He couldn't help but contrast the lives he was voyeuristically observing, with the dark, pointless, lives that he knew most of the members of MS-13 led. If MS-13 came for them, he would be ready to do whatever was needed to protect them and punish anyone who tried to harm them.

He eased backwards out of his hide and continued walking back towards the main road he'd come in on trying to put himself in the mindset of a potential attacker and envisioned the way the road would look after dark, likely places they might park a vehicle, and possible approaches they might take to the house once they were on foot.

He was about 100 yards past the house when he saw a flat area adjoining the road surface that looked as though people had used it as a turnaround. It was out of sight of the house on a gentle curve in the road, but still quite close to the house. He knew right away that this would be where the morons from MS-13 would park. He crossed the road to the turnaround area and squatted down and studied the various possible routes that a small group on foot might take if their goal were to approach the house stealthily, surprise the inhabitants, and then overpower them.

He knew with absolute certainty that if the gang members came for Callie's family, that they would split into two groups. One group would simply move up the road and then down the driveway; the second group would take the "stealthier" route through the woods and start into the brush exactly where he was kneeling. The exact route that they'd take through the woods was as clear as day to Billy as he looked back and forth several times between the turnaround and the house. Like a seer, he could almost see the future impressions that their feet would leave on the forest floor. He smiled and scoffed at the idea of the gang members being stealthy. He could already hear them blundering through the woods. And amateurs always took the path of least resistance in darkness. It was for this reason that professional soldiers never walked on cleared or game trodden trails when approaching a defended position. It was too predictable and the most logical place where a defending enemy would place mines and booby traps. Gangbangers never had military training, though. He took his backpack off and got his entrenching tool out and started to prepare the first of several surprises.

He completed his first trap in about an hour and then looked nearby for a green sapling the right size for his second trap. That took just minutes to set up and he set a third trap further on in case they somehow made it past the first two. Confident that his preparations would effectively deal with or at least substantially slow down any gang members taking the back way onto the property, Billy shifted his focus to those gang members who would likely take the road and driveway route onto the property. His strategy for dealing with this group would be to take advantage of the element of surprise, his silence, and his night vision capabilities. With his own concealment and most-likely field of fire in mind, he identified two Australian Pines that were growing just ten feet apart set back on the opposite side of the road from the driveway. It was just 100' from where he figured the gang members would park.

He strung his camouflage hammock between the two trees. He expected that if the gang made a move on the house, they would likely send four to eight gang members. They would be expecting little or no resistance and logically assume that to be an adequate number. He wanted to avoid killing them if possible because then he would have to deal with the bodies, but he also wanted to physically disable as many as possible and put the fear of God into the rest of them if they showed up.

He smiled to himself in the fading light, combed his long, black, hair out with his fingers and then tightly re-tied it into a tight ponytail. Then he foraged around in the bottom of his backpack until he found a small, plastic box about four inches square and just a half an inch thick. It contained a mirror on the backside of the hinged lid and four colors of mil-spec, woodland camouflage paint. He applied long streaks of the various colors to his face in what he hoped was a caricature of a "fearsome" look. After completing the application, he looked into the mirror one last time, bared his bright white teeth, and made a "grrrrr" sound like a growling bear. He chuckled to himself wondering what Jesse would likely have quipped at him if he were there. He sprayed on some bug repellant, picked up his hydration bladder and a bag of jerky and climbed up into his hammock.

As the sun set, Billy ate several pieces of the jerky and an energy bar, and then washed both down with some water. Then he settled further into the hammock, focused on his breath, stilled the chatter in his mind, and peacefully meditated as full darkness descended. He listened with an open heart to the thousands of male cicadas in the trees and bushes around him as they competed with the guttural vocal utterances of hundreds of bullfrogs along the banks of the Caloosahatchee. The sound of the cicadas came in great waves sometimes drowning out the bullfrogs altogether. Periodically they would stop in almost perfect unison. After a brief pause, several would tentatively flex their tymbals again like orchestra soloists tuning up. Then, with the precision of a conducted symphony, the rest of the orchestra would join in until the entire forest was completely filled once again with their song.

Billy's soul was at peace, and he realized that it had been a great while since he'd lain outdoors, completely quiet and listened to the natural world around him. It made him think of his childhood and how different his current day-to-day life was from that of his ancestors. Phones, televisions, radios, automobiles, air boats, planes, refrigerators, and the myriad list of other things that relied on internal combustion engines and the noise they produced; did any of them really add anything of value to his life? Each of them offered benefits, for sure, but taken in total, was the overall quality of his life any better or more meaningful than that of his ancestors hundreds of years before him? His other "self" listened knowingly to the conversation taking place in his mind. A great deal had been lost so that very little could be found. He resolved to explore this in more depth when he returned home. The rest of Sunday night passed without incident.

The following morning about an hour after sunrise his phone vibrated with an incoming text. It was a message from Jesse asking for a sitrep. He took a few seconds to respond.

First night. Nice ride. All quiet.

Billy kept watch over Callie's family and the road going past their house for the rest of the day. With the exception of the family's pickup trucks coming and going several times, he had seen just two other vehicles pass the house and both of them had immediately turned around at the end of the road and then left again without displaying any inordinate interest in Callie's home. One was an old Austin Healey convertible with the top down and a young couple in it. The other was a beat-up van with a bad blue paint job that also had a sticky valve. It blew smoke rings out of the tailpipe as it idled past the house. He couldn't see into the vehicle because it had smoked glass but dismissed it as a possible threat once it turned around and left the area.

That evening he once again settled into his hammock at sunset and after a simple repast consisting of an energy bar, some jerky, and spring water, fell fast asleep once again listening to the symphony of cicadas and bullfrogs that surrounded him.

Chapter 41

At 11 pm that same evening, Esteban and Marko called the small crew they'd gathered to attention. The four others who shuffled over were all minor characters in their late teens.

Esteban started once he had their attention. "Pendejos! Listen up. As I already mentioned, Diego and I found out where the little motorcycle puta lives with her family. I don't know how many people live in the house but there's no reason to suspect that anyone living there will be expecting us. I did a drive-by this morning and saw two pickup trucks in the driveway. I didn't see the girl's motorcycle, but she may have been out or maybe had her bike parked in the back. Diego really wants this girl alive. He's got special plans for her."

The youngest gang member present, Jorge, started thrusting his hips back and forth, mimicking what he imagined Diego had planned for the girl and playing to the group. Everyone but Esteban found him amusing and made cat calls and egged him on. Esteban stopped talking, angry at the interruption. He watched Jorge for two or three seconds and then took one quick step towards him and did a brutal leg sweep, knocking both his legs out from underneath him. Jorge cried out as he fell hard to the cement floor. Everyone else was immediately silent. Esteban calmly put one of his booted feet on Jorge's neck and looked down at him. "You finished?"

Jorge couldn't speak for the boot on his neck but held up both his hands in obvious supplication.

Esteban looked back up at the group. "As I was saying, the most important thing is to take the girl, alive. If she's not there we question the people who are until we find out where she is; then we kill them. If she is there, once we have her in hand, we'll kill her family in front of her. This girl has cost us a lot of money and made all of you look like maricons. Diego wants to seriously hurt this one, comprende?"

All five nodded in agreement.

"We'll leave in a half hour."

Alejandro, Jorge, Tomás and Emilio shared a gram of shitty coke before getting into the back of the van thirty minutes later. The coke had been cut with crank and they were amped up and edgy as a result. They passed a joint around in the back of the van as they headed for the young girl's house.

"Give me a hit of that," Marko demanded from the front seat. He took a long toke off the joint and then held it out to Esteban. "Want some, bro?"

Esteban shook his head. "You fools need to get your head into the game. We're almost there. We don't know exactly who will be in this house and I don't want you maricons shooting me or the girl by mistake. Get rid of that shit."

Marko took a last nervous hit and then reluctantly flicked the roach out of the window. "What's your worry, Ese? There are six of us, chill."

Esteban turned off the main road onto Callie's no-name road annoyed with Marko's cockiness. As he got close to their driveway, he turned off his headlights and idled forward with just his parking lights and the faint light from a rising half-moon to guide him.

"There's not much out here," Marko observed.

"No, they have no neighbors." Esteban could see the porch lights were still on in the house, but no interior lights. It was 11:30 pm.

"Wake up you fucksticks, we're here," Esteban uttered in a low tone. He saw a cleared spot on the side of the road about 100 yards shy of the driveway and pulled off the pavement and into that spot; parking precisely where Billy had predicted. He put the van in park, turned off the engine and sat still for several seconds with his window down. It was completely quiet.

****

CALLIE AWAKENS

The cicadas quieted once again. This time, however, they didn't restart Billy's eyelids snapped open, his pupils fully dilated, and the highly photosensitive rods in his eyes gathered every bit of available light Instantly awake, he rolled silently from his hammock, nocked an arrow in his bow and then watched through the scrub palms as a vehicle with just its parking lights on glided slowly and almost silently into the turnaround Before the engine dieseled to a stop Billy noted the same distinctive sound of a bad valve that he'd heard earlier in the day when the same beat-up van had passed Callie's house the first time. It was showtime.

****

Esteban turned in his seat and spoke in a low voice. "Listen up. Marko you take Jorge and Tomás through the woods and come in the back door I'll take Alejandro and Emilio; we'll go down the driveway and through the front door."

"How will we know when to kick it?" Marko asked.

"Just wait until you hear us bust the door in front. It's quiet as hell out here. You'll know."

Marko nodded. The reality of what they were about to do was dawning on him. They were no longer in the clubhouse telling exaggerated stories about their bravado, cleverness, and viciousness. They were about to enter the home of a group of strangers that they knew nothing about. The girl on her own was a formidable adversary, from what he'd heard. She likely had a father and might well have brothers. They weren't ganging up on some defenseless lone teenager. Adults no doubt lived in the house and judging from the two pickup trucks in the driveway, at least two of them were males.

Esteban reached alongside his seat and grabbed his machete. He nodded towards Marko. "You ready?"

Marko reached into the glove compartment and pulled out a Smith & Wesson .357 magnum revolver. The weight of the big gun felt good in his hand and buoyed his confidence. "Si." He turned to the four teens in rear of the van. "Let's go, pendejos."

409

Emilio slid open the side door and stepped down to the ground. Like Esteban he had a machete in hand. Jorge followed. He had a H&K VP 9mm that he'd borrowed for the evening from his brother. Alejandro and Tomás were last to step out into the night. Alexandro had a baseball bat in hand, Tomás was armed with a short ugly piece of iron rebar and a Maglite.

"Marko, it's going to take longer for you, Jorge, and Tomás to find your way through the woods and get to the back of the house. You guys start now. Alejandro, Emilio and I will follow shortly in the front." Esteban ordered.

Marko nodded with a confidence he didn't feel and started walking into the woods. He took just three steps and tripped over a branch and fell to the ground. He grunted as he landed.

"Fuck! Tomás; give me your goddamn flashlight."

****

Billy flipped his NVGs down and silently crept forward until he was on the edge of the road behind a Sabal palm. He watched with amusement from just 100 feet away as the bangers took their first tentative steps into the woods towards the house and chuckled silently when he heard one of them fall. There were six of them and just as he'd expected, they split into two groups. Three of the men started into the woods. The other three hung back at the van for the moment. Until he'd taken at least one man out from each of the two groups, it was his plan to stay fluid and position himself between the attackers and the house and make sure that none of them got past him and threatened Callie's family. He expected that once he had two of the attackers down and hurt, that the rest of them would quickly come to their aid. And when they realized that they were under attack from an adversary that they couldn't see or hear, that they would quickly lose heart and retreat. That was the plan anyway.

****

410

Once he was up off the ground and had Tomás's flashlight in hand, Marko started moving more confidently through the woods. Jorge and Tomás followed close on his heels trying to benefit as much as possible from the stray light coming off the Maglite. Once the three of them were into the woods Esteban touched both Alejandro and Emilio on the shoulder to get their attention and then pointed down the road towards the house. "You two lead. I want to keep an eye on Marko. Hold up shy of the front porch once you get to the bottom of the driveway and wait for me there. Alejandro and Emilio both nodded and started down the road, side by side.

****

Billy knew that his booby traps would eventually get at least one of the three bangers coming through woods and he shifted his attention to the two men who were coming down the road towards him. He was well concealed behind a large shaggy Sabal Palm and went to a full draw with his bow. While he could easily make a center-mass shot on either of the two on the road, he really didn't want to have to deal with the bodies and the attention they would draw afterwards. He just wanted to incapacitate, and he shifted his aim lower, to the righthand thigh of the one closest to him. His site picture, while green from the NVGs, was nevertheless perfect, and as soon as they'd closed to a comfortable distance, he let his first arrow fly. He watched without moving as the entire arrow accelerated and took flight through the arrow rest. He held his form long enough to hear it impact.

The target stumbled three or four steps before falling to the ground, his leg no longer responding to commands. Billy knew that the arrow had missed the femur bone in the center of the thigh. If he'd hit the man in the femur, he would have dropped like the temperature on an arctic night and he wouldn't have taken the extra stumbling steps.

Alejandro heard a slapping sound like the one you hear at the meat market when the butcher throws a piece of meat down onto the chopping block. Emilio stumbled and reached out towards him looking for support.

411

But before he could offer any, Emilio fell to the ground. Alejandro quickly knelt at his side assuming he'd simply fallen. Emilio also didn't understand yet what had happened beyond knowing that his leg had suddenly collapsed. He reached down to the backside of his thigh and cut his hand on the razor-sharp Broadhead arrow that was protruding from it.

"What the fuck?" He looked down at his leg in the low light and then moved his hand around to the front side of his injured leg. There was a three-foot-long arrow coming out of his thigh. "Fuck, fuck, fuck; I've been shot, Alejandro!"

Almost simultaneously with Billy's arrow impacting Emilio's leg, Billy heard the shriek of one of the bangers in the woods as he broke through the thin branches that covered the punji stick pit he'd dug. Billy felt slightly guilty for using such a tired, old-fashioned trap as the punji stick pit, but they really were effective, especially at night. He inadvertently grimaced as he envisioned the small hardwood stakes that were no doubt now sticking out of the feet, shins and knees of the attacker who'd fallen in. He expected all three of the men in the woods would be tied up for several minutes trying to extricate the one who'd fallen in and returned his attention to the two men on the road.

He advanced towards them through the woods, a second arrow nocked and ready to fly. The man he hadn't wounded was back on his feet and looking wildly in every direction for some sign of the person who'd shot his friend. He was holding a baseball bat at the ready and was clearly freaked out. Billy stepped out of the woods and onto the road in plain sight of him. The moon had risen sufficiently so as to provide enough light for the second man to see him. Billy was at full draw and advanced towards him projecting a nightmarish visage to the bat-wielding man as the green light from his NVGs spilled out the sides and highlighted his overdone war paint.

"Drop the bat, or I'll drop you," Billy threatened in a quiet voice as he closed to within twenty feet of the man.

Alejandro was terrified. He'd never had to face a violent opponent on his own. He was used to confrontations where he and other members of the gang inflicted damage on defenseless individuals. The man approaching in the near darkness was something out of a nightmare, a clearly competent,

412

trained, warrior. Alejandro anxiously looked behind wondering where in the hell Esteban was. He was frozen with fear.

Alejandro's look back over his shoulder reminded Billy that he'd forgotten about the largest of the gang members. Three had taken the back route through the woods and three had started down the road. One was missing. It was no time to get sloppy or overconfident and he let his second arrow loose. It traveled the short distance with a hissing sound and soundly impacted into Alejandro's shoulder causing him to drop the bat and fall to the ground. Billy nocked a third arrow in less than three seconds and shifted his attention from the road to the woods while still moving towards the two fallen gang members on the road.

Jorge was the one who'd fallen into the punji stick pit and he was crying and shrieking in agony from the sharpened sticks that had penetrated one of his knees and both shins. He'd never felt such pain. "Tomás, Marko! Help me!" he sobbed. He'd dropped his H&K pistol into the darkness of the pit when the first punji stick had penetrated his knee. It was now forgotten amidst the pain he was in.

Not fully understanding what had just happened to his fellow gang member, Tomás stumbled back several steps tripping Billy's second trap; a two-inch-thick green sapling that snapped viciously into his face and forehead puncturing one of his eyes and cutting a deep two-inch-long gash across his forehead. Blood immediately started to pour down his face effectively blinding his remaining good eye. He fell to the ground.

Billy got to the two men in the road who were both on the ground. He kicked the baseball bat off to the side and knelt down facing them.

"You are not to touch the young girl or her family!" Billy hissed at Alejandro and Emilio. He was holding his bow with a nocked arrow in his left hand and drew his big, razor-sharp, Marine, K-Bar knife from his chest sheath with his right hand, for emphasis. Alejandro was terrified of the long-haired man with war paint crouching in front of him, but he was certain that somehow Esteban would come to their aid in the next few seconds and managed a weak threat. "Fuck you, pendejo! I will piss on your grave."

Billy knew he had to get off the road and into the woods. He was a sitting duck, crouching where he was.

"Wrong answer, *pen de jo*." Billy spelled out. He took two steps, put his foot on the banger's knee, rolled it and the attached leg sideways; then jabbed downward with the K-bar into the space between the Achilles tendon and the end of the fibula, and cut his Achilles tendon. Alejandro screamed out and started flopping back and forth on the ground, apoplectic with pain and fear at the violence that had just been inflicted on him.

Despite having effectively hobbled both bangers, Billy didn't pause to count coup or assess the damage he'd just wreaked. He was already moving before the razor edge of his K-bar completed parting the man's tendon, ducking his head, spinning, and bringing his bow up in a defensive sweep move.

Billy had sensed Esteban's impending attack before Esteban even moved from his concealed position in the woods. It was like an ancient Spidey sense that Billy had inherited from his ancestors and learned to pay close attention to during his days as a Marine. He had no idea what weapon was being brought to bear against him, but he knew from long experience that his head and body core were the likely targets, so even as he was bringing up the arm that held the bow in a swiping motion, he was also pivoting his head and his body away from the threat. That instinctual swipe and pivot saved his life in the next second as he deflected Esteban's machete blow from one which would have split his skull down the middle to one that deflected the cutting edge of the blade sideways before the machete impacted his left shoulder. It was a brutal concussive blow, and he dropped the bow when his left arm was hit. That arm was now completely useless, but he was still in the fight.

He quickly danced backwards as Esteban took two more wild swipes at him with the long machete. Billy still retained the K-Bar in his right hand, but the length of the machete gave his opponent a decided advantage and he knew that he was in some trouble. Esteban continued to alternatively circle and swing the machete in vicious arcs. He was a formidable adversary and nothing like the skinny teens Billy had already taken out. He taunted him.

"Nice tattoos, your mother must be very proud."

Esteban swung at him again in answer. The tip of the blade passing within a half inch of Billy's chin. Before Esteban could draw the blade back into a ready position again, Billy kicked him hard in the femur and then withdrew just out of range, again, before the blade came swinging back.

"What's up with the big holes in your ear lobes, you ugly motherfucker? Were those your momma's idea too?" Billy feinted one way, then the other and then with blinding speed, lunged in a third time, and flicked his K-Bar upwards. One of Esteban's ear lobes fell to the ground.

Esteban stopped his attack and looked down in disbelief at his detached body part and reflexively brought a hand up to the side of his head to check that it was really gone. His anger exploded, and he charged Billy like a rampaging bull. Billy had expected him to take another swing at him with the machete and hadn't anticipated the kamikaze-like charge, and it knocked him to the ground. But on the way down he was able to inflict a surface shoulder wound with his K-bar before both of them dropped their weapons as they hit ground. Billy ended up underneath Esteban in a clearly inferior position and Esteban started beating Billy in the face with both fists. With his left arm out of commission from the initial machete strike, Billy was almost defenseless to Esteban's superior position, rage, and fierce blows.

Marko was trying to absorb what had just happened to Tomás and Jorge. One was in a pit of some kind crying like a baby and the other was on the ground shrieking incoherently and holding his head. Both were obviously in excruciating pain. Marko started turning in circles with the .357 pointed out in front of him desperately seeking a target. Someone or something was taking them out one at a time. He could hear the sounds of Billy and Esteban as they fought out on the road, but still had no idea what or who had taken out his two friends. He was freaked and inadvertently fired the .357 at a nearby palm tree mistaking it for an attacker. The high velocity magnum shell shattered the night with its distinctive sound.

Billy was almost blind and unconscious from the repeated blows to his face and eyes when he heard Marko's .357 go off. His first thought was, *So much for stealthy protection of the girl's family. No way are the people in*

415

the house going to sleep through that. The second thought he had was, *Why the hell am I letting this ugly, bald headed gangbanger beat me to death when I can just shoot him?*

Billy reached for the 9mm Sig on his hip with his good arm, wrenched it free of the holster using muscle memory, and blindly fired two rounds up towards the man beating him. Esteban saw the gun come out of nowhere and started to move off and away, which saved his life. The first shot missed him, but not by much and he went immediately deaf in one ear from the gun discharging so closely to his ear. Billy's second round, however, caught him in the fleshy part of his left arm. It was a through and through and didn't do any serious damage, but as he scurried backwards from Billy, he was unsure whether or not subsequent rounds would be coming and retreated towards the van.

Alejandro and Emilio had already dragged themselves back to the van as Billy and Esteban fought. Esteban got to the side of the van a few seconds later.

"Where are Marko and the others?"

"No idea, man, just leave them. We need to get to a hospital!"

Esteban looked to the woods where they'd originally started and then towards the house. Lights were going on in every room in the house. He realized he only had a minute or two.

"You worthless putas!"

He ran into the woods in the direction Marko, Jorge and Tomás had originally taken and stumbled down the path. He ran into the three of them almost immediately. Marko was dragging Jorge backwards by the armpits and Tomás was walking like a blind man with his arms out ahead of him trying to follow.

Esteban grabbed Tomás by the shoulder. "Hang onto my shoulder and follow me. We need to get out of here!"

Marko was the only one to have avoided injury at Billy's hands but was stopped and sobbing despite his good fortune. "I don't know what happened man. We were just walking along and both of them went down."

Esteban slapped him. "Get your shit together. You're almost back to the van. Grab Jorge again, we need to get out of here before the people in the house or the police get here," he hissed.

The four of them regained the safety of the van several seconds later. Esteban and Marko got Tomás and Jorge in the back along with Alejandro and Emilio and then jumped into the front seats. Esteban started the van and then did a quick 180 on the road. The last thing he saw in the rear-view mirror as he accelerated away, was the man he'd fought, on his belly, dragging himself and his bow off the road and then slithering into the woods on the far side of the road from the house. He was reminded of a large python. What in the hell had just happened to the six of them?

Billy hurt everywhere but especially around his face and eyes where Esteban had repeatedly struck him. He lay silently in the woods for several minutes catching his breath and taking an inventory of the damage to his body. His lip was broken, and his eyes were caked with blood and swollen nearly shut. His biggest concern was his shoulder which had limited mobility. It had been a long time since anyone had gotten so many good shots in against him in a fight. He took out a small LED tactical flashlight, clicked it on, and looked at his shoulder. It wasn't bleeding, but he knew he'd suffered concussive damage to the muscles and tendons under the skin. He tentatively moved the arm in a small circle. It was going to be tender and of limited use for several days, but he'd gotten lucky, he could have lost the whole arm.

He heard a door slam and then voices, quickly turned off the flashlight, and lay completely still in the thick brush and watched as three men rushed from the light of the house into the darkness of the front yard and then as they ran up the driveway. They'd no doubt heard the gunshots and possibly the van full of damaged gangbangers as they'd accelerated away. Two of them were armed and the third was shining the light back and forth into the woods on either side of the driveway as they ran up it towards the road.

RIP CONVERSE

Chapter 42

Crab Claw started barking from the living room before the first gunshot rang out. Harley Sr. threw off the covers and turned on the light next to the bed at the sound of his barking.

"What in the heck is wrong with that dog?" he wondered out loud as he got ready to berate him.

"Probably just raccoons in the trash," Frances mumbled.

The distinctive crack of a .357 magnum shell pierced the night.

"That, was no raccoon, Frances!"

"It was right outside, Harley!"

He quickly pulled on a pair of pants and dashed from the bedroom to the front hall closet and took a shotgun out of the corner and nervously loaded two shells into the side-by-side barrels. Callie's brothers Harley Jr. and Damon, half dressed, joined their father at the door as he prepared to go outside.

"What do you want us to do, Dad? Sounded like a gunshot right outside to me."

Two more gunshots rang out, not quite as loud as the first one but also close to the house and the three looked at each other.

"I'll get my gun too, Dad," Damon said. He ran back down the hallway to his room and quickly returned, snarking .22LR shells into the side of his 22 rifle as he joined his brother and father at the door.

"Get a flashlight, Harley," he directed his son. "Frances, we're going to have a look around outside. It was probably just some kids, but if you hear anymore gunfire call the police and make sure you tell them that we're outside too."

"I will. Be careful, Harley!" she yelled back.

They arrived at the top of the driveway just in time to see the taillights of the van as it disappeared around the first turn of the main road.

"They must have been in that car," Damon observed.

"But what were they doing here?" Harley Jr. asked as he shined the light around the area at the top of the driveway. The two empty brasses that had discharged from Billy's gun winked back at him in the light of the flashlight. He walked over, reached down, and picked one of them up. When he bent down to pick up the shell, he also noticed spots of blood all over the ground.

"Looks like blood."

Harley Sr. held out his hand and Jr. handed him the shell casing.

"Nine-millimeter? Doesn't make any sense at all. No one's going to be out trying to jack deer with a nine-millimeter. This is very odd for sure, boys. Something else was going on here. I also don't understand why we heard two different guns."

Harley Jr. saw something else in the road that he couldn't immediately identify and bent down again and poked it with his finger. It was some sort of round black ring surrounded by....

"Look at this! I'm not certain, but this looks like part of someone's ear!"

Harley Sr. and Damon both knelt down next to him as he shined the light on the piece of flesh.

"The only person I've ever seen who has a pierced ear like that is the night-loser who runs the register at the Loves Travel Stop out on Bayshore," Harley Jr. noted.

"What in the hell boys?" Sr. asked out loud.

"Something intense went down here tonight, that's for sure," Damon observed. "Whatever it was, at least they seem to be gone now."

Billy lay still in the bushes just twenty feet away from them, invisible in his camouflage and the low light and smiled. He'd forgotten about the ear and almost chuckled out loud at the suggestion that it might belong to some convenience-store clerk. The men talked for a few more minutes and then made their way back to house. After Callie's family went back inside, Billy slowly got to his feet, walked to his hammock, and then got in it, wishing he had a couple of ice packs to put on his shoulder and face.

420

He did a quick after-action assessment. He'd been lucky with the big, bald, gangbanger. He wasn't some gangly punk teenager. He'd been a formidable opponent and despite his putting four and possibly five of them out of commission, the young girl and her family were likely still in danger. He didn't feel quite so bad about his injuries as he recalled the moment he'd parried in and flicked his wrist and took the earlobe off his opponent with his razor-sharp K-Bar. He wondered whether the people in the house had left the ear on the road. He toyed briefly with the idea of going back and getting it and making a necklace out of it. If he ever ran into the owner again it would be fun to see the look on his face when he noticed his ear on a necklace hanging around his neck. *No,* he thought. *It would smell. I may be a chief, but I'm not a savage* He smiled at the thought though before eventually falling asleep.

RIP CONVERSE

Chapter 43

Esteban had no choice but to go to the hospital after fleeing Callie's house. He knew that the hospital was required to alert the police whenever people showed up in the ER with weapons-wounds and he and his crew certainly qualified with the various gunshot, knife, and arrow wounds that all but one of them had sustained. They had agreed in advance that they would all tell the same story of having been jumped by Lake Boyz gang members that none of them could identify.

The police knew they were being lied to and the questioning had continued for hours, but all of them kept to the same story and ultimately none of them were taken into custody simply because the police couldn't tie them to any specific crime. They were simply victims.

Esteban's arm was sore, but it didn't bother him nearly as much as the loss of his earlobe. He hit the steering wheel in the van in frustration thinking about it as he drove towards Diego's house with Marko, Jorge, and Emilio. Tomás and Alejandro had been admitted to the hospital due to the seriousness of their wounds. Who was the wild man in the woods who had so severely wounded five of them? What was his connection to the little girl? Most troubling of all, he now had to share with Diego the fact that they'd failed to get the girl and that four more gang members were now out of commission. Diego was going to be crazy mad. He turned into Diego's driveway and after parking, sat still for several seconds trying to figure exactly what he would say to him. He looked at the three gang members before going in and hit the steering wheel again.

"Putas!" he shouted at them before exiting the van and walking towards Diego's front door.

He had to knock loudly on the door for several minutes before Diego finally answered.

"Quién es?"

"Esteban."

"Come in."

Esteban opened the door and was almost bowled over at the stench that hung in the air. It was worse than the last time he'd come by. Diego was sitting on the couch and bent over the coffee table snorting coke from a large pile. He jacked the powder into the back of his nose and sat back on the couch.

Esteban looked at him. His hair was hanging in greasy unwashed tendrils, he was glassy eyed, and he hadn't shaved in days. He was wearing the same clothes he'd last seen him in.

Diego looked up. "Did you get the girl?"

Esteban tried to avoid the question. "How is your mother doing, Jefe?"

"She's about the same."

"You know, it smells really bad in here?"

"Yeah, I forgot to take out the trash. Why're you avoiding my question and what's up with your arm and your ear?"

"Sorry." Esteban reflexively felt the bandage on his ear and immediately remembered his missing lobe.

"We ran into a problem at the girl's house."

"What problem?"

"Someone laid some sort of a trap for us outside the house, and we never got in."

Diego stood up on unsteady feet and shuffled over to him. He looked into his eyes and then, with surprising speed, punched him hard in the gut.

Esteban folded over but stayed on his feet.

"Don't bullshit me, tell me what happened."

Esteban stood upright again and took a few seconds to get his breath.

"I took five guys. We parked up the street from her house and then we split up into two groups; one was going to go in through the back of the house and my group was going to go in through the front door."

Diego held out his hand and made a "give me more" gesture with it.

424

Esteban continued. "I'm still not 100% clear on what happened next but best I could tell some Indian-looking cocksucker came out of nowhere and shot both Emilio and Alejandro with a fucking bow and arrow. Once Alejandro was down on the ground, he also cut the tendon in his ankle."

Diego screwed up his face in disbelief. "Que? You mean like an Indian Indian?"

Esteban nodded. "I know it sounds crazy, Jefe, but I swear on my mother, this big motherfucker looked just like an Indian. He was dressed in camouflage and was wearing these weird green goggles, but I could tell he was an Indian. He had long black hair tied back in a ponytail and..." Esteban knew the next part would sound ridiculous but said it anyway. "He had on warpaint."

"Warpaint?" Diego nodded his head like he believed him. "Course he did; you fucking moron! And where were you when this big scary Indian took out the pendejos you brought with you? I thought you were with them headed for the front door!"

"I was hanging back some waiting to see if the other three got through the woods in the back. As soon as I heard Emilio and Alejandro go down on the road, I ran right to them and confronted the Indian."

Diego slapped Esteban's wounded ear and then his bandaged arm. "And I can see from these that you were really successful at taking him down!"

"I did, Jefe! I beat him good."

"Obviously, that's why the little motorcycle girl is kneeling here in front of me, working my fucking knob!"

"Well, then he shot me in the arm."

"And what about the other three who were supposed to go in the back?"

"I don't really know. The Indian laid several traps in the woods and both Jorge and Tomás got really fucked up. Tomás lost an eye and Jorge fell into some pit full of sharp sticks!"

"And then what, you just drove off?"

"Sí. What were we supposed to do? The girl's whole family was wakened by the gunshots and I'm guessing had called the police, and five of us are wounded. What would you have done?"

Diego paced with his head down as he listened to Esteban's story.

"When Alejandro was down on the ground and the Indian cut him, he said that the Indian told him, 'don't touch the little girl.'"

Diego looked up as he tried to take in and make sense of Esteban's story. "Well, we wouldn't want to do anything that would annoy the big, scary Indian now would we?"

"Jefe?"

Obviously, someone was looking after the girl's family and Diego thought for a few moments before speaking again. "Here's what I want you to do. You know that martial arts studio where she goes.?"

Esteban nodded.

"According to Benicio, when he and Tomas went into that studio to get the girl, she seemed very tight with some gangly fuck. This afternoon you park outside there, and wait until the little puta or her boyfriend comes by. Then you take one of them or both of them. Bring as many men as you need. If the girl's not there, grab her boyfriend instead and we'll use him as bait to draw the girl to us. But you go. Don't leave it to anyone else."

"Sí, Jefe. And then what?"

"Bring them here, you fool! I can't leave mi madre, but I want this one in the worst way. We'll put her in the basement with the other two and keep her alive for a couple of days until we wear her out. Then we either kill her or sell her. Comprende?"

"Sí, Jefe, you won't be disappointed again." Esteban felt lucky to still be alive and almost ran out of the door.

Diego shut the door behind him, went back to the coffee table, bent over, and snorted two more lines.

Chapter 44

Nancy and I left Boston at 10:30 that morning from runway 22-L. The jet we flew back on was a Learjet 35 and to my eye not nearly as exciting as the Embraer Phenom 300 that we'd flown up on. Outside, it was still cold and overcast with intermittent snow showers. The departing runway was significant because our flight path, after takeoff, took us directly over that portion of Boston Harbor that Meredith and I had departed from in her Contender and then we flew directly over Thompson Island. I was actually able to see the dock where we'd helped Nate pump out his boat and the pier we'd walked down to get to the boathouse.

I tapped Nancy's shoulder and pointed down through the window. "That's the Outward-Bound island that Meredith and I went to on Saturday," I said excitedly. "And that's where that guy who offered me a job was working on one of the pulling boats."

"Sounds like you and Meredith had a good time."

"We did. I like her and she's a really good captain. The weather was just like this." The island below suddenly disappeared as we climbed through the overcast sky as if to emphasize my point. "She's a great navigator and has really good judgment."

"Two highly desirable skills, I imagine, that one should always seek out when going boating and picking a captain." Nancy flipped a page in the magazine she was reading.

"Someone seems in a not too good mood. I'm serious, she's a good operator."

Nancy held up her hands. "Relax, I believe you."

I did as she suggested realizing that I must have sounded a little defensive. I just couldn't quite believe how quickly my life seemed to be changing in so many areas. And so much of it was due to Nancy.

Fifteen minutes later we climbed through the ceiling into blue sky, and I looked down at the soft, white, fluffy, clouds moving beneath us. The towering cumulonimbus clouds moved independently, each with a life of their own, one folding over another, two merging, another bubbling upwards towards us. I was thinking about all that had taken place over the past week in Boston. My acceptance to Babson was not certain, but I was now comfortable with making a commitment to a place like it that emphasized entrepreneurship, independent thought, and problem-solving. I did not yet feel a compulsion to necessarily follow the same path as Aunt Nancy, but I was comfortable with the inherent value that an entrepreneurial education would provide and the potential freedoms and flexibility it would afford me.

I still wanted to be a ship captain, but I also wanted to be a pilot and likely a hundred other things that I hadn't even thought of yet. Simply acknowledging and accepting that thirst in my personality as opposed to trying to shoehorn myself into a single discipline or career, felt incredibly freeing. Instead of one thing, it was now my plan to do it all and hopefully the choices I made after attending Babson, or a school like it, would enable me to pursue all my varied and eclectic interests and also provide me with a sense of purpose. A key to all of this would be the process of generating wealth which was something I'd never cared about. I'd squared my disdain for wealth by simply changing my definition of it. Wealth didn't have to mean acquisition, excess, and control. It could also mean, freedom, fulfillment, and opportunity.

"Nancy, how much did you sell your company for?"

"A lot," Nancy said without looking up from her magazine.

"No really?"

"Really, I sold it for a lot." Nancy put down her magazine and turned to me. "That's kind of a personal question. Why are you asking?"

"I'm trying to figure something out. Never mind, I'll just look it up on the Internet." I opened my phone and started typing.

She put her hand on my forearm. "Callie, what's got you all wound up this morning? It's not a national secret, it's just not something I would normally discuss with someone your age."

"What does my age have to do with it? Do you think me knowing how much money you have would somehow change my opinion of you or how I live my life?"

"No, of course not. You just took me by surprise is all. Okay, I sold my company for three hundred and fifty million dollars."

"What did you pay for your house?"

428

"Callie!"

"Please, just tell me."

"Eight million. There, are you happy?"

"It doesn't make me happy or unhappy, I'm simply curious. Why would a book publishing company be worth so much? I thought people were reading less and that bookstores are going bankrupt all over the country. I wouldn't think a publishing company would be worth so much."

"Both statements are true. In the end, book publishing was just a small part of the revenue stream of my company. Back in the 90's as the internet and television grew and reading declined, I saw the writing on the wall and I diversified and started publishing electronically. That did so well that I branched out and started acquiring the digital rights to various musical artists. That was also lucrative and eventually we developed a specialized niche in the music world."

"What was it?"

"Deceased artists."

I scratched my head. "How does that work?"

"You buy the rights from their heirs or from the estate of the artist if there were no named beneficiaries. I discovered that many of the heirs of successful artists were unambitious near-do-wells and more often than not people who'd grown up spoiled and who never did much on their own. They simply rode the coattails of their famous relatives. Typically, these heirs had expensive tastes and habits, and at some point, they could no longer meet their monthly obligations as the work of their artist-relatives became less popular and generated lower royalties. I developed a financial model that allowed me to predict future royalties pretty accurately and my company would offer one-time, up-front cash buyouts to these heirs for their predicted future income streams."

"And your offers built in profits for you." I finished for her, suddenly getting it.

"Exactly. What is it you're trying to get at with all your questions about my finances?"

I fidgeted for a few seconds before responding. "I'm trying to reconcile my Babson decision."

"How so?"

"I'm just trying to square choosing the business school, wealth-generation model over the single career model I'd been pursuing and thinking about all the types of things I could do with money if I were successful. My basic wants and needs are incredibly simple. From the moment I get up in the morning till the minute I go to sleep at night all I think about is doing and learning new things. That's what excites me and drives me. If I were able to generate the type of wealth that you did, that would leave a whole lot left over to do other things."

Nancy nodded her head in agreement with my self-assessment and conclusion.

"Given all that, I'm trying to think of the positive side of having lots of money and all the different ways I could spend it to give more meaning to my life and to the lives of others."

Nancy stared at me for a long time, then shook her head. "Are you serious about all that? You aren't just trying to figure out how many Bentleys and motorcycles you could buy? You're actually thinking about giving back?"

Her suspicion took me aback. I nodded. "Of course I am. The reason I was asking you what you sold your company for and what you paid for your house was that I just wanted to have some idea in my mind of the types of resources I might have available to me if I were as successful as you; you know so I could figure out the types of things I could do and the impact I might be able to have on those around me."

I was silent for a few moments as I thought about Nancy's surprise that I would have an interest in philanthropy. "You know, when you took me to that battered women's shelter, I wasn't just interested in the Krav Maga. It wasn't lost on me how desperate those women must have been to leave their homes, move in with strangers, and start their lives over with no money and few skills. That must be terrifying. And the self-esteem issues all of them must have after having willingly lived with an abusive man; I can't imagine thinking so little of myself!

"Or that girl I saved from MS-13; there are probably millions of other Karens out there living on the street with drug habits and nothing to look forward except more of the same each day and then an early death. What if that were me? What if I didn't have all the advantages that I have? Going forward I'd really like to do something to help people like her break out of sad lives."

Nancy put her arm around me and leaned her head in against mine. "You're so unique. I wish I had half of your wisdom when I was starting out. Why did it take me until I was in my forties?"

"I don't know, why did it?"

"It was a rhetorical question, dear."

"I know you do positive things with your money, but your home and your cars and your lifestyle only account for about three percent of what you sold your company for. What's your plan for what you'll do with the rest of it?"

"That, is a great question and one which I'm embarrassed to admit I've not spent nearly enough time thinking about. I do have another home on Nantucket and an apartment in Paris which I've never mentioned to you. That said, I do give quite a bit to charities every year and I have a couple of pet-projects like the battered women's shelter. But all that seems unimportant right now within the context of what you're asking. The short answer is that I make much more every year than I currently spend on myself and give away in charitable ventures and its high time I got organized about maximizing how to better use my wealth. How would you like to work with me on ways I could better give back if I were to start a foundation?"

I was flattered with the trust and faith that her offer implied and thought about it for a minute. "I might. Let me think about it some. I'm not sure what I'd add at this point. You're a very clever woman and I'm just starting out at all of this."

Several minutes passed with both of us silent and caught up in our own thoughts. The muted sound of the twin Honeywell turbofan engines outside the plane was hypnotic. It got me thinking once again about flying.

"Nancy?"

She opened her eyes and turned to me.

"Any chance we could budget a private jet into your foundation? I'd fly it of course."

"Of course, you would."

We landed in Fort Myers an hour later and as we taxied up to the ramp at Alexander Aviation, I confess I was excited at the prospect of seeing Stuart and sharing all the details of my trip with him. Both Nancy and I had texted our estimated arrival to him and Court a half-hour before arriving and the two of them were standing outside the flight center door as we rolled to a stop. Nancy had changed her clothes and freshened her makeup just prior to us landing. I couldn't resist jabbing her some.

"Nancy's got a boyfriend; Nancy's got a boyfriend," I whispered in a sing song into her ear as we taxied.

"Shut up, you nasty little girl. You are without a doubt the biggest mosquito I've ever known."

"Ouch, how scathing. I'm sooo hurt that you think of me that way although I must admit I'm confused. How can I be the smallest yet the biggest at the same time?"

"You simply never stop! Here, read my lips. *Shut up, shut up, Callie.*"

"Oh…, that really clarifies things. You want me to be quiet so that you can savor the background violins that are probably playing in your head. I get it now. Jeesh…. okay already I'll—"

Nancy clamped her hand firmly over my mouth cutting me off mid-sentence, looked me in the eye, burst out laughing, and then kissed me on the forehead.

"I love you, Callie. Let's do something like this again soon. Now, why don't you run along and go play with your boy toy or ride your Italian motorcycle or do something else and leave me alone. I've got work to do."

I couldn't resist one more jab. "Work, that's what they're calling it now? My generation calls it hooking up." I then grabbed her by the neck, pulled her in towards me, and kissed her back on the forehead. "I love you too. Thanks for this week."

I locked eyes with Stuart as we came down the steps of the jet. I'd really been looking forward to seeing him, but I slowed up a little when I saw him looking back at me with big, pathetic, puppy-dog eyes. His fawning look made me acutely aware that there would likely be consequences, which I wasn't sure I was quite ready for yet, if I were to greet him too effusively.

I felt like giving him a hug, but as we came face to face, I dialed that back and instead offered him a big smile and put one of my arms around his waist. I'm pretty certain that if I'd put my arm around his shoulders, he would have gathered me into his arms and possible leaned in for more. I just wasn't yet ready to accept that elevated level of intimacy. I liked him too much to let him think that's where our relationship was at. Immediately I saw a flash of disappointment in his eyes, but he accepted my modes greeting and did not push for more.

"Hi, Stuart. Are you good?"

"I'm okay, how was your week?"

"It was a super busy, but it was also really fun. I think I'm a lot closer to knowing what I want to do next."

"Are you going to move to Boston?"

No small talk there. I really didn't want to get into that discussion right then, so I deflected.

"Nothing's firm yet, but it's a possibility. Let's not talk about that right now. Did I miss anything going on around here while I was gone?"

He shrugged. "Let's walk inside."

We walked into the flight center. Nancy and Court were talking privately and clearly not interested in engaging with us or anyone else. We sat down on one of the couches.

"I've been to class a couple of times and Eva told me she thinks that someone's been watching her dojo."

"Shit! Sorry. I was a little worried about something like that happening. When you were there did you seen any sign of people or cars parked outside that didn't look like they belonged?"

He shook his head. "I looked a couple of times, but I didn't."

"These gang people are scary, Stuart. I'd feel awful if anything ever happened to Eva."

"I'm worried that they're still looking for you."

What he said made sense. I'd hoped that with almost two weeks having gone by without me going to the dojo, that the gang would have forgotten about me and moved on. It sounded like that wasn't the case.

"They're not exactly the brightest group of individuals I've ever seen. I mean who breaks into a martial arts studio full of Krav Maga students in the middle of the day like the two who were after you?" he added.

"No kidding, but still, they're dangerous. My Aunt Nancy totally wigged out when I told her about what'd happened to me. I guess if anyone can take care of themselves its Eva."

I suddenly just wanted to go home and do nothing for a while. The entire week away had been intense and I didn't feel like I had the bandwidth to engage with Stuart on what was likely percolating in the back of his mind and took the cowardly way out.

"I guess I better get going. I haven't been home in a whole week and I'm sure my parents will want to know I'm back and find out how things went in Boston."

"Sure; I understand."

I could tell he didn't though. "Stuart?"

He looked at me.

"Forget it," I said, chickening out.

"What?"

"Nothing. Let me get squared away and back into my world here. I'll go check in with my parents and drop off my stuff. Then I'd like to go by the dojo and see Eva. Do you want to meet there later? We can talk more then."

He nodded. "Sure, that sounds good. I just missed you, and now I'm suddenly feeling uncomfortable and guilty about that."

I smiled, grateful that he'd put some of what I'd been thinking into words I couldn't say. I reached up and touched him on the face.

"I know. We can talk about that. You're a good guy. I'll meet you around 3:30."

His hope, I suppose renewed, he broke into a smile. "I'll be there."

"Good, see you then."

I said a brief goodbye to Court and Nancy and then walked with Stuart out into the hanger and turned the key in Velocitá. She started right up. The familiar sound of her engine instantly made me feel more grounded and back at home. I put on my helmet.

"Thanks for watching my girl."

"You're welcome. Follow me out, I'll get the gate for you."

I followed him around the side of the hanger to the gate and after he swung it open, I thanked him again, idled through it and out onto the road. Once on the other side I flipped down the smoked face shield and accelerated up to the speed limit. I felt guilty and then mad at myself for feeling guilty. I wasn't used to feeling guilty about anything and asked myself whether I'd led him on in some way. I couldn't think of anything in particular that I'd done or said that was disingenuous. Was there was something wrong with me? My experience with boys and relationships was pretty much limited to my brief, naïve, infatuation with the would-be rapist Christopher which didn't exactly make me an expert on relationships.

Once I reached Route 75, I accelerated to an irresponsible speed which demanded sharp focus. Like magic, my guilt was forgotten, and I got into my groove of moving much quicker than the traffic without pissing anybody off. It was an incredible release and a space that I was extremely comfortable in. I came up on my exit before I knew it and downshifted and braked on the ramp until I was traveling at the speed of traffic again and thought about all I had to tell my parents.

I got to our house ten minutes later and stopped at the top of the driveway and looked down it before entering. My father and brother's less-than-perfect pickup trucks were casually parked at odd angles to the front porch. There was a pile of old lumber on one side of the driveway with weeds and bushes growing through it, and on the other side there was stack of crab pots that hadn't been there when I'd left. There was one patch of scruffy grass in front of the porch and a few others on the sides of the house, but all of it was spotty and badly in need of a mowing. I didn't care a whit. It was all I'd known my entire life.

Boston, the Ritz Carlton, and the private jets had all been new and exciting, but they'd also felt foreign and somewhat intimidating. The simple unassuming lifestyle I'd grown up with was more me. It felt good to be home. I found myself hoping that my parents would react to my news and decision to go to Babson in a positive way.

At the sound of Velocitá's distinctive idle at the top of the driveway, Crab Claw pulled himself, paw over paw, out from under the front porch like a commando and came bounding halfway up the driveway mewling and whingeing; unsure, I imagine, whether to scold me for having been gone a lifetime or to bite me with delight at me finally being home. He bounced up and down next to me as I idled down the driveway. As I put Velocitá up on her stand, he lay on his back with all four legs in the air and squirmed with rapturous joy at my return. I got down in the dirt with him and rolled around and wrestled with him, grateful that I still had on my leather jacket and helmet as he pawed at me. When he finally realized that his public display of affection was a bit over the top, he jumped to his feet shook the dirt off, and snorted twice. I lay there for several seconds staring

ip at the sky with him staring down at me with his tail swishing slowly
from side to side.

"Hi, girl."

I looked up at the sound of my father's voice. He was at the top of the
porch steps and had obviously been watching Crab Claw and me. "Hi, girl,"
was actually quite a sentence for him to have vocalized.

"Oh hi, Daddy. I didn't hear you come out." I stood up, undid my
helmet, and hung it on Velocitá's rear view mirror.

He grunted an unintelligible response, which was more like him.

"Did you miss me?" I asked, not really expecting an answer.

"A little."

I thought I'd misheard him for a second. His admission that he'd missed
me "a little" gob-smacked me. I don't think I'd ever in my life felt warmth
from my father and for him "a little" actually meant "a lot" and my heart
swelled. I know this all probably sounds ridiculous to those of you who
grew up with adoring parents, but those two words coming out of his mouth
spoke volumes to me. I ran up the steps and gave him an over-the-top hug,
which was not reciprocated.

"I knew it! I knew this moment would come when you would finally get
in touch with your inner love for me!" I gushed with exaggeration.

"Now you're just talking foolish, Cat. Are you high or something?"

"Darn, you figured out my secret. Yes, Aunt Nancy and I were doing all
sorts of drugs with that liberal cabal of leftwing whackos that she hangs
out with when she's not being a capitalist pig."

"Well it shows."

My mother came out next. "Callie! You're home!"

I beamed back at my her and gave her a real hug that was reciprocated.

Those moments on the porch with my parents were seminal. When I'd
returned several months earlier from my summer with Nancy, I was still
Callie, their little girl and my return then had been no different than if I'd
spent just a single night away at a friend's. When I got back from Boston
that day, something had changed. Mind you, all of us had been living a
very static life for as long as I could remember. We three kids had gone to
school, my father had shrimped and put food on the table, and my mother,
working quietly in the background, had provided a solid framework and

constancy that all of us had dwelled and sheltered in. She'd been like a stalwart grove of mangroves at the ocean's edge and we three kids had been like juvenile fish that had slowly matured and grown strong enough, in the shelter of her roots, to finally leave the safety and protection that she and my father had afforded and were now ready to swim out into the open sea on our own.

This had started with Damon's announcement that he was joining the Marines and would not be shrimping with my father and Harley. It was continuing now with me. My parents didn't yet know specifically what had happened in Boston or what I might have decided, but all of us sensed and accepted that big changes were afoot, and I suspect they knew intuitively that they had about as much control over me as the mangrove roots have over the little fish once it decides to swim into the ocean. All of this flooded over me in those moments on the porch. Their quiet acceptance of these changes left me with new love and respect for both of them.

"Come inside and tell us all about your trip, Callie," Mam suggested.

We went inside and all of us sat down at the kitchen table. My father cupped a coffee mug that he must have poured earlier.

"Would you like a cup of coffee or a water, Callie?" my mother asked.

"No thanks, Mam." I could barely contain myself wanting to share with her the appraisal that David Firestorm had given on her bracelet. I unzipped a side pocket on my knapsack and carefully took her bracelet out and laid it out on the table.

Both of them looked back and forth between me and the bracelet wondering what I was doing. My father spoke first.

"What's that, something your aunt bought for you?"

It was clear that my father had never seen the bracelet before and his lack of recognition for the distinctive look of the bracelet made it clear that he didn't have any idea of the level Mam's work had risen to.

"No, silly. Mam made it for me as a gift."

Daddy looked closer at the bracelet and then back at my mother.

"Your work has gotten really good, Frances. That's a nice bracelet."

Mam kept her gaze on me, wondering what I was up to.

"When Nancy and I were in Boston, she took me into a really fancy jewelry store that she knows." I paused.

My mother kept looking at me and finally asked, "And..."

I broke into a huge smile. "And…. I showed it to the owner of the store and asked him how much he thought the retail value was."

"Were you thinking of selling it?" my mother asked.

"No, of course not. Nancy had seen it on my wrist and told me that the workmanship was outstanding. I think she actually said, 'incredible.' Anyway, we asked David, the owner, what he would appraise and sell a bracelet like that for in his store."

"What did he say?" Mam asked somewhat flatly without near the excitement I'd expected. She was probably nervous like any artist would be that their work wasn't valued highly.

I let the moment build and said nothing for several seconds.

"What did he say Callie?" Mam pushed.

I broke into a huge smile. "He said that if he were to sell that in his store, he would price it at…." I let the moment build a moment longer.

"Callie!"

"He said that he would price it at $90,000."

There was absolute silence in the room. I think even Crab Claw stopped panting at my feet. No one said anything for what felt like minutes, so I filled in the silence.

"He also said that he personally wouldn't pay over $70,000 for it, but still, that's a boatload of money."

My parents looked back and forth at each other with disbelief written all over each of their faces.

"Callie, are you joking around?"

"No, Mam, I swear to God. Can you believe it? He also said that he'd buy anything that you made."

Tears started to run out of the corner of Mam's eyes and her lower lip trembled. She didn't say anything for the longest time, and it suddenly dawned on me how incredibly powerful, the information that I had just cavalierly dumped on my parents, was. Seventy thousand dollars and the promise of more was an absolutely life-changing amount of money for the two of them.

I also realized, just a second later, that I had also likely just changed the dynamics of the roles between them; roles that had been cast in stone since they'd known each other. In one sentence I had changed everything in my parent's lives, and I suddenly wondered if I'd done the right thing.

Daddy didn't say anything for the longest time, and I wondered what was going through his mind. He was still trying to process it, I'm sure. The idea that Mam could make more money with a month or two of effort than he had ever cleared on his best *two years* of shrimping must have been difficult for him to take in. He'd never thought of her beading as anything other than a distraction for her. He pointedly stared down at the tabletop and drummed his fingers lightly on the surface. Both Mam and I stared at him. He moved his hand to the bracelet and slid it across the table till it was in front of him. Then he carefully picked it up and handled it as gently as I'd ever seen him touch anything and he looked more closely at it.

I honestly had no clue as to what was in his mind. Was he contemplating his diminished capacity as the family breadwinner or was he realizing that maybe both he and my mother would finally have the full health-insurance coverage they'd always wanted but could never afford? Was he wondering whether his wife of twenty years would continue to stay with him and put up with his surly, silent nature now that she no longer had to, or was he thinking that maybe now they could re-roof the house? I had grown up in a home where real feelings were never shared. I had no idea what his response was going to be.

He put the bracelet down on the table as gently and as reverently as he'd picked it up, pushed back away from the table and stood. Mam and I followed him with our eyes, neither of us willing to say a word, waiting to see what he would do or say next. After looking back and forth between us, he walked slowly around the table to Mam's side, put his hands on her shoulders and then bent his head and kissed her forehead with more warmth and passion than I'd witnessed in all the years I'd known them. He had tears in his eyes.

"Frances, I know I haven't been the sweetest husband all these years and I probably won't ever change, but please know that I am proud to be your husband. You have worked your fingers to the bone for all these years and never complained, not once. It couldn't have happened to a more wonderful woman."

His simple compliment melted her to the core, and she got up and embraced him with tears running down her face. They stood there hugging for about a half a minute which was about twenty-five seconds longer than any other display of affection I'd ever witnessed between the two of them.

They had been silent the entire time they were hugging but had obviously communicated a great deal to one another in that silence. After they'd taken their seats again, my mother spoke, removing any doubt as to her long-term intentions.

"I know it's still a few years off, Harley, but where on earth will we retire? We already live in Florida."

Daddy smiled at her. "I'm sure we'll figure something out."

I suddenly felt very self-conscious as though I was intruding on a very private moment and moved my chair back and started to rise in order to give them some space.

"Wait, Callie. Aren't you going to tell us how things went for you?" Mam asked.

"I can tell you later."

"No, tell us. We'd love to hear what happened."

"Are you sure?"

Chapter 45

Mam nodded and I told them all about Harvard, Mass Maritime and Babson and my decision to go to Babson if the school decided they'd have me. And then I told them about the flights up and back on the private jets and what it was like to stay at the Ritz Carlton and about my boat trip in a snowstorm and my new friendship with Mer Norgen. I must have prattled on for forty five minutes. Throughout, I noticed a new acceptance on their part of my relationship with Nancy and the fact that I was growing up and making big decisions on my own. After I finished my download and was about to head to my room to unpack, my father remembered the evening before.

"Callie, something very strange happened here last night."

"What?"

"About an hour after we all went to bed Crab Claw started barking and we heard three gunshots right outside the house."

"What? That's crazy! Who was shooting?"

"We've got no idea. Your brothers and I went outside to see what was going on but there was no one out there by the time we got outside."

I cocked my head, a sick feeling starting to come over me.

"What do you think it was, someone jacking deer?"

"I don't know. We saw the taillights of a car or maybe a van disappearing down the road when we went outside to see what was happening and we found a couple of shell casings, but this is the strangest part..." He paused without finishing.

"What?" I asked.

"Your brother Damon found what we think was maybe an earlobe."

"An earlobe? That's crazy!"

"Couldn't really tell. You know those stupid black rings that convenience store clerks sometimes wear to make holes in their ears expand? You know, the things that say, 'I never want to get a real job'?"

I knew exactly what Daddy was talking about and it wasn't lost on me that all three of the men in the van who'd tried to kidnap Karen were wearing rings like that in their ears. I felt sick inside. Nancy had been right about MS-13 and the danger they represented, and I had been ridiculously naïve to think that just because I was in Boston, that they'd stop looking for me or go after my family.

I nodded absently in agreement with my father about the hole expanders. "Yes, I know what you mean." But my head was elsewhere.

"Well, we couldn't tell for certain, but that thing that Damon found at the top of the driveway sure looked like one of those rings and it had some type of flesh around it.

"Did you call the police?"

Daddy shrugged. "They were already gone by the time we got outside. What would have been the point?"

I almost told my parents right then what I suspected, and I should have, but I didn't want to ruin the news about my mother's bracelet, and I doubted the gang would do anything in broad daylight.

"We should keep the doors locked and keep our ears open," I lamely suggested.

"We will. You can be certain of that," My father assured us.

I looked at my watch. It was just two o'clock and I wanted to look around outside and then talk to Eva. She'd know what to do.

"Would you guys mind if I took off for a while? I want to check in with Eva and see what's going on at the dojo."

"That's fine, Callie, just be back for dinner at 6:00," My mother responded.

I went into my bedroom with my knapsack, took my baton out, and slid it into the inside pocket of my leather jacket, then walked back through the kitchen.

"See you all later."

My parents were talking quietly at the table and barely acknowledged me as I went out the door. Crab Claw followed me. I started to reach for my helmet, then thought better of it, and with Crab Claw following, I

442

walked first up to the top of the driveway and then down to the turnaround looking on both sides of the road as I went. I wasn't sure what I expected to find but I wondered if the gang might have left something behind that would point more definitively to them.

The ground looked disturbed on the edge of the turnaround, and I walked into the woods towards the house. Almost immediately I noticed blood spots on the ground. I walked further in and stopped at some sort of pit that someone had dug. It was full of leaves and broken branches and I pulled some of them aside. There were dozens of small, sharpened stakes and more blood spots in the bottom of the pit. I looked closer and could see the grip of some sort of gun. I reached in and carefully pulled it out. I'd never fired a handgun of any sort, but I knew from the look of the gun that it was one of the ones that you have to pull the slide to load and that it had a clip inside that held the bullets. I was completely confused at this point. Obviously, someone had fallen into this pit and gotten hurt and dropped the gun, but who had dug the pit in the first place, and why?

I didn't want to leave the gun there, but I also didn't dare tuck it into my pants and wasn't yet ready to share with my parents all that had gone on with MS-13. I wasn't sure whether it was loaded or not and looked more closely at it. "VP9" was engraved on the slide. I knew enough not to squeeze the trigger, but I certainly wasn't going to tuck it into my waistband.

I got up off my knees and looked around. It was quiet and I hadn't heard anything alarming, but I had the distinct feeling that someone was watching me. Eva was always saying, "trust your instincts." Mine were dinging at that moment and I also saw that Crab Claw was on alert with his ears cocked. I looked in the direction that he was looking and slowly started walking in that direction with the gun hanging in my hand at my side. We crossed the road, and after pausing to listen again, parted the branches and looked into the woods on the other side. A voice came out of nowhere.

"You must be Callie. You aren't going to shoot me, are you?"

I almost jumped out of my skin at the sound of the voice, but I didn't see anyone. Crab Claw started barking and snarling and darted towards a clump of short palmettos. The palmettos suddenly changed shape and a man dressed in full camouflage appeared out of nowhere. He went down on one knee, held out his hand out towards Crab Claw and made several clicking sounds with his tongue. Crab Claw immediately stopped barking, halted his charge, went down on his belly, and then crawled right up to the man who reached out and petted his head.

I walked several steps closer holding the gun out in front of me, but not pointing it directly at him. I was scared, and not yet certain whether or not he represented a threat. He'd addressed me by name, was kneeling and petting my dog, and he wasn't making any moves towards the clearly visible weapon that he had holstered pistol on his hip. Taken together it seemed that he didn't have hostile intent. The stranger had long black hair with silver streaks in it pulled back into a ponytail and was clearly of Indian descent. His eyes were black and swollen as though he'd been in a fight, and he had stripes of color on both sides of his face.

"Is that war paint?" I asked, and immediately felt foolish for my question.

Billy put his hand to his face and grimaced at the touch. "I strive to be authentic. You're one to talk; are you on your way to a Blondie concert?"

I smiled at his obvious reference to my riding leathers. "You obviously know me, but I don't know you. I'm going to go with a wild guess here and surmise that you're not MS-13?"

The stranger shook his head. "What gave it away?"

"Your age for one. You're way too old to be in a gang."

"Ouch. Young girl speaks with vicious tongue." The man slowly got to his feet and stood there and stared at me. After several seconds, he spoke again. "I'm Billy, Billy Rainwater."

"Nice to meet you, Billy. And no, I'm not going to a Blondie concert. These are riding leathers."

He nodded. "I figured as much. Sorry I'm not more at the top of my game. I had a rough night last night."

"MS-13?"

He nodded again. "There were six of them and just one of me. You should see what they look like."

"I think I saw some of your work."

"The punji-stick pit, the earlobe, or something else?"

"The pit. I heard about the earlobe though. Did you happen to take it off a big, ugly, bald guy with tattoos everywhere?"

"I did. He was a bit of a surprise. MS-13 are usually skinny little punks. He was a monster. At least I got a round into his arm although I think it was just a through and through."

"What's a through and through?"

"I think you civilians call it a flesh wound. The bullet I fired at him went through the fleshy underside of his arm and didn't impact any major muscle or bones."

"Well that's unfortunate."

"What is?"

"The fact that you didn't do any major damage to the guy. His name is Esteban and he's number two or three in the local chapter of MS-13. According to a police detective I know," I added.

Billy nodded.

"Are we really having this conversation, Mr. Billy?"

He smiled "We are." He was silent for a few seconds. "I hadn't counted on the dog."

I cocked my head at him.

"When I was briefed on this mission, no mention was made of a dog and I failed to ask. You see, my protection was supposed to be quiet and discreet. In that I have failed."

"You saved my family though."

"I did."

"For that I will be eternally grateful. I feel like an idiot for not realizing the danger I put them in."

Billy shrugged and continued to pet Crab Claw's head. "The cub is not responsible for the sins of the wolf."

"Is that some ancient Indian saying?"

"Nope, just made it up."

I laughed and approached the strange Indian man to look more closely at his wounds.

"You aren't going to shoot me, are you?" Billy asked pointing to the gun I still held awkwardly in my hand.

I looked down at it. "I expect not. I don't know anything about firearms. I'd likely shoot myself." I held it out to him with the barrel pointed downwards. "Would you like it?"

"Yes, I'd feel more relaxed if that were secured." He reached out and gently took it out of my hand. Then he pressed the button on the side of it with his right hand, caught the ejected magazine in his left, slid it into one of the many pockets in his Cargo pants, then deftly pulled the slide on the top of the gun ejecting a round into the air then onto the ground, then cycled the slide on top of the gun open again, peered inside, and slid it into his waistband.

"You should get some ice on those eyes. You look like a rabid raccoon," I suggested.

"That would have been nice last night, but I didn't have room on my motorcycle for a cooler."

"You ride a bike?"

"Sometimes. Mainly I travel in a big 4 x 4 or my seaplane. What do you ride?"

"A Ducati Monster 796. She goes like the wind."

Billy nodded, apparently enjoying my enthusiasm. "So how did you get into this mess with such an undesirable group?"

"They were trying to snatch a girl on the street, and I messed up their abduction."

"How?"

"I took two of them down, threw the girl onto the back of my bike, and took off."

"And how did you take two of them down, my lionhearted friend?"

"Palm strike, kick to family heirlooms, three knees to face and then punch to throat and side kick to knee."

"Krav Maga?"

I nodded. "I didn't even try to fight the big ugly one that you fought last night. I ran from him."

Billy laughed. "Like the wind, no doubt and I'm glad for it. He's a pretty fearsome character for a banger."

I brought our easy banter to a screeching halt with my next question. "What are you doing here, Billy?"

He didn't answer me for several seconds. "An associate of mine, whose name isn't important, asked me to undertake the protection of you and your family. He's quite busy with some other matters right now or he would have done it himself."

"But why? Why does this unnamed individual care about me and my family?"

"Do you have a doting aunt?"

"I do, Mr. Rainwater." I made the connection right away but was conflicted. I resented Nancy's secret intrusion into my life but, was also incredibly grateful that nothing had happened to my family. I nodded. "That explains your presence, although I'm not sure why you were supposed to be so discreet, which you aren't by the way," I added.

"I'm not sure of her reasons. That was not made clear to me. I gather that she quite presciently perceived the imminent danger you and your family were in and acted on her fears. You should be grateful. Those men did not come here to chat. They came with guns, bats, rebar and machetes."

I wiped a tear from the corner of my eye. "Thank you, Mr. Rainwater."

"You're welcome. Sometimes all of us need the help of friends."

"So are you just going to hang out here in the woods?"

He nodded. "For a while."

"How long is 'a while'?"

He shrugged. "Time means different things to different people."

"More ancient tribal wisdom?"

He laughed. "No, I broke my watch when I was scuffling with the bad hombres."

I reached out and punched him softly on his bad arm unaware that it was damaged.

He winced. "Ouch."

"Ouch! Here I am thinking you're some mystical, powerful warrior."

"I thought so too. Don't tell anyone, especially a guy named Jesse if you ever meet him. I'll never live it down."

I nodded. "Listen, I'm going to head over to my friend Eva's dojo and find out what's been going on around here while I was gone. Can I bring you anything when I come back?"

"A handful of Ibuprofen would be nice. I took all that I had. But listen, Callie."

"I'm listening."

"I'd like to ride along behind you and cover your six. It will leave your family unprotected, but I doubt MS-13 would make another run against them here in broad daylight."

I thought about his offer for a few seconds. "I appreciate that, but I'd really prefer that you stay here and watch over them. I'd die if anything ever happened to them. I'm pretty good at taking care of myself and I'm just going to the dojo where I'll be surrounded by a group of other martial artists. I'll be back before dark."

"These people who made a run at your family last night are the real deal. Sure, they're inept, but they're also persistent and amoral. This isn't over yet."

"I'm starting to gather that, Billy."

"I want you to be hyper-alert. I'm not expecting them to try anything in broad daylight, but I can't be here at your family's house and watch you at the same time."

Billy was silent for several seconds before speaking again. "Do you trust me?"

For some reason I didn't have to even think about it. "Yes."

With no warning other than his question about trusting him, Billy suddenly attacked me. He executed a perfect leg sweep, knocked me to the ground and before I could respond, withdrew his K-bar from the sheath rig on his chest and started a downward stabbing motion towards my chest. I was completely confused by his sudden attack on me but responded reflexively and swept his arm to the side and struck him hard in his already swollen nose with a palm strike before rolling to the side, regaining my feet and assuming a ready stance. "What the hell are you doing!" I shouted.

Billy stepped back, sheathed his K-Bar, and gently touched his nose. "I was afraid you'd do that."

"Do what! Are you crazy?"

"Hit me in the face. I had to find out for myself how fast you are and whether or not you can take care of yourself."

I understood what he'd been trying to do but was still shaken up and angry at his sudden aggression. I reached into my coat, drew my steel baton, quickly snapped it open and started a full two-handed swing down towards his left shoulder. I checked myself right before striking his collarbone, made pointed eye contact with him, then punched the ground with the baton and smoothly returned it to my jacket before speaking again.

"Maybe warn me next time."

Billy nodded once. "Fair enough. You're fast. Your instructor Eva must be very good."

"She is. She was an instructor for the Israeli Defense Force."

"Well, it shows with your skill level. The IDF has some of the best soldiers I've ever known."

"I gather that I passed your little test?"

He nodded.

"Okay then, I'll see you in about an hour and a half. I'll bring back some Ibuprofen."

"Callie, before you go let's exchange cell phone numbers. If I'm going to be around for a few days protecting you and your family, it makes sense that we be able to communicate."

I nodded in agreement. "Good idea." I asked him for his number and then sent him a text. He saved me as a new contact, I did the same.

"Do me a favor?"

"What?"

"Call me if you see anything suspicious, anything at all, or if you're going to be delayed. I'm not comfortable with you going off on your own after what took place here last night."

"I know; I'll be okay though. Just keep an eye on my family."

"I can do that, but I'd really prefer you just hang around here where I can keep an eye on all of you at the same time."

"I don't want to give these dirtbags all that power over me. I'll be fine." I got up and started to walk away, then stopped and turned back to him,

I pointed to the gun in his waistband. "Would you show me how to operate one of those sometime? I can't stand it when I don't know how to work something."

He thought about it for a few seconds. "Perhaps."

"Okay then, Mr. Rainwater, now I'm really going."

"You want your dog?"

"No, he seems happy as a clam, with you. He'll come home when he's ready. You're incredibly good with him, are you a dog whisperer?"

He nodded sagely as though he knew the secrets of the universe, then totally surprised me with his answer. "No, not at all. I've never even had a dog. Seems like a nice enough animal though."

I shook my head and started to walk away, then looked back one more time to see whether the kind, fearsome looking man was real. He wiggled his fingers in a goodbye gesture which seemed completely out of character but somehow still worked and belied his self-assurance. I walked out of the woods, down the driveway and started up Velocitá. *What a character*, I thought to myself as I put on my helmet.

Chapter 46

Billy returned to his hammock and thought about his unexpected meeting with Callie. She was mature and confident for her age, yet also vulnerable as she'd shown when he'd told her about the attempt on her family. As soon as she was out of sight and he heard her Ducati start, Billy pulled out his cellphone again, and dialed one of his "favorites." His call was answered after two rings.

"This is Chyrel."

"Chyrel, Billy."

"How're you, stranger?"

"Fair to middling for an aging Indian."

"I'm sorry to hear that. Fair, middling, and aging aren't the most positive expletives that I've ever heard. What's going on and how can I help?"

Billy had worked with Chyrel many times over the years. A computer and communications wizard, Chyrel had cut her chops as a computer analyst for the CIA and then the DHS and the CCC (Caribbean Counterterrorism Command). Currently she was doing contract work for McDermitt & Livingston Security and Armstrong Research; both companies that Billy and Jesse worked with.

"I'm in Fort Myers helping Jesse out by protecting a young girl and her family."

"That doesn't sound like a project you guys would normally take on."

"Well, you know Jesse. He acts tough as nails with everyone, but he's got the heart of a teddy bear. This girl is something, and she probably reminds him of his own daughters. Anyway, the primary on this is a young teenage girl named Callie. MS-13 has been coming at her hard and I'm just one person and I'm trying to keep an eye on both her and her family. I need you to track her phone for me."

"Sure, what's the number?"

Billy gave it to her.

"That's it?"

"That's it."

"Well right now she's on 75S coming up on..."

"You're amazing, Chyrel. I don't need her location now, she just left me!"

"You said..."

"I know, I should have been more precise. I was just giving you a heads up. I'll call you if I need her location."

"I'll be here."

"You always are. Thanks, Chyrel."

"Anytime."

Billy pressed the end button on his phone.

Chapter 47

I stopped at the Walgreens on Colonial on my way to the dojo to get Billy a bottle of Ibuprofen and then continued on to Eva's dojo. I parked behind the building and went in through the rear door.

Stuart and Eva were the only two people in the dojo when I walked in. They were seated on the floor facing each other and laughing about something."

"What'd I miss?"

"Callie!" Eva said jumping up. She wrapped me up in a big hug and then held me at arm's length with her hands on my shoulders. "We were laughing about you if you must know, and your fascination with big powerful machines. Stuart was just telling me that I should have seen the look on your face when that private jet taxied up to you. I knew exactly what he was saying."

I blushed in embarrassment and then decided to play along. "I can't help it. When I see big, powerful machines I get all weak in the knees. Do you two think I need help?"

Eva hugged me again. "Absolutely! But we love you anyway."

I looked at her, glad to be home. "I missed you."

"Ahhhh, did you hear that, Stuart?" She turned towards him as she spoke. I instantly took advantage of the distraction by putting her in an arm-bar hold and then tripped her forward. She laughed as I leveraged her to the floor and fell down on top of her. We grappled on the floor, neither of us gaining a definitive advantage as we were laughing too hard. We stopped when we heard the rear fire-door I'd come in through, slam shut. All three of us looked up.

Five MS-13 gang members were standing there, led by Esteban. Three of them had handguns, Esteban was carrying a short heavy Billy club. He was smacking it into his open palm as the five of them spread out in a rough half circle around Stuart, Eva, and me.

Stuart, with little thought but a great deal of courage, made a sudden, instinctual movement to get up as if he were going to somehow defend us. With incredible speed, Esteban took a single quick step towards him and backhanded the Billy club into his forehead. The cracking sound it made on contact was sickening and Stuart crumpled to the floor. I immediately crawled over to him and pulled his head into my lap and gently swept his hair back. He was out cold. I couldn't see a crack in his skull, but a large egg immediately started to form under the skin where the club had made contact and he started to bleed where the skin had been broken. He was completely unconscious, and I wondered whether his skull was fractured.

Eva slowly got to her feet. I looked back and forth between her and my nemesis. He looked every bit as large and fearsome as I'd ever imagined, and I wondered what she was thinking. There was no way she'd be able to overpower him and the other four men at the same time in the same way that she'd overpowered the other two gang members who'd tried to take me the week before.

"You think that makes you a big man knocking out a teenage boy?" Eva asked. "Why don't you try the same thing with me."

"Esteban, you want I should just shoot the bitch?" Marko asked.

Esteban smiled at Eva. "No es necessario, Marko. The day I need help with a puta like this will be the day I go to a nursing home. You just watch the other two."

Esteban turned square to Eva and thrust out his chest. "I'm going to beat you like you like I beat my hookers when they try to hold back money."

I could see the hatred in Eva's eyes as she slowly brought her open hands up to the sides of her face and drew her right leg back slightly and went up on the balls of her feet. The muscles in Esteban's arms were massive and corded and he smacked the Billy club into the palm of his left hand several more times. He looked indomitable and I tried thinking of ways that Eva might possibly hurt him without a weapon. I drew a complete blank.

In an instant, without telegraphing her intention in any way, Eva's right foot lashed out in lightning strike towards the side of Esteban's face. He batted it aside like a pesky fly without even flinching. Eva returned to her feet undeterred and almost immediately unleashed another kick with the other foot going after Esteban's knee. Despite her speed, Esteban instinctively dipped downwards right before her foot made contact against his locked knee. Instead of taking out his knee as it would have done to any other fighter, the joint remained whole, and the top of her foot ended up slapping against the side of his thigh. It was a good hit, but not a debilitating one.

Esteban maintained his eye contact with her and smiled again revealing his hideous grille. "That's it? That's all you've got, a little love tap? Are you in love with me? You know, when we leave here, we're going to take your little friend with us. We will show her our love over and over and over again. And then, if she's still alive, we'll introduce her to drugs and then to many men from all over the country. Would you like to join us? I could make that happen if you liked."

Esteban's words must have cut like a knife into Eva's heart and damaged soul. In answer, she struck out again with her other foot to the other side of his body, made good contact with his kidney, and then immediately bored in with everything she had.

"Krav Maga is not about hitting and evaluating and then hitting and evaluating. It's all about delivering an explosive, continuous, unrelenting attack on your opponent until he is no longer viable." Those had been Eva's words to me and the other women in the shelter the first night we'd met. After her kick to his kidney she immediately pressed her attack inward, without pausing, and went first for his throat and neck with punches, and then for his eyes with rigid fingers. Each strike was focused and powerful, and I could barely see her hands as she struck. But no matter how fast or aggressive she was, Esteban would move just enough so that every strike, was just off. Her throat punches glanced off both sides of his throat and her jabs to his eyes ended up striking his forehead and then one of his temples. His speed was blinding, like nothing I'd ever seen.

After avoiding Eva's second eye strike Esteban leaned in to meet her attack and swept both her hands with his left arm, drew back his right arm and hit her with the club hard, in the stomach. He really put his weight into the strike and Eva was lifted right off her feet and thrown backwards to the floor where she lay gripping her stomach, heaving, and gasping for air. Esteban did not stop, though. Once she was on the floor, he started a brutal, methodical, beating and worked his way around her prostrate body hitting every part with short hard strokes; her back, shoulders, kidneys, thighs, and calves. After hitting her ten or twelve times he stopped and looked down to check his work as if to make sure he'd beaten her in every available spot. He was winded from his efforts and started to walk away from her broken body. Then suddenly, he turned back, drew his right leg back and kicked her in the face. The room was silent, except for my screams.

Without even being cognizant of it I had been screaming for him to stop from the moment he'd started his beating. He looked down at me like some insignificant bit of lint and hit me over the head with the club. My lights went out and I didn't come to until fifteen minutes later. I awoke on the floor of their van, tied, gagged, and blindfolded with an incredible headache.

Chapter 48

B illy looked at the time on his cell phone. It was 7:30. Callie had left at 4:00 and indicated that she would be back by 5:30. He pressed the redial button and listened as his phone rang and rang until it finally went to voicemail. He'd already left three messages. Something was definitely wrong; he could feel it. Callie's failure to return on time, answer her phone, or call him was inconsistent with both her personality and what she'd promised. Billy dialed Chyrel.

"Chyrel, it's Billy."

"I can see that. What's up?"

"You know that phone number I gave you earlier?"

"I do."

"Where's that phone at now?"

"Give me a second, I've got to pull up my map overlay."

Billy paced back and forth impatiently as he waited.

"Okay, once she left your location it looks as though she went downtown to a Plaza called Dick's. Looks like she was there for about fifteen minutes. Then she went to a house on Carrell Avenue. It looks like she's still there."

"What's the street number?"

"7355."

"I think my client might have been snatched and is being held there. What's the tactical situation at that address?"

"Looks like a run-of-mill-residential street with neighbors close on both sides and also across the street. You should be able to get right up close to the house using the houses around it for cover. Course that assumes there aren't any lookouts outside."

Billy remembered what Callie had told him about her Krav Maga instructor and had another thought.

"Can you give me the address of that Dick's Plaza also?"

"Sure, it's in the 4,900 block of South Cleveland."

"Thanks, I've got to run."

"Let me know if there's anything else I can do for you."

"I will."

Billy pressed "End on his phone and then quickly broke down his compound bow and put it into his backpack, then instinctively, as he walked, checked his Sig for a round in the chamber and verified that he still had three extra magazines. He continued through the woods and once out of sight of Callie's house, got on the road and hustled to the end where his motorcycle was cached. Before leaving he pulled up the Map App on his cell phone and reviewed the location of both Dick's Sporting Goods and then the Glenwood address that Chyrel had given him. When done he hurriedly pulled the cut bushes aside that concealed his Indian, started it up, and roared off towards downtown.

He wasn't at all certain what had happened to Callie but knew that if the gang had somehow gotten their hands on her it was likely that there had been a number of them. He also knew he wasn't at 100% because of the beating he'd taken the night before and had no idea if Callie's Krav Maga teacher Eva would be at the Dojo, but it seemed prudent to check first and see if she might be available to help him. At the very least, she might have intel on where Callie had been headed when she left.

When he got to the Dick's Plaza, he started at the North End with the idea of looking at each of the tenants. Pilates by Laurie and Eva's Krav Maga was the first retail location South in the Plaza and he stopped right in front of the studio, hopped off, and tried the front door. It was locked. He looked in through the glass. All the lights were on, but no one came to the door when he banged on it. He got back on his bike and drove around to the rear of the building to see if he could find another way in. He parked, drew his Sig, went up to the rear fire door and listened for several seconds before trying the knob. It was unlocked. He prepared himself and then pulled the door halfway open as fast as he could, took a quick peak into the room from a crouched position, then withdrew, to see if he drew any fire. He waited a few seconds, then kicked the door the rest of the way open, made a cautious entry, and seeing no threats, quickly made his way the rest of the way into the room sweeping his gun from side to side as he went.

He caught a glimpse of himself in the floor to ceiling mirrors as he panned the room. He paused to look over the visage staring back at him. Some of the camouflage paint he'd painted on the night before remained. It now seemed to simply highlight his swollen and bruised face. His upper and lower lips were both scabbed over from being bashed against his teeth, and he was still wearing head to toe camo. Over that was his tactical rig with his upside down, sheathed combat knife and spare magazines, in his hands, a silenced Sig Sauer. *You look like a damned lunatic!* he thought to himself.

"Hello!" he yelled out, and then listened. He had a bad feeling and looked more closely around the room. Dark brown stains in the middle of the mat immediately stood out and caught his eye in the otherwise clean and organized space. They looked like dried blood.

"Hello...is anyone here?" he shouted out again. This time he heard a muffled, banging sound coming from behind a door in the rear corner of the room in apparent answer to his calls. He brought his Sig into a halfway-up position and moved quickly but silently across the room to the source of the sounds and listened closely. It sounded as though there was someone on the other side of the door trying to yell through a gag. He pulled it open.

Inside, there was a woman tied and gagged on the floor and bleeding from a head wound. He holstered his gun and knelt down next to her. She looked up at him nervously, clearly unsure of whether he was friend or foe. He made a gentling motion with his hand to reassure her, then carefully removed her gag.

"It's okay, I'm a friend and I'm here to help," he said in a gentle voice. He looked over the ropes that bound her hands and feet, unsheathed his K-bar, and cut them. Then he helped the woman out of the hot closet and into a seated position with her back resting against the outside mirrored wall.

"Are you Eva?" he asked.

Eva took several huge gasping breaths, grateful that her gag was off and that she was out of the stifling closet. "I am."

"Tell me what happened here, Eva. I'm worried about your student, Callie."

She had big dark circles around both eyes, and large bruises on both of her arms. She also appeared concussed, and absently felt around with two fingers in her mouth and pulled out a loose tooth and stared at it for several seconds before responding. She was groggy but seemed to be coming around.

"Who are you, what are doing here, and how do you know Callie?"

"My name is Billy. I'm a friend of hers."

Eva had never heard Callie mention someone named "Billy" but there was something about him that she instantly trusted.

"They took her. MS-13 took her and another one of my young students named Stuart."

"How long ago?"

"I'm not sure, maybe a half-hour ago." Eva became more alert as she spoke and struggled to stand up. "We've got to call the police and get them to start looking for her! We have to do it right now! They're planning to do some terrible things to her!"

Billy reached out with a hand and put it on her shoulder trying to calm her and prevent her from jumping up. "I'm aware of the danger; that's why I'm here. I think I might know where they've taken her."

Eva's eyes came into sharper focus. "How do you know Callie?"

"It's a complicated story which I'll share with you when we have some time, but right now I need to get back on the road and see if I can find her and intervene before anything more happens to her. I came here because I understood from her that you'd done some time in the IDF and I was hoping you might be able to help. That's obviously not going to happen though, with the condition you're in."

Eva slapped his hand away and struggled to her feet. "Try and stop me!"

"Eva, you can barely stand. How're you going to help me?"

"You've obviously never dealt with a pissed off Israeli! You got another one of those?" Eva pointed to Billy's hip and the holstered semi-automatic.

He smiled. "As a matter of fact, I do."

"Then why are we just standing here? Let's go!"

"Fair enough."

"Just give me thirty seconds to wash some of this blood off my face so I can see."

A minute later Eva emerged from the restroom and followed Billy out the fire door. He noted that she was unsteady on her feet and had some difficulty walking.

"Are you sure about this, Eva? You look pretty shaky."

"I'll be okay.

Billy took off his backpack as the fire door closed behind them and held it out to her. "Do you think you can wear this?"

Eva looked at him questioningly and he pointed to his 1,200 CC Indian Roadmaster.

"I don't have a backrest and if I wear the pack, you won't be able to get your arms around me to hold on."

Eva nodded and he held it up so she could get her arms through the shoulder straps. He slowly settled the full weight of the pack onto her bruised shoulders. She winced but didn't complain and allowed him to swing his leg over the seat and start the big motorcycle before carefully climbing on the back.

"You know what you're doing on this thing?" Eva asked.

"Not really, but how hard could it be? I'm sure I'll get the hang of it after a few minutes."

"Funny man."

Billy rapidly accelerated up the access road, across the parking lot, and stopped for traffic before turning onto Cleveland.

"You know where you're going?" Eva asked.

Billy nodded. "I grew up around Fort Myers."

"Why are you trying to help Callie?"

"I'm doing a favor for a friend. Callie's aunt talked him into providing protection for Callie and her family."

"These are some rough people, Billy. You don't look much better than me. I hope you can take care of yourself."

"I took out four or five of them last night when they made a run at Callie's family. But I screwed up today by not staying close to her."

"So I take it you know your way around weapons and fighting."

"I was a special forces Recon Marine for quite a few years, although I've got to admit, one of the men I fought last night was more than expected. I'm moving a little slower than usual as a result."

"Was he big, bald, tattooed, ugly, and missing an earlobe?"

"That's the one. I was the one who took his earlobe. I also got a round into him last night, but I'm not sure I did any real damage."

"He's still functional. Told me he was going to beat me like a hooker who owed him money."

Billy thought of the number of bruises he'd seen on Eva's face and body. "You must have owed him a lot of money."

Eva was silent as they roared through the streets doing rolling stops at stop signs and red lights, driving right through them when safe.

"Billy, we've got to find her. The big ugly one told me what they're going to do to her, and I'll tell you right now that I won't let that happen. She's an incredibly special girl and what they're planning will destroy her if she lives through it."

Billy nodded. "I got that impression from the little time I spent talking to her."

"Can you go any faster?"

"I don't see how. We're almost there though."

"What's our plan?"

"I don't know yet, other than to save Callie and kick enough ass so that these dirtbags are no longer a problem for her."

"If they've done anything to her, I'll kill every one of them. I swear this to you."

"Not if I do it first."

Chapter 49

Esteban backed down the side of Diego's mother's house until the side door of the van was adjacent to the kitchen door, just as he'd done when transporting Heather and Laura to the house. He looked carefully around for neighbors in their yards, passersby, or other potential witnesses. Marko was in the passenger seat. Bones, Razor, and Reny were in the back. Callie and Stuart lay on the floor between them, back-to-back with their hands tied behind their backs with filthy bandannas secured over their eyes and rags stuffed into their mouths. As Esteban put the van in Park, Stuart started to come around and struggle against his bonds. Esteban turned around in his seat.

"Keep him quiet while I go in and talk with Diego. When I tell you, drag them both inside and then down into the basement."

"Sí," Marko acknowledged.

Esteban got out of the van, walked to the front of the house, knocked, and then waited for a minute. He peered through the sidelight of the door and seeing no one in the living room knocked again and then rang the doorbell. He doubted Diego was out with his mother as sick as she was and the two teenage girls still there, tied in the basement. *Perhaps he's in the basement*, he thought to himself and tried the front door. It was unlocked and he called out Diego's name several times as he slowly pushed it open.

The stench that assaulted him as he walked in was absolutely putrid, much worse than the last time he'd been there, and his eyes immediately started to water. All the windows he'd opened the last time he'd been there were closed again, and the temperature in the house was uncomfortably warm, as though the air conditioning was out.

He called out Diego's name several times more and then peered down the dark hallway where he knew the three bedrooms in the house were. All the doors were shut. He was uncomfortable with opening any of them and decided instead to first check the basement. Maybe he was just downstairs feeding the two girls. He walked into the kitchen, opened the basement door, and called down. "Diego, are you here? It's Esteban." There was no response from him, but he clearly heard the two girls call out. "Help! Is there someone there!"

He went the rest of the way down the stairs and once he got near the bottom, called out Diego's name again. The stench in the basement was almost as bad as upstairs but smelled more like a port-o-potty than rotten food.

Diego was sprawled on a filthy old couch, unconscious. The coffee table in front of him littered with empty beer bottles, a mirror with cocaine residue, and several empty disposable syringes that had no doubt been used on the two, young, suburban teens. Esteban looked farther into the room and into their pleading eyes. They were both still manacled to the lally columns with the short pieces of chain. Both were filthy with puddles of urine and feces at their feet. To Esteban they were just putas, but their desperation and fear was so intense that it shocked even him.

"Please, mister, please! Can we have our shot and some water and use the toilet?" they begged.

Esteban looked at the washer, dryer and sink in the corner and then back at them. The chains they were restrained by weren't long enough to reach the sink and the water tap. Without saying anything he walked past them to the sink, filled a dirty, old Tupperware container with water and then placed it on the floor between them. He watched for a few moments as they shared the water back and forth between each other.

"How long has he been out?" he asked. Neither responded as they continued to drink. He kicked Laura, the younger of the two. She cowered away from him.

"How long has he been out?"

"Since last night. He came down last night, sat on that couch, drank beer, and did drugs until he passed out. Please, mister, please; can we have our shots and use a bathroom?"

"Maybe later." He walked over to the couch and looked down at Diego who looked only marginally better than the two girls. His oily hair hung in his face, he was dressed in the clothes he'd been wearing for an entire week and urine stained the front of his pants. Esteban was disgusted at his condition and used his foot to push against Diego's leg until he slowly came to.

"What? What!"

"I have the motorcycle girl and her boyfriend outside. You want I should bring them in?"

"Diego rubbed his eyes and then looked through the mess on the table and picked up several of the bottles and held them up to the light, no doubt looking for one that still had some dregs remaining. All of them were dry and he yelled out in apparent frustration. "Fuck! What happened?"

"You must have fallen asleep, Jefe. I was asking if you wanted me to bring the girl and her boyfriend in."

"Yes, you fucking moron. Bring them in and tie them to two of the other posts. There's rope in the corner over there. I've got to clean up, get a beer and check on my mother."

"Sí, Jefe."

"What's that smell? It smells like shit down here."

Esteban nodded at the two young girls. "You didn't let them go to the bathroom. They did what they had to. Upstairs still smells too. What's going on with you, Diego? This whole place is a shithole."

Diego stood up and pushed Esteban out of his way. "Es mi madre. Esta es infermo (It's my mother, she's sick)."

"Sí, I know that, but you can't care for her properly if you're fucked up in the basement all night."

Diego stared at him for a moment with hate in his eyes at being called out. He knew Esteban was right, though. He couldn't properly care for his mother if he were passed out in the basement.

"Bring the puta and her novio (boyfriend) in and secure them. I'm going upstairs to tend to mi madre and clean up. I'll be back in a couple of minutes."

Esteban nodded his assent and stood back to allow Diego past him. He followed him up the stairs. At the top, Diego continued into the interior of the house. Esteban stopped at the kitchen door and looked out. It was almost dark. He opened the door, and signaled Marko to bring Callie and Stuart in. The side door on the van immediately slid open and Bones, Razor and Reny dragged the two of them out of the van, into the kitchen, and then down the stairs. Stuart was fully awake when they brought him in and struggled as they brought him down the stairs. Razor hit him in the stomach to squelch his resistance. When they all got to the bottom, Esteban pointed to two of the lally columns near the girls.

"Tie them separately to those two columns. You can take off their blindfolds but leave the gags in their mouths for now." Esteban sat down on the couch and turned to the newest and ugliest of the other four gang members, Reny. He was a whiney little prick and Esteban didn't like him. "Reny."

"Sí?"

"Clean up that shit and the piss on the floor."

Reny looked around the unfamiliar basement helplessly. He knew he was the lowest man on the totem pole but had no idea how to do it. He didn't even see a mop in the area near the utility sink in the corner. "How should I do it?"

"I don't care how! Lick it up, for all I care. Just get rid of it. Go upstairs into the kitchen and get some paper towels or something, pendejo."

Reny shrank back from Esteban's sharp tone and meekly went upstairs to look for paper towels. He ran into Diego at the top of the stairs. He was reaching into the refrigerator for a bottle of beer and looked at him like he was one of the turds he was supposed to clean up.

"Que?"

"I'm looking for some paper towels, Jefe, to clean up after the girls."

Diego pointed to the counter. "Right there. Don't be going around my house without my permission."

"Sí, Diego. Esteban sent me."

"Go! Get the paper towels and follow me back downstairs."

Diego sat down next to Esteban on the couch. He had a beer in one hand, a cigarette in the other, and a small, zippered toilet kit under his arm. He went back and forth between the cigarette and the beer bottle until both were finished.

"How's your mother?"

"Better, she's quiet and she's been sleeping with no pain."

Esteban nodded. "That's good, Jefe, glad to hear it."

Diego pulled a baggie of coke out of the toilet kit and dumped several grams of cocaine onto the mirror. "You want some?"

Esteban shook his head. "Gracias, pero no."

Diego shrugged, chopped several lines, snorted them, and then paused with his eyes closed to savor the potent drug as it came into contact with the tender receptors in the back of his sinuses. Finally, he ran his fingers through his greasy hair, opened his bloodshot eyes, and looked across the room first at Heather and Laura, then Stuart, and finally Callie. Reny was just finishing cleaning up the urine and feces on the floor and held up the soiled mess of towels.

"What should I do with these, Jefe?"

Esteban answered for Diego. "Take them outside and put them in the trash and then I want you to keep an eye out on the street."

"What about the girl?" He whined.

"What about her?"

"I want a turn with the girl."

"What, your sister doesn't give you enough? Just do what you're told. If she's still alive after, maybe you'll get a turn."

Reny reluctantly climbed the stairs with the foul-smelling wad of paper towels and went out the kitchen door to look for a trashcan. He found one on the side of the garage and after disposing of the human waste he walked around to the front of the house and sat down in one of the cheap plastic lawn chairs on the front porch, lit up a smoke, and thought about what he was missing in the basement.

****

Both Billy and Eva knew what was at stake and what might be happening to Callie. They were silent for the last two blocks. Billy pulled to the curb three houses back from the house her phone was pinging from and shut down the Roadmaster. They sat silently for several seconds scanning the neighborhood and letting their eyes adjust to the reduced lighting. Eva got off first. Billy threw out the side stand on the bike, dismounted, and turned to her.

"Let me get that off you," he said, and took the backpack off Eva's back, set it on the ground, and unzipped the main opening. He rummaged around inside for several seconds and then withdrew the gun and the magazine that Callie had found in his punji pit and handed them to Eva. She reflexively slammed the magazine home, cycled a round into the firing chamber and then flicked the safety on and off several times. While she was doing that Billy took out his bow and assembled the three separate pieces. Eva watched him with interest as he completed the assembly and nocked an arrow.

"I wondered if you were a native American from the way you look. You just confirmed it with the bow and arrow."

Billy sighed. "And we were doing so well before you started in with the stereotypes."

"I didn't mean—"

Billy held up a finger and put it to her lips. "Shh, I'm just messing with you. Let's move nearer the house real sneaky-like and see what we're up against. We don't know whether they have anyone outside keeping watch."

Eva nodded. "You know, 'sneaky-like' may be culturally insensitive to many."

Billy smiled at her quip. "Touché." He liked the spirit of this woman who battered and bruised was so willing to put her life on the line and still had the presence of mind to joke with him.

She followed in his footsteps as he cautiously moved towards the house. He stopped one house down from the target house and they both crouched low behind a large oak tree bordering the sidewalk. They took a few seconds to carefully surveil the dark house in the low light provided by a streetlight. Initially, they didn't see Reny, the junior gang member that Esteban had sent to act as a lookout, because he was seated far back in the shadow of the porch. His cigarette, however, and the bright orange glow from it gave him away. Billy put on the night vision goggles for a closer look. The man had a gun in his waistband.

"Doesn't look like an innocent homeowner to me." Billy observed. He took off the NVG's and passed them to Eva.

She put them on and looked at the man on the porch. "He's not. That's one of the men that took Stuart and Callie." She passed the NVG's back.

"Eva, too much time has gone by since they took her. We need to get in there. I'm going to take the one on the porch, out. Do you have a problem with that?"

Eva shook her head. "None at all. I've only got a problem if you don't Put him down."

Billy drew back his arrow and started to sight in on Reny's neck. He wanted to take him down in such a way as to prevent him from drawing his gun or otherwise alerting the gang members in the house by yelling out. It would be a tough shot, but Billy was confident he could make it. When he got to full draw, however, his wounded arm started to wobble throwing his aim off. He held his draw for several seconds hoping the arm would settle down but gave up after several more seconds and slowly let off the bow tension without letting the arrow fly.

"What's wrong?" Eva whispered.

"Last night I took a hit to my shoulder. My arm won't stay steady."

"Your left arm?"

He nodded.

Eva reached up with both hands and started to massage and manipulate Billy's stiff, corded, shoulder muscles. "Does this help?"

Billy rotated his head several times and took a deep breath as Eva massaged his shoulder. Initially her massage of his shoulder was painful but as she continued it slowly started to loosen up. He let her continue for a few more seconds. "Let's see."

Eva stopped and Billy took his arrow back to full draw again. His sight picture was steadier, but still not perfect, and the broadhead arrow tip described short circles around the perimeter of Reny's throat.

"Eva, my shoulder's better, but if I miss, I'm going to rush the porch and see if I can take him out with a silenced round before he can yell or get a shot off." Billy took two more slow, deep, breathes and after identifying the pattern in the wobble besetting his arm, let the arrow fly at precisely the right moment. It left the bow like a smart missile, traveled the 100' in under a half second, and thunked into Reny's spinal column right between the C3 and C4 vertebrae severing his phrenic nerve. It sounded like the arrow had impacted an oak tree as it hit Reny's spinal column. On its way there, the arrow first severed his trachea and then his esophagus. It was a devastating wound and Reny fell out of the chair and onto the ground like a high-tension power line in an ice storm.

Billy was in motion and sprinting towards the porch the second the arrow left his bow. He retained his bow in his left hand and drew his Sig with his right, ready to fire on the gangster.

Eva was right behind him and followed into the shadowed shrubbery that ran around the perimeter of the deck. They held up there and looked through the porch railing at the dying teen. Their eyes were at the same level and Billy could see the confusion and fear on his face as he tried to understand why he was suddenly prostrate on the porch and why his limbs would no longer respond to commands. Blood and foamy air bubbles pulsed through the gaping neck wound and around the arrow shaft with every beat of his slowing heart.

Billy had watched many men die during his years as a Marine. It was always unpleasant and all the more so when the individual was young. He knew that the gang member had no chance of survival after looking at him, took pity, brought up his Sig, and fired a single, silenced, hollow-point bullet into his heart. Reny's eyes quickly dimmed, and then winked out altogether. Eva flinched at the sound of Billy's round cooking off and seeing the body jump when it impacted but felt absolutely nothing for the young man as she watched him die.

Billy turned to her, bent close and pointed to his left. "You go around that side. I'll take this side. We'll meet in the back. Keep to the shadows as much as you can and see if you can determine what room they're in. Eva nodded her acknowledgment, bent over, and scurried briefly through the light at the bottom of the steps and then back into darkness as she worked her way around the left-hand side of the house.

Billy went right, first looking into a living room which was vacant and then past a dining room which was also empty. He continued down his side of the house to a kitchen door. The van was still abreast of it in the driveway. He peered in through one of the small, divided light windows. The lights were on in the kitchen, but it too was vacant of people. The kitchen was the last room on his side of the house, and he was getting frustrated. Just before turning away to head into the backyard, he stopped himself and took a second, closer look, at a doorway in the kitchen that he'd initially dismissed as being a closet door. On his second look he realized it was door that led down into a basement. There was a stairway leading down, just inside the doorway. This was very unusual in Florida and he continued into the backyard wondering if he would find a bulkhead door. There wasn't one, but there was a small window at ground level. He held up at a small back porch and waited several seconds for Eva to complete her circuit.

"Anything?" he asked as she crouched next to him.

She shook her head. "Three bedrooms on my side; two of them vacant a sick, elderly, person in the third. But no Callie or Stuart or gang members What about your side?"

Billy shook his head but then pointed to a single small paned window to his left down at ground level that had bright light spilling out of it. It was located on the left side where the back porch came away from the rear of the house.

"When I passed the kitchen, I saw a stairway going down into what looks like a basement."

"I've never seen a basement in Florida."

"They aren't common, but it looks like this house has one. Let's take a look."

They crawled over to the small window, got down on their stomachs and looked in.

Callie and Stuart were standing with their hands tied behind their backs around two separate steel Lally columns. There were also two very young teenage girls chained to two other columns. In addition to the captives there were a total of five gang members. Two were seated on a couch, the other three randomly spaced around the room.

"It looks like we got here in time," Eva observed after seeing Callie. "It doesn't look as though they've hurt either of them yet. The other two girls must be the two middle school girls that Callie told me were kidnapped. They look terrible!"

At the sight of the two incredibly young, girls who had obviously been beaten and abused, Billy felt a very primal anger stir inside. "There's the one whose ear I took and who beat you." He pointed to the couch.

They both watched as the man sitting next to Esteban got up and started across the room. He had two syringes in his hands.

471

"Billy, we have to get in there! It looks like he's going to inject them with something."

"Easy, if he just wanted to kill them, he wouldn't have bothered to bring them to the house. If we just rush in from the kitchen and down the stairs now, they'll hear us coming and slaughter us right there in the stairwell. It's nothing but a killing box and we'll both die before we can help anyone. Hang tight."

Chapter 50

I came back to full consciousness in what looked like a basement. My hands were tied behind my back and around a steel post. Stuart was tied in a similar fashion to a post next to me and next to him were Heather and Laura the two missing, middle-school girls. They were chained to their columns and both of them looked terrible. Their clothes were filthy, their hair greasy and unwashed, and both of them had bruises on their faces and arms. Stuart didn't look much better, and I suddenly felt tremendous guilt at having been responsible for putting him in the position he was in. He had a huge subdural hematoma on his forehead that had bled quite a bit and his face was covered in dried blood as a result. He was looking at me with both fear and sadness in his eyes. I had to somehow overpower our captors.

I stood up and stretched against the rope that was holding my wrists trying to gauge if there was any play at all so that I might pull one of my hands through. I would have happily broken one of my own thumbs if doing so would have allowed me to pull a hand free, but whoever had tied us had done too good a job. The only hope I had, and it was very faint, was that someone would somehow track us by my phone. It was still in my back pocket, with the ringer silent from when I'd entered Eva's dojo. I was long past due home for dinner and hadn't met Billy as I'd promised. I'd felt the phone vibrate with incoming calls earlier, over and over again, but I didn't know whether Billy had the presence of mind or the knowledge to track it. I looked at the two men on the couch. I knew Esteban, of course, but recognized the second man from when Camila had shown me photographs of the gang. The second man was Diego, the leader of these craven misfits. He got up and started across the room towards the four of us. He had a syringe in each hand.

473

Billy and Eva continued to watch from outside. The man with the two syringes walked right by Stuart and Callie and then knelt down at the feet of the young girls and deftly injected them both, one right after the other, between their toes. Neither of them cried out in pain or distress and instead appeared to be excited and grateful.

"What did he just do to them? That must have been incredibly painful, and they didn't even flinch. And why between the toes?" Eva whispered.

"It was probably crystal meth and he probably shot them up there so they wouldn't have visible track marks that customers might see."

"Billy, those two girls are just thirteen years old. That may be the vilest, most evil thing I've ever seen. I'm going to kill that man."

What had caught Billy's attention even more than Diego's vile intent, was the apparent gratitude of the two girls. "He is a dead man walking for certain," Billy hissed back.

Diego stood back up after injecting the girls and walked over to Callie. He looked closely at her face and reached out and touched her hair and then turned to Esteban.

"So finally, this is the girl that has caused me so much trouble. Esta es muy hermosa (she is very beautiful), Esteban. You didn't tell me she was so cute. She looks like a gentle little lamb." He paused and then continued. "Right before slaughter of course."

Diego moved closer to Callie and ran his hand over her forehead and then through her hair, sweeping it back and behind one ear.

"Can you say, 'choo, choo,' little girl?" He raised his arm into the air, and slowly pumped it up and down several times imitating a train engineer sounding his horn. Then he leaned in closer and taunted her. "Oh yes, little puta, you're going to have a memorable evening tonight. You should talk with the two other little putas over there and let them tell you how much fun we've been having. They will tell you what a lover I am."

I watched Diego move across the room to Heather and Laura and then watched in horror as he knelt down and used the syringes to inject both of them with something, between their toes. In just seconds both girls' eyes rolled back in their heads and each slowly slid to the floor, the tortured, sac expressions on their faces, replaced by rapturous ones.

I wondered which one was Heather and which one was Laura. Jus seconds ago they'd been sobbing in perfectly explainable fear and humiliation at what they'd likely endured during their weeks of captivity It was hard to conceive of anyone being to take anything further from these two girls, yet Diego had obviously found a way. When he injected them even their righteous and justifiable fear and humiliation was stripped from them, and they were reduced to something less than human as the obviously powerful drugs reached their starved bloodstreams and made them uncaring of what had been done to them and what they would likely be forced to endure in the future. I felt an absolute fury wash over me.

Diego watched them for several seconds and smiled at their reaction. Then he turned towards me and walked over. When he got close enough he reached out and inside the front of my leather jacket and crudely ran his hands over my breasts.

I tried to squirm away from him. Stuart strained against the rope and the steel pole preventing him from coming to my aide. He screamed out in frustration against the gag in his mouth.

Diego shifted his attention to him. "Does this excite you, boy? Is she your woman? She's about to be mine, you know." He paused, smiled, and pointed to every gang member in the room in turn. "And his, and his, and his, and his, and even that ugly little motherfucker who went upstairs."

Tears started running down Stuart's face.

Diego leaned in closer to me and touched my hair again, grossly misjudging the intimidation value of his words and my physical capacity to strike back. He seemed completely oblivious to my disgust and the all-encompassing hatred I was feeling for him.

I struck like a rattlesnake, with absolutely no thought of the consequences and rocketed my forehead directly into his face and felt the satisfying crush of his nose cartilage as it collapsed beneath my forehead. Simultaneously, I snapped my knee into his groin. He went to the floor like the drug addled dirt bag that he was and lay there curled into a fetal ball with blood streaming out of his broken face for almost a minute.

There was sudden and complete silence in the room. No one, I imagined, wanted to inadvertently draw Diego's attention by visibly bearing witness to his humiliation. Eventually, he got up into a sitting position and silently contemplated the blood as it streamed out of his nose, over his mouth and chin, and then down onto the front of his shirt, soaking it.

Eventually, he got to his feet and looked around the room. Every single person was mute, eyes averted, too terrified to say anything, except for me. I stared right at him.

Once he was back on his feet, he turned towards me, shuffled close, and delivered a massive haymaker to my unprotected stomach that knocked every bit of wind out of me. I folded over in agony. Then he grabbed me roughly by the hair, pulled my head towards him until the rope binding my wrists was tight, and hit me in the face, probably trying to duplicate what I'd done to him. My nose was hurt and bled, but he hadn't broken it. He was holding my head up by my hair so hard, it felt as though it was going to tear out of my scalp.

"I was just going to run a train on you, puta, and then put you out to work in our stable, but I've changed my mind. After we've all had our way with you, I'm going to disfigure you and then slowly cut your boyfriend up into small little pieces with my mother's pruning shears and a saw, right here in front of you. And after, I will beat you to death."

I looked into his bloodshot eyes and felt something I'd never felt before in my life, total and absolute hatred for another human being. I lunged towards him with my teeth bared like an animal. If I'd been able to get my teeth into his throat, I would have torn it out. But his hand was still in my hair pulling me to the limits of my bonds and my movement was completely ineffectual.

He laughed at me and then hit me with two humiliating slaps. I spit some of the blood in my mouth into his face. He wiped it away and turned to Bones and Razor. "Get most of her clothes off, bend her over that sink over there and then tie her hands to the taps. I'm going to have another beer and a few more lines to get in the mood." He walked back to the couch, sat down, and turned to Esteban. "You sure you don't want something?"

"I'm sure. I just want to be done with this little puta. She's cost us too much."

Chapter 51

Billy and Eva continued to look in through the window and watched as Callie delivered her head butt and then her knee to Diego's face and crotch.

Billy couldn't help himself and whispered to Eva. "Nice hits. That girl is a warrior."

"Forget that, we need to get in there!"

Billy put his hand out and restrained her. "If the two of us simply storm down the basement stairs, there's a good chance that some or all of those kids will be hurt or killed. We need to do this carefully. The three bangers standing there all have pistols and the big ugly one who got both of us could kill any one of the kids in a second if we just storm in."

"So what should we do?" Eva asked, frantic.

"We continue to watch for now and wait for an obvious opening."

Diego eventually got up off the floor and hit Callie a tremendous shot in the stomach. It was a ferocious blow and Eva reached for Billy's arm in shock at the savagery of it. They continued to watch as he held Callie up by the hair and punched her and then slapped her. Then he turned to two of the standing gang members and said something that they couldn't hear. They watched as one of them walked behind Callie and started to untie her.

"We might be about to get our chance. Give it a second more." Billy suggested. "With her hands free I've got a feeling that chaos is about to shortly ensue which will provide us with the cover and distraction that we need to get down those stairs and take out a couple of them without the kids getting hurt."

Eva looked into his face. "Did you really just say, 'chaos is about to shortly ensue'?"

Billy shrugged. "Just striving for accuracy. Did I not mention that besides being a doer of good and a protector of innocents, that I'm also a licensed attorney?"

"No, you failed to mention that. Are you really joking with me at a time like this?"

"I was just—"

"Shhh!"

I felt a faint ray of hope when Diego told his men to get my clothes off and tie me to the sink. To do that they would need to untie my hands. That would probably be the only opportunity I would have, and I was determined to do everything within my power to prevent them from raping me and killing Stuart. I didn't care what the cost was. I wasn't going to let that happen. I knew without any doubt that I could take two of them if I had freedom of movement. I would hold nothing back. What they had done to Laura and Heather and what they planned to do to me was so amoral and wrong that I decided in that moment that if I had the opportunity, I would do whatever I had to, even if it meant blinding or killing one or more of these men. They didn't deserve to live and continue ruining other lives.

The ones Diego had called "Bones" and "Razor" started moving towards me. I was still bent over from Diego's punch, but I was no longer incapacitated from it. I was playing possum. The second one of my hands was free I planned on bolting across the room out of their grasp, drawing the baton that was still in the inside pocket of my jacket, and then turning first on them and then on Diego and Esteban. I got ready as Razor bent down behind me and started to untie the rope.

"Alto (Stop)!" Esteban shouted from across the room. "Are you two stupid maricons really going to free her hands?"

Razor stopped untying my hands and looked up with a questioning look on his face.

"She may be tiny, but that little puta is going to seriously fuck you up if you free her."

I almost cried in frustration and watched as Esteban got up off the couch, walked behind me, and wrapped one of his gorilla-like arms tightly around my neck. Then he lifted me right off the ground by my neck. He leaned in close and whispered to me. "If you try anything, I'm going to break your scrawny little neck. Understand?"

I couldn't speak but moved my head forward and back several times to let him know I'd heard.

"Good." He nodded at Razor who then untied one of my wrists. Then Esteban carried me by the neck to an area in front of the sink and lowered me until my toes were just touching the floor. But he continued to maintain his choke hold, and I was helpless to make a move.

"Get her pants off while I'm still holding her, then her jacket, one arm at a time. Then tie her hands to the sink taps."

I cringed as I felt Razor and Bones paw at my pants, unzip them and then pull them down, but I didn't cry. I hadn't given up yet. After they pulled off my jeans, they went to work on my jacket and pulled it off one arm and then the other. Hector discovered my steel baton and held it out towards Esteban with a questioning look on his face.

"That's a police baton. Finish securing her and I'll show you how to use it."

Billy and Eva watched in frustration as Esteban wrapped an arm around Callie's neck. They both knew that any chance Callie may have had of breaking free and creating a distraction, had just been thwarted. Then they watched in horror as Callie's clothes were stripped off and her hands retied to the sink taps in the corner of the basement.

"Billy, I don't care what the risk is, we are not going to just sit here and let Callie get gang raped. I will not watch that happen to her."

"I agree. I have an idea. How good a shot are you?"

"I used to be pretty good, but I'm rusty. Why, what are you thinking?"

"Do you think you can hit any of the gang members shooting through this window? If you miss, there's no telling where the ricochets might end up."

Eva studied the window, the room, the gang members, and the angles. "I think I can put one in the one who untied Callie's hands. Then what?"

"First, give me a minute to get into the kitchen and partway down the stairs. Then, take your best center-mass shot on whoever you think you can hit. The instant you fire, all of their attention will immediately shift to this window and that should give me the opportunity to get to the bottom of the stairs undetected and hopefully take out a couple more of them. Just make sure you roll away from this window the second you take your shot, because they're bound to pour a ton of fire at the window right away in response. As soon as you roll away, start running for the kitchen door and get down the stairs as fast as you can to back me up."

Eva nodded her agreement with his plan. They both turned to the window again. Esteban was beating Callie on her bottom and the backs of her legs with the steel baton. Diego had gotten up off the couch and was rooting him on along with Bones, Razor, and Marco.

"Go, Billy, now, before Callie gets hurt any worse."

Billy turned with a new sense of urgency and sprinted out of the back yard towards the kitchen door. Eva brought her handgun into a two-handed prone position with her elbows planted on the ground and sighted down the barrel. Her earlier confidence at being able to hit one of the bad guys disappeared through her sight-picture. All of the bangers had moved since she'd given her initial assessment to Billy and continued to move as they egged Esteban on. Downrange of the cluster of gang members, stood the three other captives. If she took the shot that she'd initially described to Billy, one of the hostages would very likely be hit.

The kitchen door was unlocked. Billy entered and swept his Sig back and forth several times on the off chance that there was someone else in the house. It was silent and the first floor of the house felt empty. He moved quickly to the basement door and started down the stairs. From the raucous sounds the gang members were making and all the gunfire, he was certain that none of them would hear him coming.

Eva tracked Esteban first, figuring he was the most dangerous of the four gang members, but the beating he was administering to Callie caused him to keep moving. Then Eva tracked Diego for several seconds, but he was mostly side-to, to her, and Stuart was right behind him. It was too risky a shot. All at once Marko stopped moving and began to undo his trousers. He was square-on to her. Eva took a bead on the center of his chest and started to take up the slack in her trigger.

But she stopped, noticing the oblique angle she was firing at through the window. Would the bullet travel in a straight line from the gun barrel to the center of Marko's chest or might it deflect on contact with the glass? She simply didn't know, and Laura and Heather were directly behind him if she missed.

I felt self-conscious as Razor and Bones had pulled off my jeans, but to be honest with you, modesty was the last thing on my mind. I was disappointed that I wouldn't get a shot at all of them with my hands free but the pain from getting hit with my own baton, quickly became my focus. Esteban's first strike went right across my buttocks, and it hurt, a lot. After several strikes there he started striking the backs of my thighs and that hurt a hell of a lot more. He definitely had my attention. Despite the pain, I could tell he was holding back some because if he'd wanted to, he could easily have broken my coccyx and possibly even my femurs if he'd hit me hard enough. I knew he had that kind of power. I suspected that he wanted me very much alive to feel the sadistic humiliation and pain they were apparently planning for me. I wasn't thinking about the emotional trauma of being gang-raped so much as I was thinking about how much I would hurt all of them if I could gain my freedom. That became my focus to the exclusion of everything else.

Eva said a quick silent prayer and pulled the trigger. The gun bucked and she saw the window shatter as the bullet passed through it, but before she was able to tell whether or not her bullet had hit and disabled Marko, she had to roll away from the window. She sprinted for the kitchen door, entered the house in a ready stance, swept her gun back and forth quickly looking for targets as Billy had. Seeing no one, she continued on to the basement stairs and started down.

The sounds of gunfire echoing up the stairs from the basement were horrific as Bones, Marko, and Razor poured return fire at the window she'd shot through. Eva started down the stairs grateful for all the noise that muffled her approach but stopped halfway down. She'd had training in house-to-house combat when she'd been in the IDF, but the only actual close-quarters firefight she'd been in was the one was when she'd been taken by the five Arab terrorists eight years previous.

481

During that brief but intense firefight Eva had been shot in the leg and her friend Ronny had suffered a devastating neck wound. The panic and helplessness she'd felt when she'd vainly tried to apply a compress to an uncompressible, gaping, hole in her friend's torn neck combined with the pain she'd experienced from the bullet wound in her leg, all came flooding back. She was suddenly terrified and froze.

The screams of Laura and Heather and then the cough of Billy's silenced weapon reminded her that this wasn't just about her. Billy, Callie, Stuart, Heather, and Laura were all depending on her. She took a deep breath, pushed through her fear, and started moving again. One she reached the bottom of the stairs she crouched low and did a quick sneak-peak into the room. It was absolute chaos and a round immediately impacted into the sheet rock next to her head. She instinctively ducked without having gotten a real sense of how many, if any, of the gang members were down.

When Eva fired her single round through the window, Billy rushed the rest of the way to the bottom of the stairs certain that everyone's attention would be on the window. He did a quick threat assessment to prioritize his firing order. Diego had fled away from the window and behind the couch. Esteban wasn't far behind him and was headed in the same direction. Bones, Razor, and Marko were still mid-room pouring a steady stream of return fire through the small basement window. Billy could see right away that Eva's shot had hit Marco from the exit wound visible at the top of his back, but he was still clearly in the game and Billy wanted to try and take out all three of the men wielding guns before worrying about Esteban and Diego.

Esteban yelled a warning in Spanish from the side and Marko immediately wheeled and tried to bring his gun up. Billy was a full second ahead of him, however, and had already quick-sighted the middle of his chest and let loose four rounds. Marko knew he'd lost the quickdraw competition before he could bring his own gun to bear and moonwalked backwards in a staccato fashion with a surprised look on his face as all four of Billy's rounds ripped into his chest making him look like a possible contender for some obscene dance competition. He folded to the floor like a cheap suit, done.

Bones wheeled towards Billy next. Billy was able to get off one quick snapshot in his direction but caught movement out of the corner of his eye and started to wheel towards the new threat before he could finish Bones or redirect his fire at Razor. Callie's steel baton crashed unexpectedly into Billy's right wrist knocking his Sig from his hand and onto the floor.

Esteban had retained Callie's baton when he'd retreated from the window and quickly counterattacked while Billy's attention was on Marko. When Billy's gun fell to the floor, Esteban's mouth opened into a wide grotesque, smile that revealed the gold, grillwork in the front of his mouth and he started moving menacingly towards Billy. A gunshot went off behind both of them and Esteban's smile disappeared as a chunk of his side blew out. Eva had shot him from behind.

Without missing a beat, Esteban spun around and swung the baton down on Eva and hit her shoulder. The strike hurt like hell and Eva watched in horror as her gun also fell to the floor. Billy took advantage of the distraction and quickly drew his K-Bar and moved on Esteban. He drove the incredibly sharp six-inch blade into the rear of his shoulder all the way to the hilt and then rotated his body to Esteban's front which put Esteban between him and still armed Marko. Marko didn't dare fire out of fear of hitting Esteban by mistake. Esteban bellowed in rage as the knife cut through the muscle and sinew in his back.

Diego had taken cover back behind the couch right after Eva's shot through the basement window at Marko. When Billy entered the basement seconds later Diego had cowered down to the floor. Once Eva and Billy were fully engaged with Esteban, Diego moved around behind the couch and then up the stairs. Callie watched him flee up the stairs like a suddenly exposed cockroach and jerked wildly at her bindings trying to pull free from the two faucets she was tied to. He couldn't be allowed to get away!

Eva went down to the floor after her gun the moment Billy plunged his knife into Esteban. She was also trying to keep Esteban between her and the still armed gunman. She got her gun back, scooted behind the couch, and after a quick three-count, sprung up from behind it. Razor's gun was now empty, but Eva didn't know that, and she fired five rounds, one after the other, center mass into Razor causing him to jitterbug backwards until he came to his final rest against the wall and slid to the floor: the new winner of the obscene dance contest. She steadied herself, re-aimed and fired a final round directly into his forehead.

She anxiously looked around for other threats. Marko and Razor were down, Diego was nowhere in sight, and Bones was wounded and struggling to reload with one arm in the corner. Billy was the priority, and she turned her attention back to Billy and Esteban. They were both still on their feet and fighting despite the knife in the top of Esteban's shoulder and his now missing liver. Eva was suddenly seized with new anger over the cruelty and senselessness of the gang, their violence, and their inhumanity and she struck out at Esteban's throat from the side with a powerful throat punch, then struck him again with a vicious side kick to the side of his knee, shattering the joint and destroying all the ligaments in it. He came crashing to the floor landing on it with his lower leg jutting out to the side at a completely unnatural angle. Billy let go of the knife handle as Esteban fell and they both stood there silently watching him bleed out on the floor struggling to breathe through his damaged trachea.

Bones, unable to reload his gun with just one arm, and seeing the direction the fight was going, darted quickly and quietly up the stairs and then out the kitchen door while Billy and Eva finished Esteban.

In the seconds after, clouds of cordite hung in the air near the ceiling. In the sudden near silence, Billy and Eva locked eyes and reached out to one another sharing some sort of post battle connection.

"Are you okay?" Billy asked.

Eva nodded as a tear slowly tracked down her cheek. "You?"

He nodded his reply and then the two of them looked around the room, each with an arm around the other's back. Marko, Razor and Esteban all lay in pools of blood. It was over and none of the hostages appeared wounded.

"Two of them got away," Eva noted.

"While perfection is a laudable goal, sometimes we must be content with progress. At least we were able to recover all the innocents, and you and I survived."

Eva smiled warmly at the man she'd met just an hour before, but now felt as though she'd known her entire life.

Heather and Laura started crying again in what I suppose was some sort of PTSD relief and Stuart and I looked at one another simply wondering what on earth had just happened.

Billy holstered his weapon, put his foot on Esteban's shoulder next to his K-Bar, reached down and pulled it out of his shoulder in one quick motion. Then he sheathed it after wiping it off on Esteban's shirt. He looked around the room making eye contact with each of us, one by one. The fury in his eyes turning to sadness as he looked at the two, young crying, middle schoolers and contemplated what they'd been through.

Eva wrapped one of her arms around his shoulders and leaned in until their heads were touching. She swept her hand around the room towards the dead gang bangers. "What a waste. What a complete waste of humanity these people are."

Billy nodded his head in agreement.

RIP CONVERSE

Chapter 52

Over the next few minutes Billy cut the ropes binding Stuart and me. He found the key to the locks binding Laura and Heather to the Lally columns, on the table in front of the couch. Eva gathered both of the young girls into her arms once they were free and the three of them huddled together in relief and sadness. I picked my pants up off the floor and carefully pulled them on past my very sore thighs and buttocks, then turned and gathered Stuart into my arms. "I'm so sorry I got you involved in this whole thing, Stuart." I gently touched the lump on his forehead.

"It's not your fault, Callie."

"Isn't it? Would any of this had happened if I'd just let them take that girl, Karen?"

"Probably not, but what would have happened to Karen? You aren't responsible for the evil of others. I'm just glad that none of them will be able to keep doing what they were doing."

I looked into Stuart's eyes, grateful for his words and kissed him gently on the lips. "You were very brave."

"Handsome too, right?"

"Don't get carried away, tough guy. One of the reasons I like you so much is because you're sensitive."

"In that case, I take it back."

I released Stuart and turned to Billy and Eva. "Thank you, Mr. Rainwater and Eva. I'd almost given up. You two saved all of our lives. It's hard to believe all of this." I gestured around the basement room. The smell of blood and spent ammunition still heavy in the air. The simple basement laundry had been transformed into a medieval abattoir or torture chamber with the pieces of chain on the floor, the dead bodies of the gangsters and the six of us all beaten and bloody to one degree or another.

I looked down at Heather and Laura and Eva and knelt down with them and joined their group huddle. "I'm particularly glad we found you two." I said to Heather and Laura. I cringed inside even as I said it suspecting that their road back to any sort of normalcy would be a long and difficult one. I couldn't think of better person than Eva to offer them support, though. I stood and faced Billy.

"Diego and one of the others got away."

"I know," Billy replied. "He was the linchpin of all of this. We can only hope that the police will find them eventually."

I shook my head knowing that wouldn't be the end of Diego. "I'm kind of afraid of that. Some of us or all of us will have to testify against him and that will put all of us back where we started."

"That's true," Billy agreed. "You and these two young girls shouldn't have to go through anything more."

I silently wished that there were some mechanism or way to put animals like Diego away without all the fallout that inevitably fell on innocents like Heather and Laura.

I think Billy sensed my frustration. "Don't let the behavior of others destroy your inner peace, Callie."

I thought about his wise sounding words for a moment. "That sounds like good advice. Is that ancient tribal wisdom from your Calusa forefathers, Billy?"

He looked back at me, smiled, and then shook his head. "No, it was the Dali Lama who said that, but it sounds like something a sage Indian would say."

"Well, excuse me for a minute. I want to use the ladies' room before the police get here and start trying to sort all of this out."

Eva noticed me heading up the stairs. "Would you like some company, Callie?"

I looked back her and thought about it for a second. It did feel creepy heading upstairs into a house I didn't know after what had just taken place, but she still had her arms around Heather and Laura, and they looked like they needed her more than me at that moment.

"Thanks, but I'm good." I replied. "I'll just be a minute. Stay with the two girls."

Eva looked dubious but nodded. "Okay, just yell if you need me."

"I will."

I was incredibly sore from the baton beating I'd received at Esteban's hands and limped slowly up the basement stairs. Despite the pain, I knew I'd heal in short order and reflected on just how lucky all of us had been.

It was amazingly quiet upstairs after all that had taken place in the basement. My ears were still ringing from all the gunfire that had taken place in such a small, enclosed space. Besides the eerie quiet, the other thing I noticed immediately on getting to the top of the stairs and entering the kitchen was a foul smell I and wondered when they'd last taken out the garbage. It was awful and didn't get any better as I moved through the living room and then into what looked like a hallway full of bedrooms. *How can anyone live like these people?* I wondered.

I found the bathroom, dropped my trousers, and peed. After I finished, I sat quietly for a second more and focused on a faint almost electrical sound I could hear coming through the vent above my head. It sounded a little like the sound a transformer makes as you walk underneath a power pole. It was, however, muted and somewhere else in the house and I dismissed it as I pulled up my pants and then washed my hands in the sink.

I shut off the water in the sink and looked around for something in the dirty bathroom to dry them on. Thought better of it and simply wiped them on my pants and then opened the door. I could hear everyone starting up the stairs from the basement and also the faint sound of distant sirens. Both were reassuring.

I walked out into the hallway and looked down it. There were three other doors in that hallway besides the bathroom, and all of them were shut. I started to walk down the hallway towards the living room. As I walked past the second door, I heard the electrical buzzing sound again, and confess that my curiosity got the better of me. I should have known better. I opened the door to see what was making the strange noise.

The moment I opened it a veritable tsunami of olfactory nastiness flooded out of the room and into the hallway almost bringing me to my knees. I'd never smelled anything so putrid and put my hand over my face as if that might somehow mitigate it. Along with the smell came a huge cloud of fat, black flies that swarmed out of the dark room and into the hallway. *What on earth?*

In for a penny, in for a pound, I reached in through the doorway and felt around for a light switch. It was where my hand expected to find it and I flicked it up. An overhead light in the middle of a ceiling came on and with it, another great, thick, cloud of blue/black flies rose off something on the bed. I'd never seen so many flies! The smell was so horrendous that my eyes started to gush tears and partially blind me, but not before my brain registered what I was seeing.

Propped up against the pillows, a rotting, elderly head peeked out from beneath the sheets. I knew the person was elderly from the clumps of gray hair that still clung to the desiccated skull. I cried out in horror, recoiled backwards into the hall, bent over, and vomited.

The next thing I was aware of was someone gripping my hair tightly, the sound of a gun cocking next to my ear, and the hard, cold barrel of a handgun poking against the back of my head.

"You shouldn't have bothered my mother, puta. Mi Madre es mucha infermo." It was Diego, the leader of the gang.

I couldn't move and felt as though I was going to completely lose my shit from first having discovered what I later found out was a two-week-old corpse, but secondly because his gun was actually touching my head and I knew that he could pull the trigger at any second.

"I'm sssorry," I managed to stutter out. "I didn't mean to disturb her."

"You have caused me a great deal of trouble, puta. Now you will die."

I felt his hand tense as he began to draw the remaining slack out of the trigger and thought briefly of possibly kicking back, but I could barely move my legs as they were, and I mentally prepared to die.

Eva heard Callie cry out and then as she vomited. She held up her hand stopping everyone behind her and then put her finger to her lips. She drew her gun from her waistband and crept the few feet to the hallway where he'd heard Callie and took a quick peek down it. Callie was less than twenty feet away and bent over. The gang leader was holding a large caliber handgun to her head. Eva knew instantly from his body language, that Callie was about to be executed and that there would be no negotiation or opportunity for distraction and further that Callie would be dead in the next second or two if she didn't take a shot. Eva wasted no time thinking and wheeled back into the hallway raising her gun-hand as she made the turn. There was no sight picture, no aiming, no time for micro adjustments of any kind. She simply had to make the shot. And as she finished her turn into the hallway her gun was still rising as she pulled the trigger and took a snap-shot at Diego's head. Her movement and the firing of her gun while it was still in motion was something that Eva had practiced many times on the range when she was in the IDF, but she hadn't practiced in years. The motion was similar to an underhanded softball pitch where your fingers release the ball while your arm is still moving forward and up. The only difference was she would retract her index finger instead of opening her whole hand and the softball would be a bullet traveling at 850 mph instead of 77 mph. She got lucky and it went on target.

A single shot rang out and I immediately felt a splash of wetness on the back of my head. My eyes were pinched tightly closed, and I wondered why I was still conscious and why being shot in the head didn't hurt more. The next thing I was aware of was Diego falling away from me and sliding down the wall next to us. Another shot rang out, this one much louder and I flinched. It was the gun still in Diego's hand. Apparently, his hand had not yet gotten the message that his brain was dead, and it was simply executing the last command it had received. Miraculously the bullet impacted harmlessly into the floor next to my foot, and not into my head. I continued to stand there, shaking, too terrified to move. The next memory I have is of waking up in Eva and Billy's arms and clinging to them like my very life depended on them. It had.

"It's okay, Callie, it's okay. It's really over now," Eva whispered to me.

RIP CONVERSE

Afterward

T he next few days were a nightmare of police interviews as the authorities tried to piece together everything that had taken place from the very first night where I'd prevented MS-13 from taking Karen, until the final moment in that hallway when Eva had taken one of the most challenging shots of her life. We were all asked the same questions over and over as the authorities tried to determine if any of us had acted improperly, particularly Billy and Eva. Thankfully, it was eventually decided that Billy had committed no crime when he'd defended my parents, and that Billy and Eva were not responsible for any wrongful deaths when they'd assaulted Diego's house and rescued the four of us.

Technically, Eva was perhaps the only one who'd been in any jeopardy at all and that was for having worn Billy's backpack with a concealed weapon inside, from the dojo to the house without her possessing a concealed carry permit in the State of Florida. It was decided that everything else they'd done as they had rescued us was lawful.

I had a great deal I had to answer to my parents for and will spend a long time rebuilding their trust in my judgment. They weren't angry at me for initially having rescued Karen and preventing her capture, but they were rightfully angry at me for my lack of judgment in not being open and honest with them about MS-13's attempts on my life after. That lack of transparency had endangered our whole family. I see that in retrospect.

Billy and Eva spent most of the first night in custody while the police questioned them. They were released on their own recognizance early the next morning with Billy's agreement that he would stay in town and make himself available for further questioning over several days. He came by my parent's house the afternoon of the day after to meet my family and to collect his gear and ended up staying for dinner. This gave my parents and brothers the opportunity to ask him exactly what had transpired in the woods and on the road when MS-13 had attempted their assault on our house. When my family heard the details of how many gang members there'd been and how they'd been armed, they became aware for the first time of just how much Billy had personally risked in defending them. They owed this quiet stranger immense gratitude and each of them expressed that in his or her own way as the evening went on. Harley was particularly interested in the fact that Billy had served in the Marines and asked dozens of questions about what he could expect in basic training and exactly how Billy had become a special forces recon Marine. When Billy was finally ready to leave, I walked him outside to his bike.

"I'm sure you could stay on our couch or string your hammock again between those two Australian Pines if you wanted" I offered.

He smiled. "That's a nice offer, Callie, but I'm good. Eva offered me a bunk at her place and I'm going to take her up on her offer."

I'd been to Eva's one-bedroom condo and blushed at the implications of what he'd just told me. All sorts of protective and defensive thoughts instantly washed over me as I thought about them sharing a bed. I immediately felt protective and defensive, and I wondered at the wisdom of her having a physical relationship with Billy; someone we hardly knew. Eva was my instructor, but she was also my closest friend, and my next thoughts were of what had happened to her at the hands of the terrorists when she was in the IDF.

I caught myself, thankfully before I spoke, realizing that I was about to fall into the same trap that her parents, her fellow soldiers, and most tragically, Eva herself, had fallen into. Would I think of her as "damaged goods" requiring special protection? Was she no longer entitled to the same opportunities for happiness and human warmth as everyone else? Would I let that one horrible experience that she'd endured as a victim, forever define her? Or would I trust that especially she, with her core goodness and strength, was perhaps *more* entitled to these things than anyone else?

I put my hand on Billy's arm. "That's wonderful, Billy. She must see something in you that I missed."

He looked at me, with a confused expression on his face.

I smiled at his discomfiture and punched him lightly on his arm.

"Relax! I'm just messing with you. Eva's incredibly special to me and you don't seem like a bad sort yourself despite what everyone else says behind your back."

He looked at me once again with confusion.

I went up on my toes, hugged him, and gave him a kiss on his cheek. "God you're easy! It's just a little game my aunt and I play. No one is saying anything bad about you behind your back. All of us feel incredibly grateful that you put yourself out there like you did, without even knowing us. So, thank you, Billy Rainwater, for everything."

"You're welcome Honiahaka, anytime."

I cocked my head to the side. "What does Honiahaka mean?"

"It means, 'Little wolf,' in Cherokee."

"I like it." I paused and then continued. "Will you teach me to shoot? His earlier answer to me of "Perhaps" hadn't really been an answer."

"When some time has passed, and if your parents approve, yes."

I sensed that I was not going to get a firmer commitment than that.

"Fair enough."

Billy put on his backpack, got on his Indian, and started it.

"Billy?"

"Yes."

"Please be kind and gentle with Eva. I know she seems all tough and everything, but if you aren't, Honiahaka will come for you in the night."

He held my gaze for a few seconds. "Message received; I believe you would. Let's keep in touch. Take care of yourself."

"You, too."

I still go to the dojo almost every day and practice Krav Maga with Eva. I'm determined to go as far as I possibly can with that in the coming year and earn my black belt. I've also added a grueling weights regimen to my work outs to develop more bulk muscle. I never again want to feel intimidated by someone like Esteban.

Stuart and I are now officially "dating," but I still haven't jumped into that with both feet because I also got accepted to Babson for the coming year and I have difficulty reconciling the idea of having a relationship with someone in Florida while living in Massachusetts. He says he can deal with it, but we'll just have to see. As it is, I see him almost every day at either the dojo or at his father's flight school and we are very close. I ended up soloing after just six hours in the air and four hours in the simulator with his father Court, as my instructor. I truly love flying and plan to take my private pilot's exam in February thanks to the generosity of my Aunt Nancy who is underwriting all my instruction and airtime.

I visited Aunt Nancy a week after everything that transpired in that house on Carrel Avenue. She and I had spoken once by phone the day after, but I really felt as though I needed to thank her in person and also wanted to share with her all that was going on in my head. MS-13 and everything thing they touched, it seemed, was dark and evil and ever since that evening, I'd felt soiled; the kind of "dirty" that no amount of soap and water will get out. I didn't like feeling that way and it was coloring every aspect of my life. I hadn't done anything wrong except perhaps been naïve. Why did I feel so guilty and out of touch with everyone around me?

The moment I drove onto the island, memories of my summer flooded back. Without me realizing it at that moment, Boca Grande would forever be synonymous with positive feelings of independence, possibility, and self-respect, and all of those things flashed into my consciousness as I came off the bridge and onto the island from the mainland. I flipped up the visor on my helmet letting the outside air in and tried to drink in those positive feelings.

It was my first time back on the island since the end of summer and keeping to the strictly enforced 35mph speed limit on the main road to her house was difficult. After turning the last corner, I could see Jesús and John clipping the privet hedges at the top of her driveway and goosed my throttle a couple of times with the clutch in, getting the attention of Jesús and John. They stopped clipping wondering I supposed at the character on an Italian racing motorcycle that was so out of character with the normal parade of BMWs, Mercedes, and Bentleys that normally coasted silently past the end of the driveway. They watched me coast to a stop in front of them, turn off Velocitá, and finally as I took off my helmet revealing myself to them.

"I'll bet you two were just saying, 'It's too bad that Callie isn't here to help us clip these bushes.' Am I right? Were you just saying that?"

Both men stopped clipping and smiled at each other. "Absolutely, Miss Callie. How did you know?" Jesús replied. "I was just saying that very thing, wasn't I, John?"

John shook his head from side to side in a "no" but said, "Yes, that's exactly right."

"You two; still up to your games of making fun of the boss's niece. It's really good to see you both."

"You, as well, Miss Callie. Rosario has been moping around the kitchen since the day you left," Jesús said.

"I've missed her also." I restarted Velocitá and put my helmet back on. "I'm going to let you both get back to it. You seem to have figured out how to clip privet without me."

"We have, Callie. That's quite a machine you have there by the way." John observed.

"Thank you, John. Her name is Velocitá. It's good to see you both."

I eased out the clutch and continued onto the white gravel driveway. The popping sound of the tiny white stones brought back a lot of memories. I parked in the turnaround right in front of the door. Nancy opened it before I'd even shut down my engine and stood there watching as I took off my helmet. She'd obviously been anxiously awaiting my arrival. She stood there silently for a moment, and we just looked at one other. My eyes started to fill with tears. I got off my bike, put the helmet on the seat, then ran up the steps and into her arms. She held me silently for a while and then she too started to cry. It was crazy. I really don't understand why I broke down then as opposed to a dozen other times I might have more logically done so over the previous week.

Up until that moment with Nancy, I'd kept it together; through the police interviews, through coming clean with my parents on everything that had transpired, and even when Eva had told me all the details of what Heather and Laura had suffered at the hands of MS-13. I thought I'd processed having watched three men shot and killed in Diego's basement and when Eva had shot Diego in the hallway upstairs as he held a gun to my head, and Diego's mother's rotting corpse and the cloud of flies that had come off it, and being chased at 130 mph by people who wanted me dead or to turn me into a sex slave and knowing about the two teenagers who were shot and then beheaded by their own gang.

I'd talked about all of those things with the police and my parents and Stuart and Eva, but I guess I hadn't really internalized all of it, not really. I hadn't even begun. Everything I'd been holding inside, and pretending wasn't a big deal suddenly overcame me and I melted into Nancy's arms and completely broke down.

I'd convinced myself that I was way tougher than I actually am, and that I could handle it, all of it. I'm here to tell you now that I'd been delusional, and I spent the next two hours projectile vomiting all of the poison floating around in my psyche out, and into Nancy's proverbial lap. Throughout, she was uncharacteristically warm and sympathetic, and I saw a side of her that I'd been unaware existed till then. I'd always known she was tough, educated, and irreverent, but I'd never seen the warm, soft, side of her that gently and reverently cradled my soul during those hours. Eventually I finished downloading all of the horrors I'd witnessed and cried myself out. After, I went into the bathroom for a few minutes to wash my face, brush my hair and generally pull myself back together. I returned to the living room and sat back down on the couch facing her.

"Okay then! Where were we."

She took one of my hands in hers again. "I'm not sure. You tell me."

"Do you think there's something wrong with me, Nancy?"

Nancy nodded her head. "Yes, tons."

"No, I'm serious!"

"Perhaps that was insensitive; how about, lots?"

I looked at her quizzically, realizing she was being serious.

"Callie, having a great mind is not just about being smart and successful and being able to solve problems. If that were the case, then we'd all worship scientists and hedge fund managers." She paused for a moment and then continued. "Truly great people, the ones we remember anyway, also have an incredible ability to empathize and sympathize with their fellow man. I call it humanity. Did you know that over the last two hours you didn't once mention yourself or your fears? Everything you related to me was about the fear, loss, and sadness of others. Most people would have talked about nothing but themselves.

You aren't weak for feeling devastated about all that transpired. That's your humanity which you are just now getting in touch with. You care deeply about people and what happens to them. And when people you know or love are threatened or hurt you want to do something about it. That doesn't make you weak, it makes you stronger. I suspect you are just as tough today as you were a week or a month ago, but I think the feelings of empathy and loss you're feeling are new ones for you and it will take some time to grow into them."

I nodded, understanding what she was saying. "Since you brought it up, what about me?"

"What about you?"

"Is there something wrong with me because I don't feel fear? In the moment anyway," I added.

She thought about my question for a few seconds. "I don't know the answer to that. I think it's out of my depth. I suspect that's something better taken up with a professional."

"You mean with a shrink, right?"

She nodded and we sat silently facing one another for a long time with our hands intertwined.

Nancy shifted gears before me. "Well, now that we've gotten all that unpleasantness out of the way, what say you to a gentle little lunch?"

I nodded my agreement and noticed that Nancy was sporting a gauze bandage just below her collar in the same place she'd had the Band-aid weeks earlier. "Hey, what's going on with that thing your dermatologist cut off? Did it get infected or something? Why the big bandage?"

Nancy absently put her hand up to her neck. "Oh, they had to go back and take a slightly larger piece out of me. It's okay now, the surgeon thinks they got all of it."

It suddenly dawned on me what had been wrong with the "freckle" they'd cut off Nancy two weeks previous. "It was cancer?" I asked with trepidation.

"Lentigo maligna melanoma they say. It hadn't gone very deep but out of an abundance of caution they like to take both the growth and a certain amount of tissue from the surrounding area to be safe."

"Will you be, okay?" I asked with tears starting to fall from my eyes again. "You're incredibly important to me. I think I'd be completely lost if you weren't in my life."

"You're sweet, but I'm certain I'll be fine." Obviously uncomfortable with the entire subject she shifted gears again before we both got maudlin. "Where on earth is Rosario anyway? I swear it gets more difficult by the day to hire decent staff! Rosario, ROSARIO!" she called out. "Where on earth has that woman gone off to?"

"She's probably folding laundry, making Beef Wellington, cleaning the pool, washing the kitchen floor, waxing your Bentley and ironing your panties or doing some other equally industrious or important task."

"Aren't you adorable with your sarcasm. Don't get fresh with me, Catherine."

I silently mimed "don't get fresh with me Catherine" back at her and stuck out my tongue.

Rosario rushed into the room and came up behind the couch in answer to Nancy's call. "Yes, Nancy. What can I get you?"

Rosario smiled and winked at me over Nancy's shoulder and then made a talking hand gesture.

"Rosario, where on earth have you been?" Nancy asked without looking behind.

Rosario continued to smile at me and flap her four fingers against her thumb. "I was having a few margaritas and watching my game shows. I must have nodded off, Miss Nancy. It won't happen again."

"I should hope not!" Nancy said with great bluster and umbrage.

I feigned a giant yawn, covering my mouth with one hand and mimicking Rosario's talking hand gesture with the other, smiling and making eye contact with Nancy as I made fun of her. I was grateful that things were back to normal.

Nancy cranked up her faux outrage. "I never!"

Rosario sat down on the couch next to me, put her arm around my shoulders and smiled at Nancy. "It's really nice to have Miss Callie back, isn't it?"

"Yes, I suppose it is. Even though she can be such a troublemaker."

END

Callie, Book II should be complete within six months. I'm never certain where one of my stories will go next so I haven't yet titled Book II. Once all the characters finish doing, saying, and going wherever it is that they decide to go next, I'm sure a title will pop into my head.

Please, if you enjoyed Callie Awakens, leave me a good rating, and also take the time to write a thoughtful review on Amazon. I know it's extra work on your part, but it makes a huge difference in my visibility and ratings on Amazon and makes it possible for me to continue writing. How do you leave a review? Just go to the Callie Awakens book page on Amazon (where you purchased/downloaded it) and then go down the page until you get to customer reviews. Right near the top of that on the left you will see a button titled "Write a customer review."

Also, if you like my work and want to be notified when I complete additional new books, go to my book page on Amazon and click on "Follow the Author" underneath the book-cover image, or to www.ripconverse.com and sign up, or start following me on Facebook . The only emails you will get from me will be announcements of new books by me.

A preview of Callie Book II starts on the next page.

RIP CONVERSE

Chapter I (Callie Book II Preview)

I was standing across from my Israeli Krav Maga instructor, Eva Dahan. We were in her dojo in Fort Myers, FL and I had a new move I wanted to try out on her.

"Explain again what it is you want me to do," she asked, looking amused by my request. "Where did you get this idea, anyway?"

"You know the rabbit hole you can go down when you're watching YouTube videos?"

Eva nodded.

"Well, I was watching some Krav Maga demonstration videos the other night and I came across this one that showed Roy Elghanayan mounting and then taking down opponents in a really unique way. I want to try the same move with you."

Roy Elghanayan is the youngest Master in Krav Maga history and the only person to be ranked #1 as the National Israeli Krav Maga Champion of the Israeli Military, twice in a row. In one of his videos he takes on and puts down sixty-five different opponents in sixty-five minutes. He's a God of sorts to both Eva and me.

"Well, if Roy came up with the move, it must be very good."

I knew that would be her reaction and chuckled. "All I need you to do is take any sort of swing at me with your right arm."

Eva assumed a ready stance. I immediately matched it and started bouncing on my toes. The move I was going to try was gymnastic in nature and I needed to explode it on her, for it to be effective.

She stepped in towards me leading with a left-hand swipe and then followed with the overhead right-handed strike I'd requested. I leaned far to my left removing my head from the path of her descending fist, reached up and inside the descending arm, grabbed her right shoulder with my right hand, and using my forward momentum, swung up onto her back and immediately locked both of my legs around her stomach and chest. With her now off balance with an unexpected hundred pounds on her back, I leaned right, then forward, and dove towards the floor, twisting left and taking her with me, keeping both my legs securely locked around her upper body, and both my hands around her right shoulder. I landed in a tumbling roll, flipping her as I reached the mat, slid both my hands up towards her right wrist and then twisted her entire arm over my right thigh with her elbow as the fulcrum point.

She tapped out within seconds, unable to move. It was clear that had I wanted I could have destroyed her elbow joint.

"Wow! That was really effective, Callie. I'm not certain I could have done the same move. You were like a monkey and on me before I was certain what you were going to do. By the time I figured it out, it was too late. I was already headed for the floor with you in total control."

I released Eva's arm and we untangled from each other.

"I'm not sure you could surprise someone with that move more than once, but it certainly could give you an advantage that someone your size needs over a larger opponent. When someone's behind you and up around your neck, there's very little you can do. Very good!"

I beamed for a moment at her compliment. Eva was stingy with them, and when they came, they meant a lot.

She looked up at the clock on the front wall and sighed. I knew what she was concerned about. We'd been working with two young teenage girls, two days a week, for the last several months. They were half an hour late. She walked over to the side of the mat, swiped at the screen of her iPhone, then shook her head. "Nothing. Let's give them a few more minutes. Maybe they just got into some traffic."

"Don't you think they would have texted or called? They've never been late before."

Eva looked over towards the coat rack area. "Laura left her knapsack last time they were here. It's heavy like it's full of schoolbooks. She must want to get that back."

I wasn't as sure as Eva that they were simply late. "Neither one seems to have their heart in what we're doing with them. I know they show up and try to do whatever you ask, but besides being physically pathetic, when I look into their eyes, nobody looks back. It's like looking into an abandoned building. I'd hoped that we would have made more of a personal connection with them by this point."

"Callie, don't take this wrong, but sometimes I think your expectations are a bit unrealistic. Not everyone is an athlete or able to compartmentalize like you. From the very beginning we both knew they were going to have a long and rough road ahead of them."

She was right about them and also about me. I do tend to have unrealistic expectations of others and I also have a somewhat disturbing ability to over-compartmentalize in not always healthy ways. I know this puts me on a "spectrum" of sorts, but I haven't yet done any work with a shrink to look more closely at those flaws.

Eva continued. "Sometimes people simply need gentle understanding and a hug more than they need another lesson. Heather and Laura are very likely drowning in guidance from their parents, their school, psychiatrists, and classmates. What they're probably not getting is unconditional love and acceptance. They didn't do anything wrong, nothing! But I'll bet you anything if you asked either of them whether people treat them the same, they'd both say no. You experienced some of the same stigma after that boy Christopher tried to rape you, right?"

"I did." I admitted.

"Everyone want's something from them and they don't have much to give. Their parents want assurance that they'll be the way they were before, the guidance counselors and the therapists want evidence that their counseling's working, and you and I want them to internalize and memorize dozens of moves that come very naturally to you and me, but not to them. They're likely feeling like they're going to explode. I just hope we can get through to them before they do."

I understood all that Eva was pointing out and immediately thought back to the visit I'd had with my Aunt Nancy in Boca Grande a week after everything had happened and how healing that had been for me.

I'd been kidnapped and beaten along with my boyfriend Stuart, by MS-13. We'd been lucky compared with Heather and Laura. They'd been held prisoners for weeks and subjected to incredible brutality including beatings, gang rape, and forced drug use. Eva, and a man named Billy

Rainwater, had rescued all of us from MS-13 and in the process killed four gang members, right in front of us. I blamed myself for much of what happened, and I'd been a mess in the immediate aftermath. I'd only able to forgive myself and start healing after I did a complete emotional download with my Aunt Nancy. Her sympathy and unconditional acceptance of me and my part in all that had happened, made it possible for me to start moving forward again. She'd asked nothing of me in return.

Eva herself was a rape survivor. During her time in the IDF she'd been shot and then held hostage by five terrorists. During that time she'd also endured incredible brutality. In the aftermath of everything that had gone on with MS-13, we'd offered to teach Heather and Laura Krav Maga, as a way of restoring their self-confidence and hopefully empowering them to move forward again without fear. They'd agreed to try it. Losing them now, after two months would be difficult, if that's what was going on.

I knew that what Eva had said was right. Everyone, including us, probably had unrealistic expectations of them. I resolved at that moment to try and offer the gentler side of myself, and to tamp down my pragmatic side. I very much wanted to be a part of their solution, not another problem for them.

****

Across town, Heather and Laura sat sprawled, facing each other, in crappy beanbag chairs that Laura had found in a neighbor's trash several weeks before. They were in their "secret place" in Laura's house. Access into the tiny space was through a small door in the back of her bedroom closet that had to be crawled through. She didn't think her parents were even aware that the space existed. If they'd ever known, they'd long forgotten about it. Both of them were busy professionals, seldom home, and decidedly not DIY types. If anything involved the basement, attic or garage they simply hired others to deal with it.

They were still in their school uniforms which included plaid skirts with matching headbands, white, button-down shirts, and patent leather shoes. Heather had her school skirt gathered up just high enough so that the incision she was making on the inside of her thigh, wouldn't be readily visible to her parents, other students, or the nuns at school. Her first cut was quite shallow and just two inches long. She'd only been cutting for a few months and watched with fascination as tiny droplets of blood just barely made it to the surface before coagulating. It didn't matter to her if Laura watched, she was also a cutter.

Laura exhaled a faint trail of white smoke from her lungs and held out the small glass pipe she was smoking. "Want a hit?" she asked.

Heather nodded absently without looking up, still mesmerized by the tiny drops of blood weeping out of the cut she'd just made.

"Well, take it then, dummy. Don't just stare at your leg. It'll still be there after."

Heather looked up. "Sorry." She reached for the pipe.

"It's okay. I think we've got enough to keep a buzz going for a few hours." Laura remembered something and after passing the pipe and the lighter to Heather, reached behind her beanbag chair and grabbed a small white paper bag. "Got you something, girlfriend."

Heather finished taking a hit, put the pipe on the low table between them and held out her hand. "Gimme."

Laura snorted. "Sister Wright would lay the ruler on you for talking that way at school."

"Like I care. Sister Wright needs to get laid, loosen up, and tighten the beads."

"Nice talk."

Heather opened the paper bag and looked in. "A smushed cupcake?"

"Yea, for your birthday. You don't want it?"

"No, I want it. Thanks. Now we're both fourteen. Whoop-tee-do."

Neither said anything for the next several minutes and instead passed the pipe back and forth several more times.

"Did, Bobby ever call you?" Laura asked.

"Yes," Heather answered disinterestedly.

"And....?"

Heather shook her head in frustration. "I'm so tired of pretending with everyone! My parents, my stupid therapist, my guidance counselor, other kids at school, none of them get it! I can't sleep at night; it's like some foul, black snake by the name of Diego is crawling through my brain and my heart and crapping inside me, then laughing. Every single thought I have is polluted by him." She wiped a tear off her face. "I'm tired, Laura, really tired."

Heather stopped talking and watched as one of her tears silently splashed on the inside of her thigh and melted one of the blood drops. The tear turned red and ran around the side of her leg and out of site.

She finally answered Laura's question. "Bobby's a dead end. He's seventeen for Christ sakes. He's not interested in me. Oh, he says he is, but he's not. The only reason he called is because he's heard all the stories about what happened to us and just assumes I'll put out. Guys are so screwed up." She paused. "I'll probably do him though. At least I won't have to feel anything for a couple of minutes."

Laura nodded, completely understanding her friend's feelings. Both of them had turned to promiscuity over the past few months as another form of escape. "Maybe we are just a couple of crack whores," she muttered.

"Let's not talk about it," Heather suggested. "Oh, I almost forgot. Look what I brought to the party." She added excitedly in a singsong voice. She looked through her purse for a few seconds and then pulled out a flatpack of capsules.

"What are they?"

"Quaaludes."

Laura pecked away at her phone for a few seconds looking it up. "A hypnotic, barbiturate-like, sedative, no longer manufactured, popular in the sixties, seventies, and eighties as a recreational drug. Sounds tasty! Where'd you get them?"

"One of the shops on Hydra."

"What's Hydra again?"

"One of my new dark web friends."

"What country did the pills come out of?"

"India,"

"Better than China, I suppose,"

Heather broke two capsules out of the glassine packaging. and swallowed them with some warm vodka, straight from the bottle. "Want some?"

Laura shrugged. "Duh! Gimme."

"That's my girl." Heather broke two more capsules out of the package and dropped them into Laura's hand.

Laura looked down and pouted. "That's it? That's all you think of our friendship. More, you pinhead. You know our motto."

"Anything worth doing is worth overdoing." They both chimed in unison, then high-fived each other.

An hour later, after consuming the last of the pills in the twenty-pill pack, along with the vodka, the girls had slid down in the beanbag chairs till they were both laying on their sides in fetal positions, their heads just twelve inches apart. They stared at one another through half open, heavy, fluttering, eyelids. Their heartrates and breathing slowed to almost nothing.

Heather's last conscious thoughts were that she'd forgotten to go by the dojo and get her knapsack earlier in the weak, and that both of them had completely forgotten their Krav Maga lesson with Eva and Callie. She felt guilty about that. Eva had rescued them from the MS-13 leader's basement four months earlier and had been trying to teach them Krav Maga to "physically empower them" and "restore their shattered feelings of self-worth."

Eva was twenty-nine and closer to her parents in age, but she was still cool. She'd been a soldier in the Israeli Defense Forces and suffered a fate very similar to what she and Laura had endured at the hands of MS-13. Eva had also been gang raped and humiliated for days. The only thing different about Eva's captivity was that her captors hadn't addicted her to drugs, which was too bad simply because drugs had been the only thing that had made it possible for her and Laura to go on as long as they had.

Callie was sixteen and closer in age to both of them, but she was different and intense. She was two years ahead of her classmates and going to college in the fall, she was a genius and barely had to crack a book to get straight A's, and, if that wasn't enough, she was also a pilot, drove a motorcycle, and had a really nice boyfriend who was also a pilot. When Eva would show the three of them a new move, Callie would get it on the first try and remember it forever, whereas Laura and her would need to be shown a new move three or four times and would forget it between one class and another.

Callie had been nice enough and understanding and had herself been a prisoner of Diego, but Diego had not had the opportunity to "break" her, in the same ways that he had wormed his way into her and Laura's souls. Alongside Callie, Heather felt ineffectual and less-than, despite Callie's patient and sincere efforts a to teach her and Laura Krav Maga.

Neither Eva nor Callie had ever asked for anything in return from either of them other than to simply show up and try martial arts as one possible path to restoring their confidence and getting on with their lives. She regretted not being able to become the person that Callie and Eva had tried to make her and hoped that the two of them would forgive her and Laura for taking the easy way out. She shut her eyes, finally at peace, and joined Laura, on the other side.

Made in the USA
Columbia, SC
04 August 2021

42980674R00312